# FAIRY IDOL Kanon

2

MERA
HAKAMADA



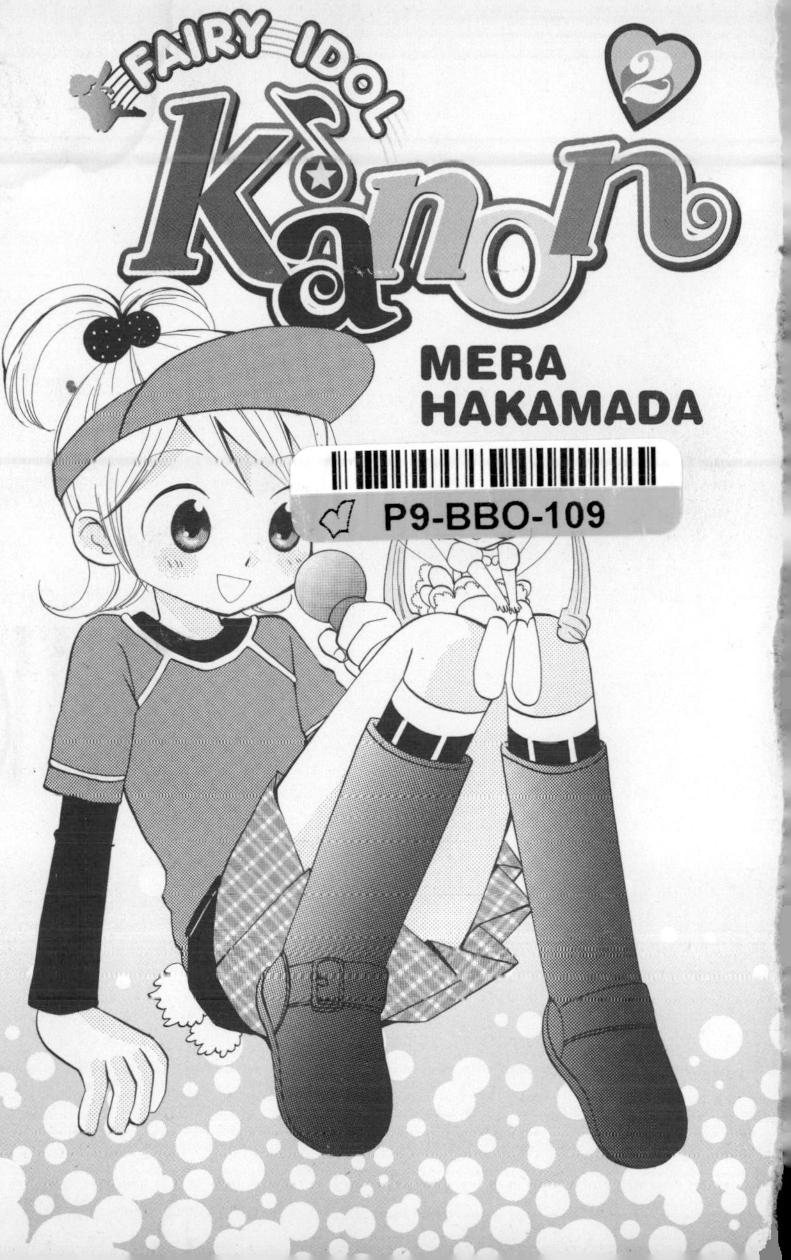

# HOW TO READ MANGA!

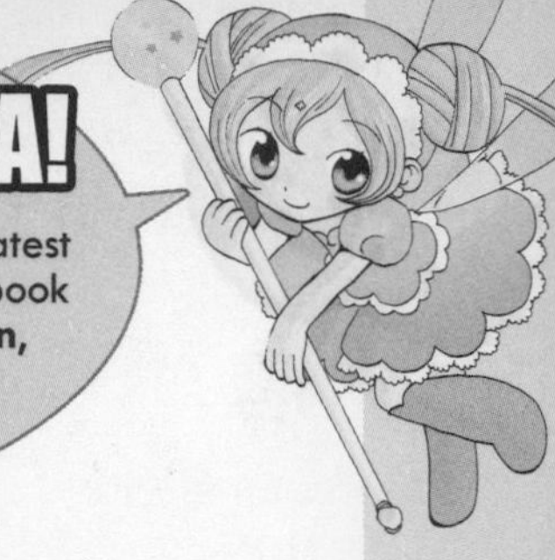

Hello there! My name is **Alto,** and this the latest chapter of **Fairy Idol Kanon**! It is a comic book originally created in the country of **Japan,** where comics are called **manga.**

A manga book is read from **right-to-left,** which is **backwards** from the normal books you know. This means that you will find the first page where you expect to find the last page! It also means that each page begins in the top right corner.

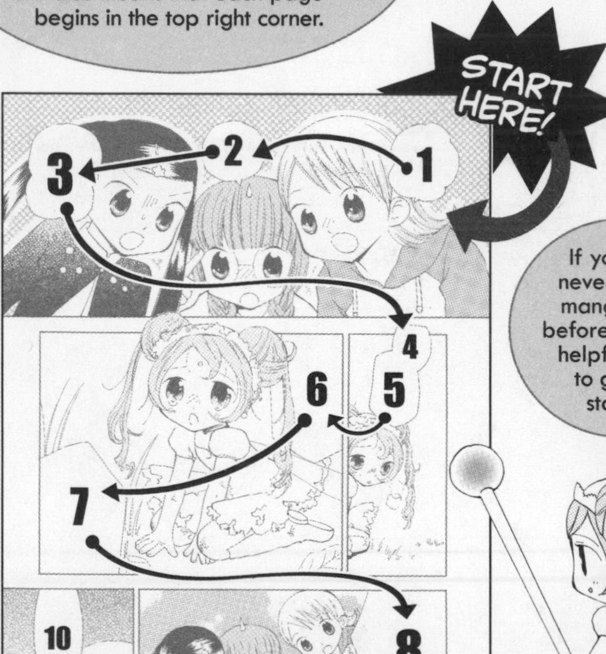
START HERE!
1
2
3
4
5
6
7
8
9
10

If you have never read a manga book before, here is a helpful guide to get you started!

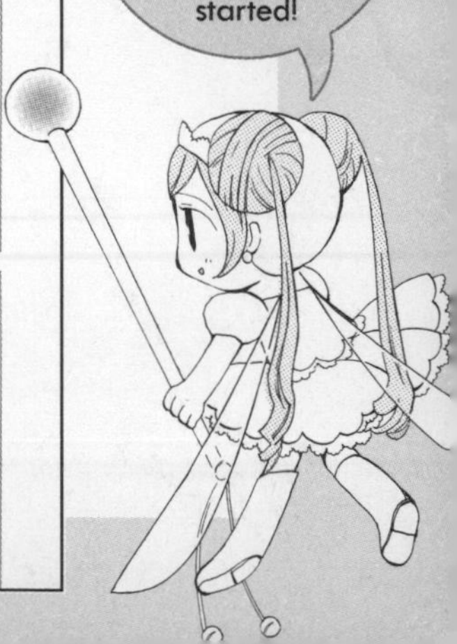

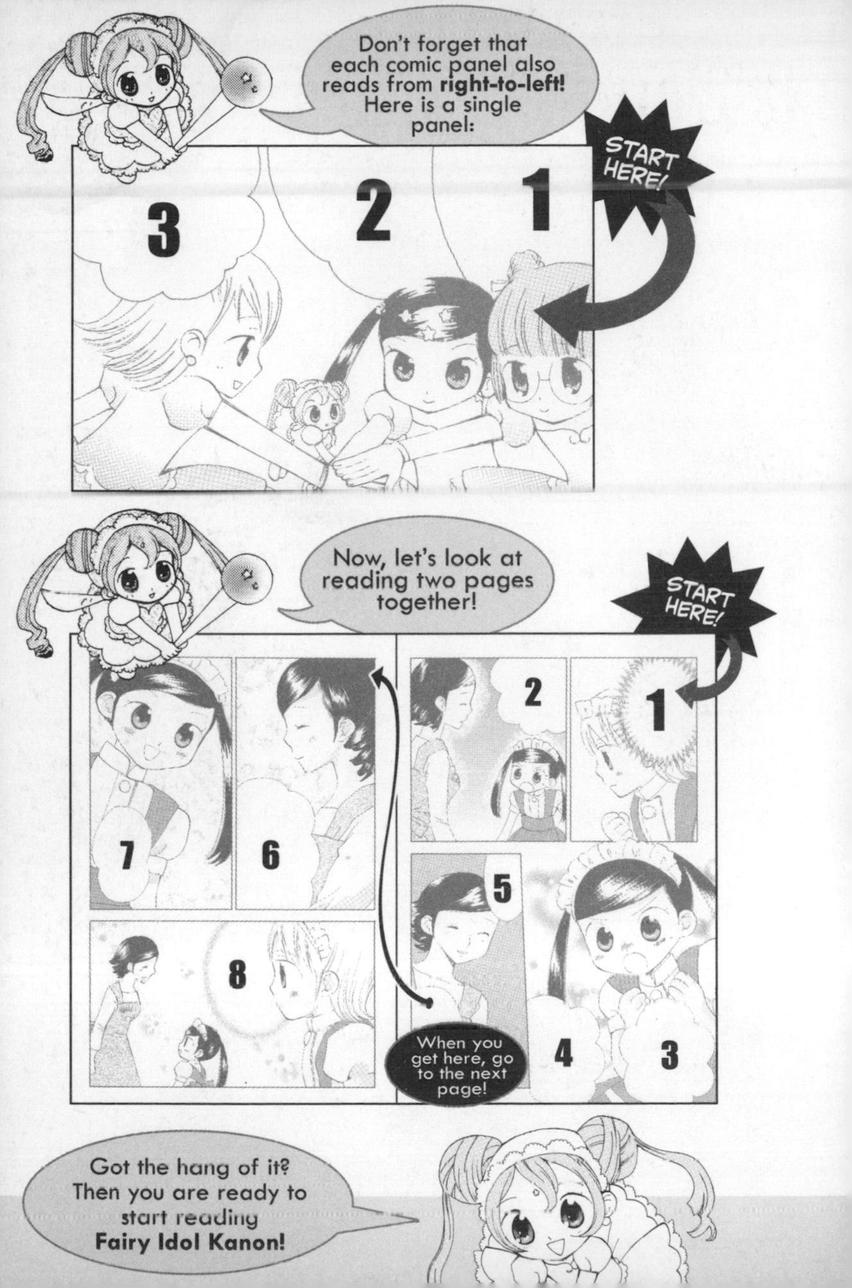
Don't forget that each comic panel also reads from **right-to-left!** Here is a single panel:
START HERE!
1
2
3
Now, let's look at reading two pages together!
START HERE!
1
2
3
4
5
When you get here, go to the next page!
6
7
8
Got the hang of it? Then you are ready to start reading **Fairy Idol Kanon!**

## The Story So Far

**Kanon and her friends have decided to try and become idols, with a little magical help from Alto, the fairy princess. They were finally able to make an appearance on an talent audition show, but Julia's interference caused Alto's takt (magic wand) to break, ruining the girls' chances. In order to repair her takt, Alto returned to the land of the fairies alone. In the meantime, the girls headed to Harajuku, a city that is known to be frequented by talent scouts. Will Kanon's "miracle voice" be enough to save the land of the fairies...?**

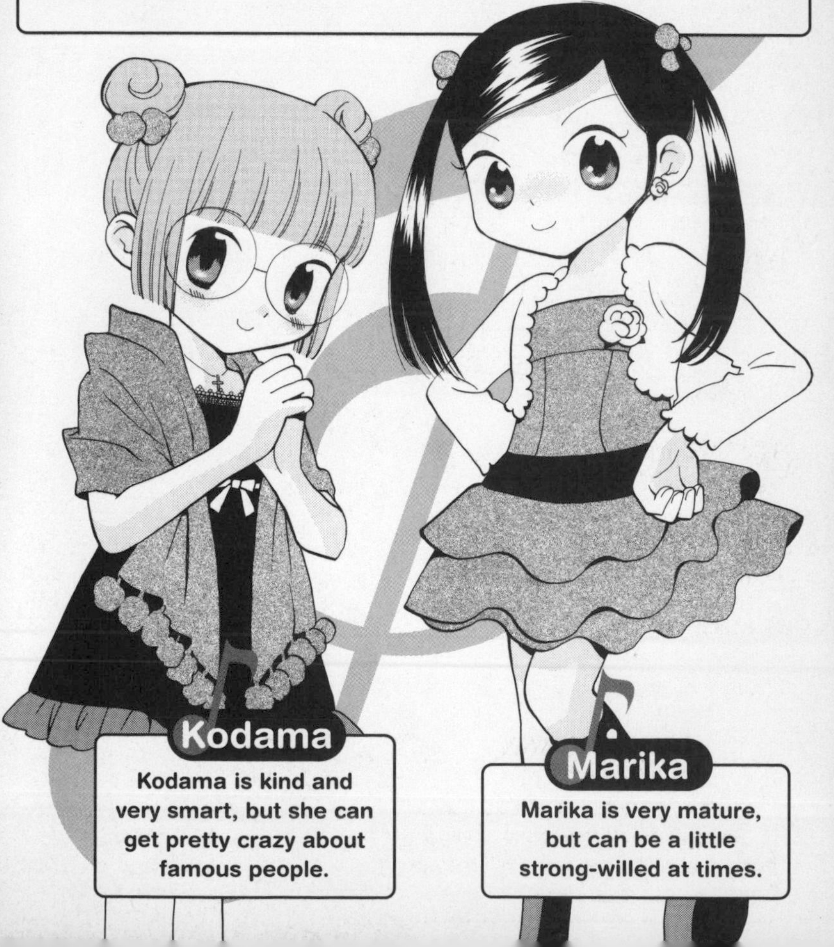

### Kodama

**Kodama is kind and very smart, but she can get pretty crazy about famous people.**

### Marika

**Marika is very mature, but can be a little strong-willed at times.**

# FAIRY IDOL Kanon CHARACTER INTRODUCTION

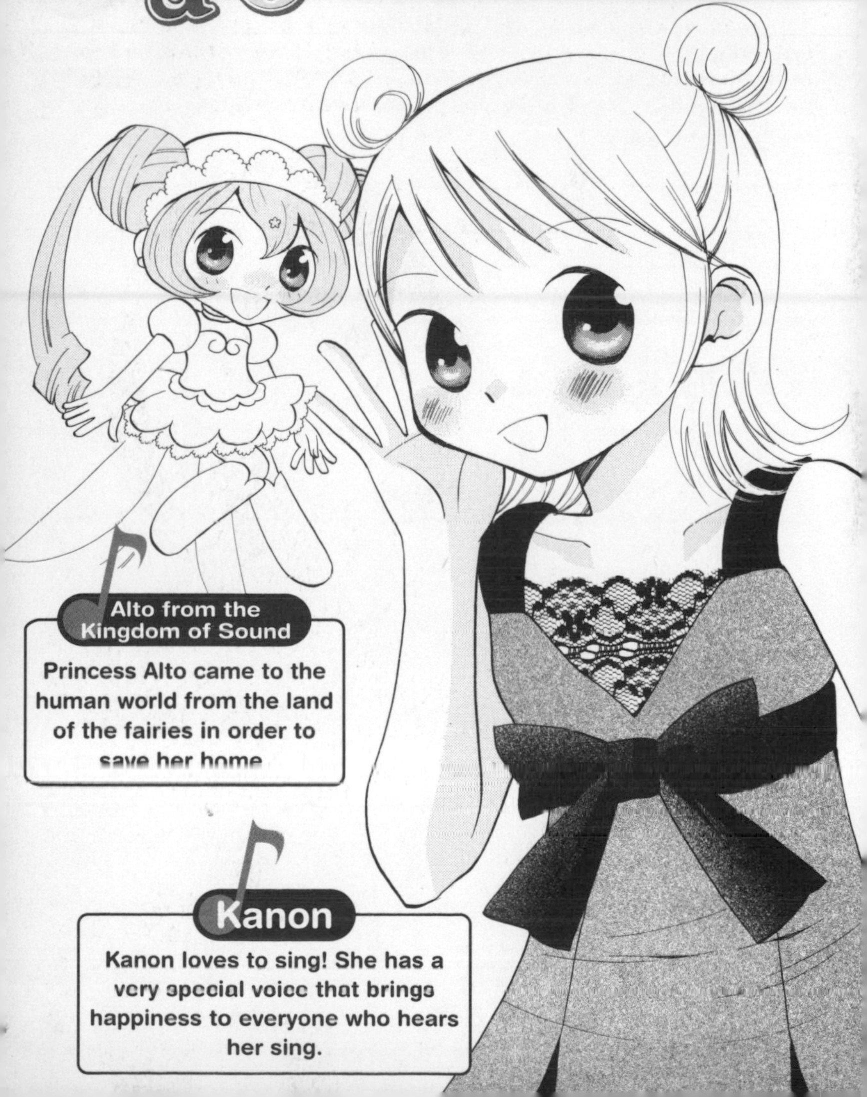

**Alto from the Kingdom of Sound**

Princess Alto came to the human world from the land of the fairies in order to save her home

**Kanon**

Kanon loves to sing! She has a very special voice that brings happiness to everyone who hears her sing.

# CONTENTS

FAIRY IDOL Kanon 2

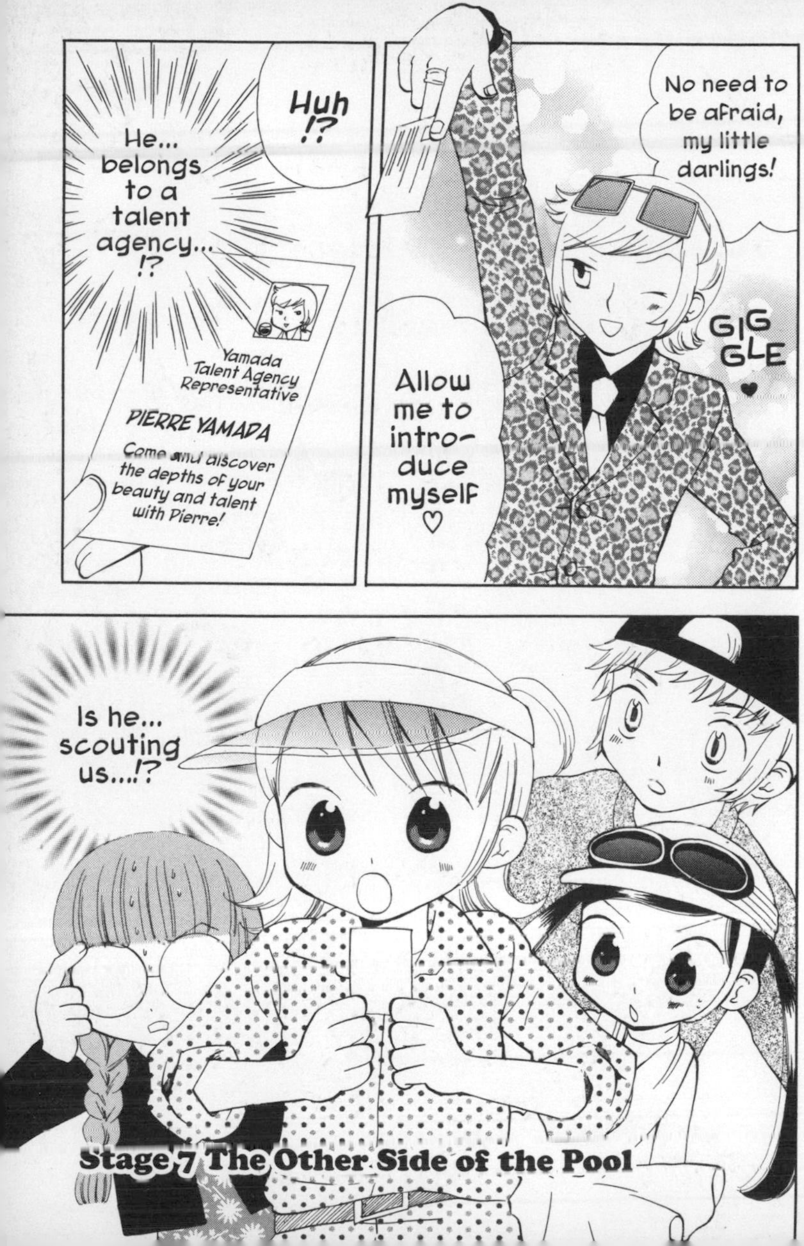
No need to be afraid, my little darlings!
GIGGLE ♥
Allow me to introduce myself ♡
Huh!?
He... belongs to a talent agency...!?
Yamada Talent Agency Representative
PIERRE YAMADA
Come and discover the depths of your beauty and talent with Pierre!
Is he... scouting us...!?
Stage 7 The Other Side of the Pool

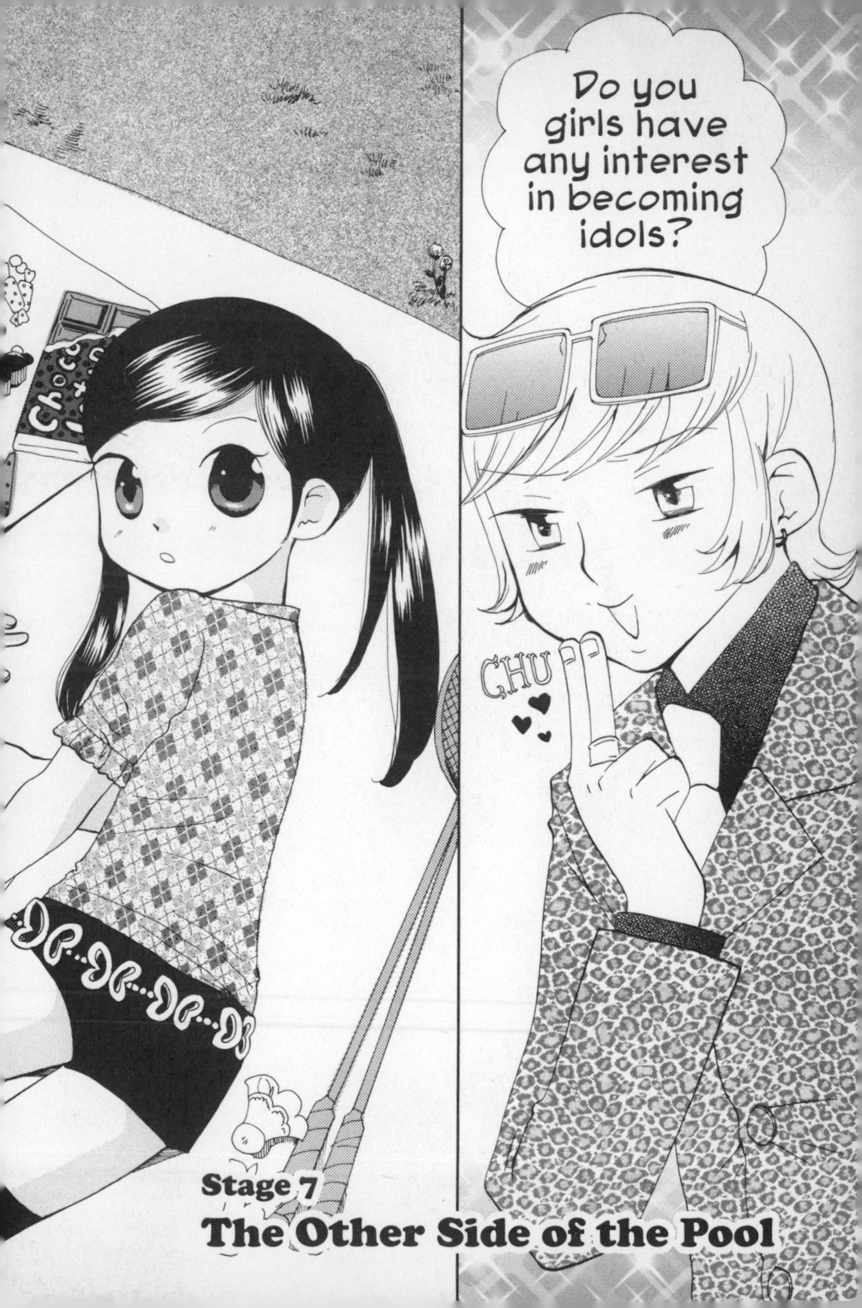
Do you girls have any interest in becoming idols?
CHU
Stage 7
The Other Side of the Pool

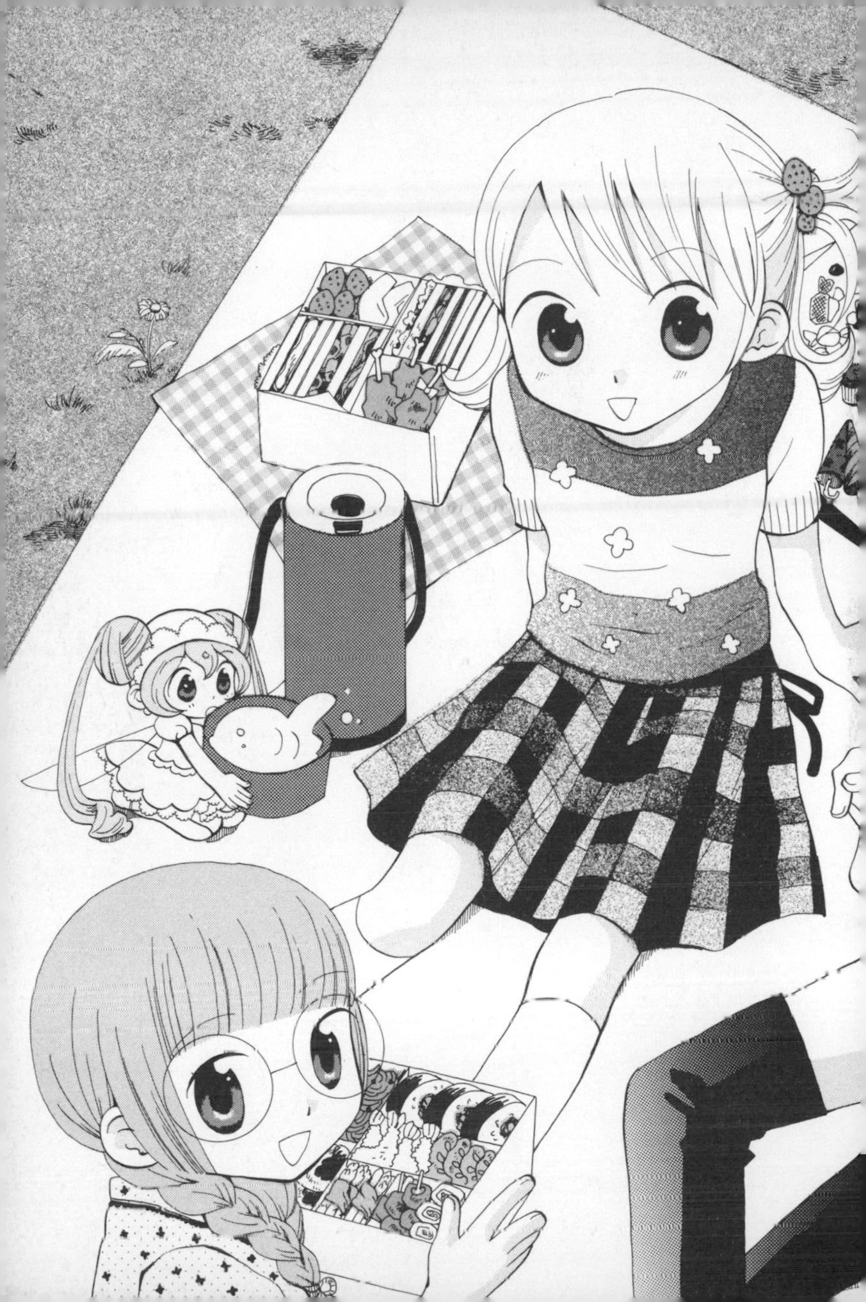

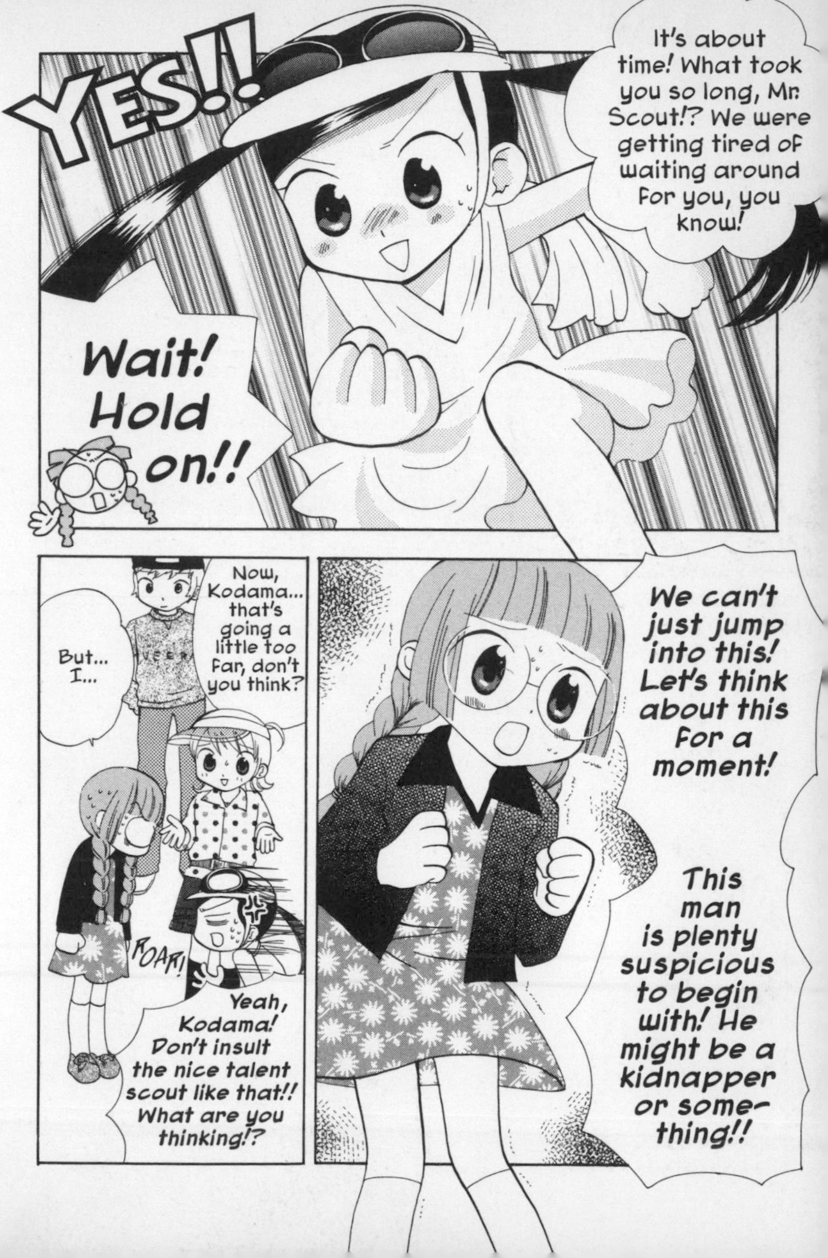
It's about time! What took you so long, Mr. Scout!? We were getting tired of waiting around for you, you know!
YES!!
Wait! Hold on!!
We can't just jump into this! Let's think about this for a moment!
This man is plenty suspicious to begin with! He might be a kidnapper or some-thing!!
Now, Kodama... that's going a little too far, don't you think?
But... I...
ROAR!
Yeah, Kodama! Don't insult the nice talent scout like that!! What are you thinking!?

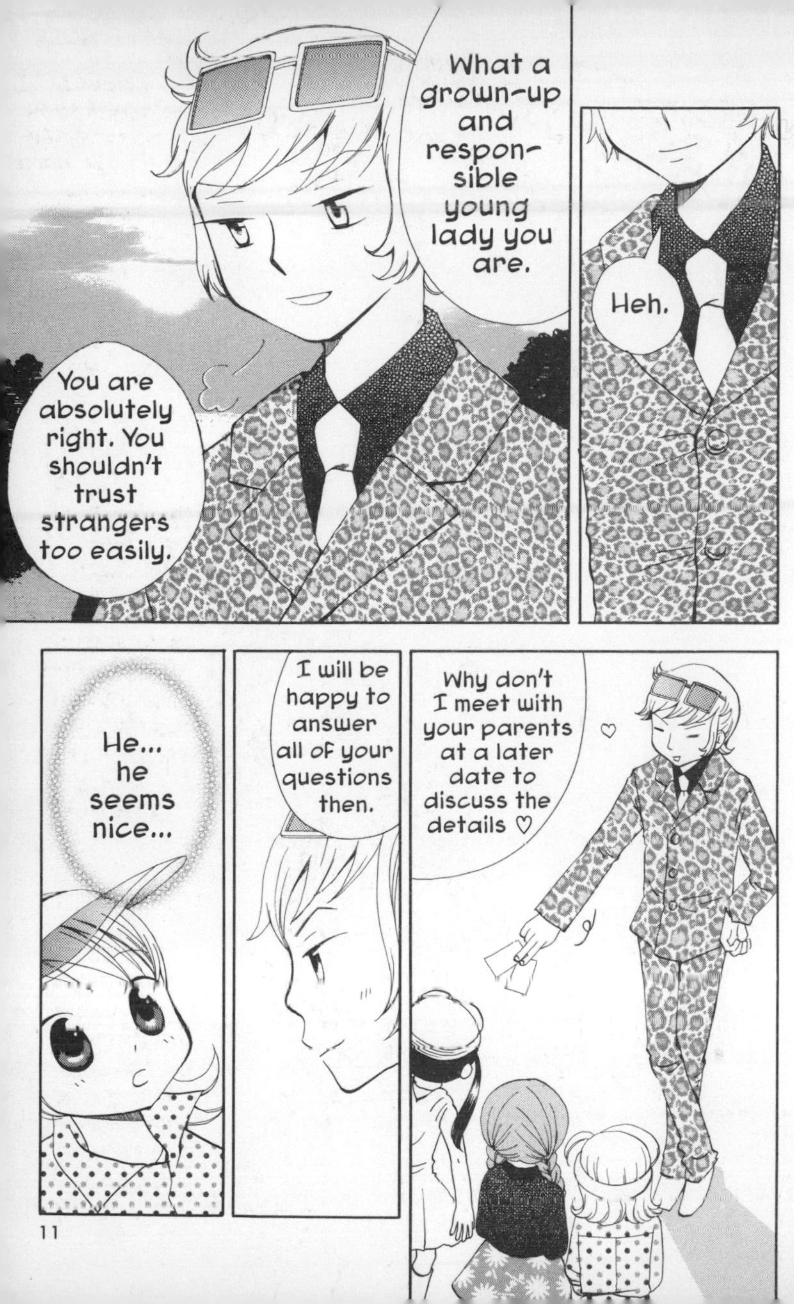
Heh.
What a grown-up and responsible young lady you are.
You are absolutely right. You shouldn't trust strangers too easily.
Why don't I meet with your parents at a later date to discuss the details ♡
I will be happy to answer all of your questions then.
He... he seems nice...

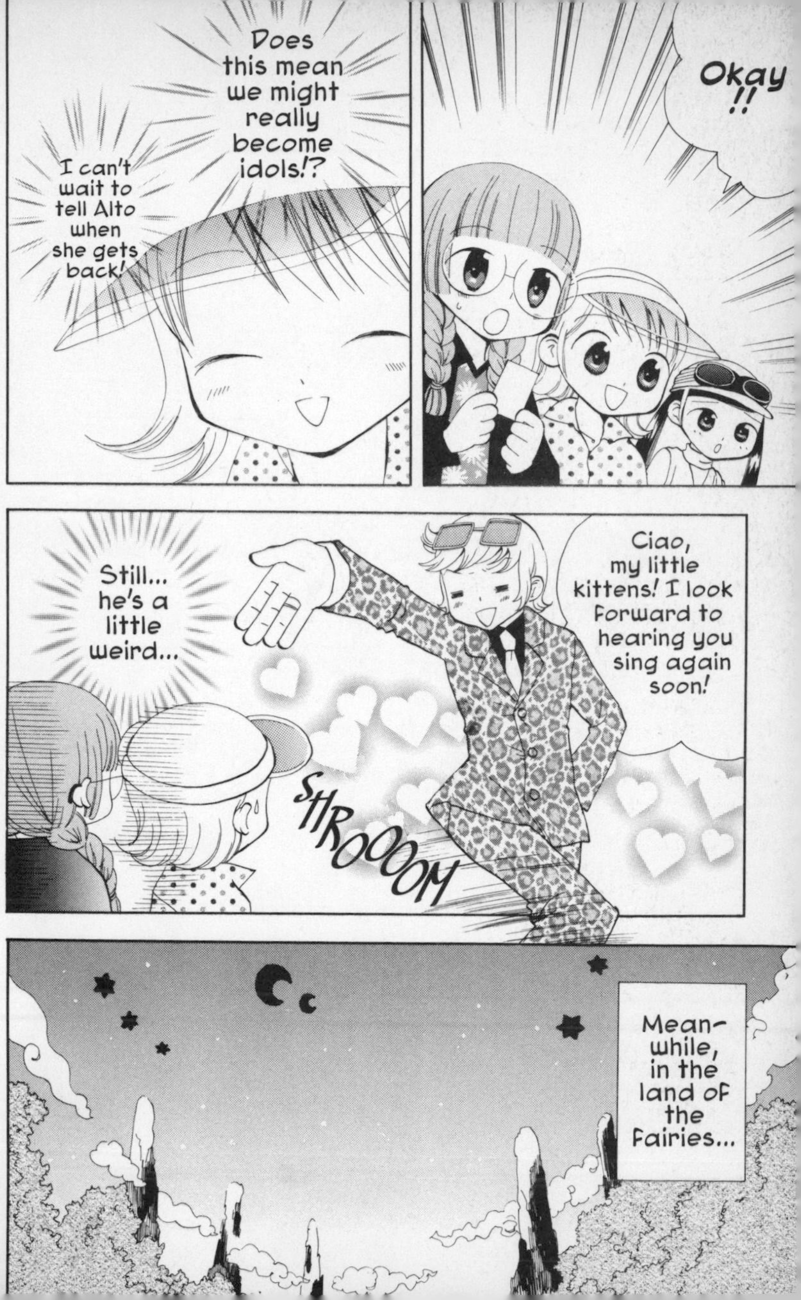
Okay!!
Does this mean we might really become idols!?
I can't wait to tell Alto when she gets back!
Ciao, my little kittens! I look forward to hearing you sing again soon!
Still... he's a little weird...
SHROOOOM
Meanwhile, in the land of the fairies...

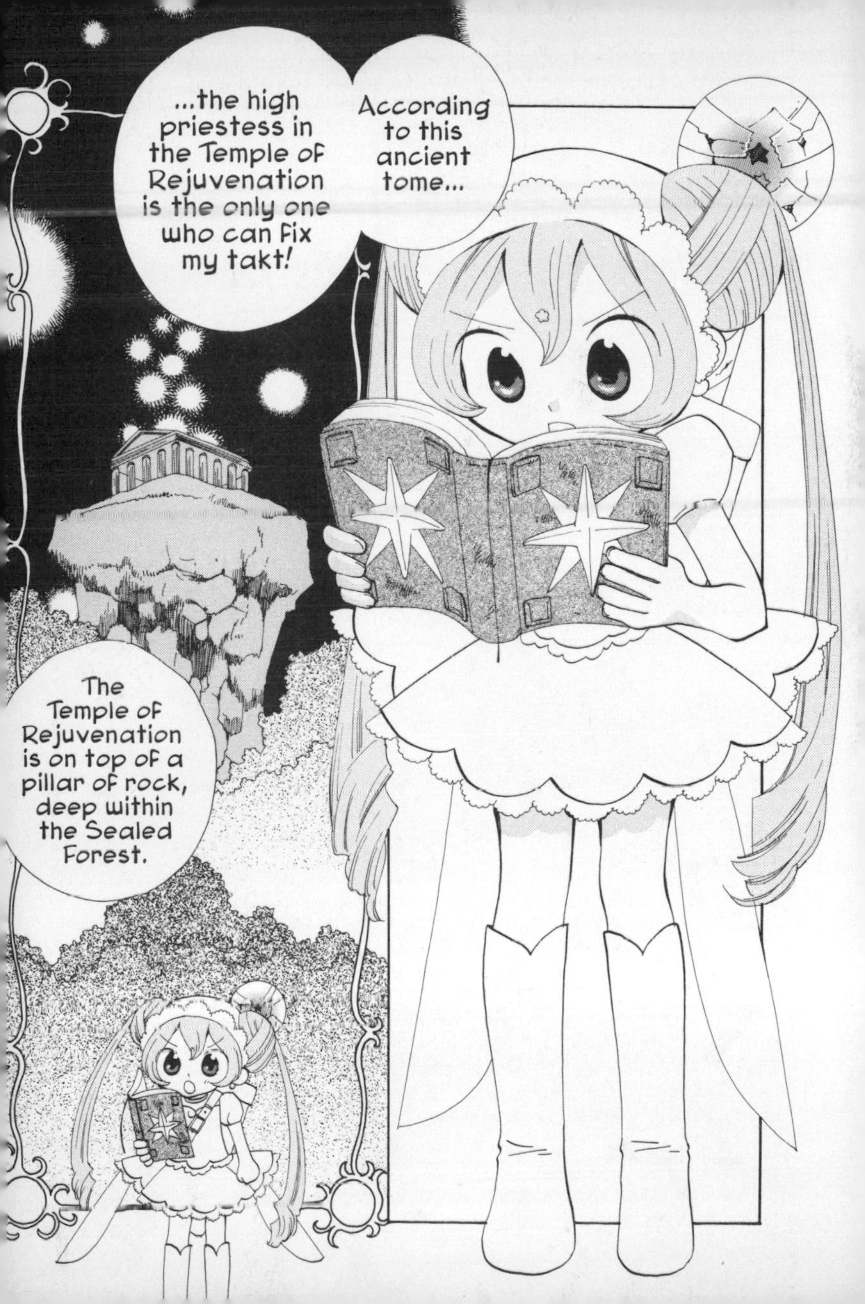
According to this ancient tome...
...the high priestess in the Temple of Rejuvenation is the only one who can fix my takt!
The Temple of Rejuvenation is on top of a pillar of rock, deep within the Sealed Forest.

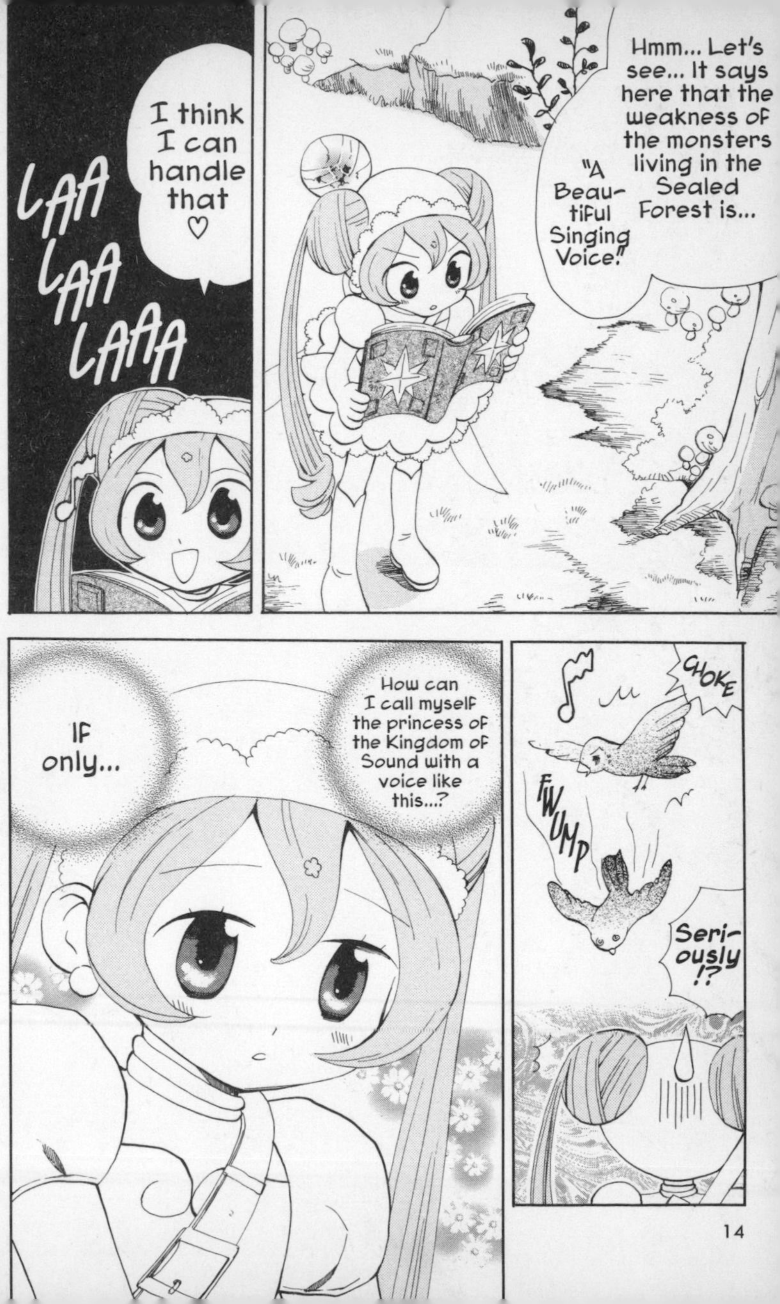
Hmm... Let's see... It says here that the weakness of the monsters living in the Sealed Forest is...
"A Beau-tiful Singing Voice."
I think I can handle that ♡
LAA LAA LAAA
CHOKE
FWUMP
Seri-ously!?
How can I call myself the princess of the Kingdom of Sound with a voice like this...?
If only...

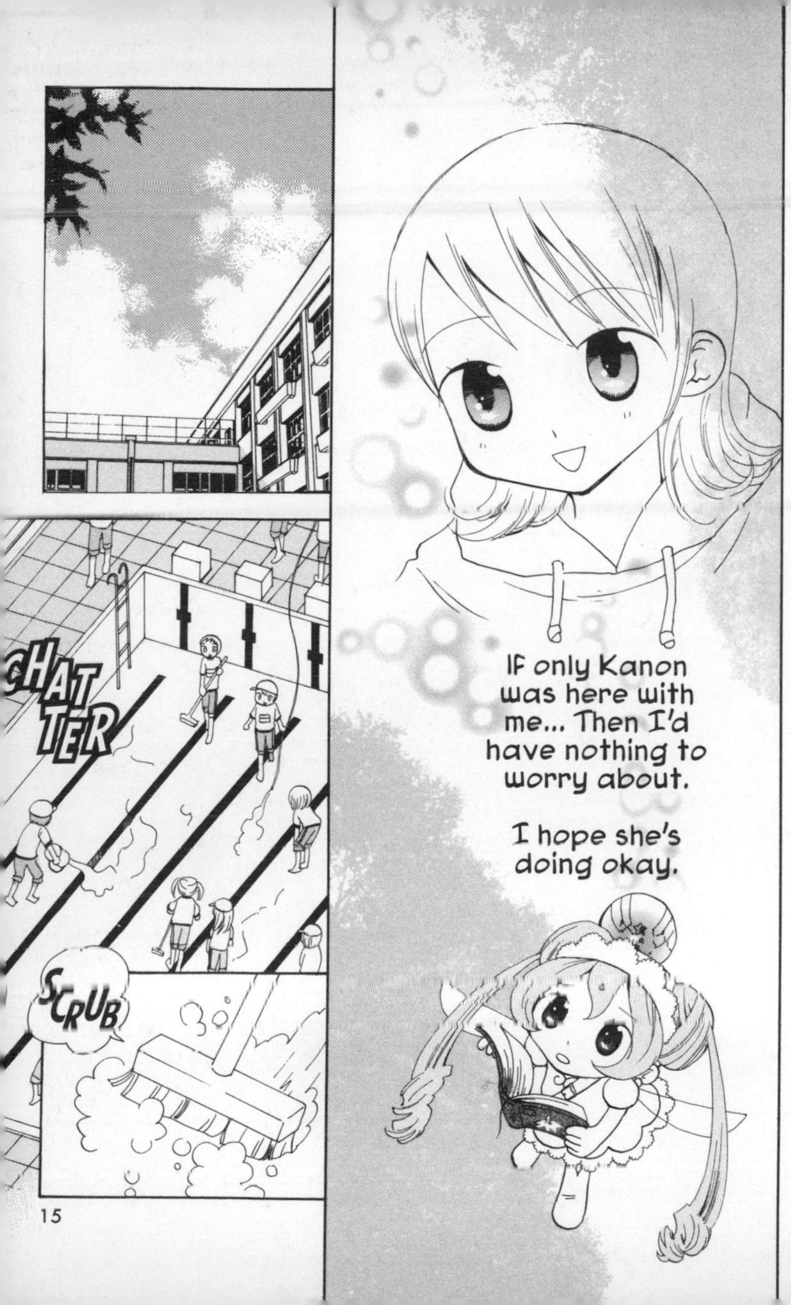
If only Kanon was here with me... Then I'd have nothing to worry about.
I hope she's doing okay.
CHATTER
SCRUB

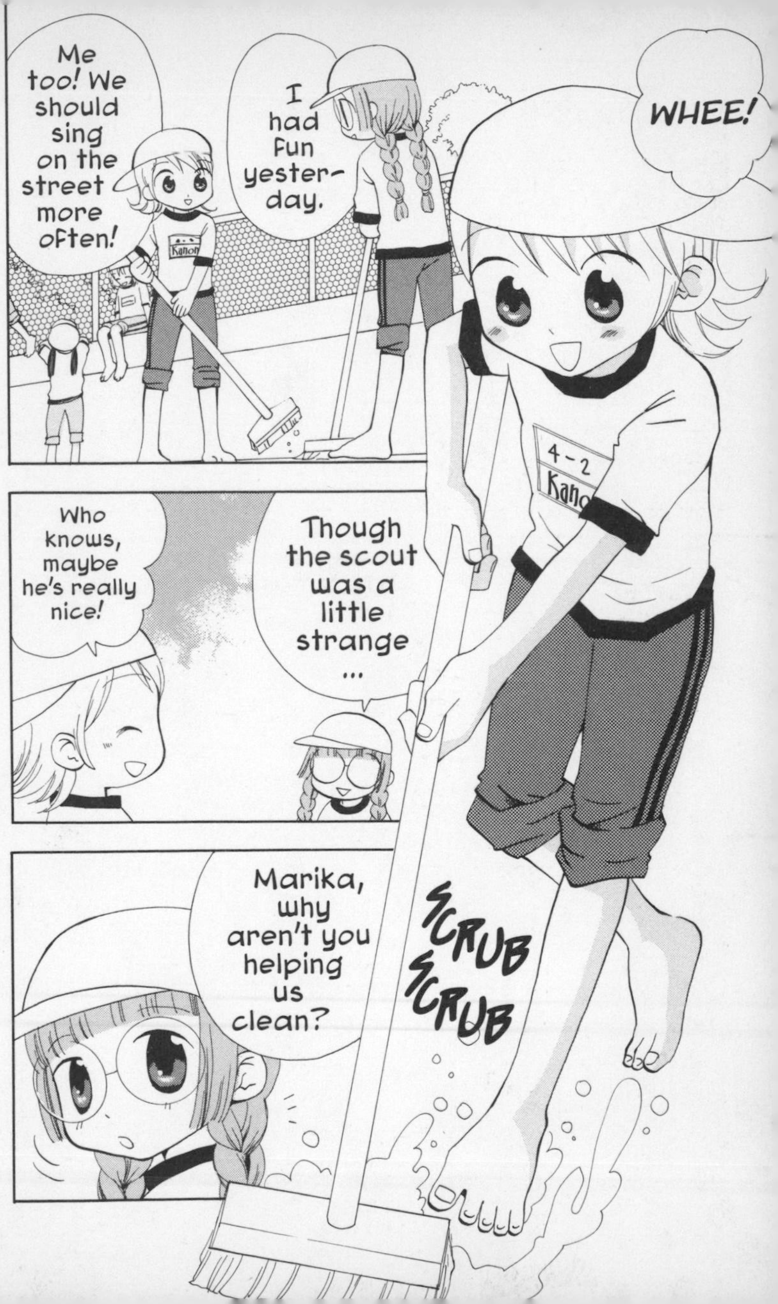
WHEE!
SCRUB SCRUB
I had fun yester-day.
Me too! We should sing on the street more often!
Though the scout was a little strange ...
Who knows, maybe he's really nice!
Marika, why aren't you helping us clean?

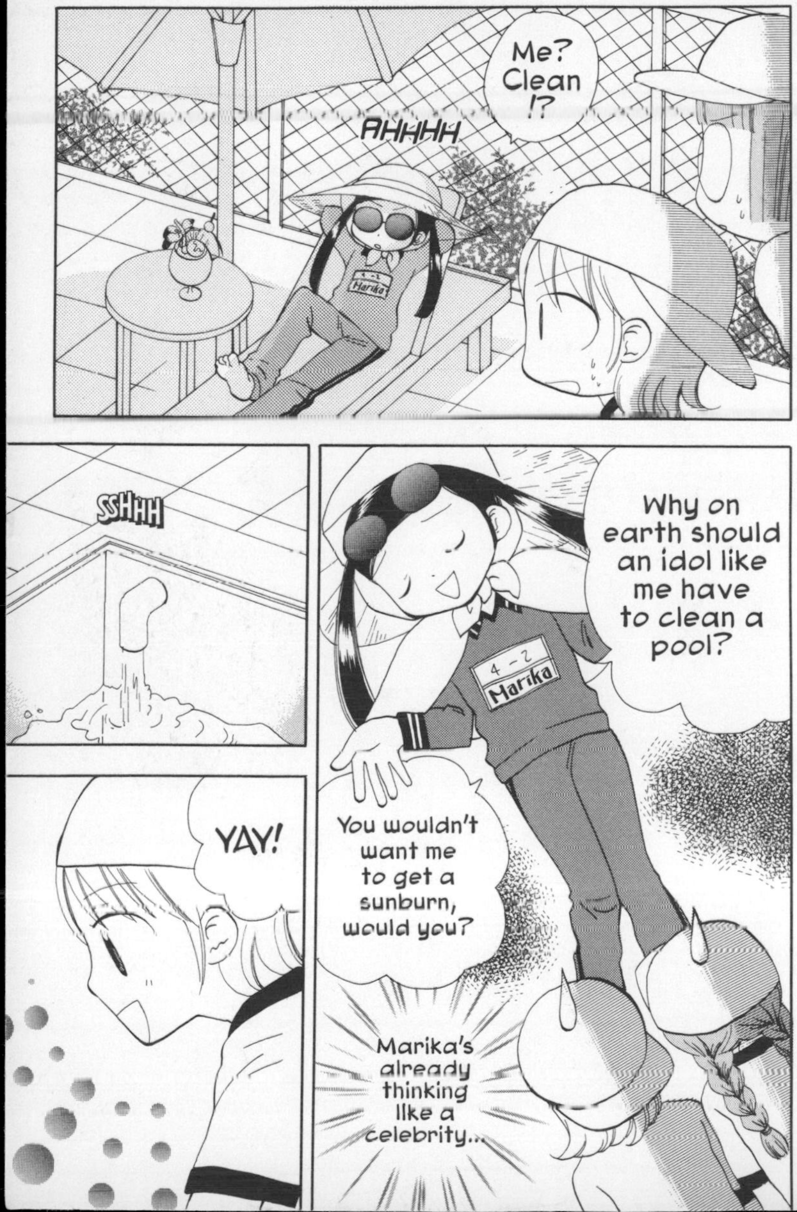
Me? Clean !?
AHHHH
4-1 Marika
Why on earth should an idol like me have to clean a pool?
4-2 Marika
You wouldn't want me to get a sunburn, would you?
Marika's already thinking like a celebrity...
SSHHH
YAY!

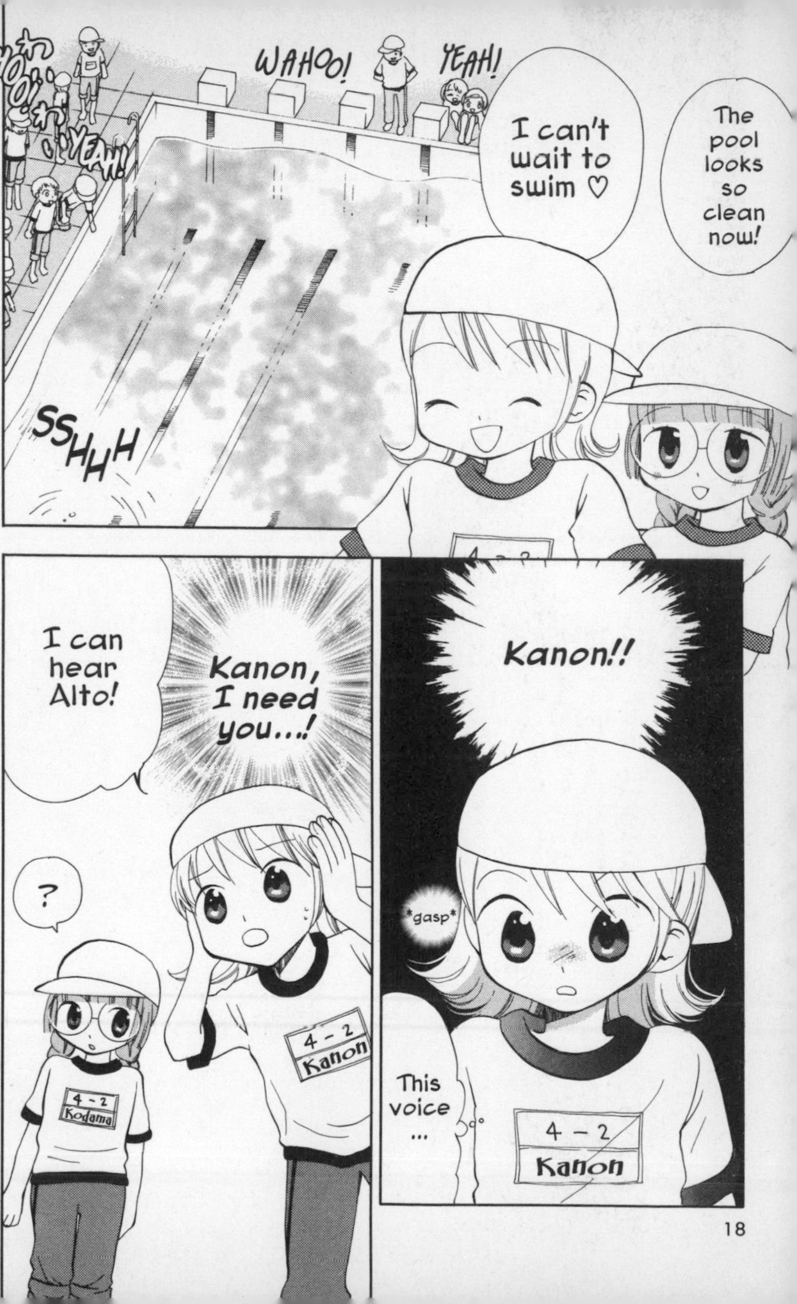
The pool looks so clean now!
I can't wait to swim ♡
YEAH!
WAHOO!
WAHOO! わ わ YEAH!
SSHHHH
4-2
Kanon!!
*gasp*
This voice ...
4 – 2
Kanon
Kanon, I need you...!
I can hear Alto!
4 – 2
Kanon
?
4 – 2
Kodama

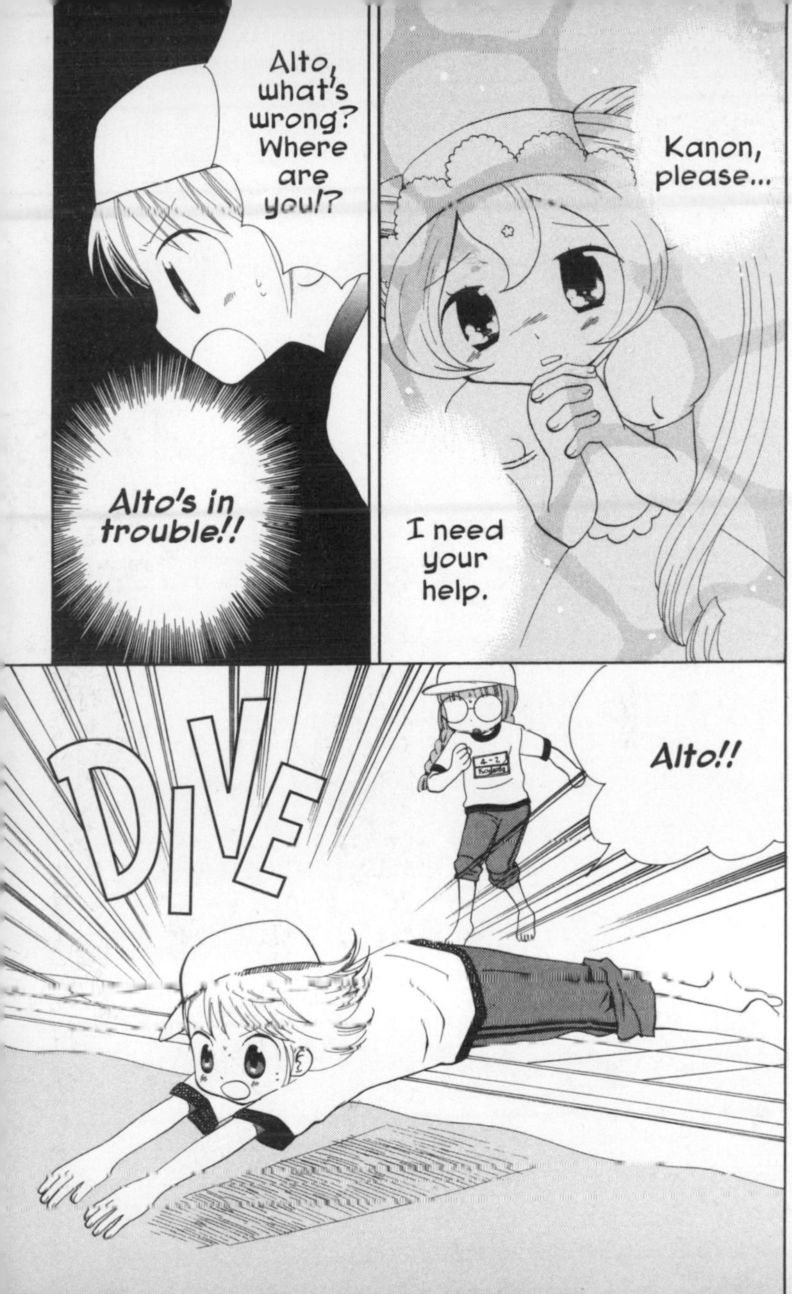
Kanon, please...
I need your help.
Alto, what's wrong? Where are you!?
Alto's in trouble!!
Alto!!
DIVE

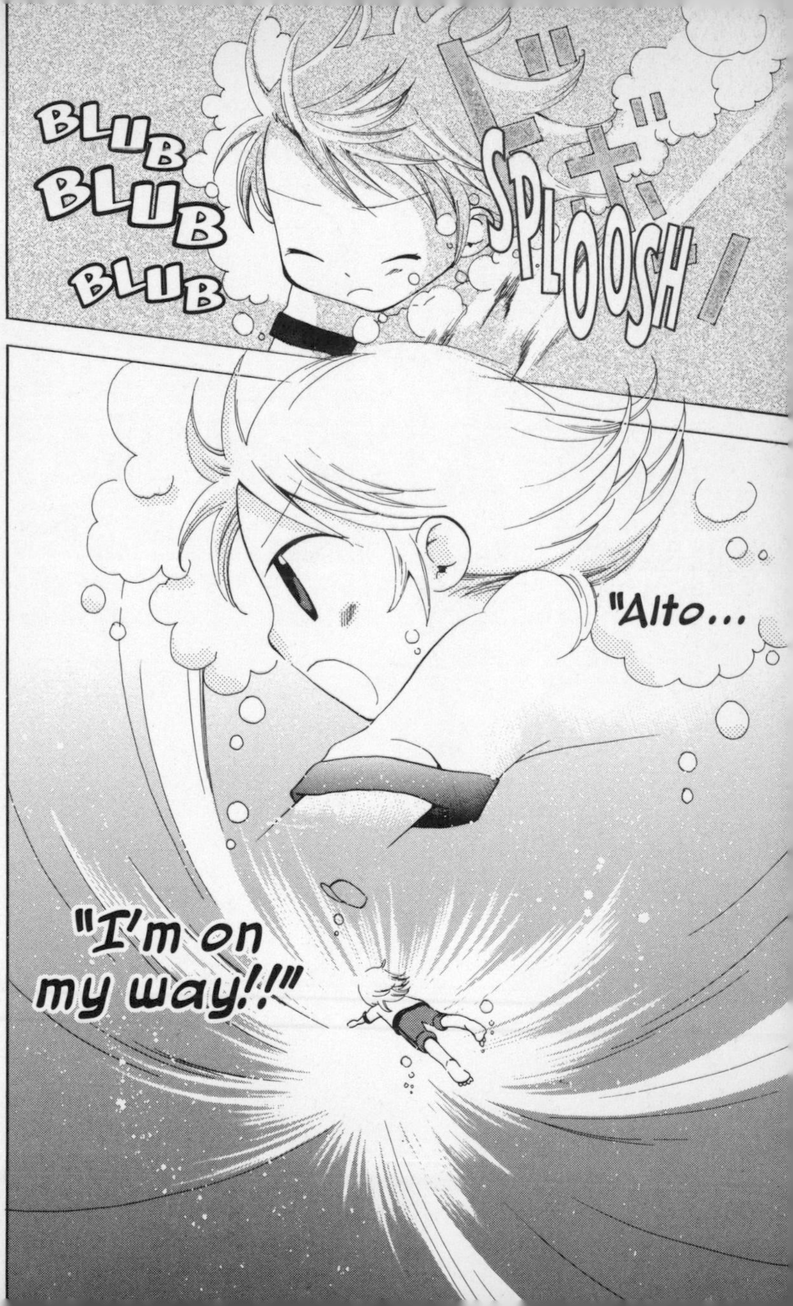
SPLOOSH
BLUB BLUB BLUB
"Alto...
"I'm on my way!!"

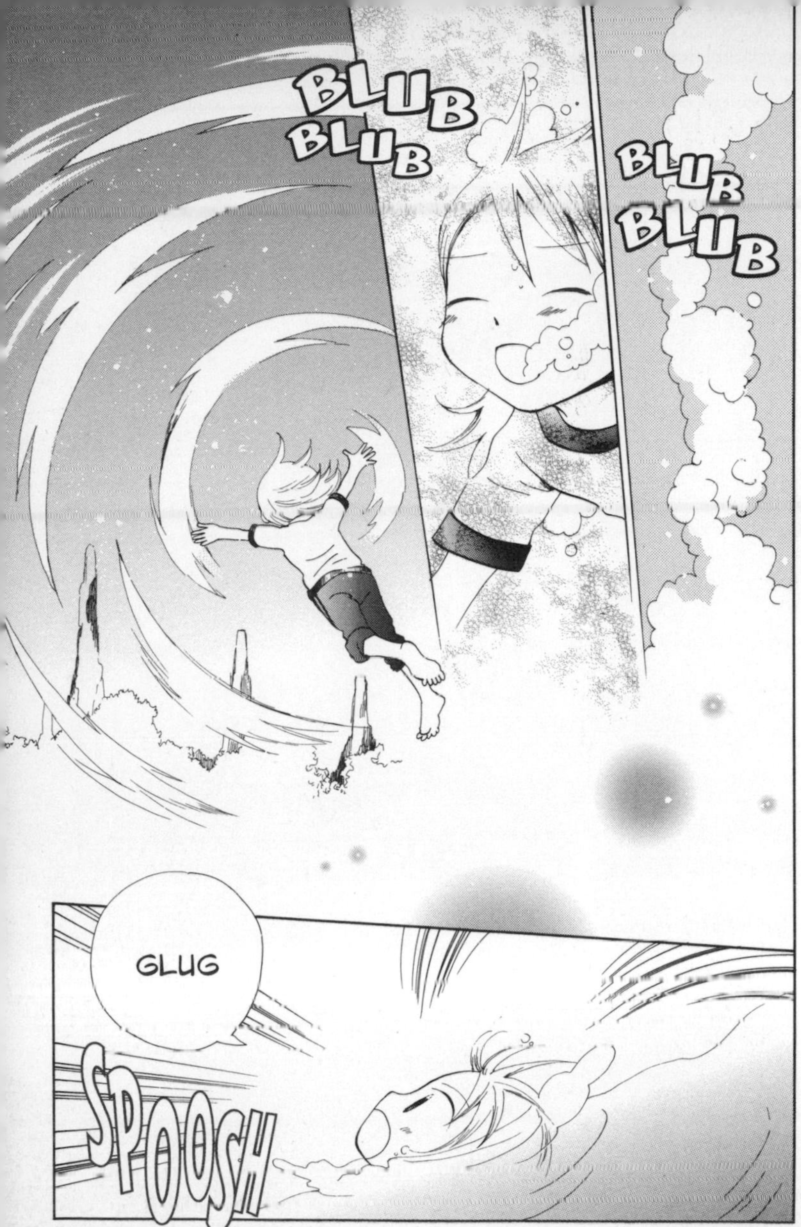
BLUB BLUB
BLUB BLUB
GLUG
SPOOSH

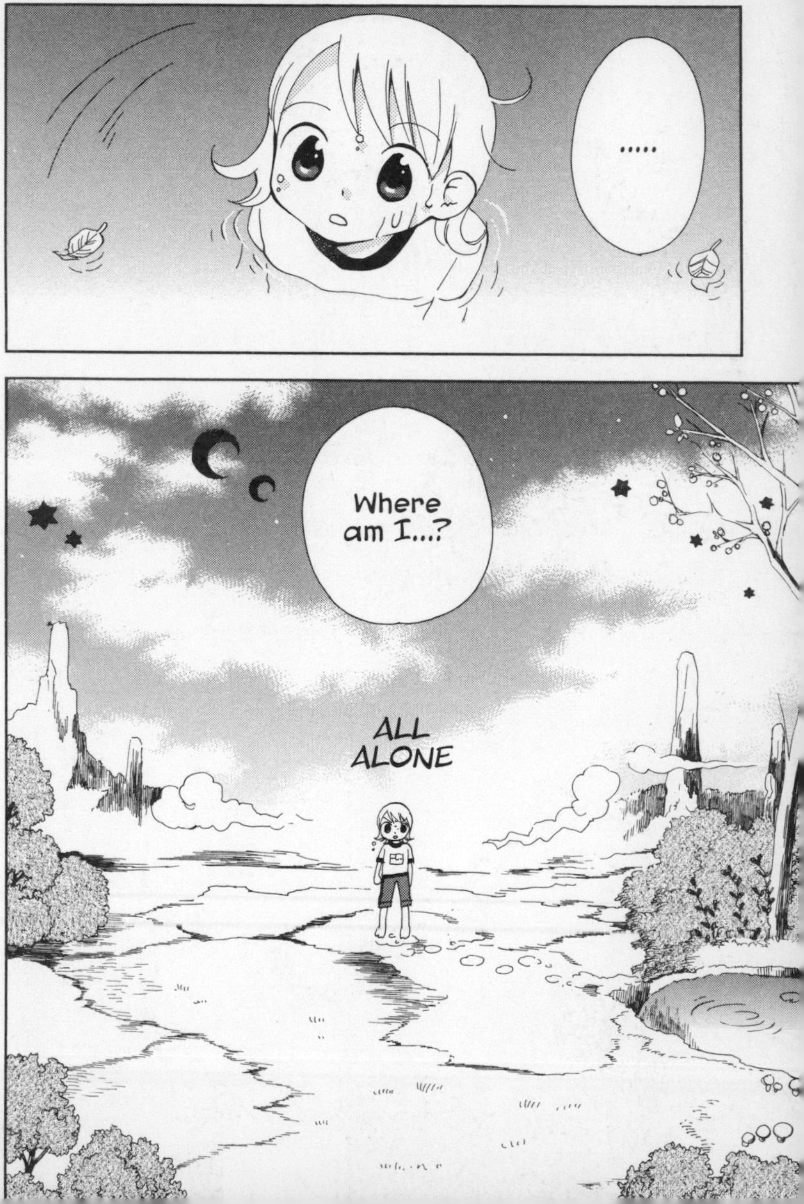
......
Where am I...?
ALL ALONE

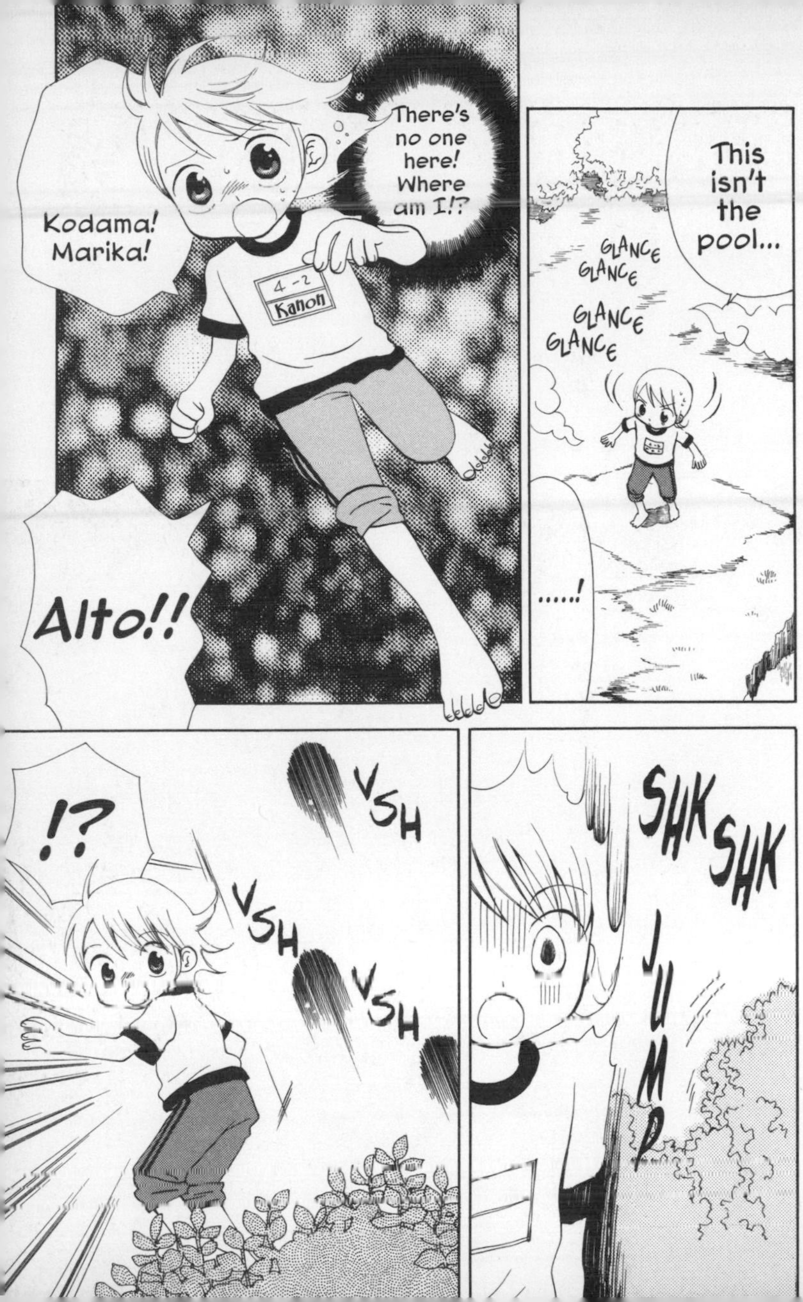
This isn't the pool...
GLANCE GLANCE
GLANCE GLANCE
.....!
There's no one here! Where am I!?
4-2
Kanon
Kodama! Marika!
Alto!!
SHK SHK
JUMP
!?
VSH
VSH
VSH

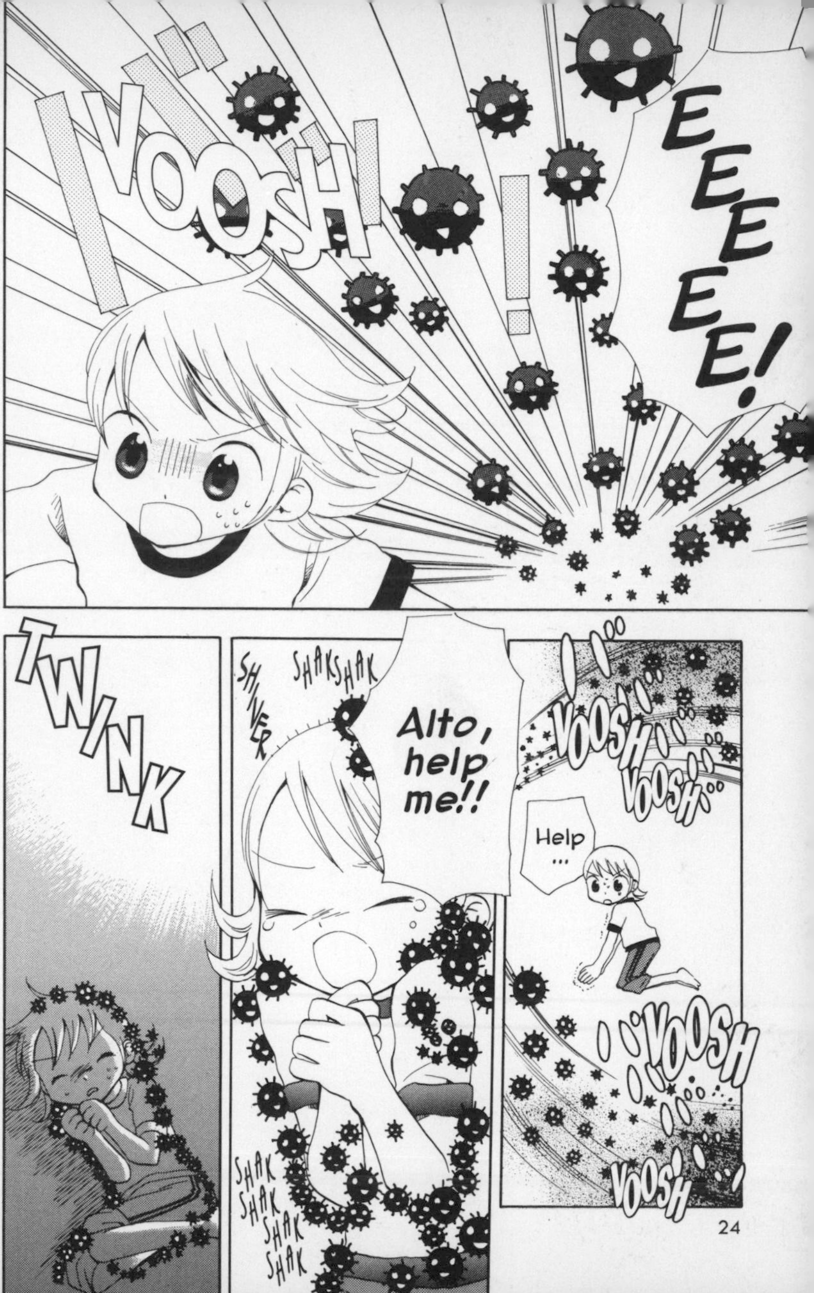

EEEEEE!
!
VOOSH!
VOOSH
VOOSH
Help ...
VOOSH
VOOSH
SHAKSHAK
SHIVER
Alto, help me!!
SHAK SHAK SHAK SHAK
TWINK

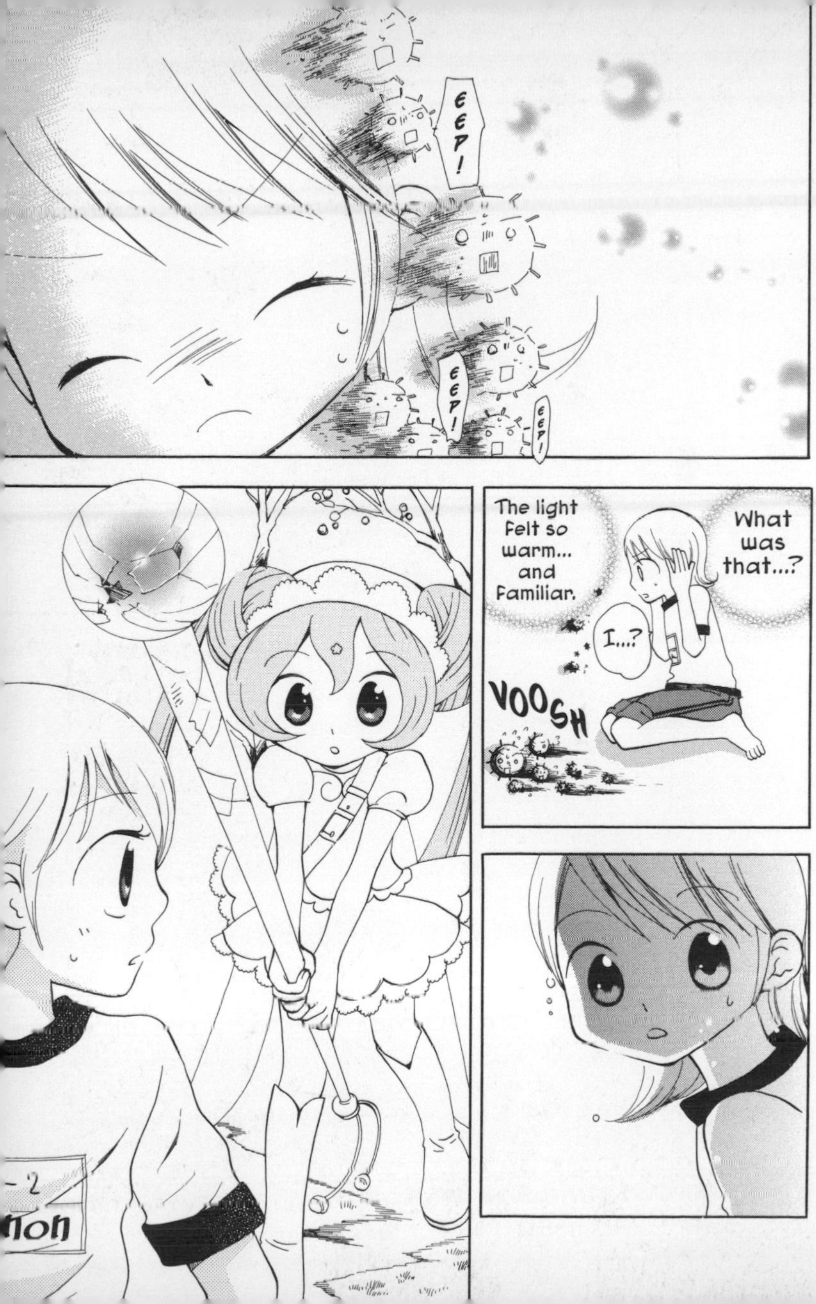
EEP!
EEP!
EEP!
What was that...?
The light felt so warm... and familiar.
I...?
VOOSH

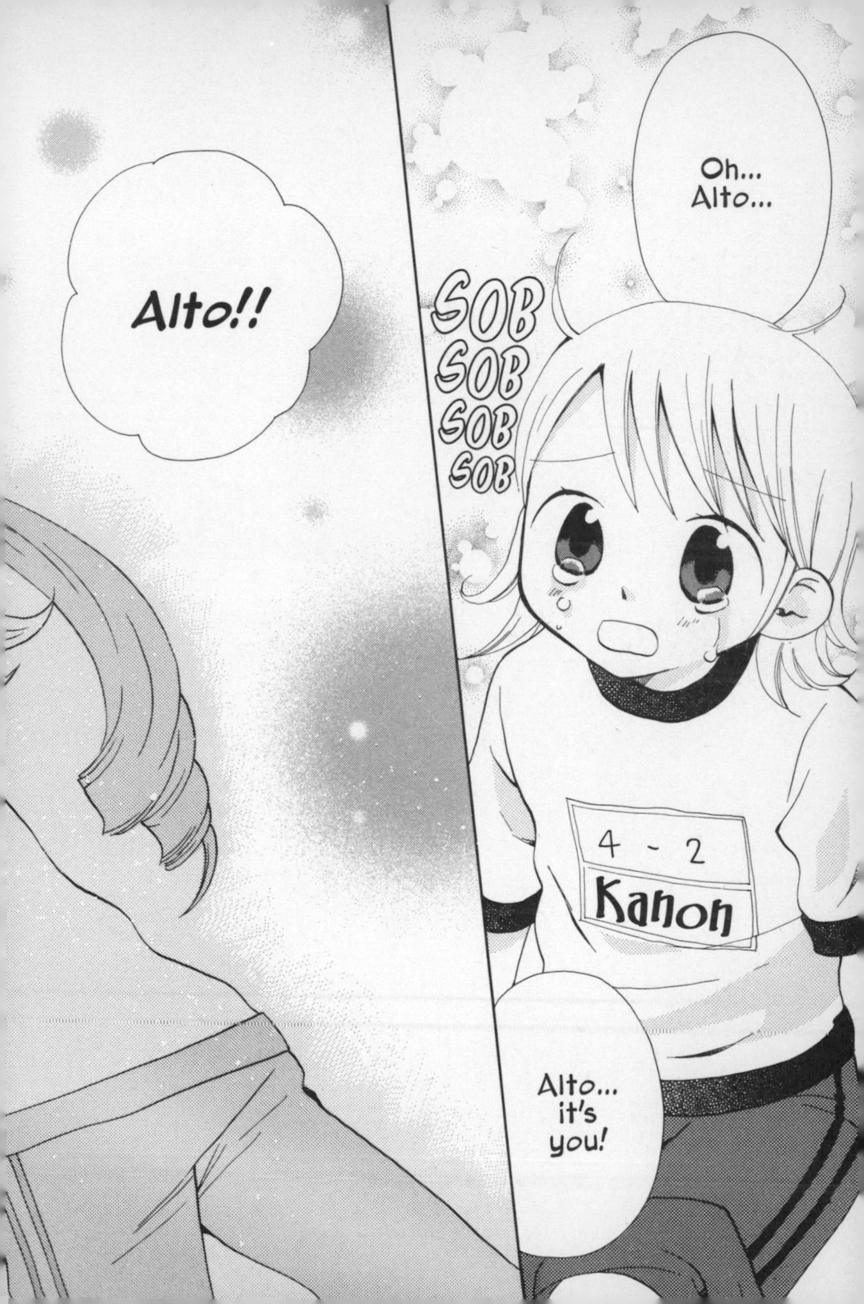
Oh... Alto...
SOB SOB SOB SOB
4 - 2
Kanon
Alto... it's you!
Alto!!

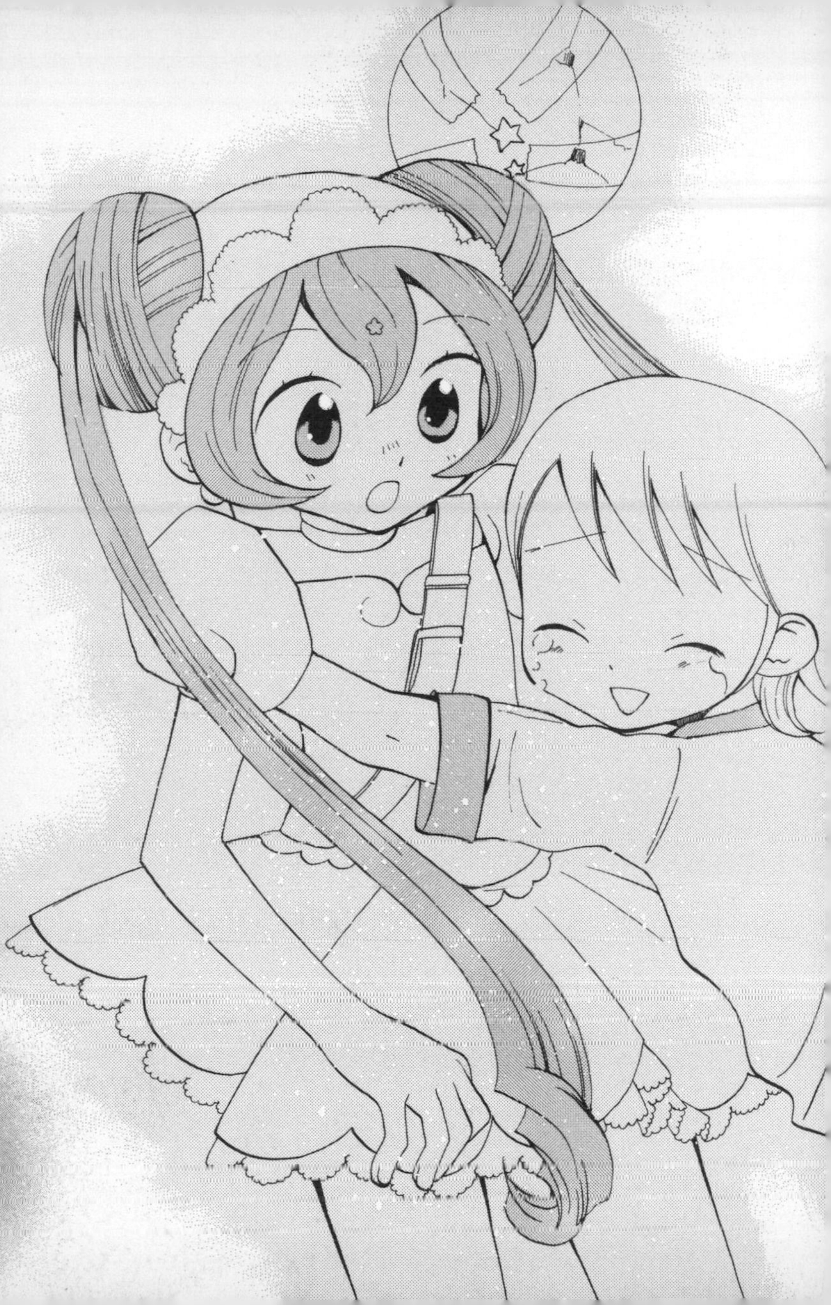

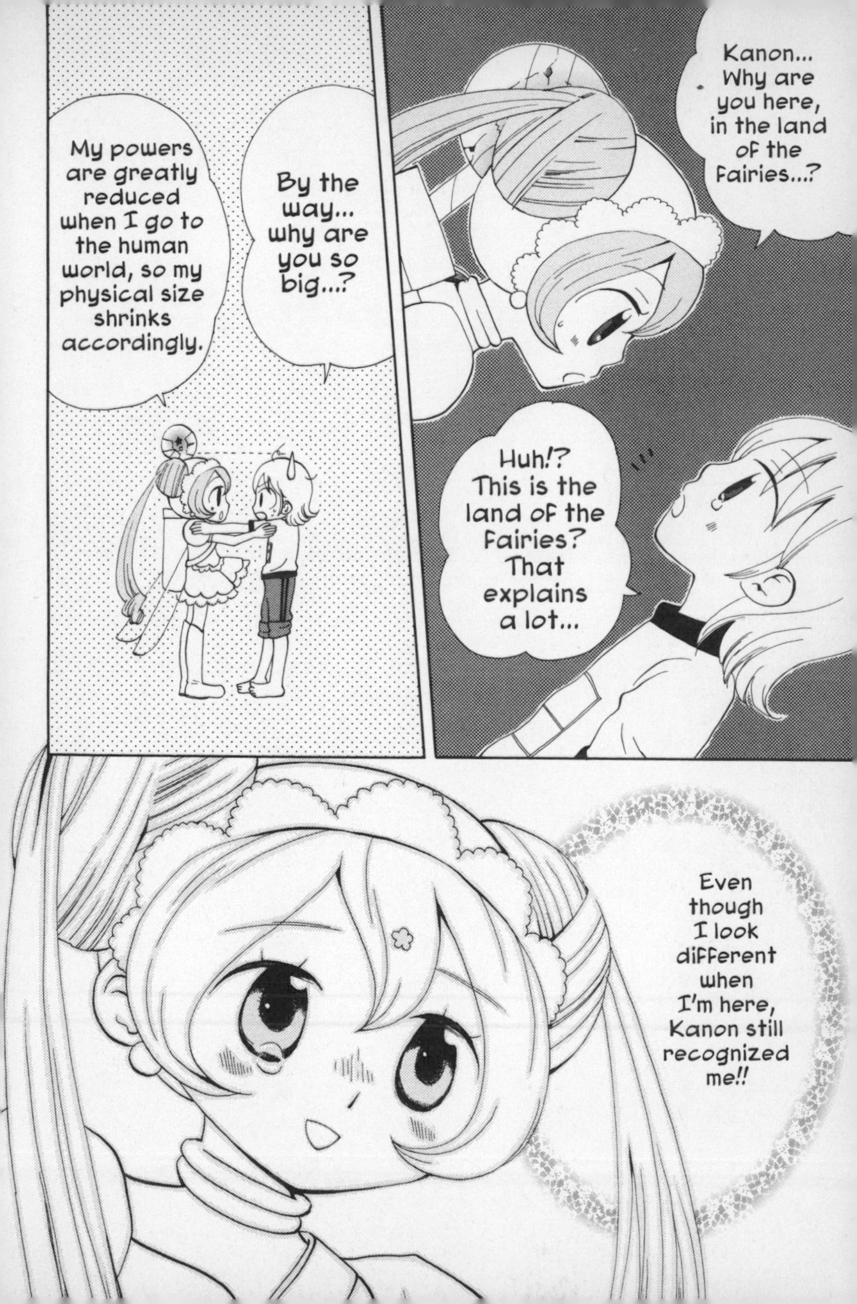
Kanon... Why are you here, in the land of the fairies...?
Huh!? This is the land of the fairies? That explains a lot...
By the way... why are you so big...?
My powers are greatly reduced when I go to the human world, so my physical size shrinks accordingly.
Even though I look different when I'm here, Kanon still recognized me!!

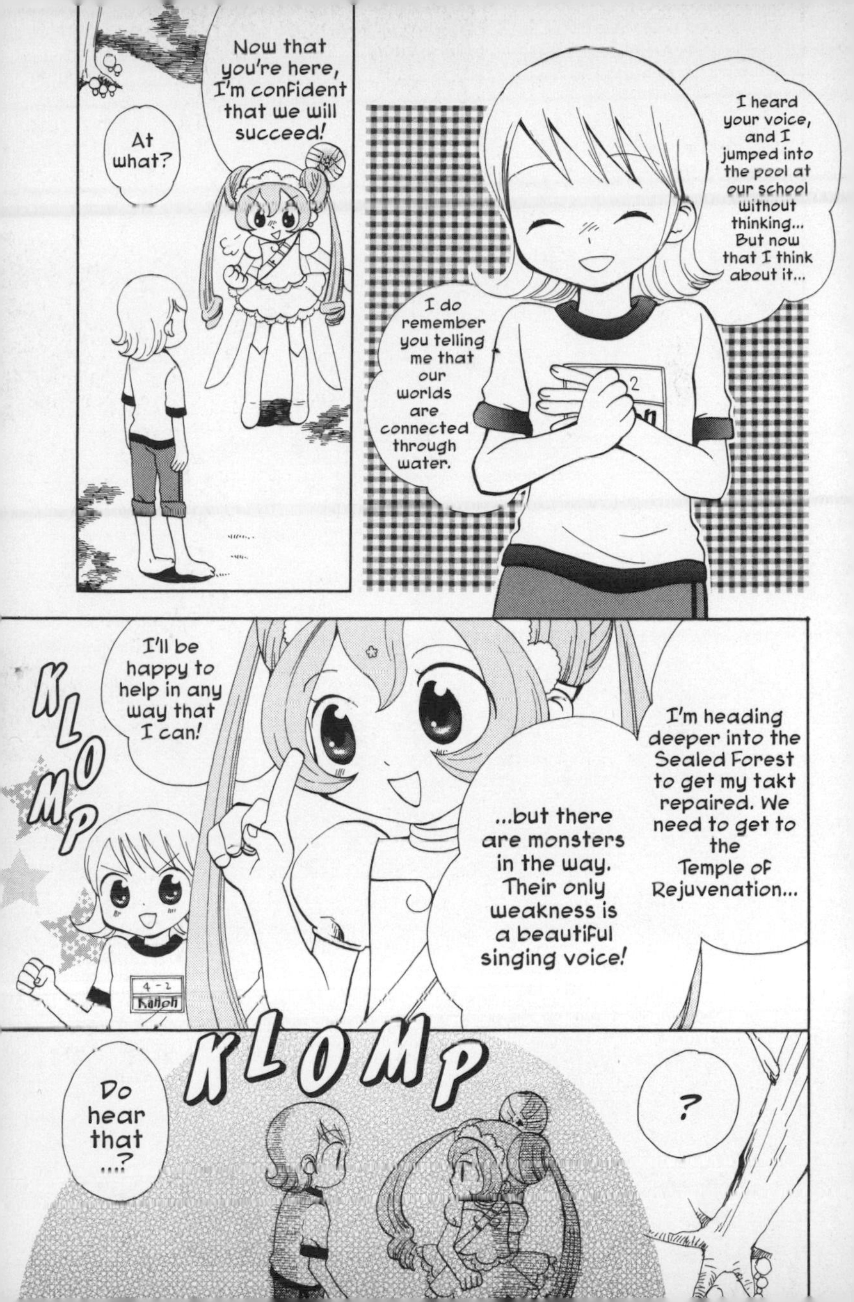
I heard your voice, and I jumped into the pool at our school without thinking... But now that I think about it...
I do remember you telling me that our worlds are connected through water.
Now that you're here, I'm confident that we will succeed!
At what?
I'm heading deeper into the Sealed Forest to get my takt repaired. We need to get to the Temple of Rejuvenation...
...but there are monsters in the way. Their only weakness is a beautiful singing voice!
I'll be happy to help in any way that I can!
KLOMP
4 - 2
KLOMP
?
Do hear that ...?

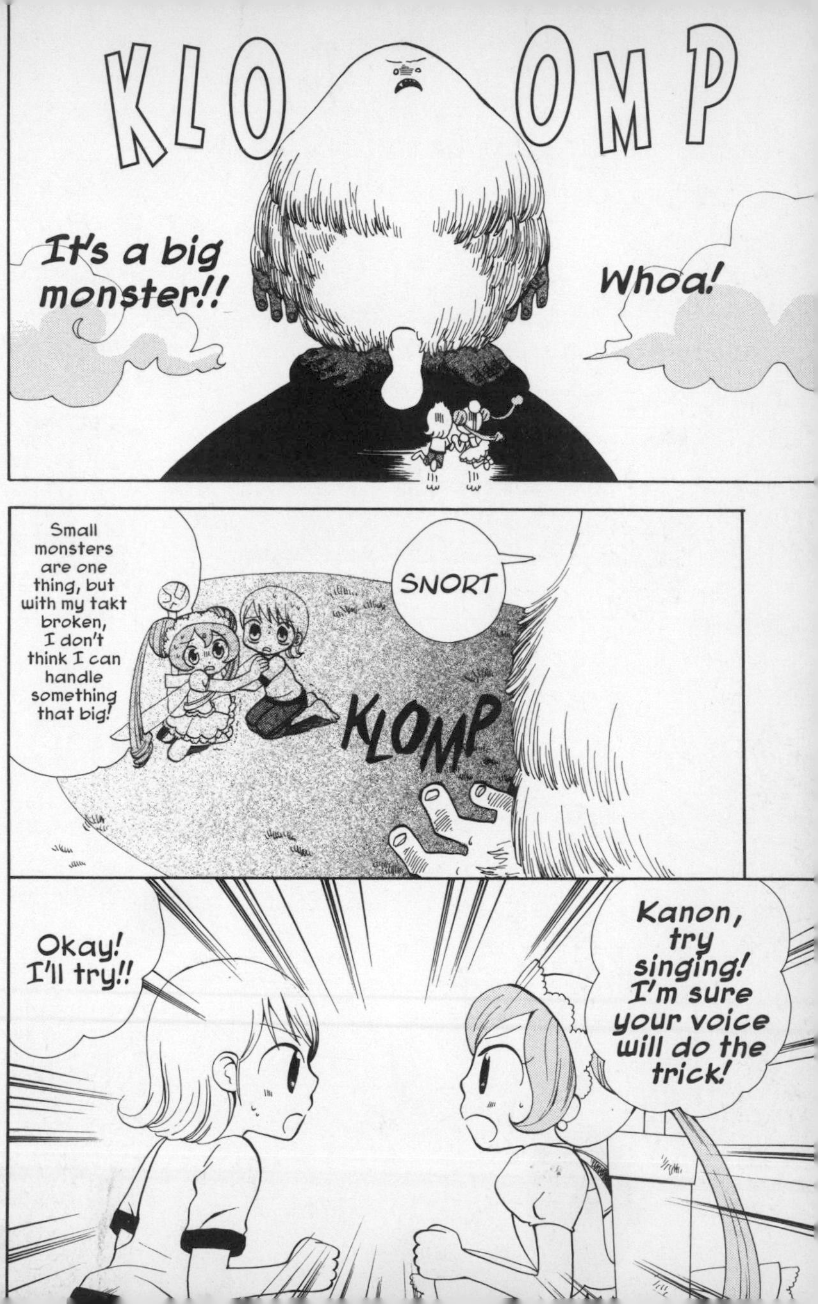
KLOMP
Whoa!
It's a big monster!!
SNORT
Small monsters are one thing, but with my takt broken, I don't think I can handle something that big!
KLOMP
Kanon, try singing! I'm sure your voice will do the trick!
Okay! I'll try!!

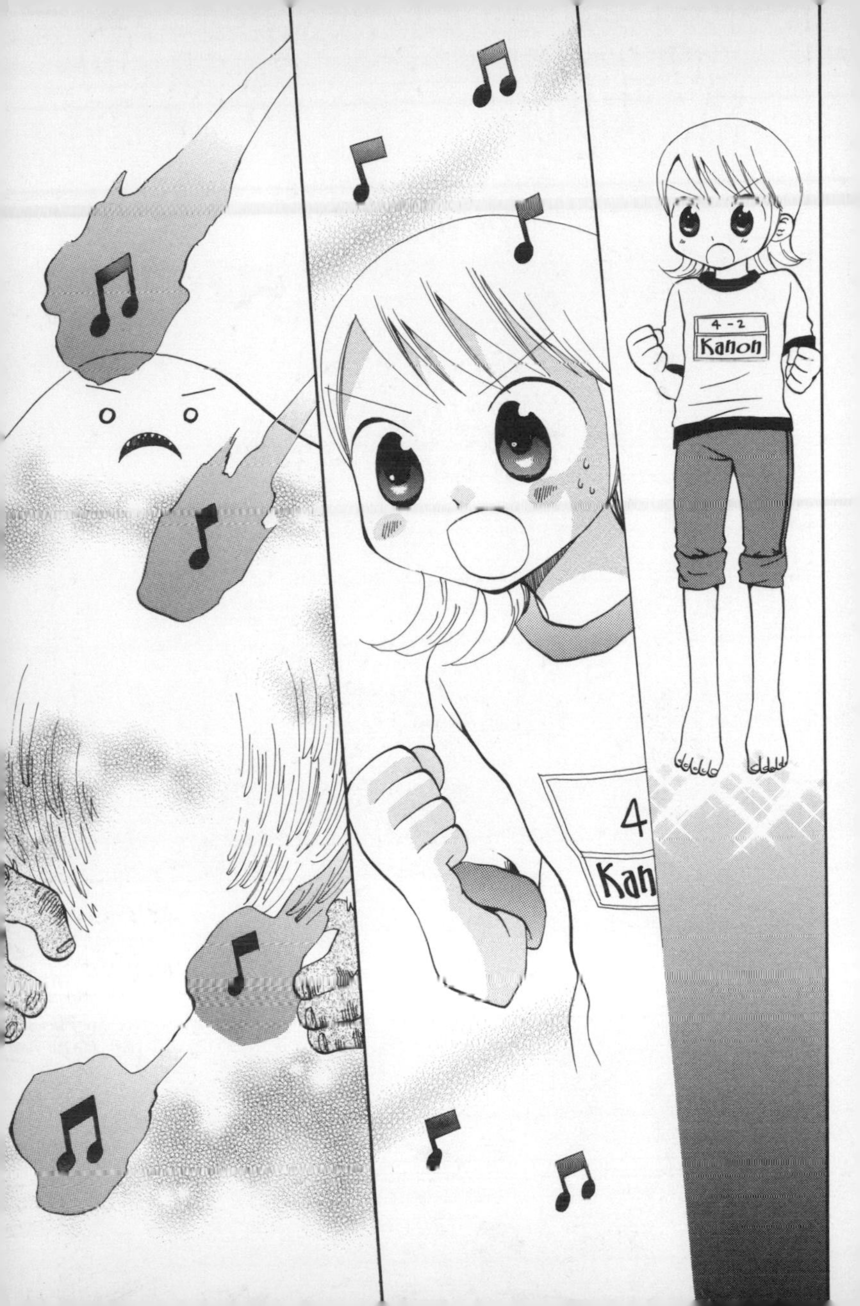
4 -2
Kanon
4
Kan

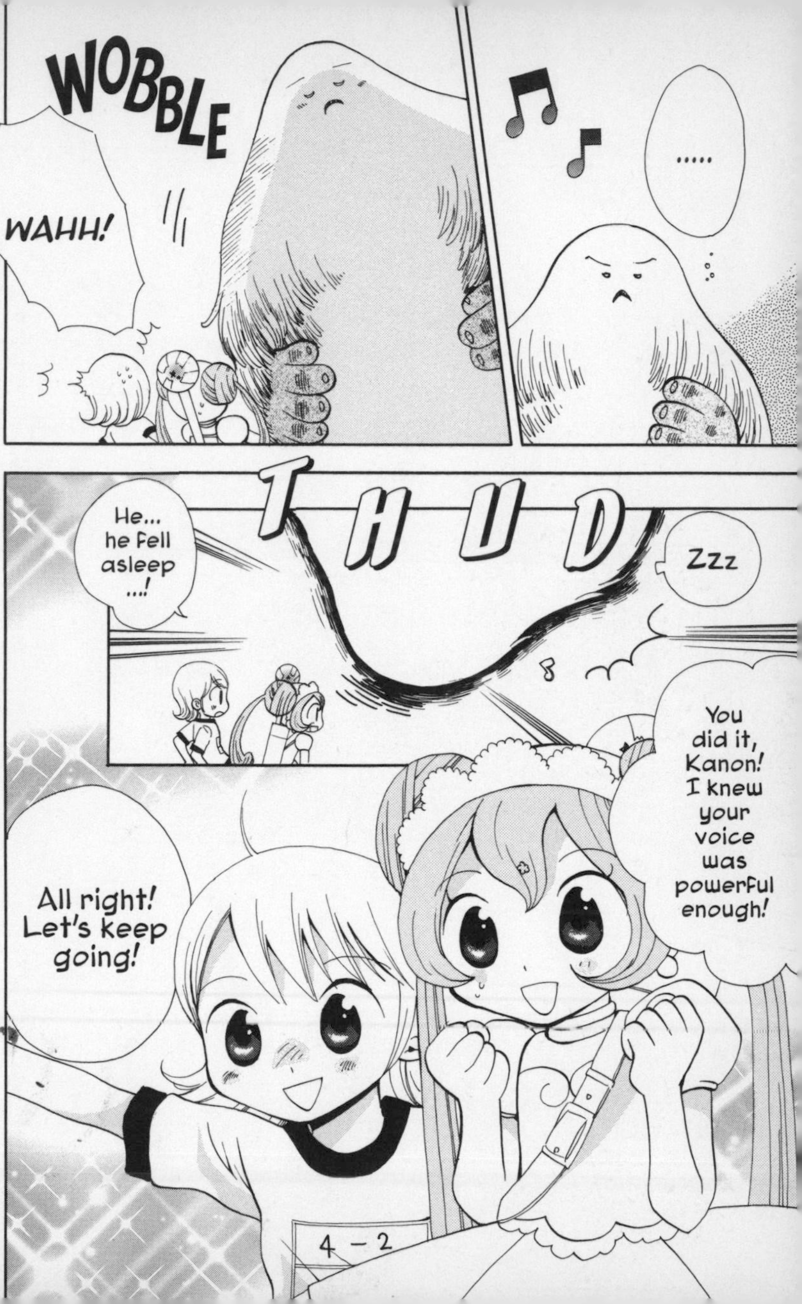
.....
WOBBLE
WAHH!
THUD
Zzz
He... he fell asleep ...!
You did it, Kanon! I knew your voice was powerful enough!
All right! Let's keep going!
4 - 2

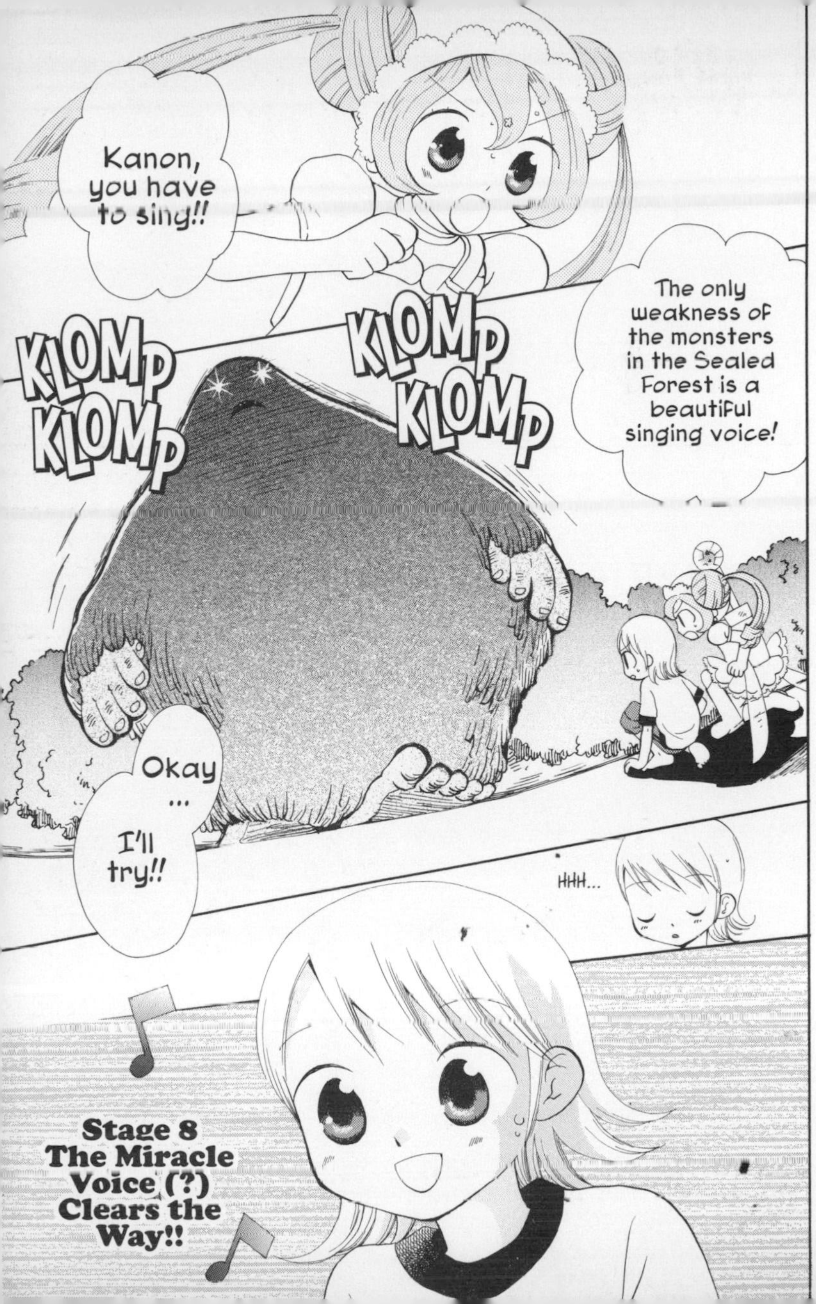
Kanon, you have to sing!!
The only weakness of the monsters in the Sealed Forest is a beautiful singing voice!
KLOMP KLOMP
KLOMP KLOMP
Okay ... I'll try!!
HHH...
Stage 8 The Miracle Voice (?) Clears the Way!!

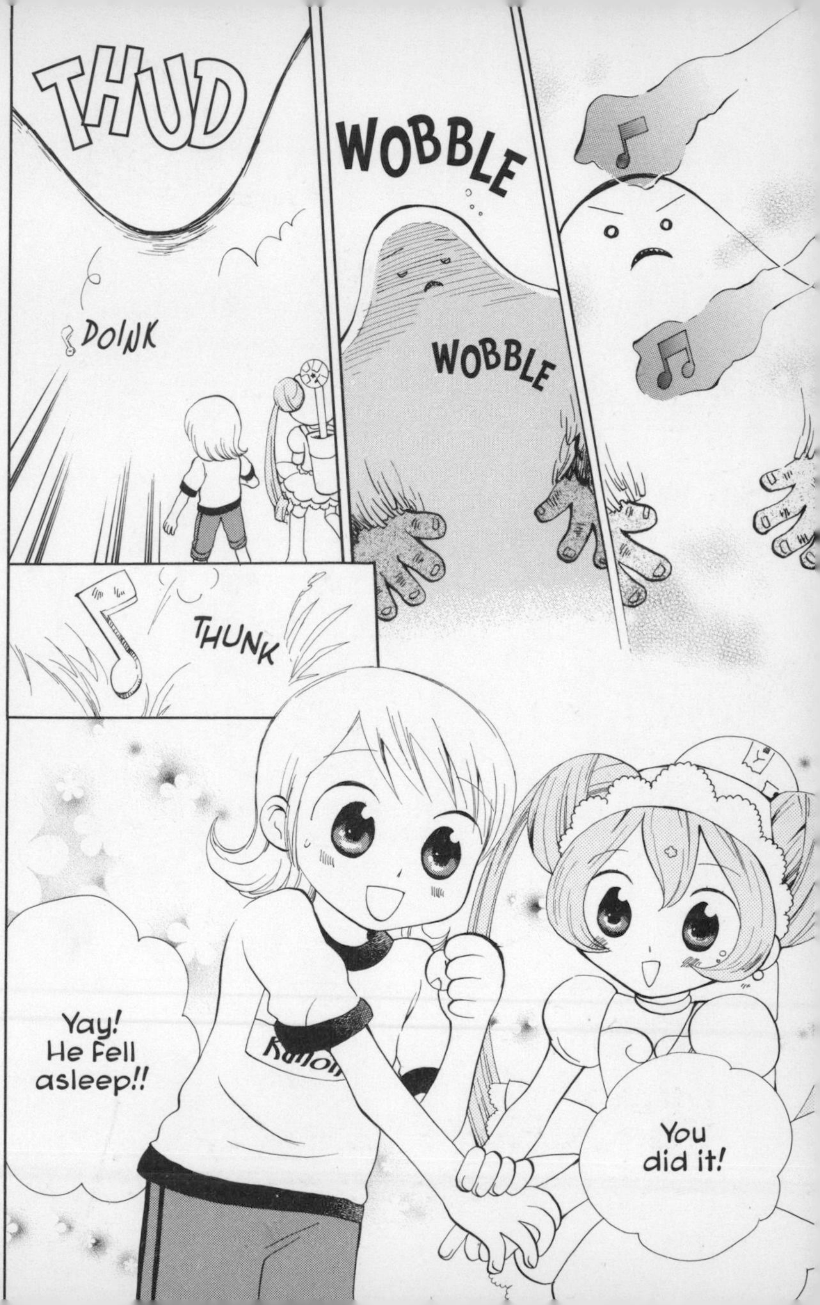
WOBBLE
WOBBLE
THUD
DOINK
THUNK
You did it!
Yay! He fell asleep!!

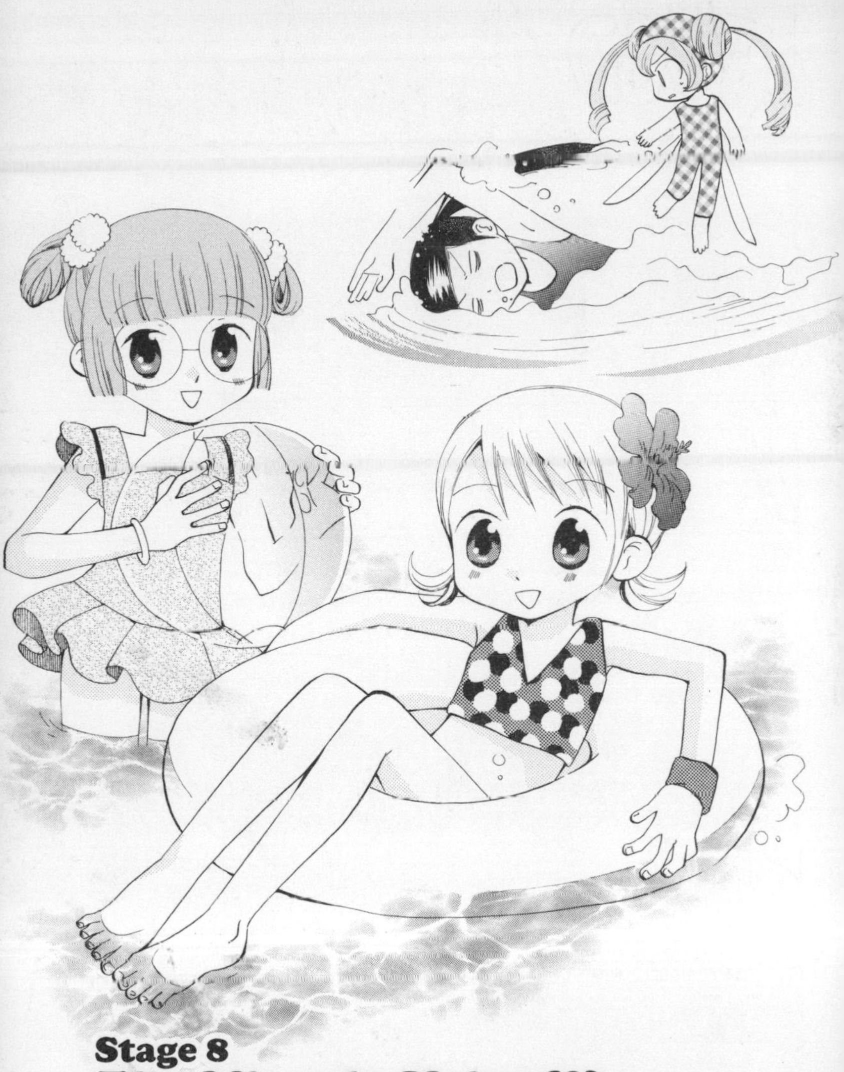

## Stage 8
# The Miracle Voice(?) Clears the Way!!

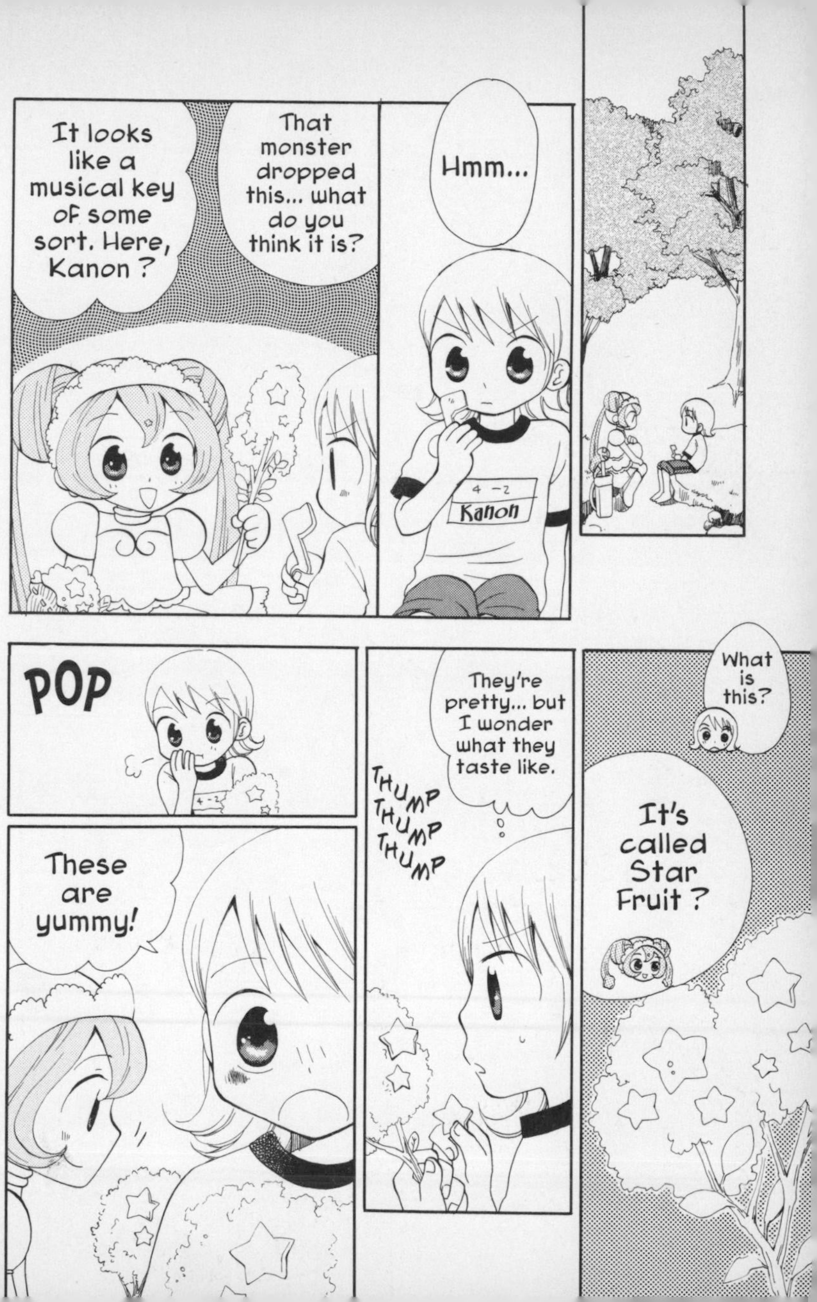

Hmm...
4 -2
Kanon
That monster dropped this... what do you think it is?
It looks like a musical key of some sort. Here, Kanon ?
What is this?
It's called Star Fruit ?
They're pretty... but I wonder what they taste like.
THUMP THUMP THUMP
POP
4 -2
These are yummy!

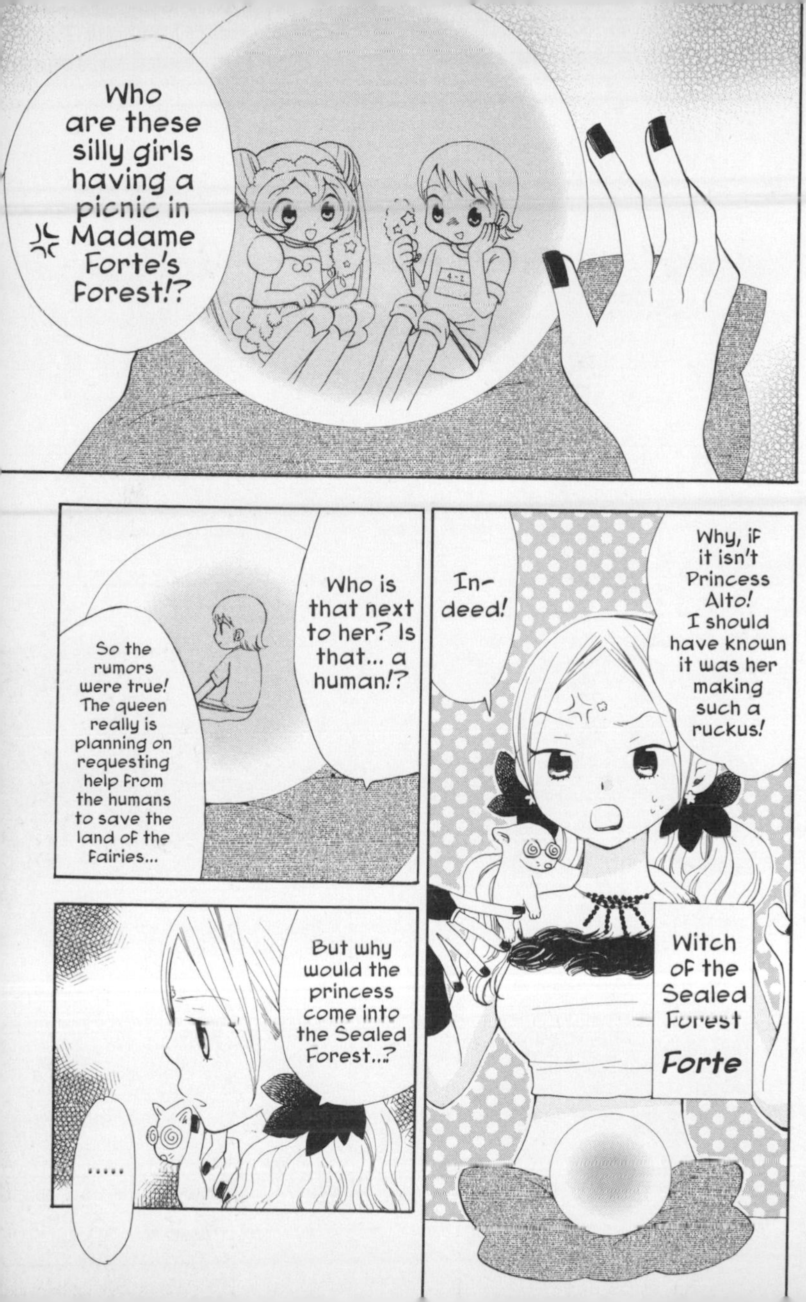
Who are these silly girls having a picnic in Madame Forte's Forest!?
Why, if it isn't Princess Alto! I should have known it was her making such a ruckus!
In-deed!
Witch of the Sealed Forest
Forte
Who is that next to her? Is that... a human!?
So the rumors were true! The queen really is planning on requesting help from the humans to save the land of the Fairies...
But why would the princess come into the Sealed Forest..?
......

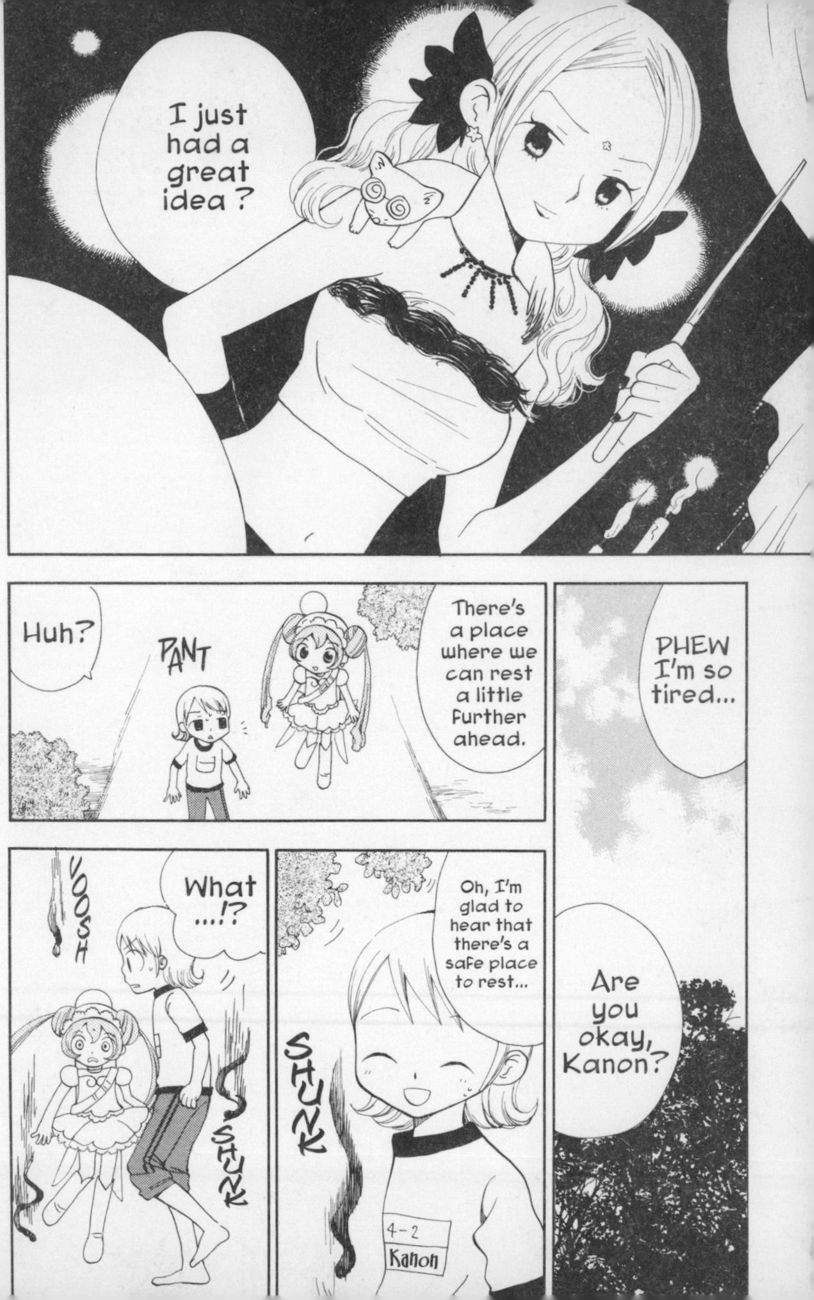
I just had a great idea?
PHEW I'm so tired...
Are you okay, Kanon?
There's a place where we can rest a little further ahead.
PANT
Huh?
Oh, I'm glad to hear that there's a safe place to rest...
SHUNK
4-2
Kanon
What ...!?
VOOSH
SHUNK

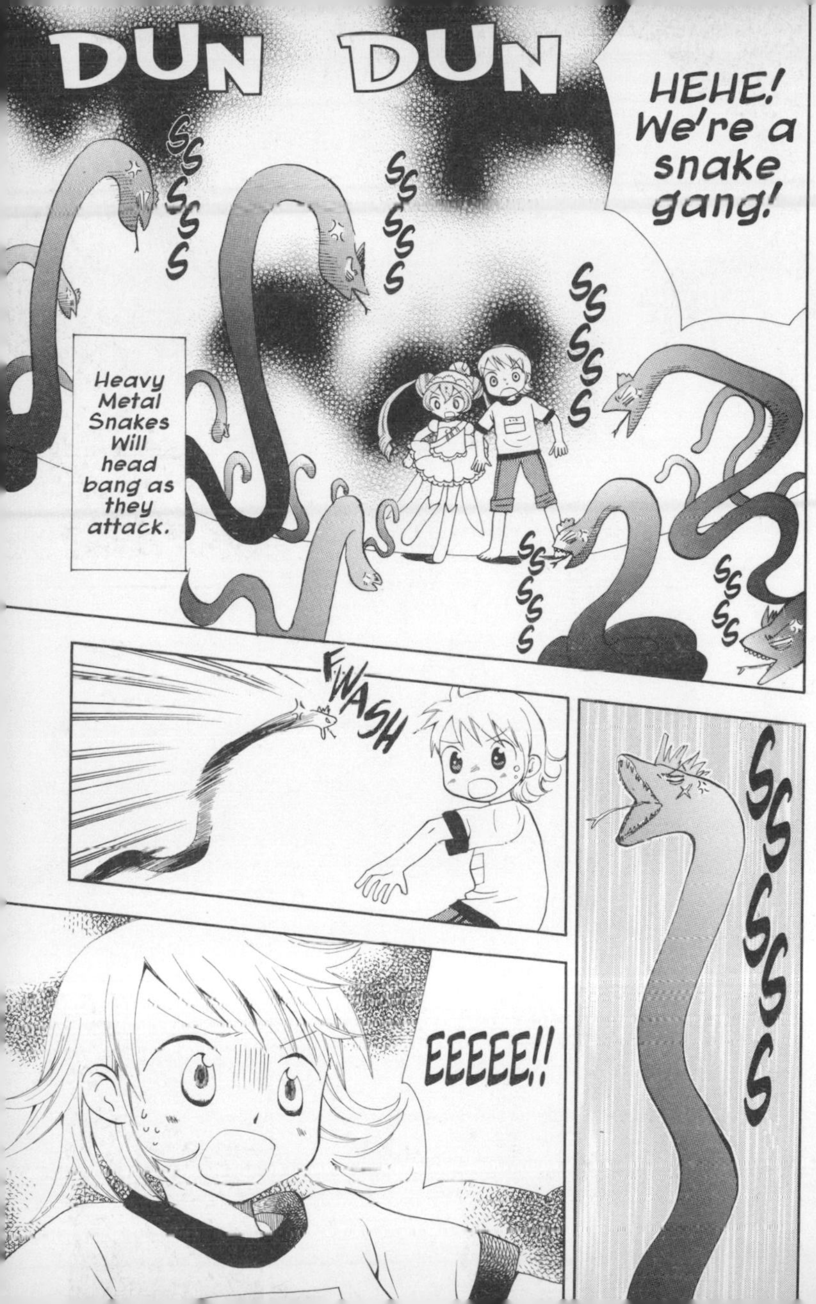
HEHE! We're a snake gang!
DUN DUN
SSSSS
SSSSS
SSSSSS
Heavy Metal Snakes Will head bang as they attack.
SSSSSS
SSSS
SSSSSS
FWASH
EEEEE!!

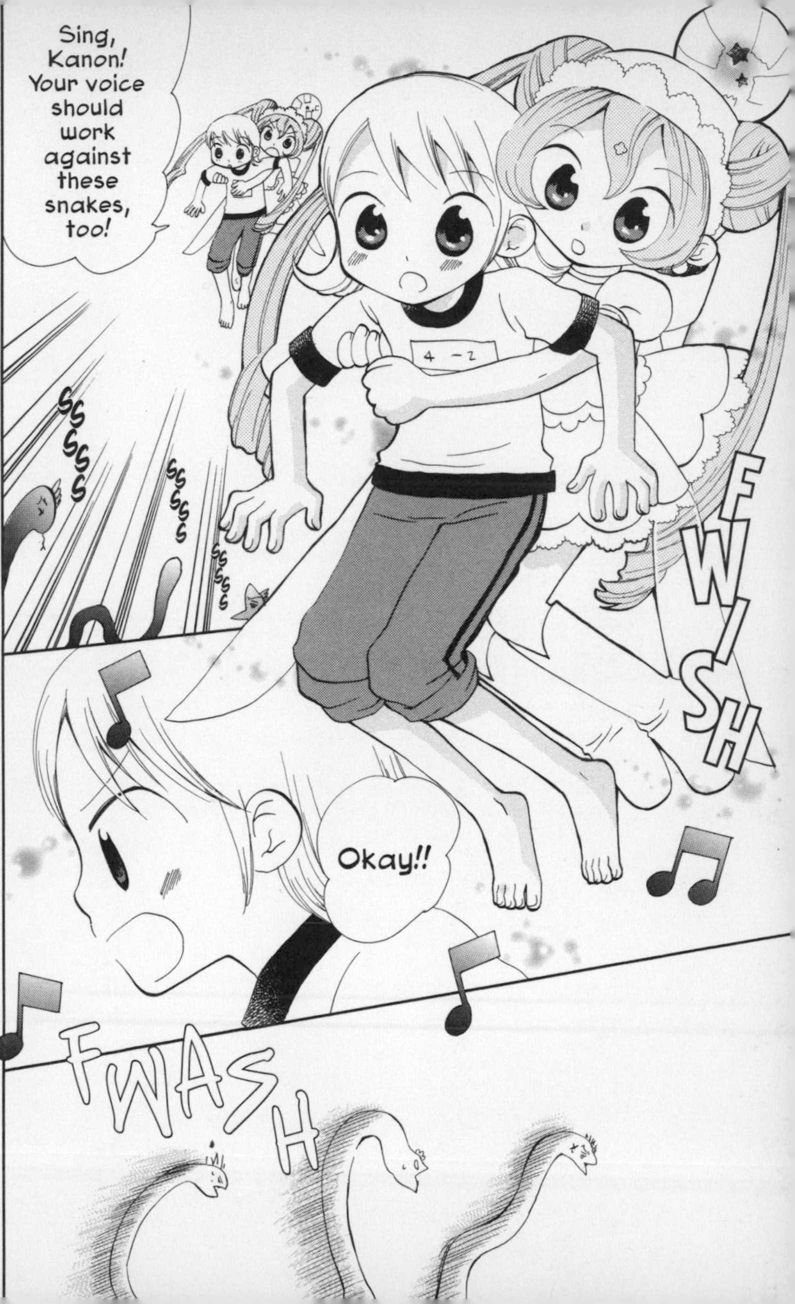
Sing, Kanon! Your voice should work against these snakes, too!
SSSSS
SSSS
SSSS
FWISH
Okay!!
FWASH

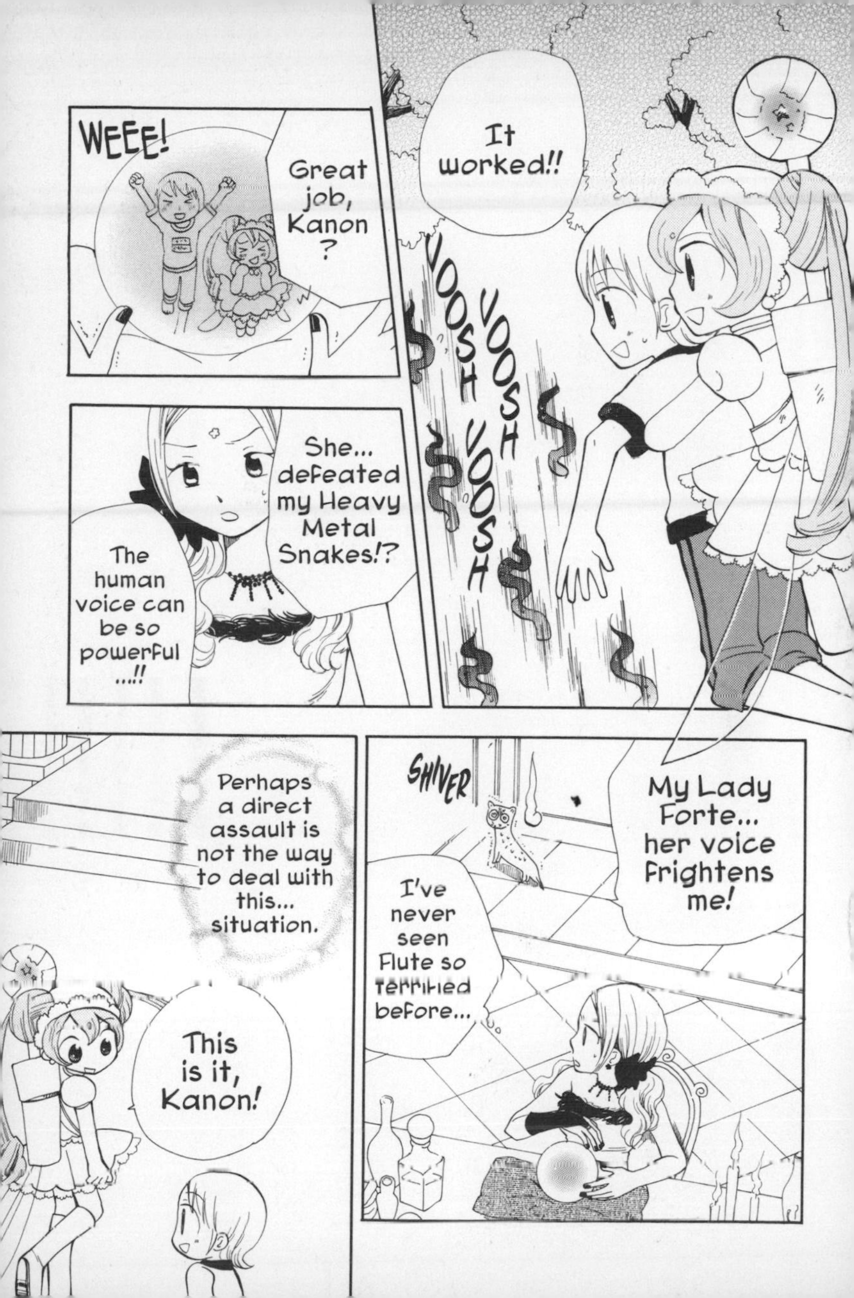

It worked!!
VOOSH VOOSH VOOSH VOOSH
WEEE!
Great job, Kanon?
She... defeated my Heavy Metal Snakes!?
The human voice can be so powerful ...!!
SHIVER
My Lady Forte... her voice frightens me!
I've never seen Flute so terrified before...
Perhaps a direct assault is not the way to deal with this... situation.
This is it, Kanon!

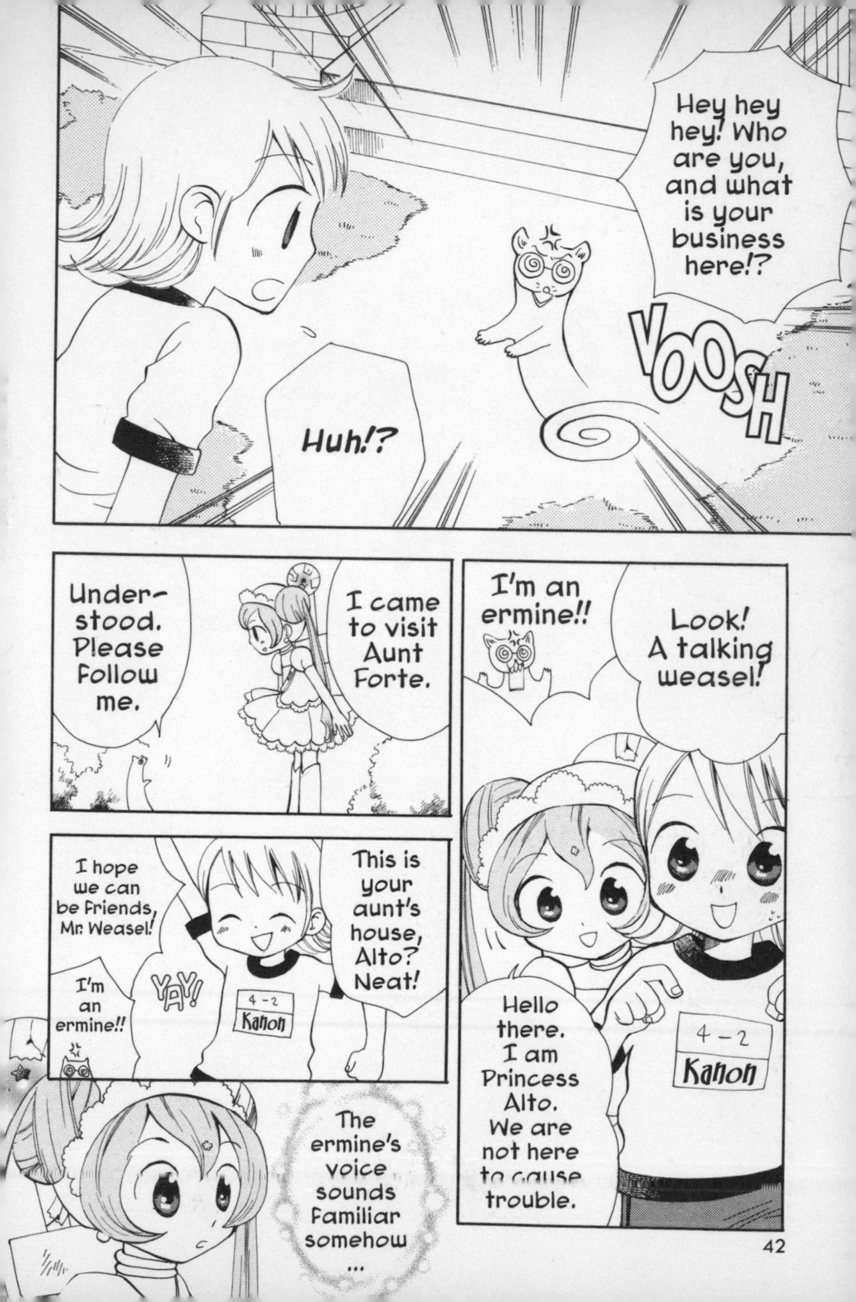
Hey hey hey! Who are you, and what is your business here!?
VOOSH
Huh!?
Look! A talking weasel!
I'm an ermine!!
Hello there. I am Princess Alto. We are not here to cause trouble.
I came to visit Aunt Forte.
Under-stood. Please follow me.
This is your aunt's house, Alto? Neat!
I hope we can be friends, Mr. Weasel!
YAY!
I'm an ermine!!
The ermine's voice sounds familiar somehow ...

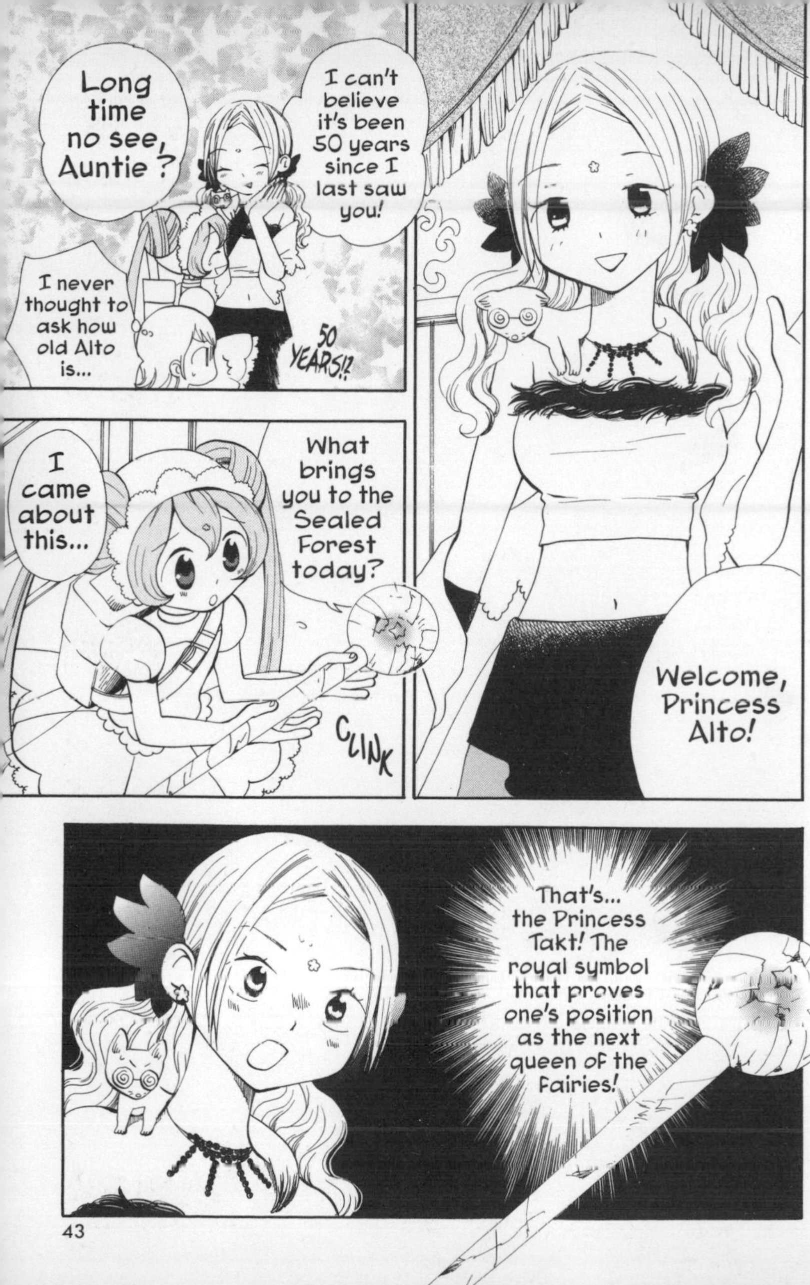
Welcome, Princess Alto!
I can't believe it's been 50 years since I last saw you!
Long time no see, Auntie?
50 YEARS!?
I never thought to ask how old Alto is...
What brings you to the Sealed Forest today?
I came about this...
CLINK
That's... the Princess Takt! The royal symbol that proves one's position as the next queen of the Fairies!

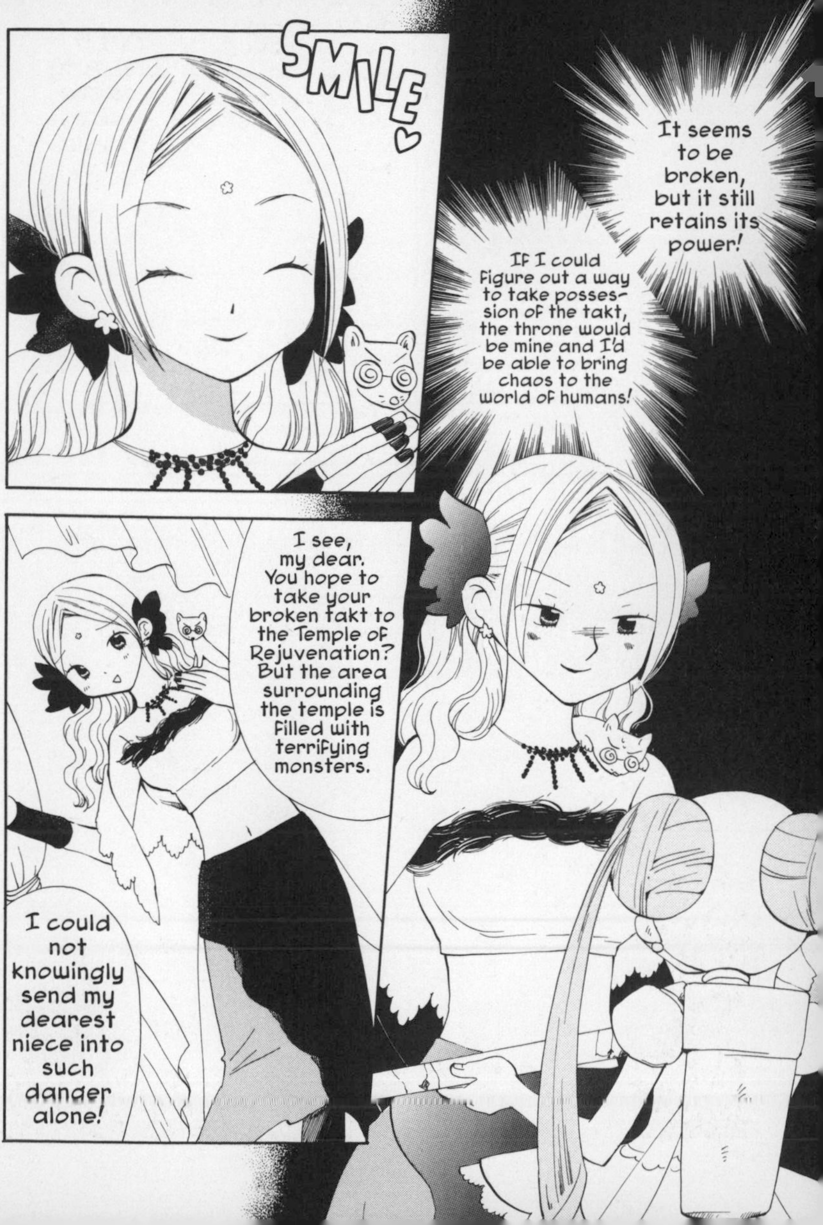
It seems to be broken, but it still retains its power!
If I could figure out a way to take posses-sion of the takt, the throne would be mine and I'd be able to bring chaos to the world of humans!
SMILE
I see, my dear. You hope to take your broken takt to the Temple of Rejuvenation? But the area surrounding the temple is filled with terrifying monsters.
I could not knowingly send my dearest niece into such danger alone!

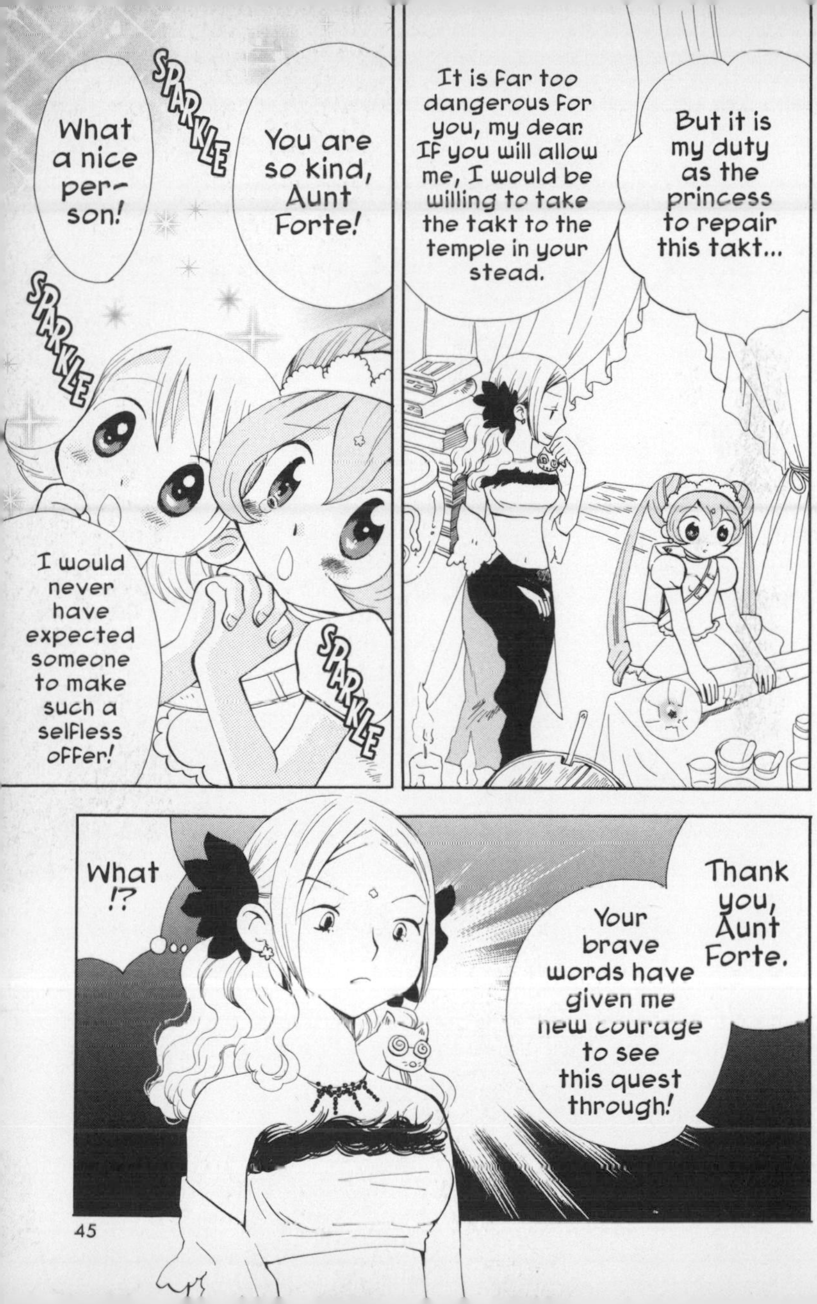
But it is my duty as the princess to repair this takt...
It is far too dangerous for you, my dear. If you will allow me, I would be willing to take the takt to the temple in your stead.
You are so kind, Aunt Forte!
SPARKLE
What a nice per-son!
SPARKLE
I would never have expected someone to make such a selfless offer!
SPARKLE
Thank you, Aunt Forte.
Your brave words have given me new courage to see this quest through!
What!?

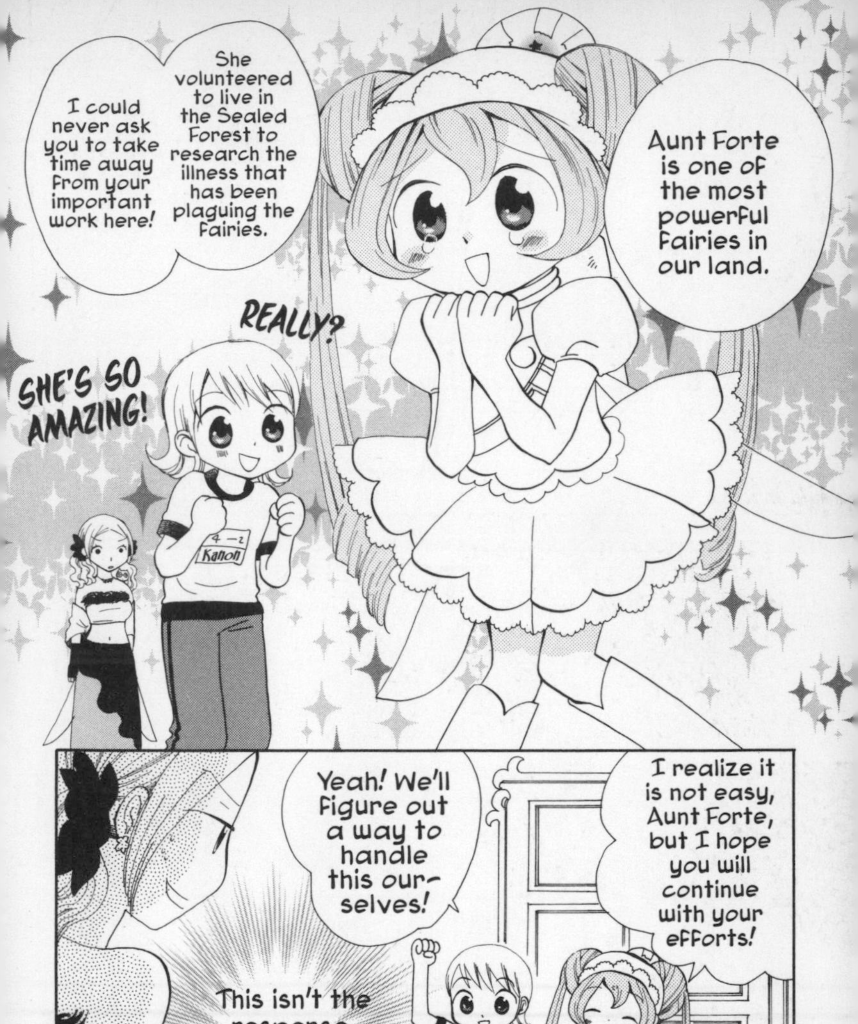
Aunt Forte is one of the most powerful fairies in our land.
She volunteered to live in the Sealed Forest to research the illness that has been plaguing the fairies.
I could never ask you to take time away from your important work here!
REALLY?
SHE'S SO AMAZING!
4-2
Kanon
I realize it is not easy, Aunt Forte, but I hope you will continue with your efforts!
Yeah! We'll figure out a way to handle this our-selves!
This isn't the response I was expecting...
4-2

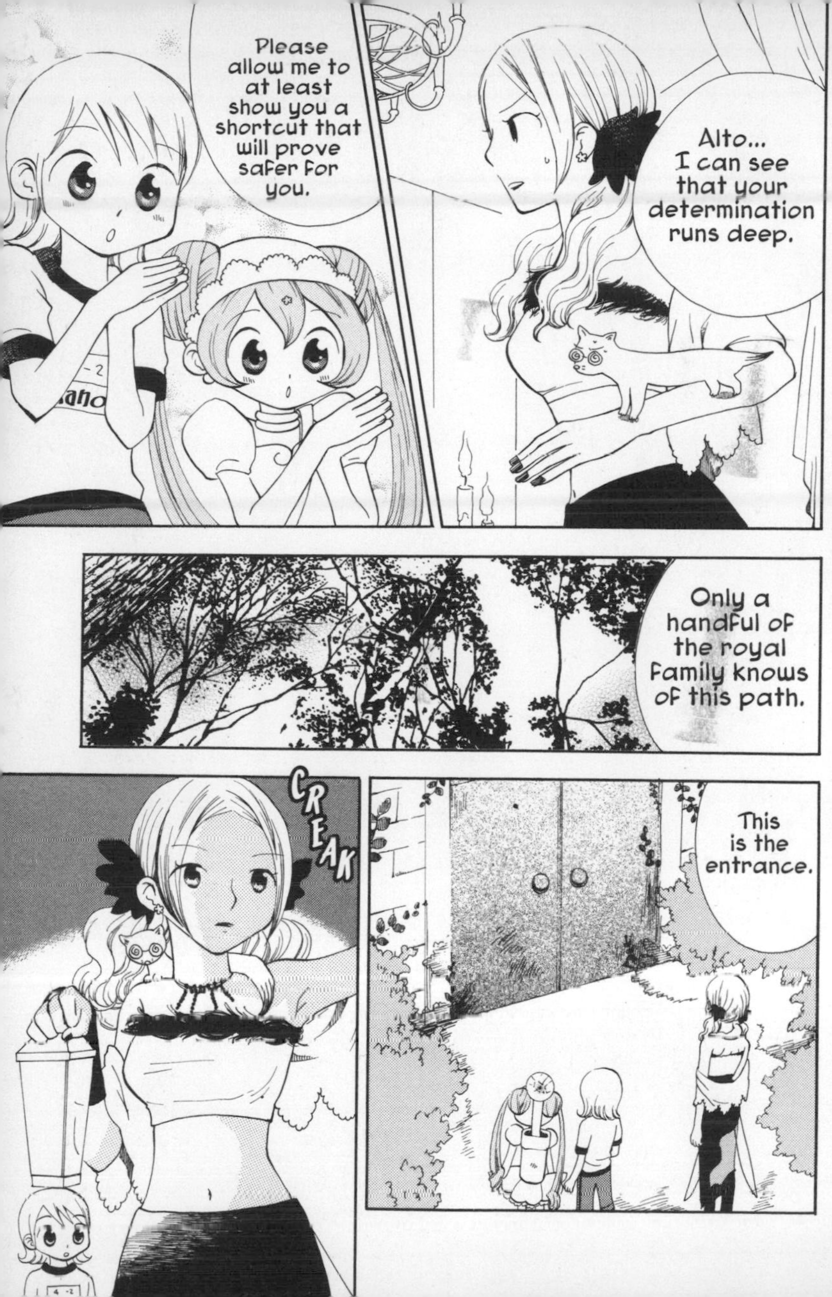
Alto... I can see that your determination runs deep.
Please allow me to at least show you a shortcut that will prove safer for you.
Only a handful of the royal family knows of this path.
This is the entrance.
CREAK

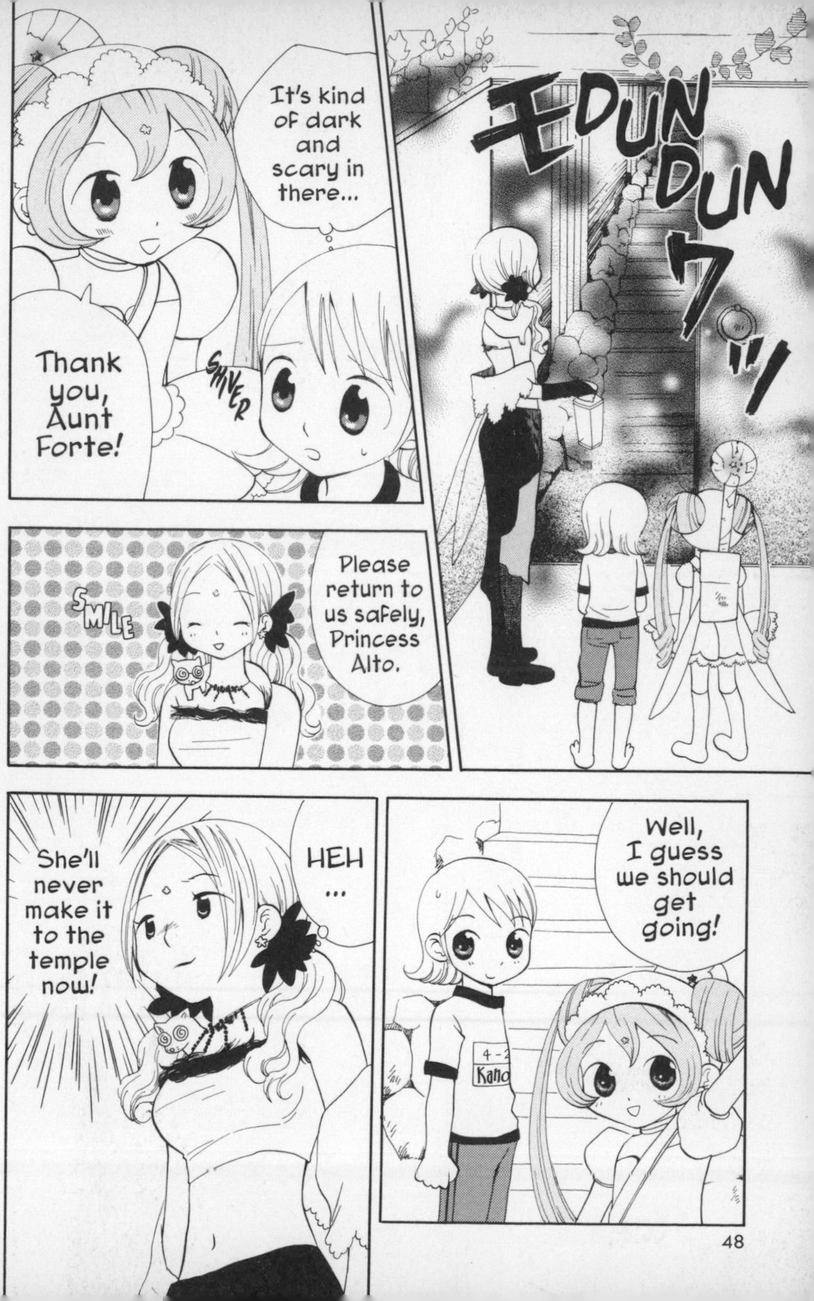
DUN DUN DUN
ウッ
It's kind of dark and scary in there...
Thank you, Aunt Forte!
SHIVER
SMILE
Please return to us safely, Princess Alto.
Well, I guess we should get going!
4-2
Kano
HEH ...
She'll never make it to the temple now!

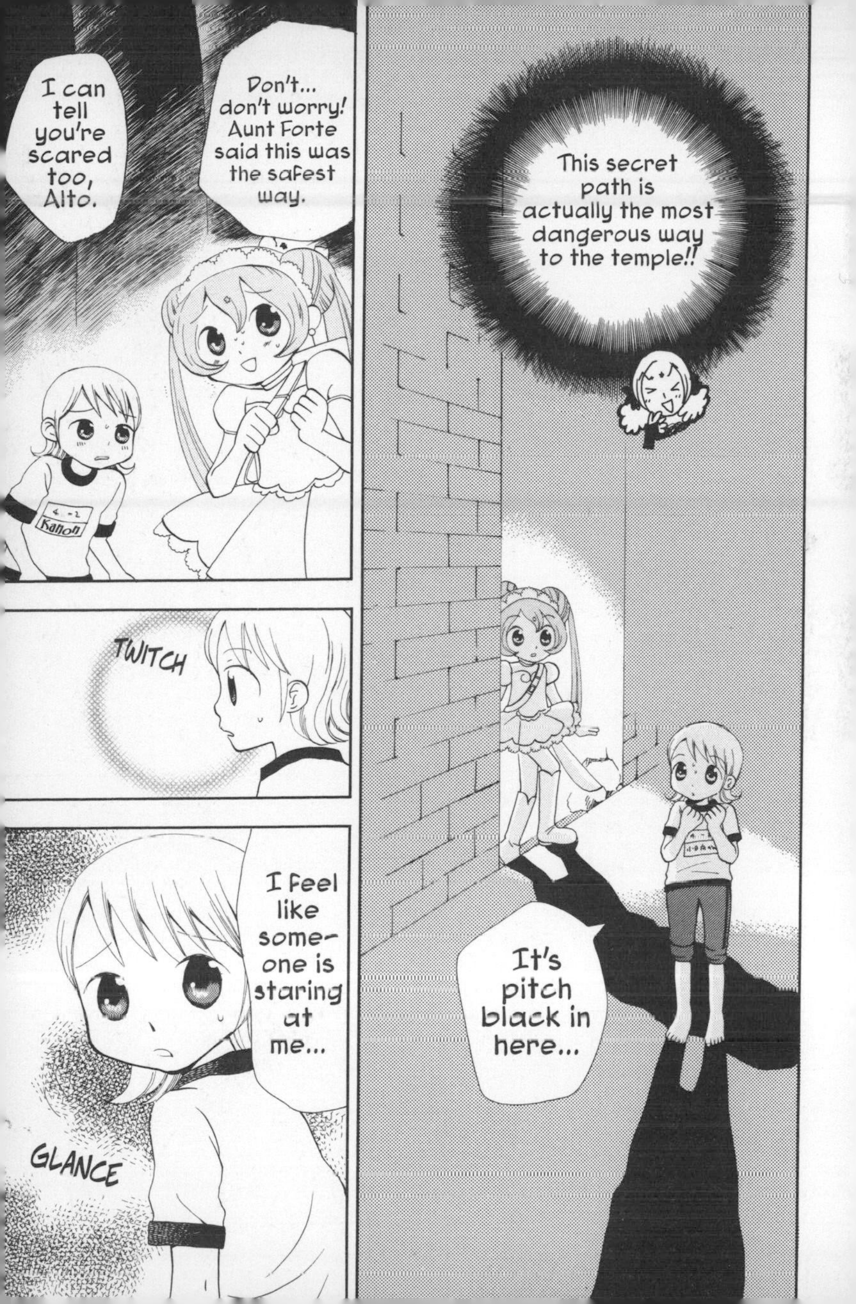
This secret path is actually the most dangerous way to the temple!!
It's pitch black in here...
Don't... don't worry! Aunt Forte said this was the safest way.
I can tell you're scared too, Alto.
4-2
Kanon
TWITCH
I feel like someone is staring at me...
GLANCE

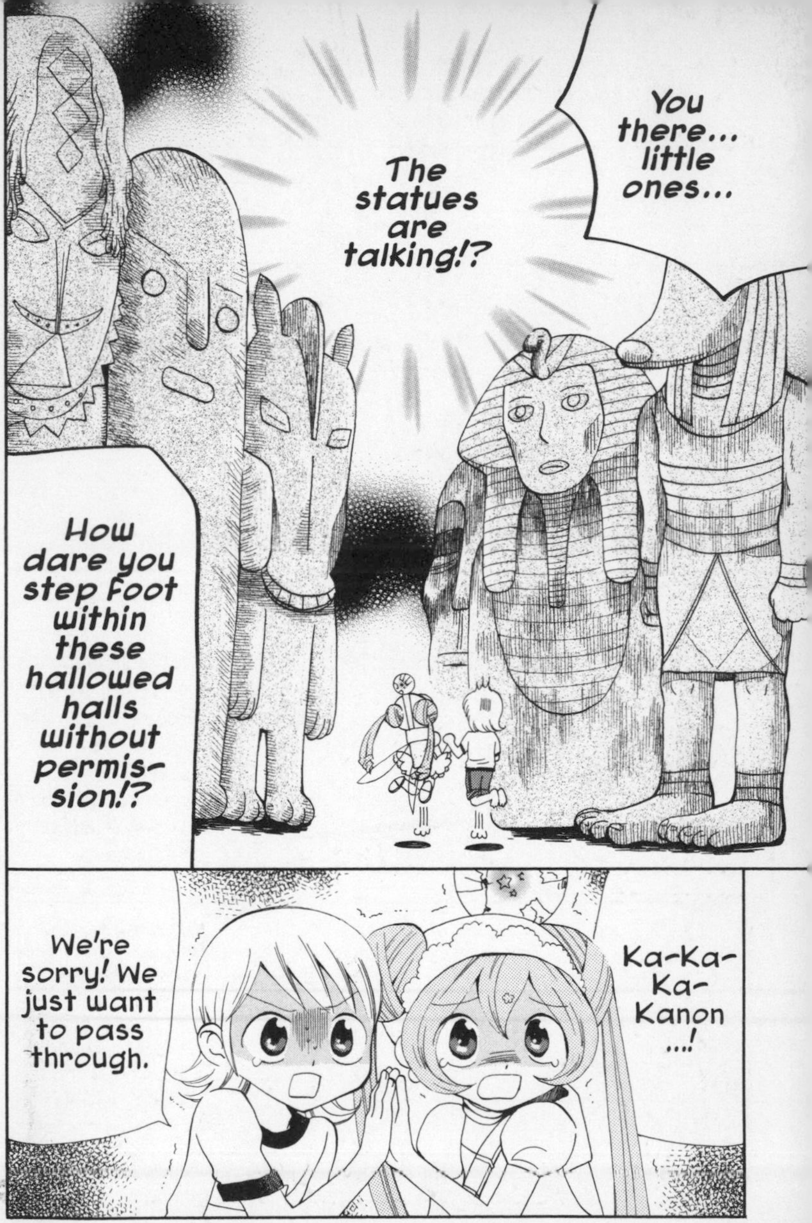
You there... little ones...
The statues are talking!?
How dare you step foot within these hallowed halls without permission!?
Ka-Ka-Ka-Kanon ...!
We're sorry! We just want to pass through.

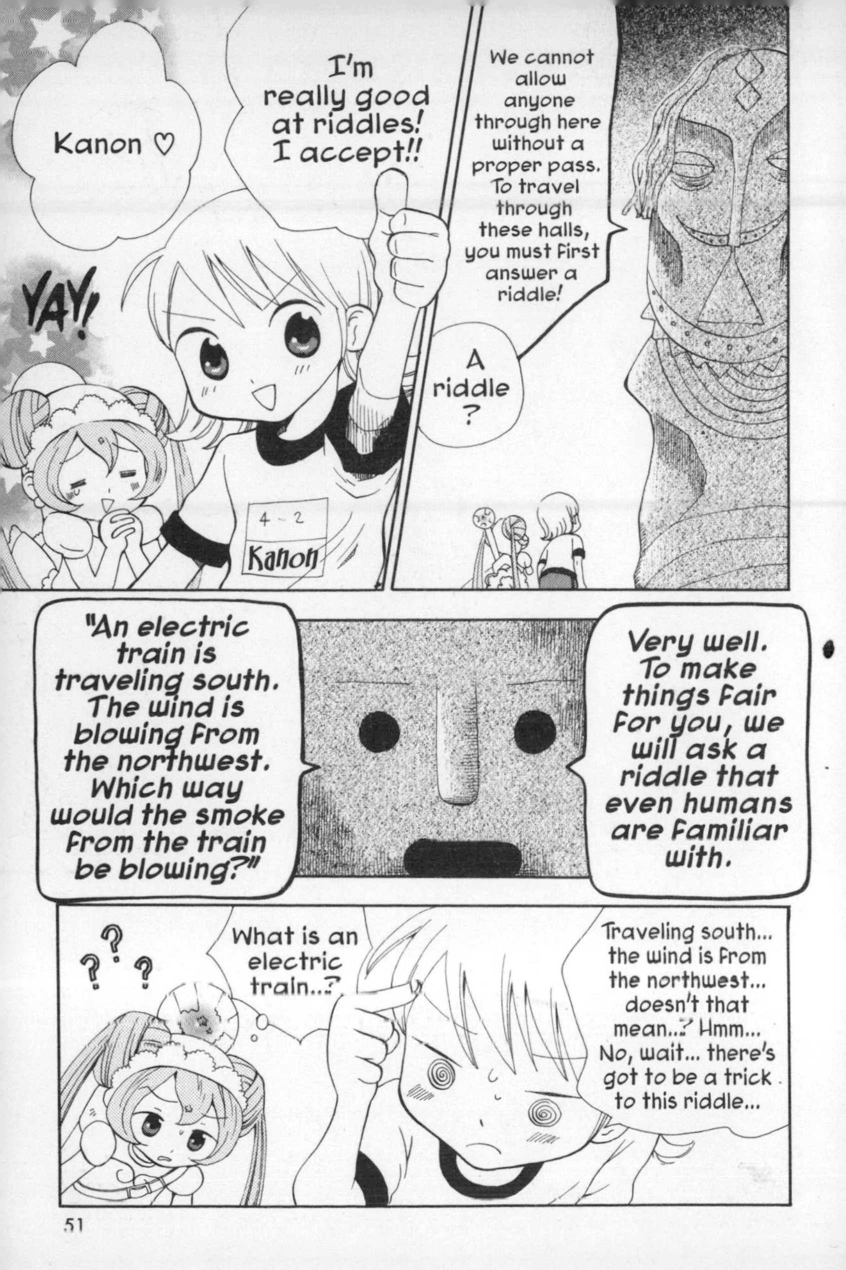

We cannot allow anyone through here without a proper pass. To travel through these halls, you must first answer a riddle!
A riddle?
I'm really good at riddles! I accept!!
Kanon ♡
YAY!
4-2
Kanon
Very well. To make things fair for you, we will ask a riddle that even humans are familiar with.
"An electric train is traveling south. The wind is blowing from the northwest. Which way would the smoke from the train be blowing?"
Traveling south... the wind is from the northwest... doesn't that mean...? Hmm... No, wait... there's got to be a trick to this riddle...
What is an electric train...?
? ? ?

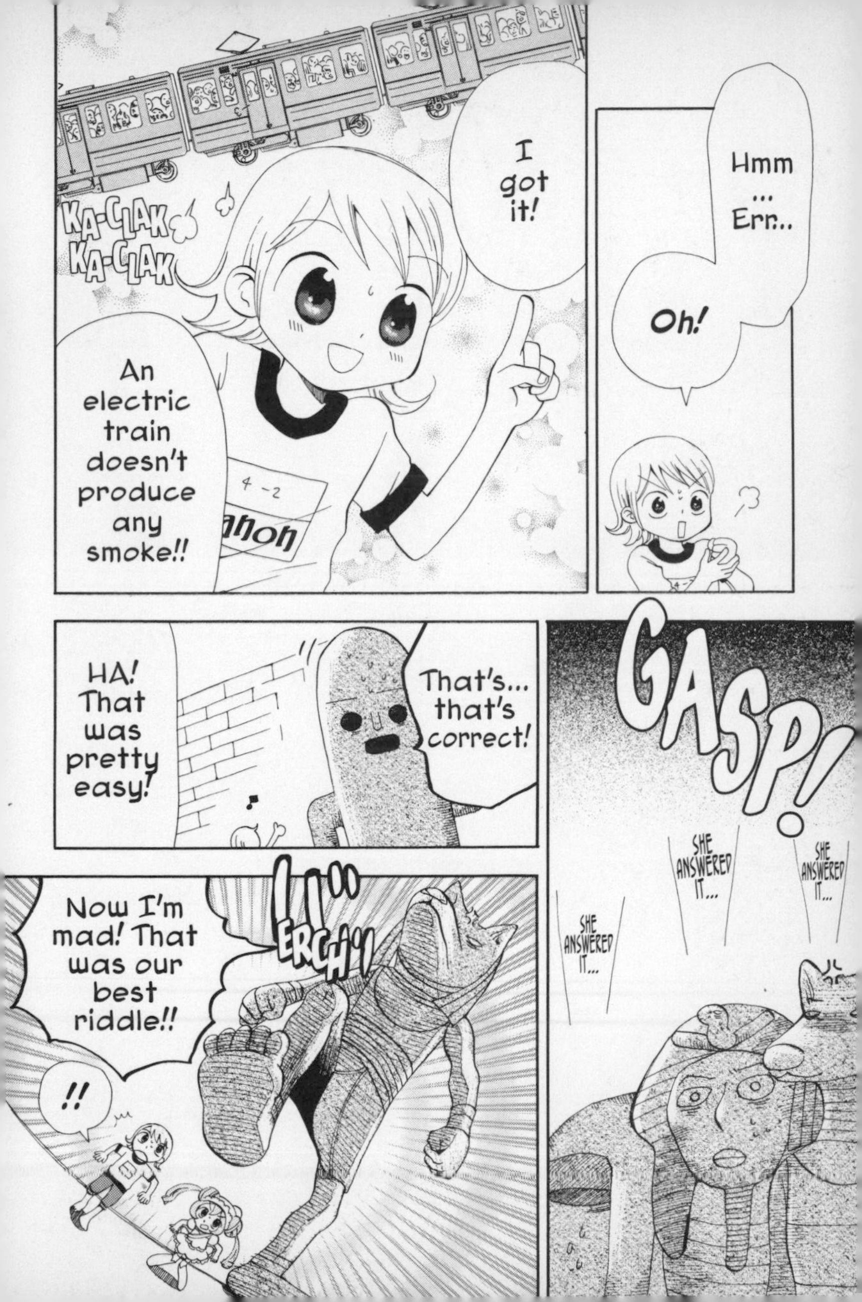
Hmm ... Err...
Oh!
I got it!
KA-CLAK KA-CLAK
An electric train doesn't produce any smoke!!
GASP!
SHE ANSWERED IT...
SHE ANSWERED IT...
SHE ANSWERED IT...
That's... that's correct!
HA! That was pretty easy!
ERCH
Now I'm mad! That was our best riddle!!
!!

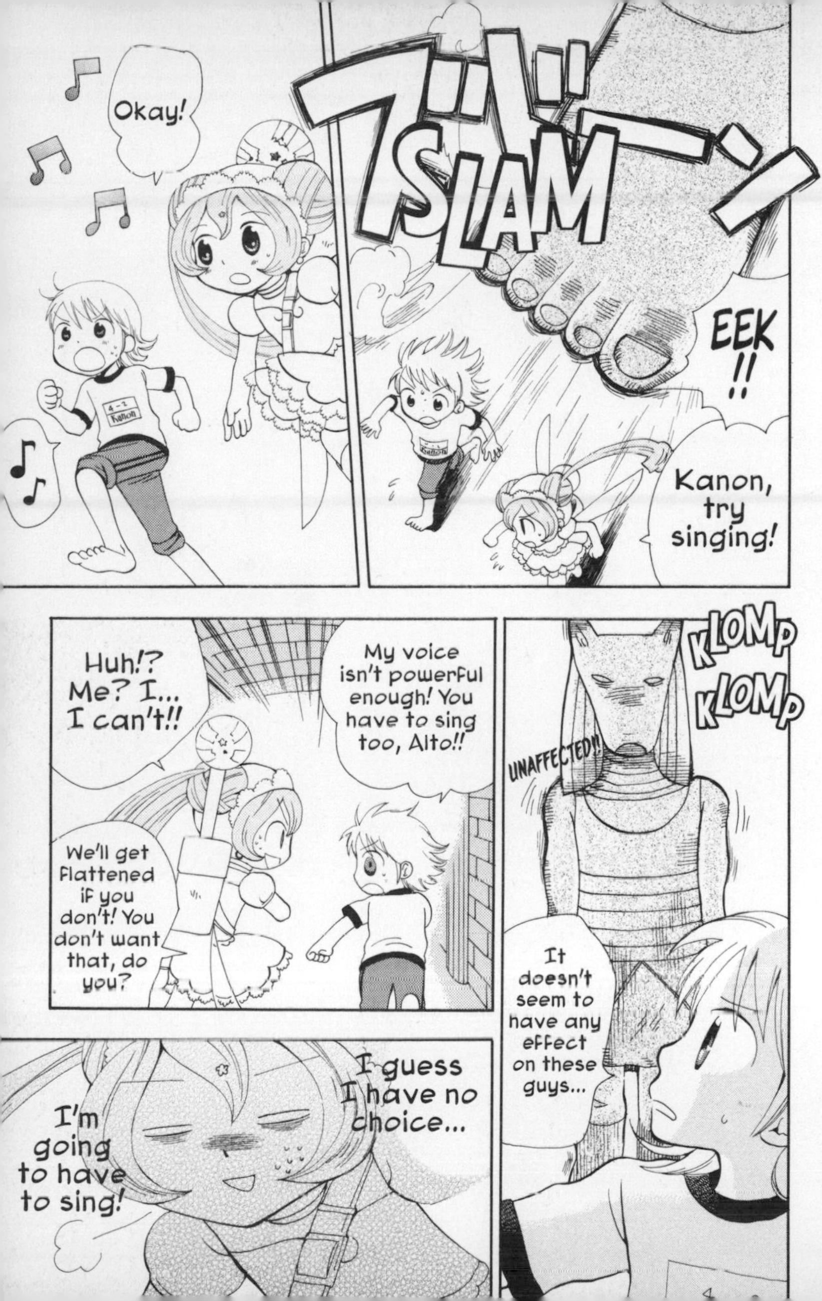
SLAM
EEK!!
Kanon, try singing!
Okay!
KLOMP KLOMP
UNAFFECTED!!
My voice isn't powerful enough! You have to sing too, Alto!!
Huh!? Me? I... I can't!!
We'll get flattened if you don't! You don't want that, do you?
It doesn't seem to have any effect on these guys...
I guess I have no choice...
I'm going to have to sing!

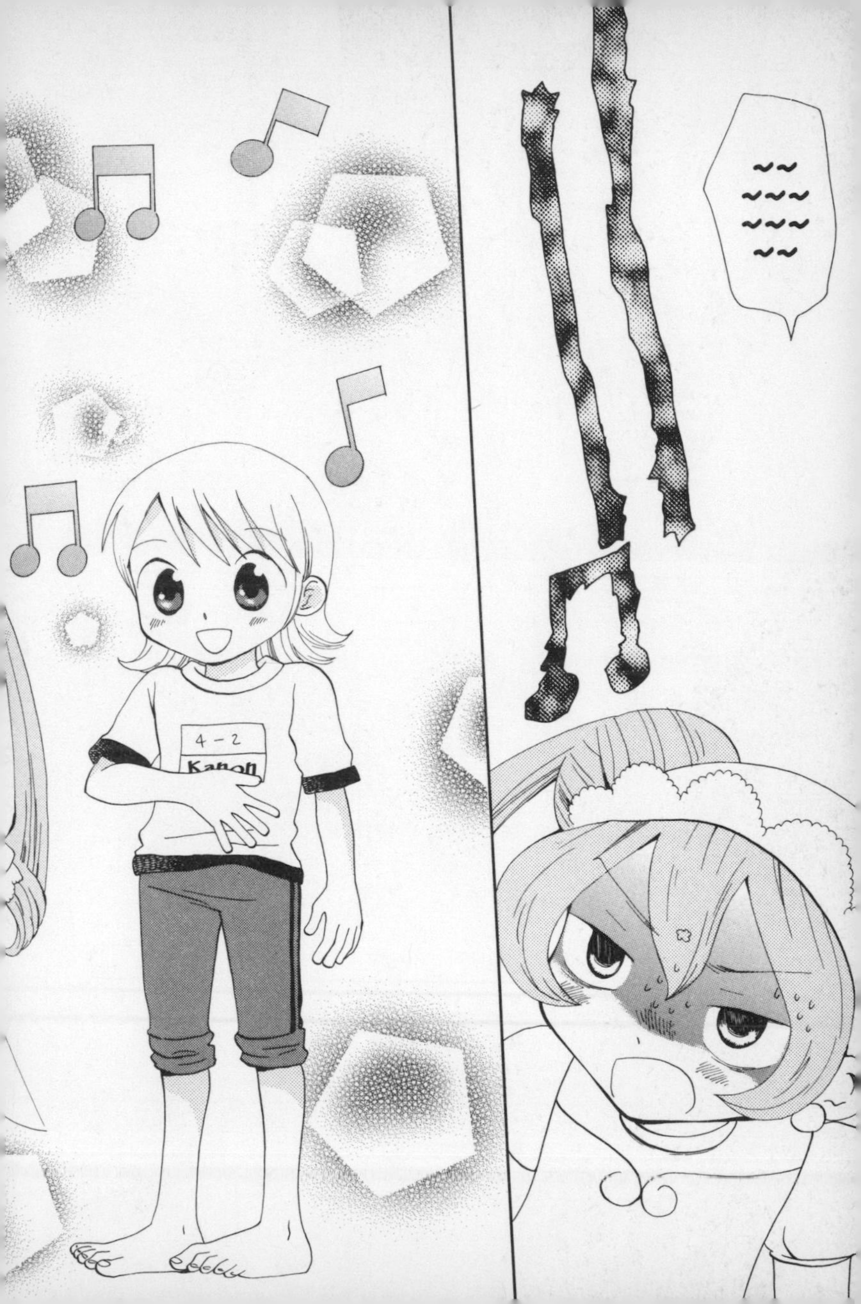
~~ ~~~ ~~~ ~~
4 − 2
Kanon

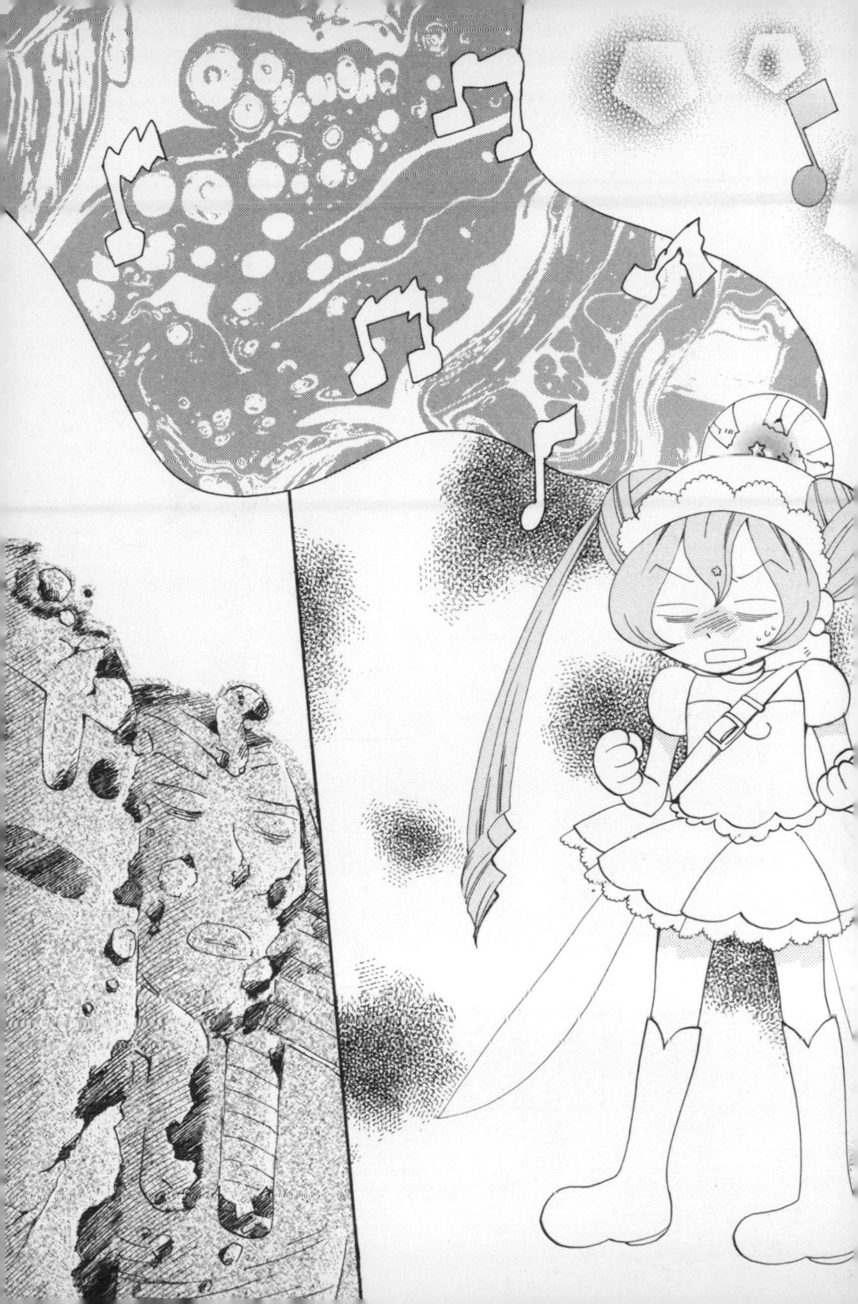

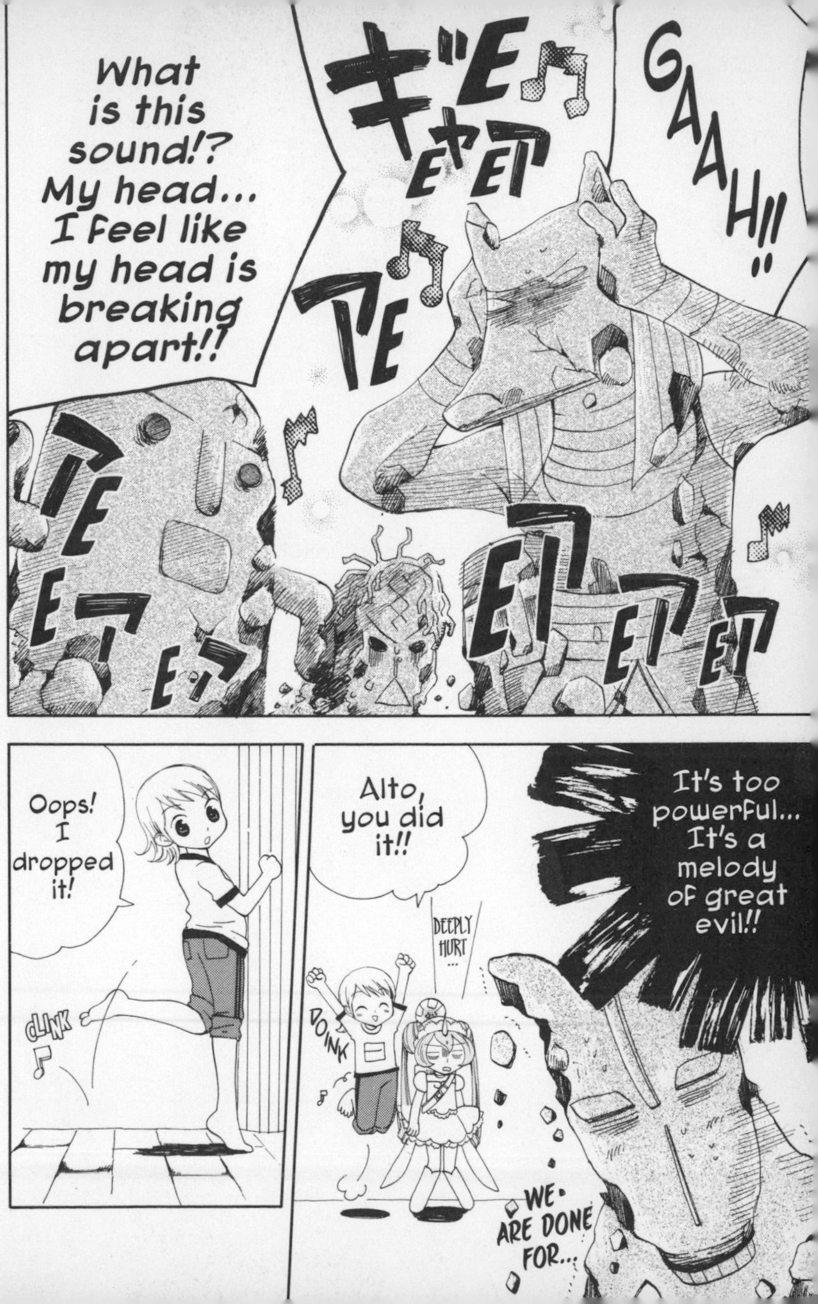
GAAAH!!
What is this sound!? My head... I feel like my head is breaking apart!!
It's too powerful... It's a melody of great evil!!
WE ARE DONE FOR...
Alto, you did it!!
DEEPLY HURT...
DOINK
Oops! I dropped it!
CLINK

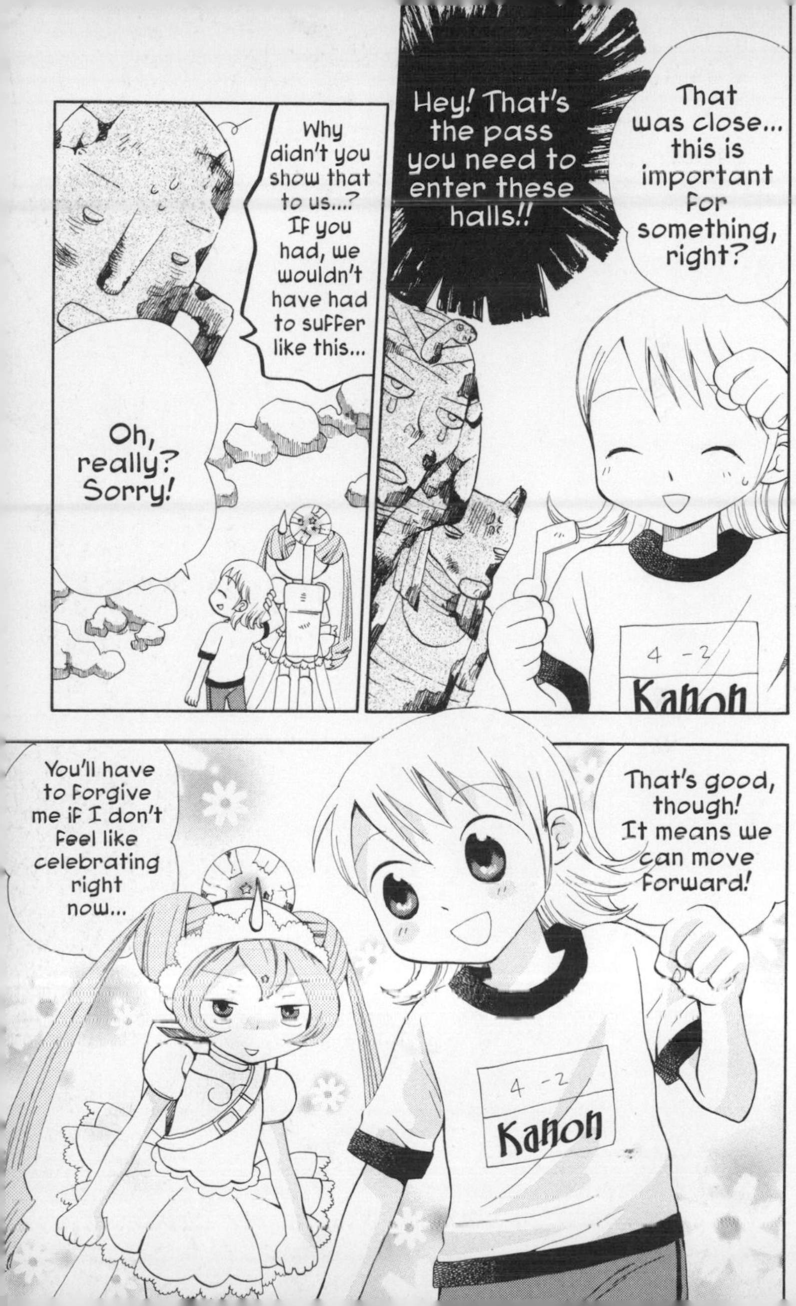
That was close... this is important for something, right?
Hey! That's the pass you need to enter these halls!!
4 -2
Kanon
Why didn't you show that to us...? If you had, we wouldn't have had to suffer like this...
Oh, really? Sorry!
That's good, though! It means we can move forward!
You'll have to forgive me if I don't feel like celebrating right now...
4 -2
Kanon

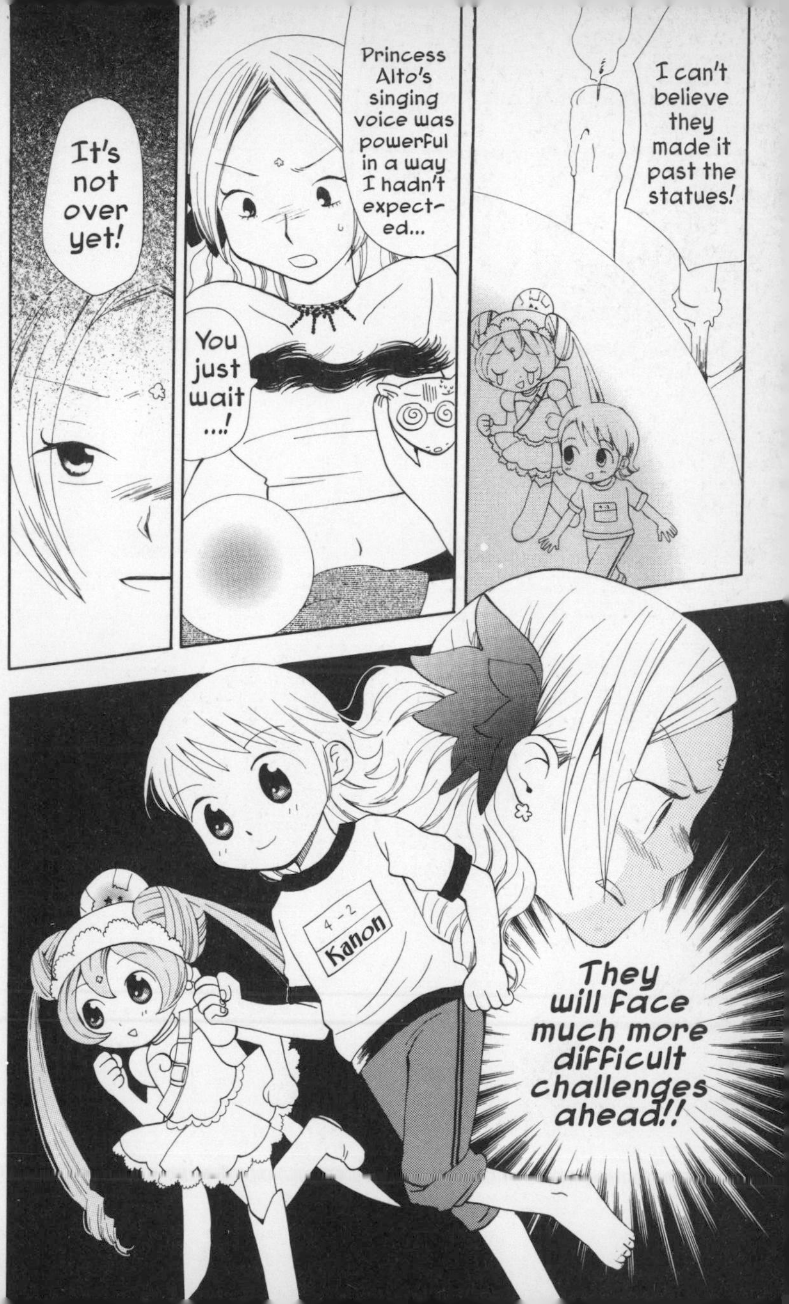
I can't believe they made it past the statues!
Princess Alto's singing voice was powerful in a way I hadn't expect-ed...
You just wait ...!
It's not over yet!
They will face much more difficult challenges ahead!!
4-2
Kanon

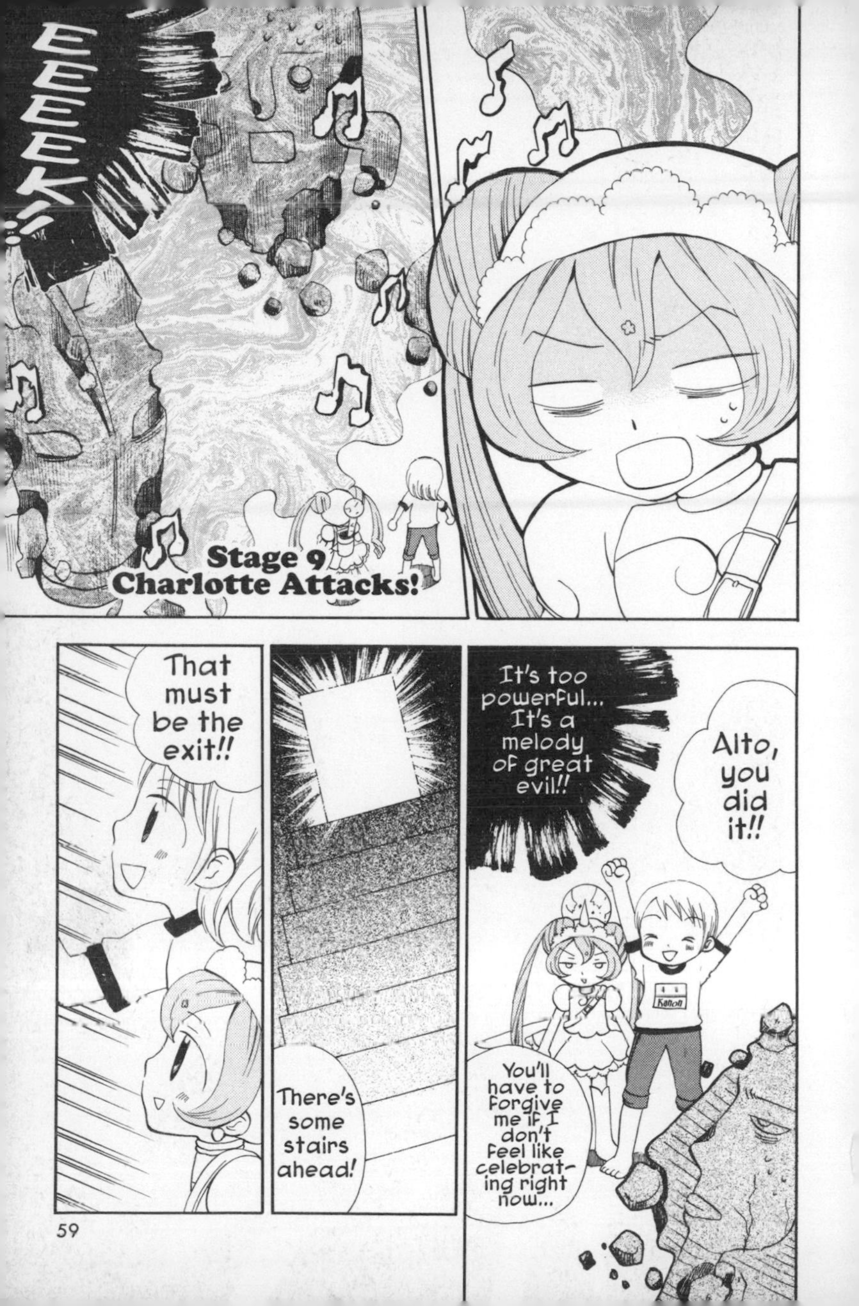

EEEEEK!!
Stage 9
Charlotte Attacks!
Alto, you did it!!
It's too powerful... It's a melody of great evil!!
You'll have to forgive me if I don't feel like celebrating right now...
There's some stairs ahead!
That must be the exit!!

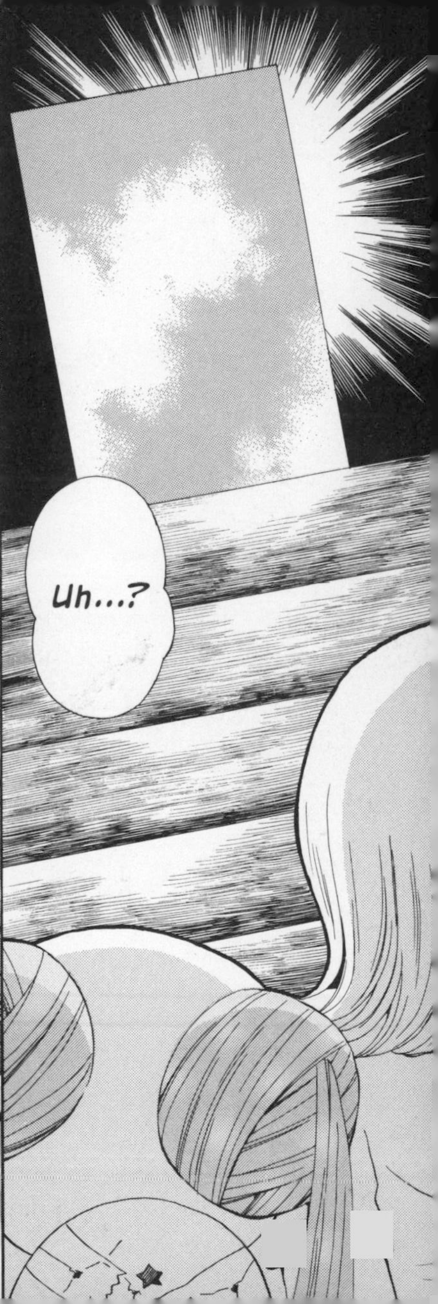
Uh...?
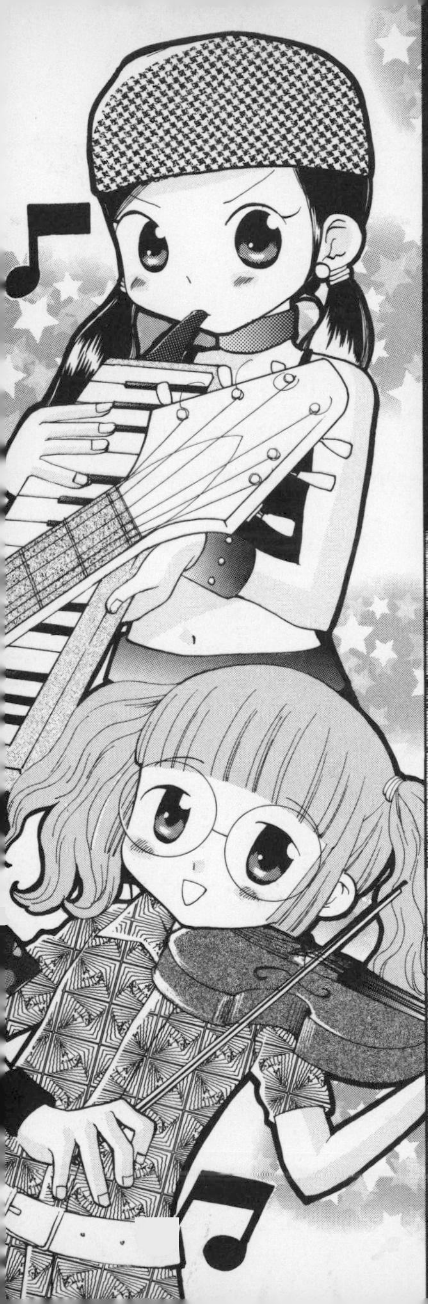

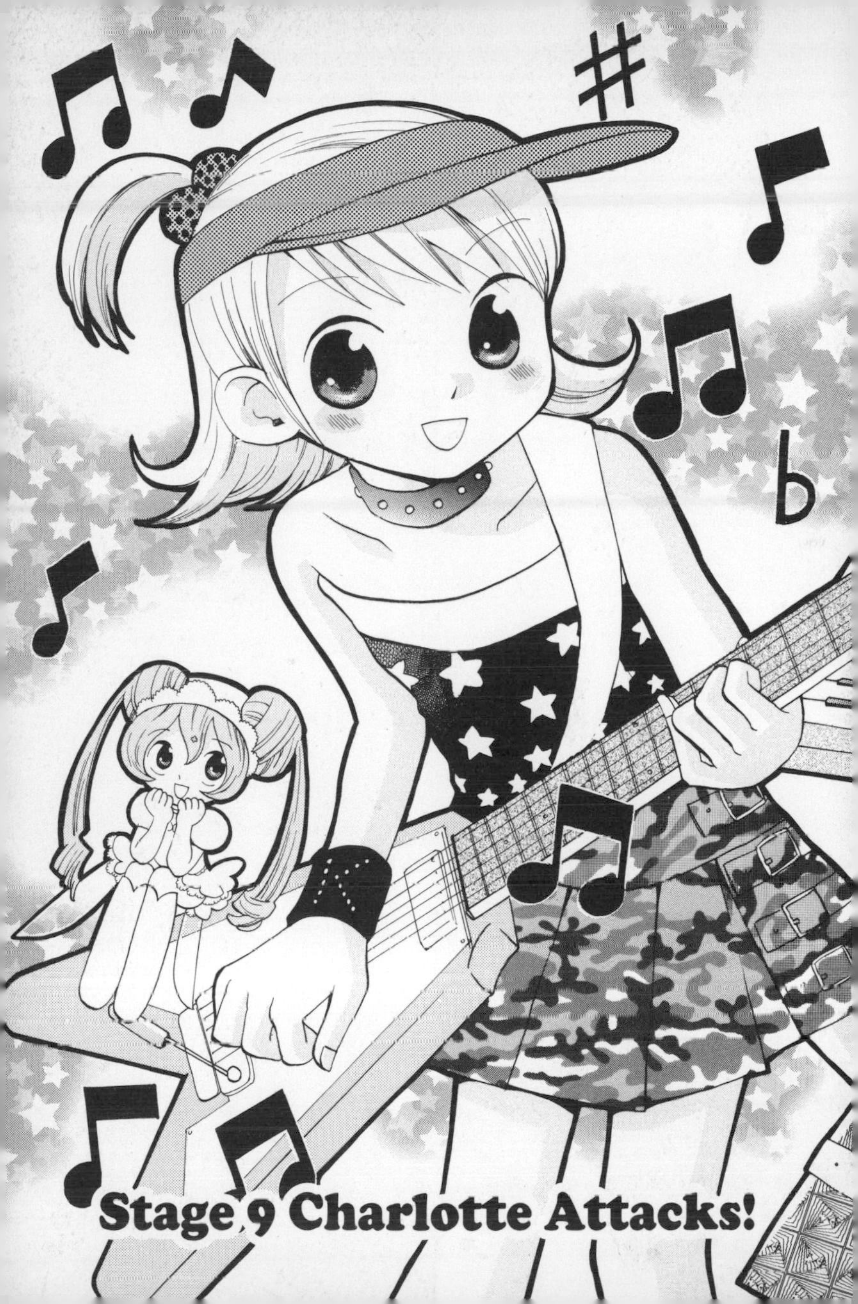
Stage 9 Charlotte Attacks!

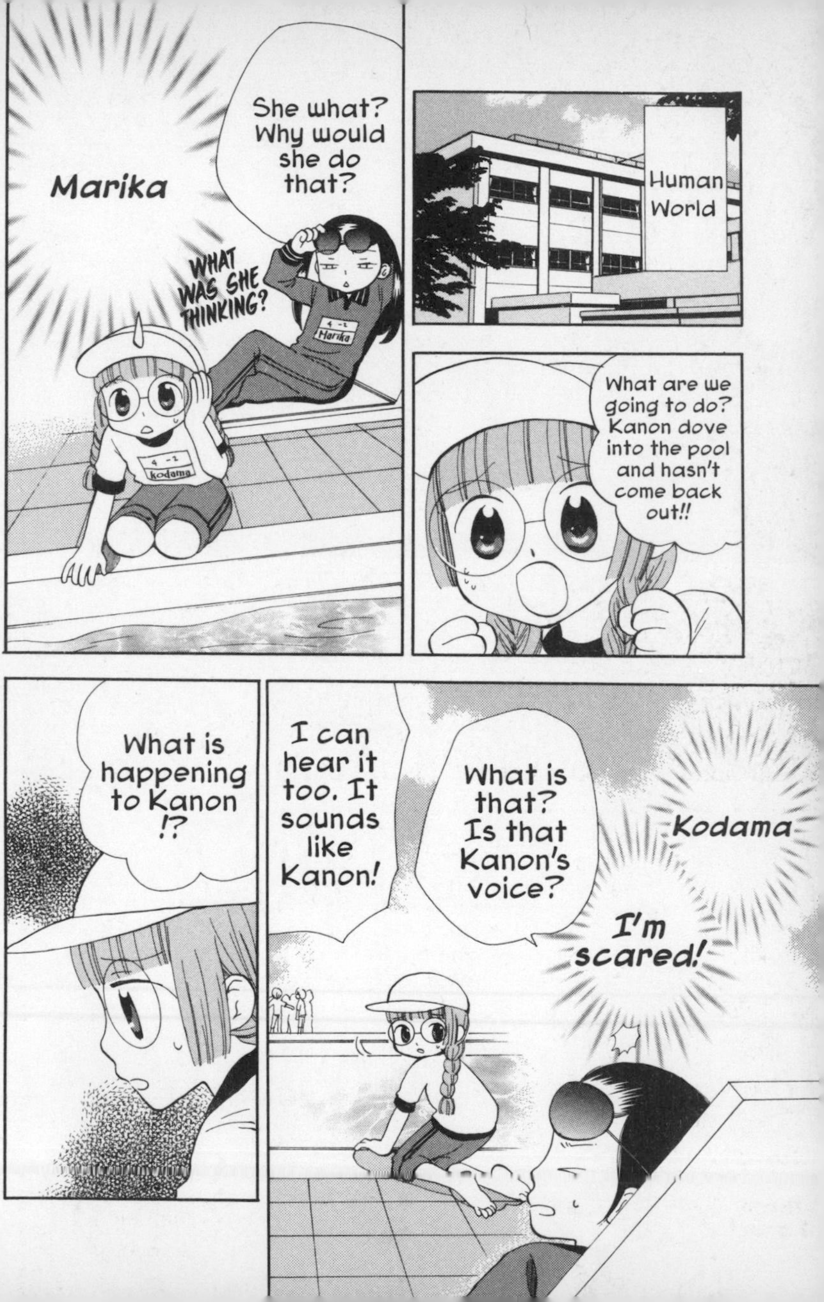
Human World
What are we going to do? Kanon dove into the pool and hasn't come back out!!
She what? Why would she do that?
Marika
WHAT WAS SHE THINKING?
Kodama
I'm scared!
What is that? Is that Kanon's voice?
I can hear it too. It sounds like Kanon!
What is happening to Kanon !?

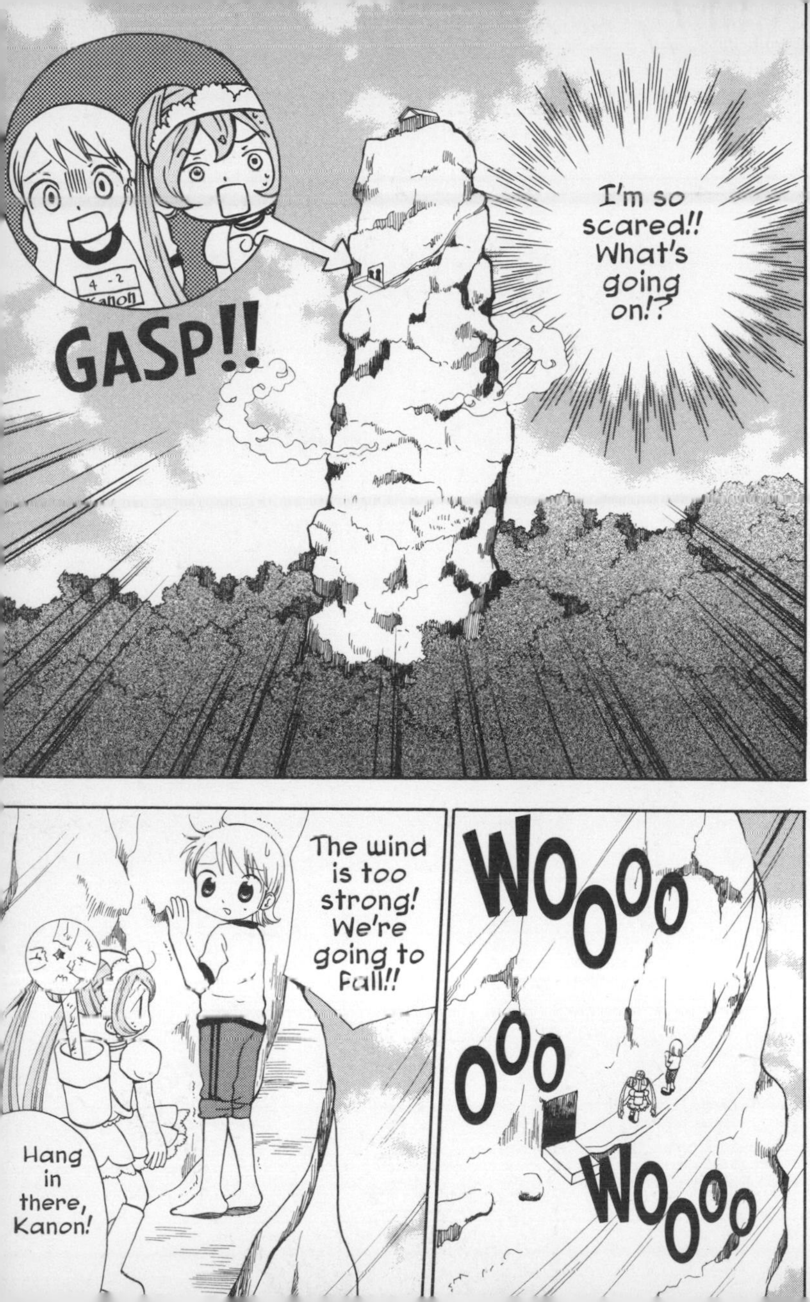

I'm so scared!! What's going on!?
4 -2
Kanon
GASP!!
WOOOO
OOO
WOOOO
The wind is too strong! We're going to fall!!
Hang in there, Kanon!

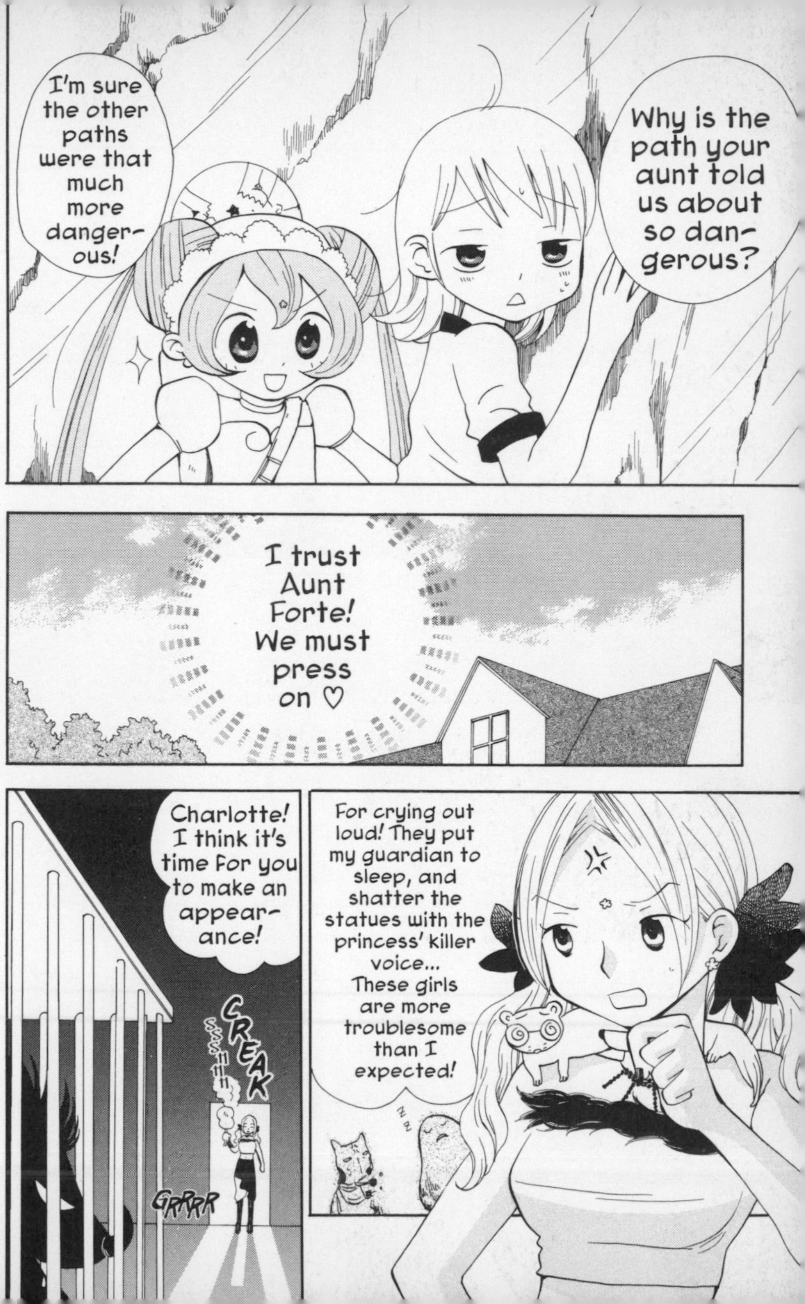
Why is the path your aunt told us about so dangerous?
I'm sure the other paths were that much more danger-ous!
I trust Aunt Forte! We must press on ♡
For crying out loud! They put my guardian to sleep, and shatter the statues with the princess' killer voice... These girls are more troublesome than I expected!
Charlotte! I think it's time for you to make an appear-ance!
CREAK
GRRRR

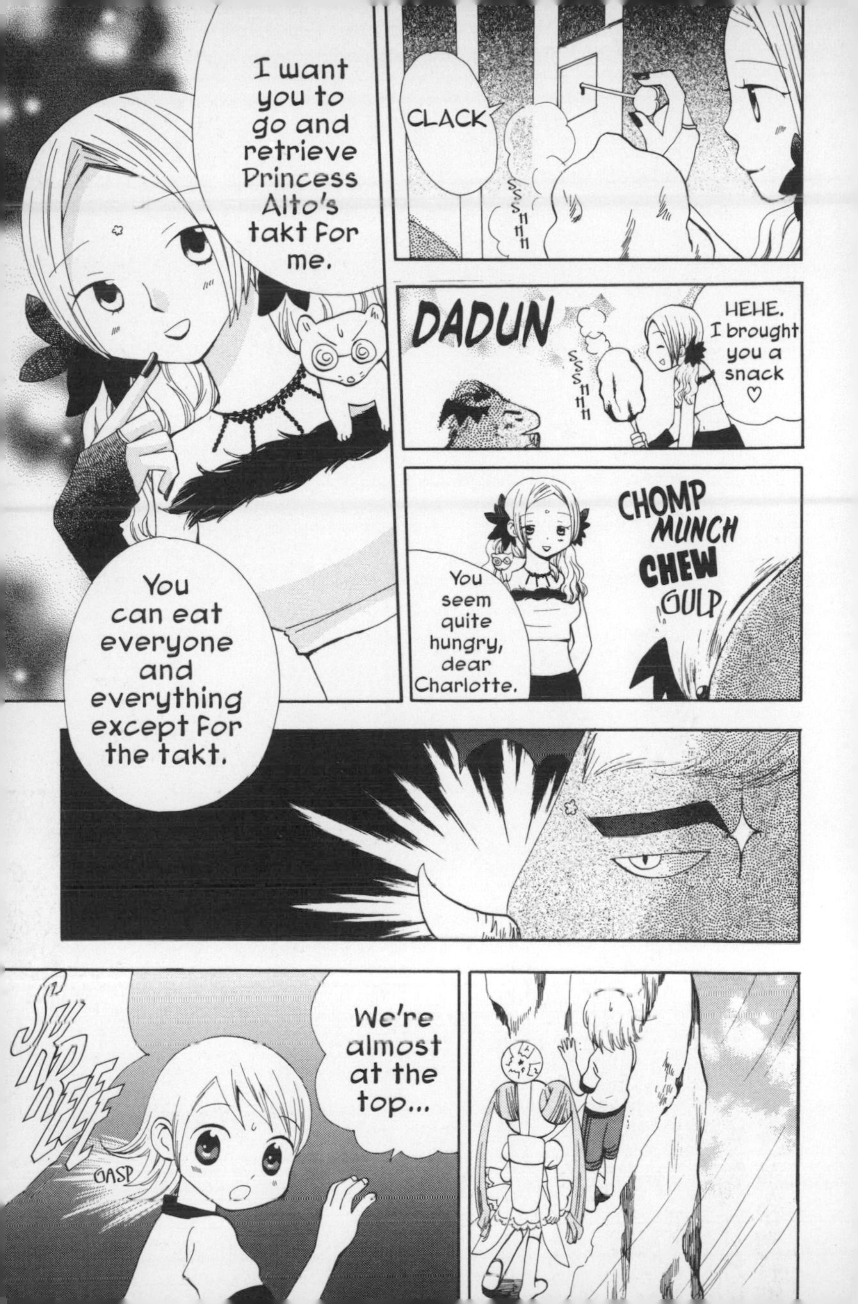
CLACK
DADUN
HEHE. I brought you a snack ♡
CHOMP
MUNCH
CHEW
GULP
You seem quite hungry, dear Charlotte.
I want you to go and retrieve Princess Alto's takt for me.
You can eat everyone and everything except for the takt.
GASP
We're almost at the top...

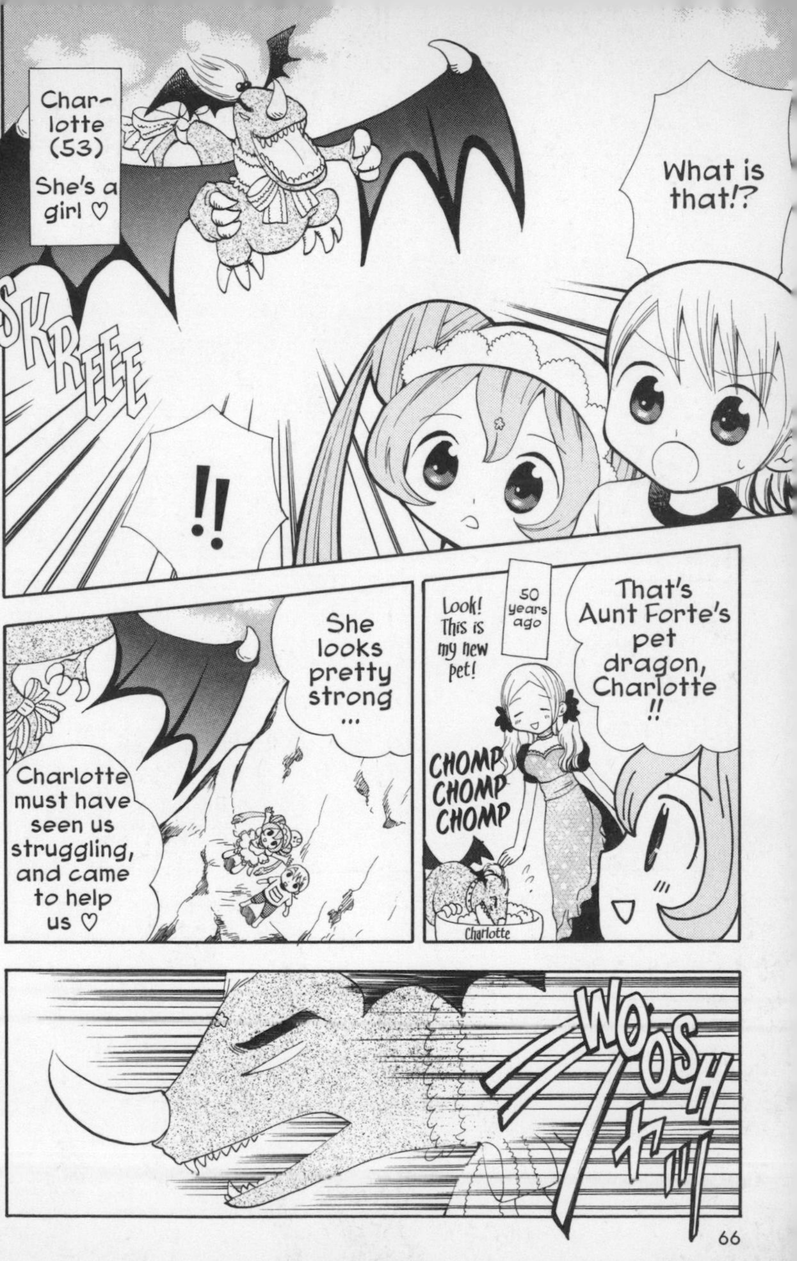

What is that!?
Char-lotte (53)
She's a girl ♡
SKREEE
!!
That's Aunt Forte's pet dragon, Charlotte !!
50 years ago
Look! This is my new pet!
CHOMP CHOMP CHOMP
Charlotte
She looks pretty strong ...
Charlotte must have seen us struggling, and came to help us ♡
WOOSH
ヤッ

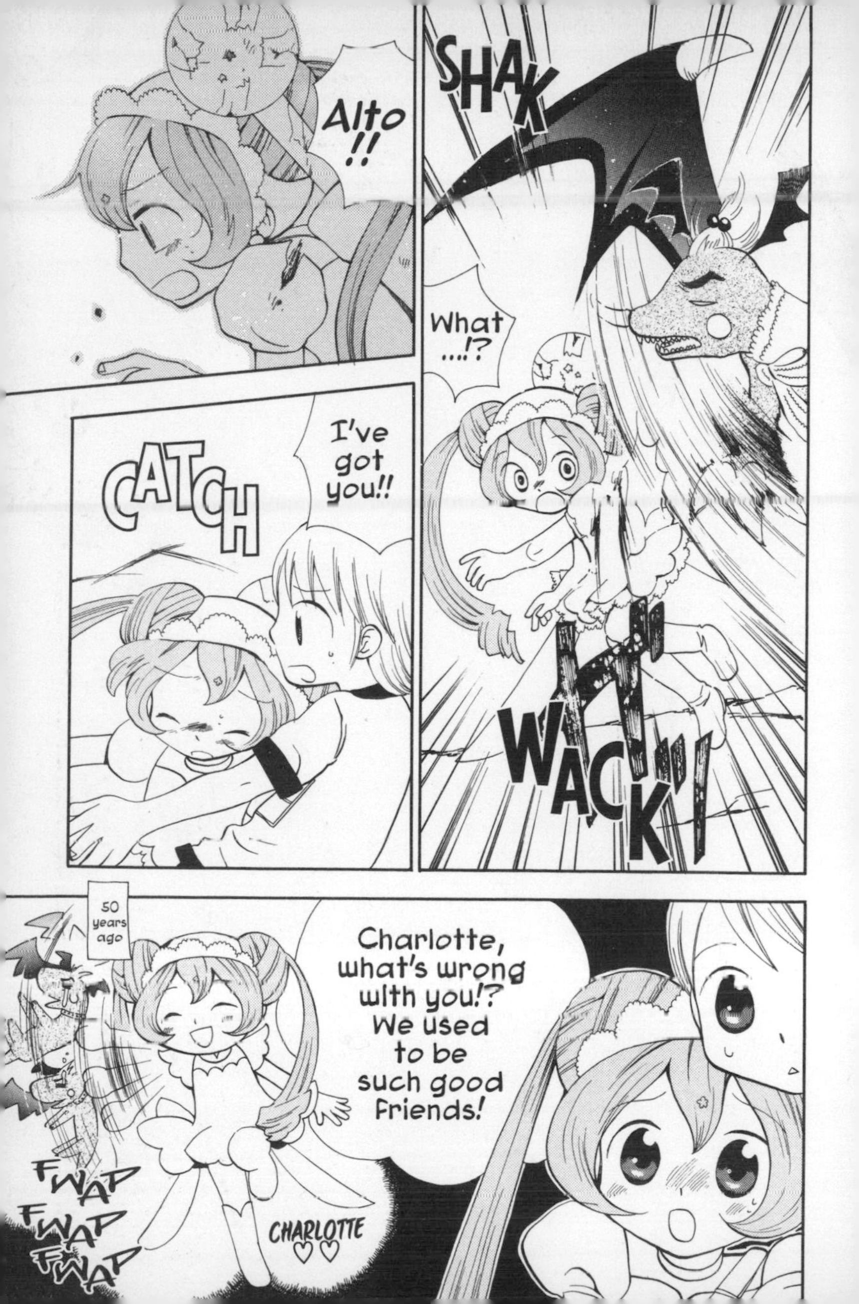
SHAK
What ...!?
WHACK!!
Alto !!
CATCH
I've got you!!
Charlotte, what's wrong with you!? We used to be such good friends!
50 years ago
FWAP FWAP FWAP
CHARLOTTE ♡♡

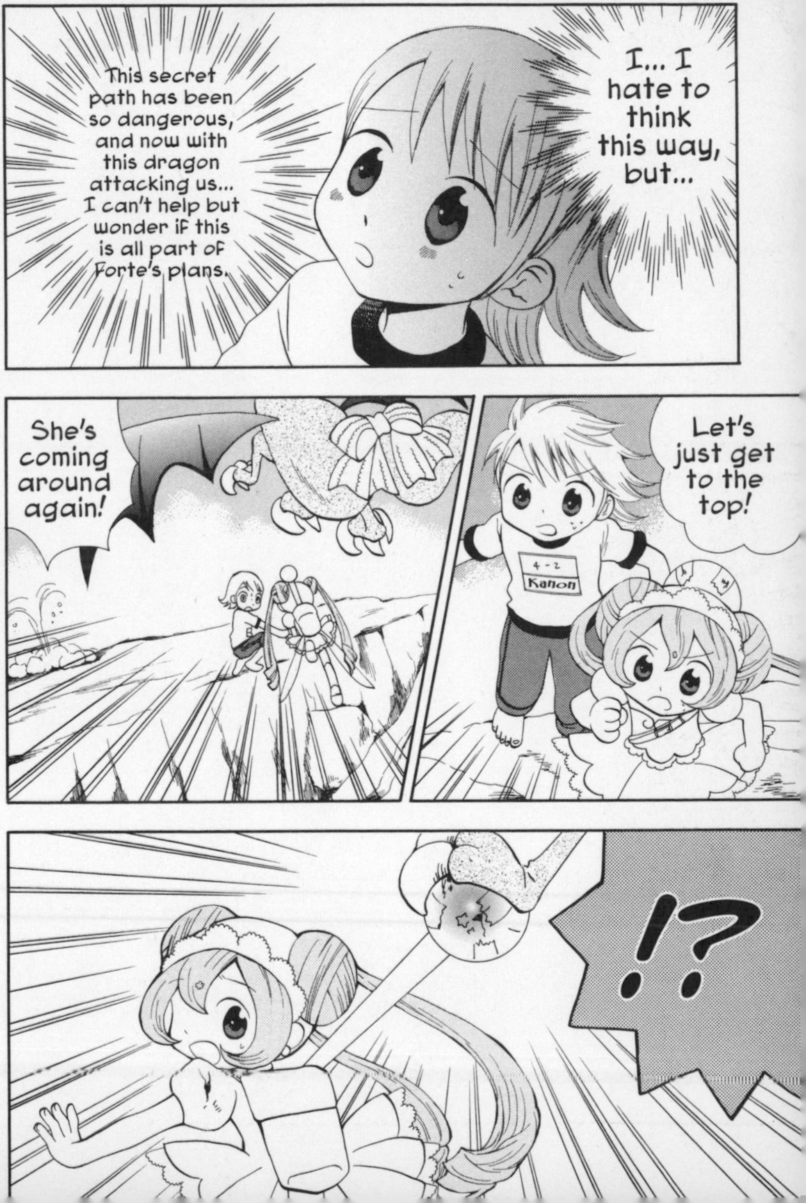
I... I hate to think this way, but...
This secret path has been so dangerous, and now with this dragon attacking us... I can't help but wonder if this is all part of Forte's plans.
Let's just get to the top!
4-2
Kanon
She's coming around again!
!?

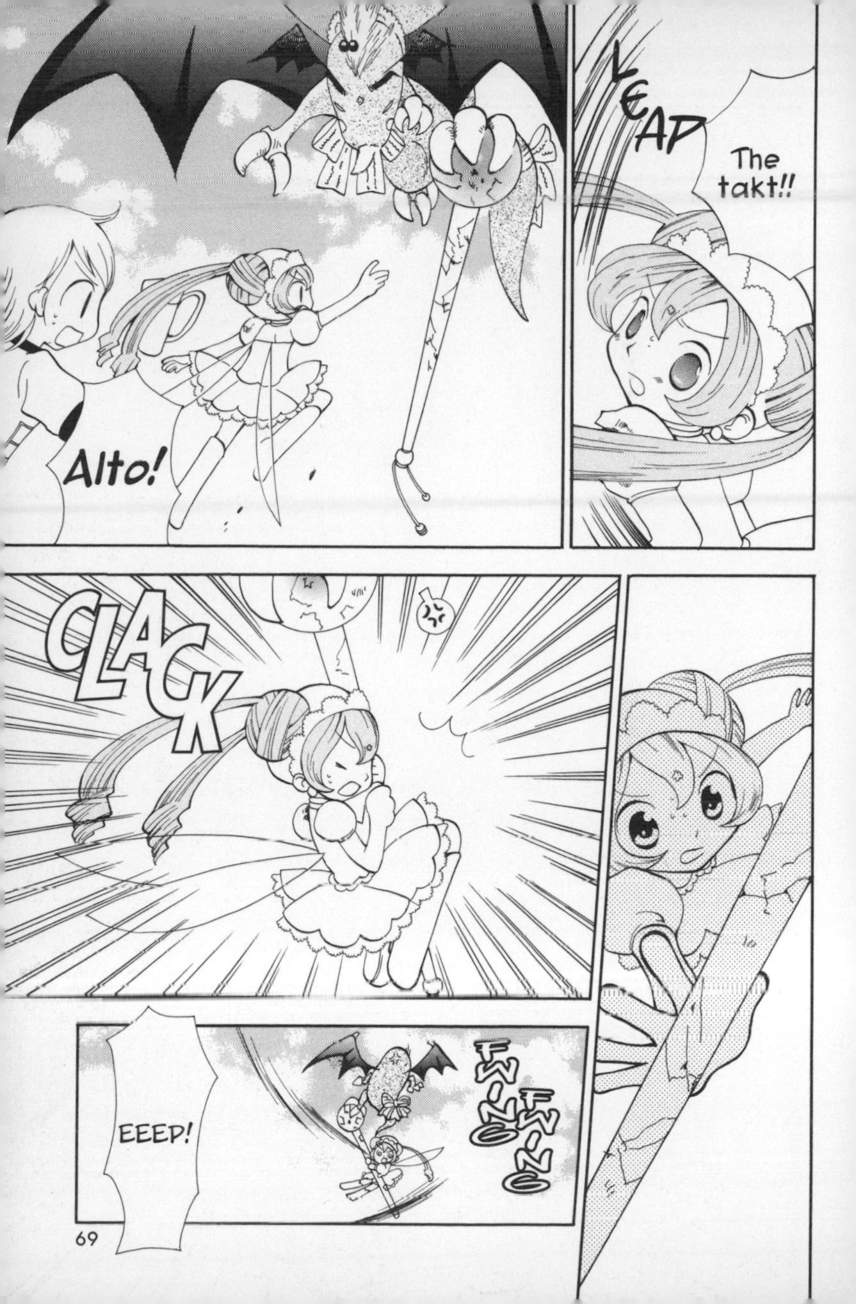
LEAP
The takt!!
Alto!
CLACK
FWING FWING
EEEP!

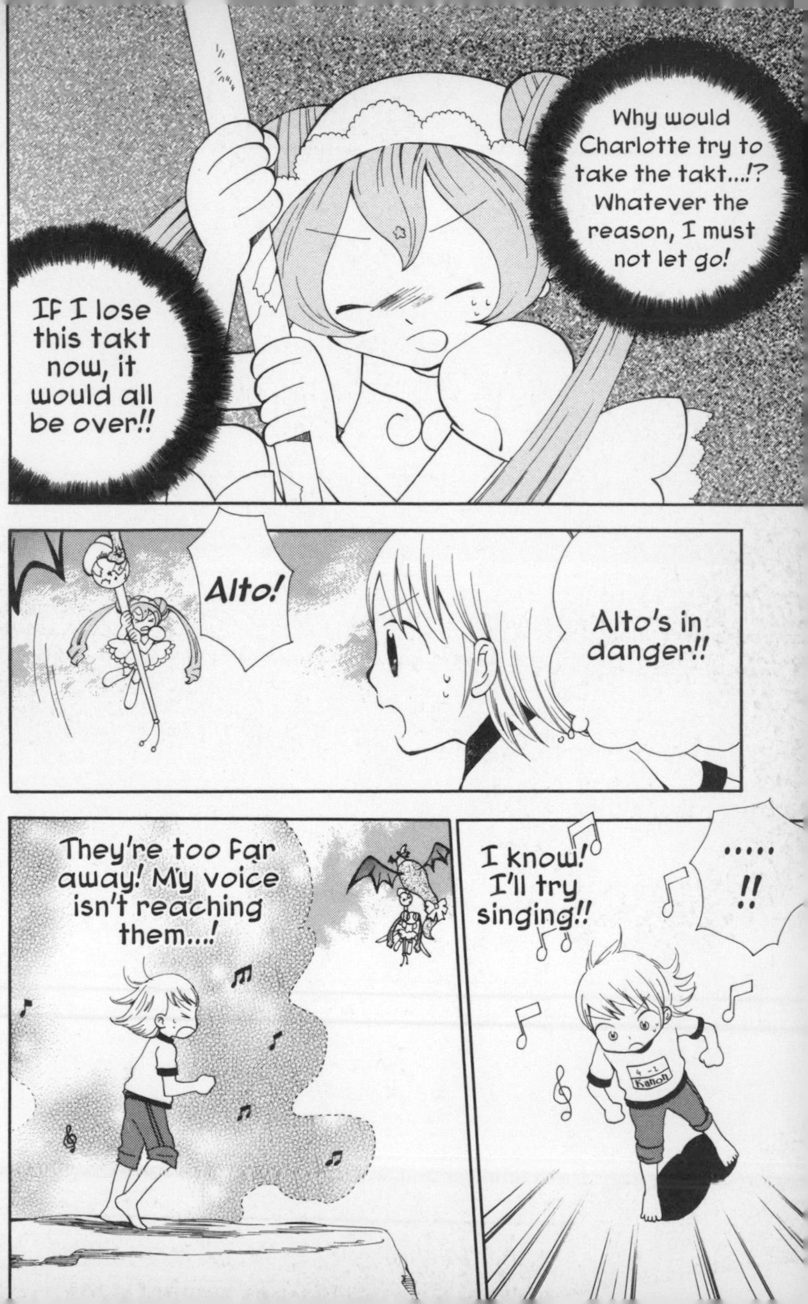

Why would Charlotte try to take the takt...!? Whatever the reason, I must not let go!
If I lose this takt now, it would all be over!!
Alto's in danger!!
Alto!
.....
!!
I know! I'll try singing!!
4-2
Kanon
They're too far away! My voice isn't reaching them...!

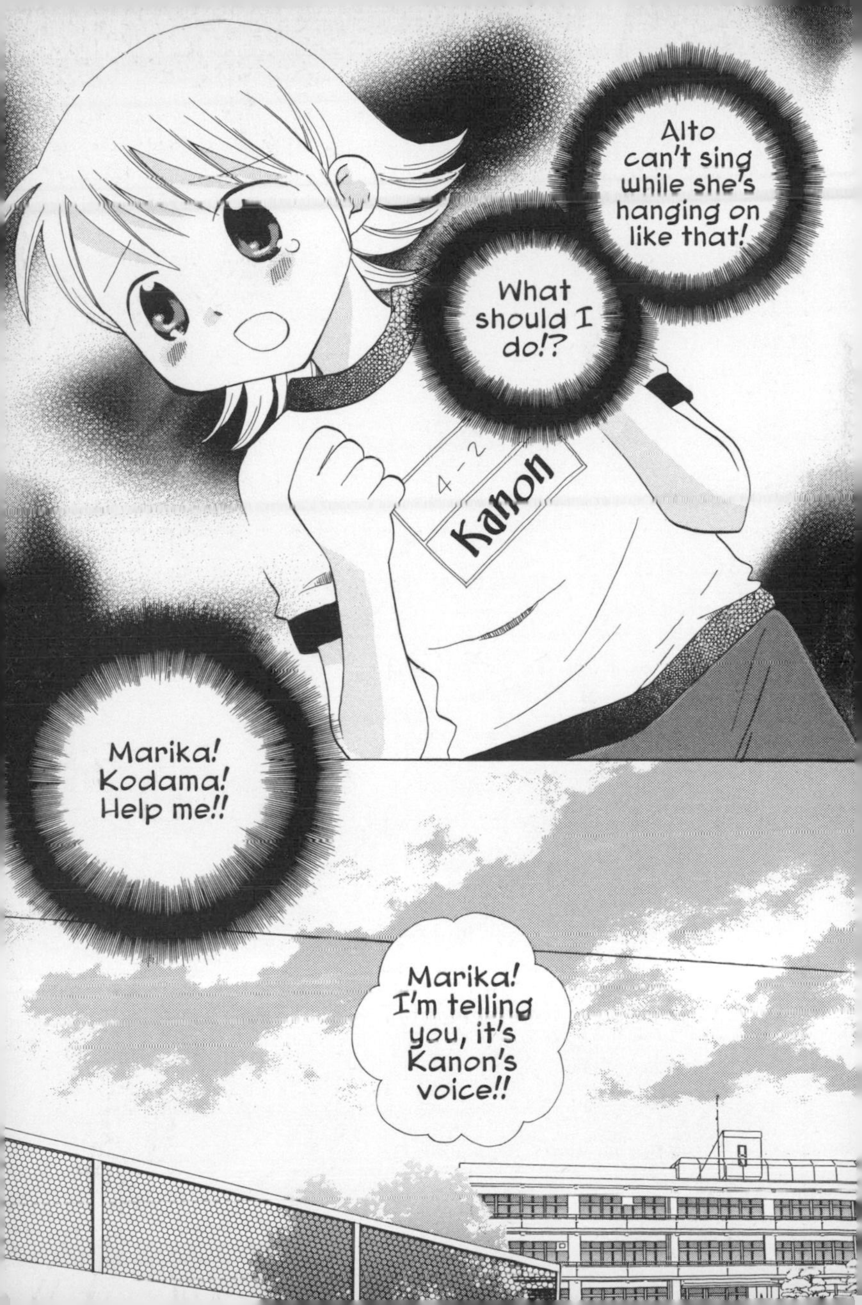
Alto can't sing while she's hanging on like that!
What should I do!?
4-2
Kanon
Marika! Kodama! Help me!!
Marika! I'm telling you, it's Kanon's voice!!

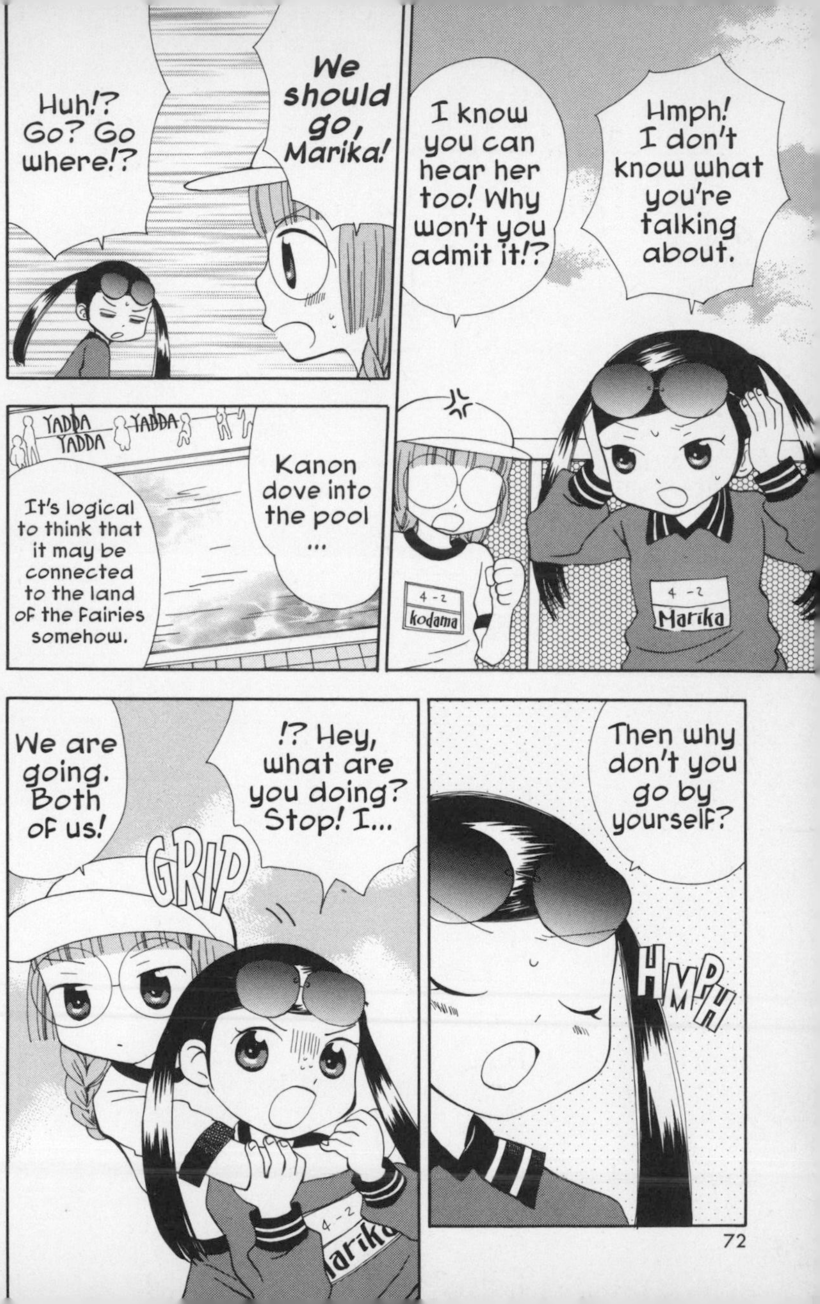
Hmph! I don't know what you're talking about.
I know you can hear her too! Why won't you admit it!?
4-2
kodama
4-2
Marika
We should go, Marika!
Huh!? Go? Go where!?
YADDA YADDA YADDA
Kanon dove into the pool ...
It's logical to think that it may be connected to the land of the fairies somehow.
Then why don't you go by yourself?
HMPH
!? Hey, what are you doing? Stop! I...
We are going. Both of us!
GRIP
4-2
Marika

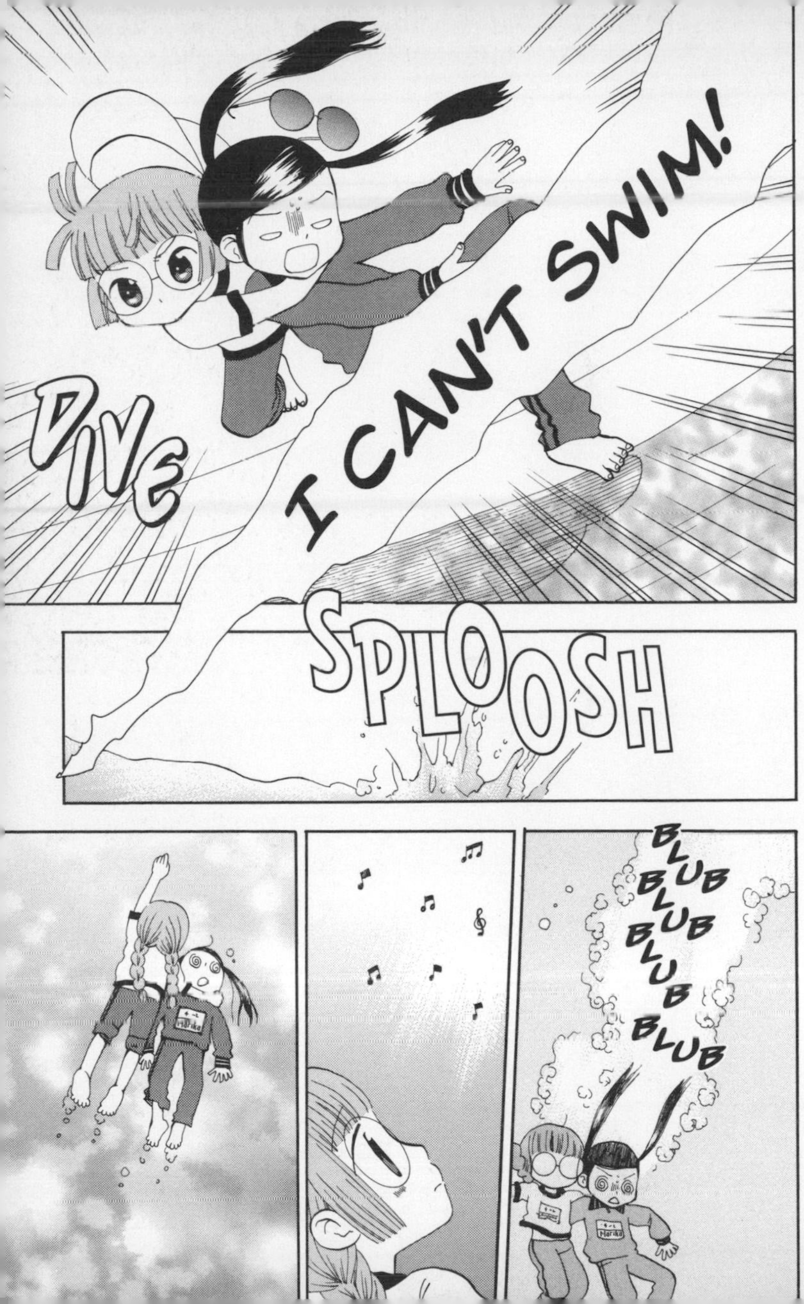
I CAN'T SWIM!
DIVE
SPLOOSH
BLUB BLUB BLUB BLUB BLUB

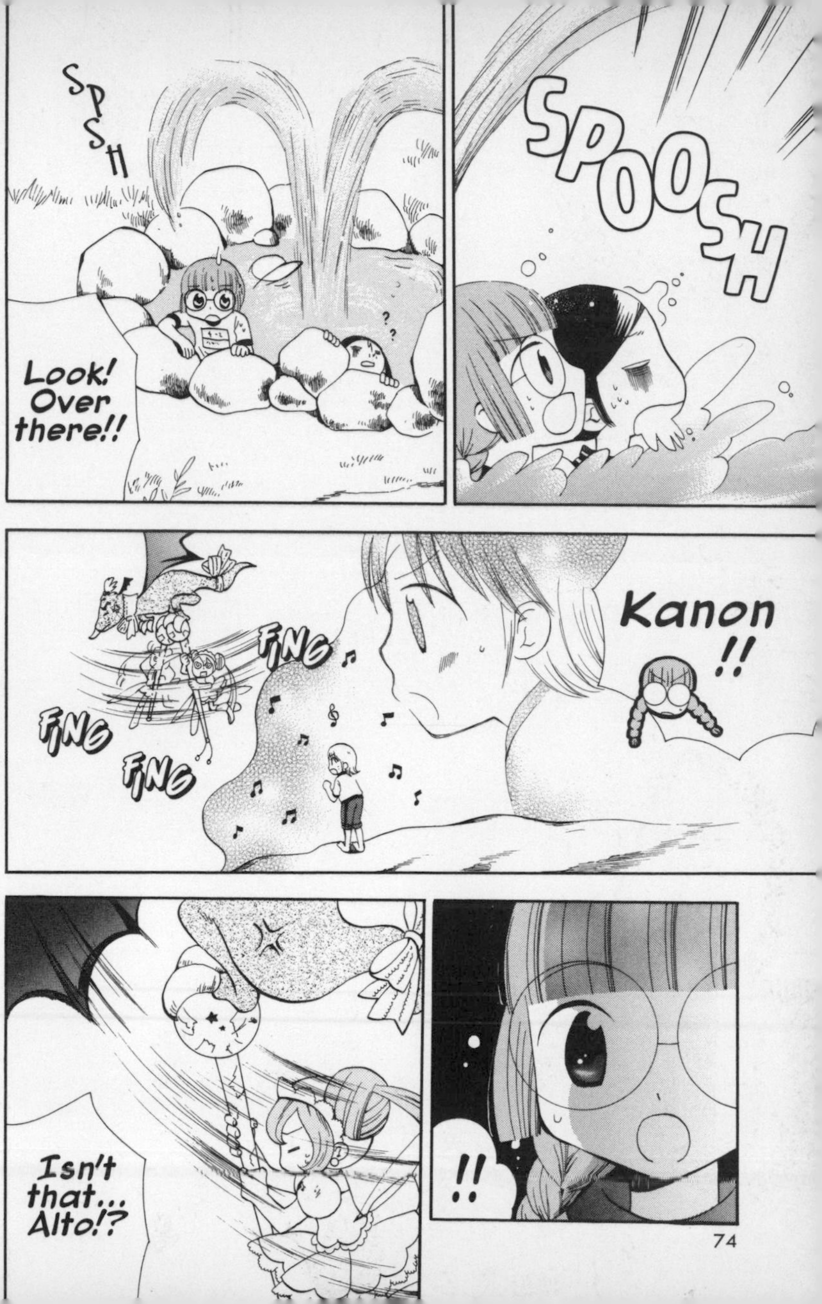
SPOOOSH
SPSH
Look! Over there!!
Kanon!!
FING
FING
FING
!!
Isn't that... Alto!?

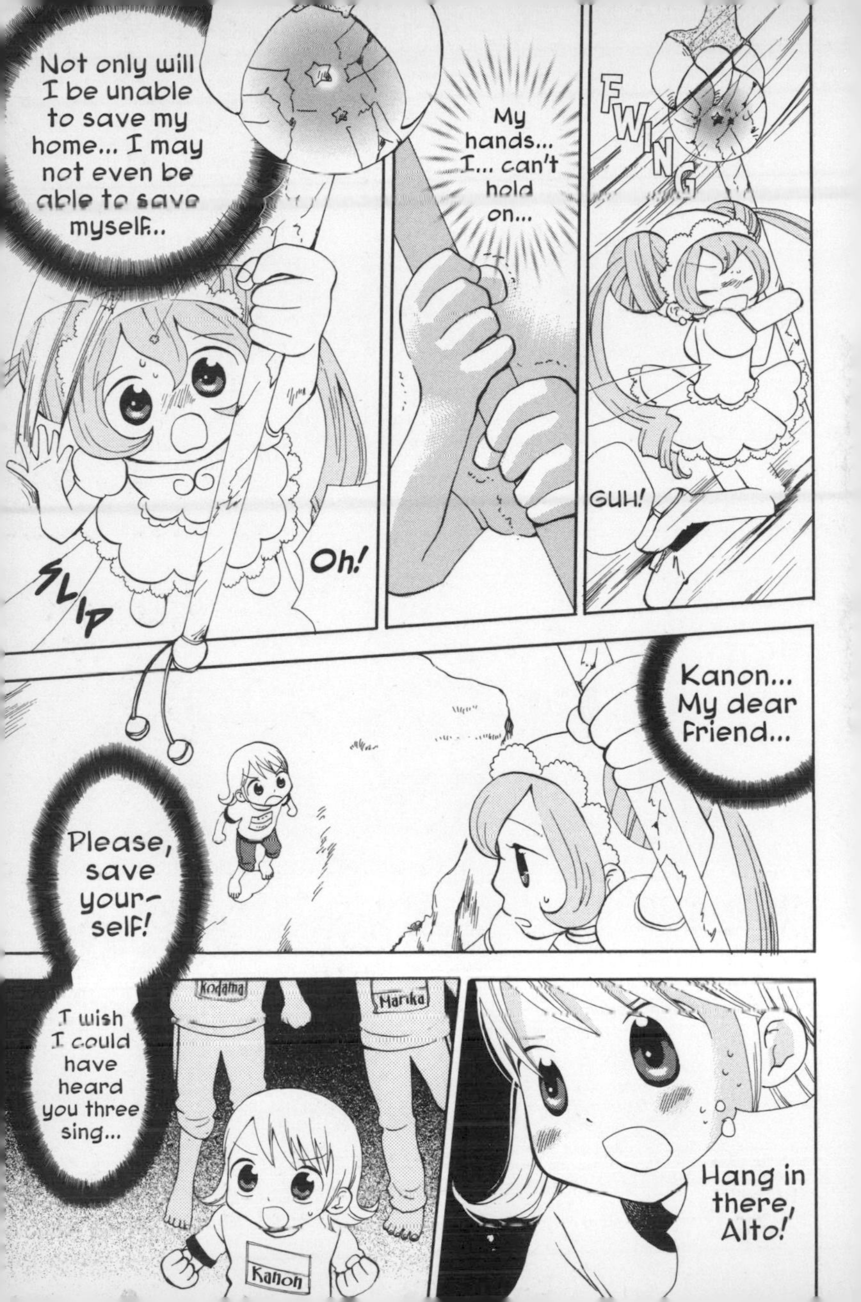
FWING
GUH!
My hands... I... can't hold on...
Not only will I be unable to save my home... I may not even be able to save myself...
Oh!
SLIP
Kanon... My dear friend...
Please, save your-self!
Hang in there, Alto!
I wish I could have heard you three sing...
Kodama
Marika
Kanon

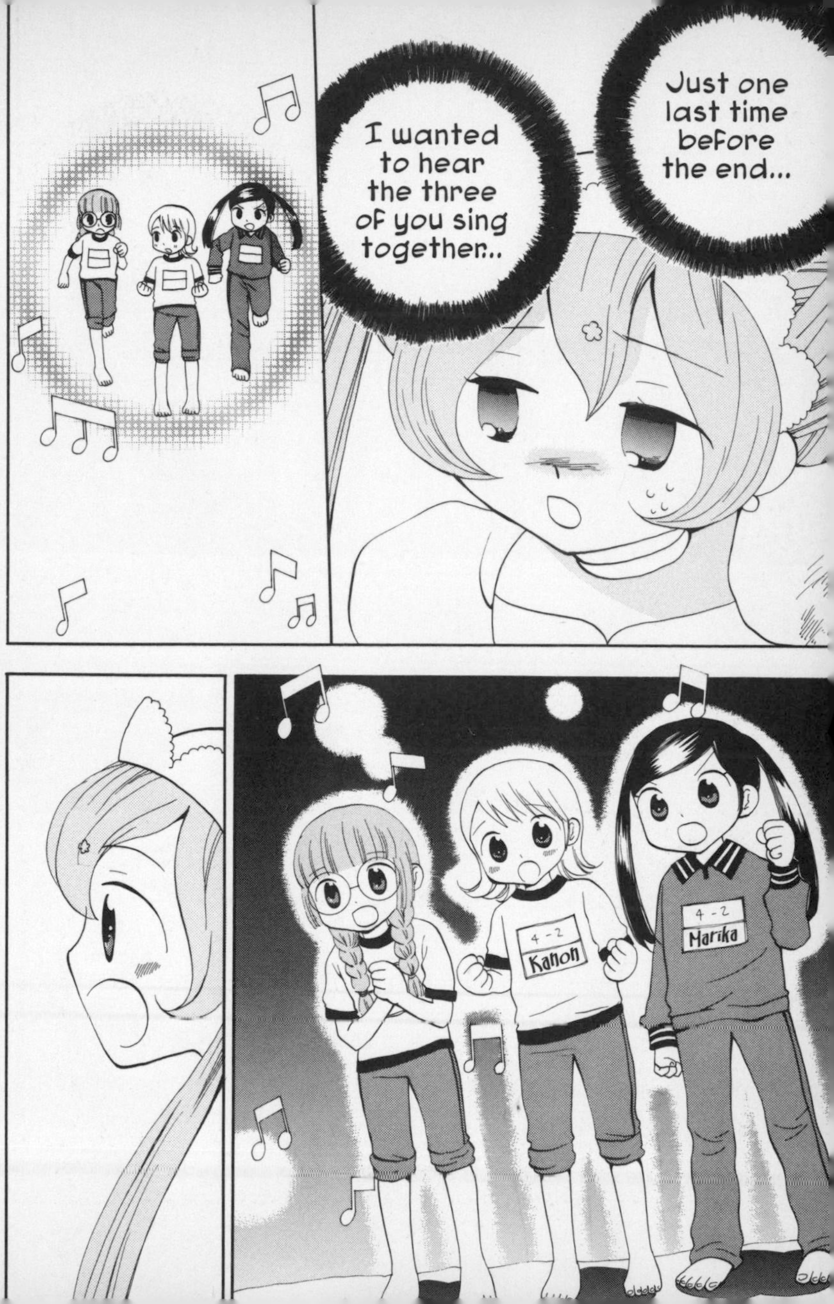
Just one last time before the end...
I wanted to hear the three of you sing together...
4-2
Marika
4-2
Kanon

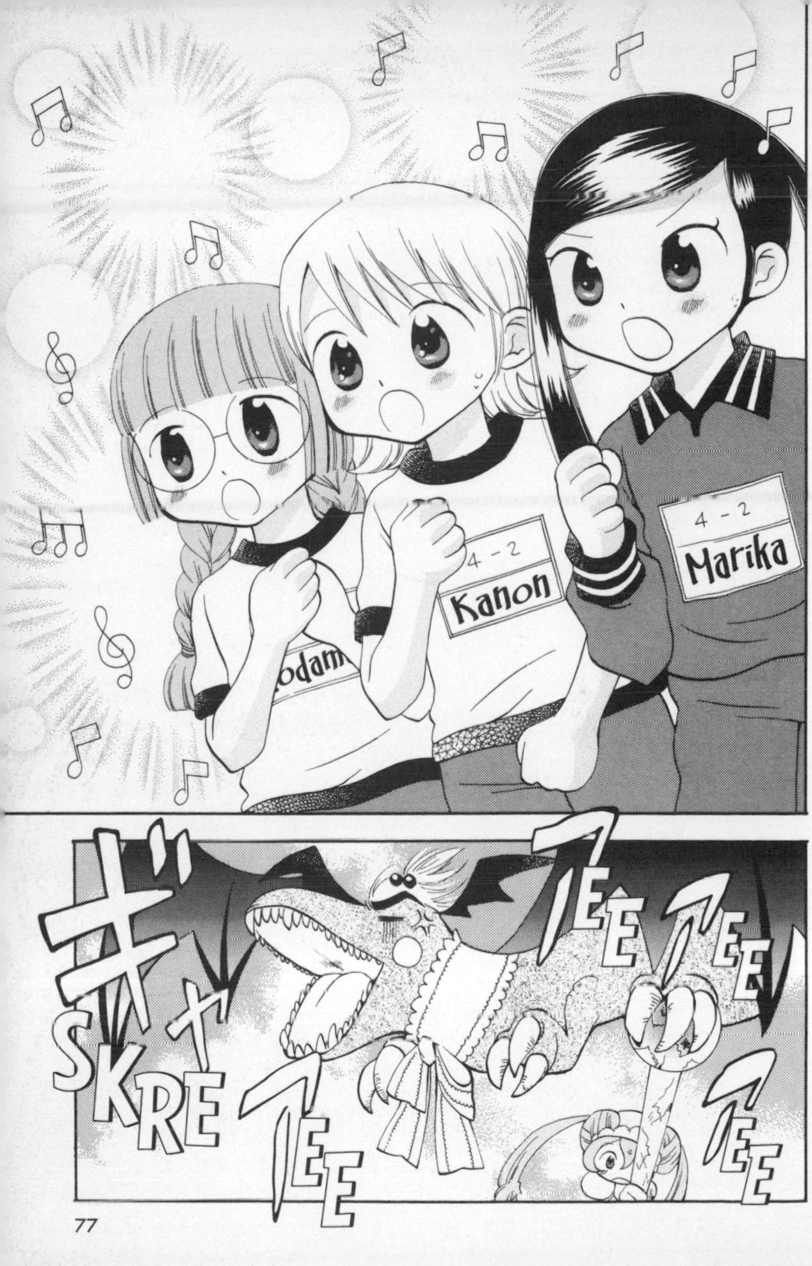
4-2
Marika
4-2
Kanon
ギャ
SKRE
EE
EE
EE
EE

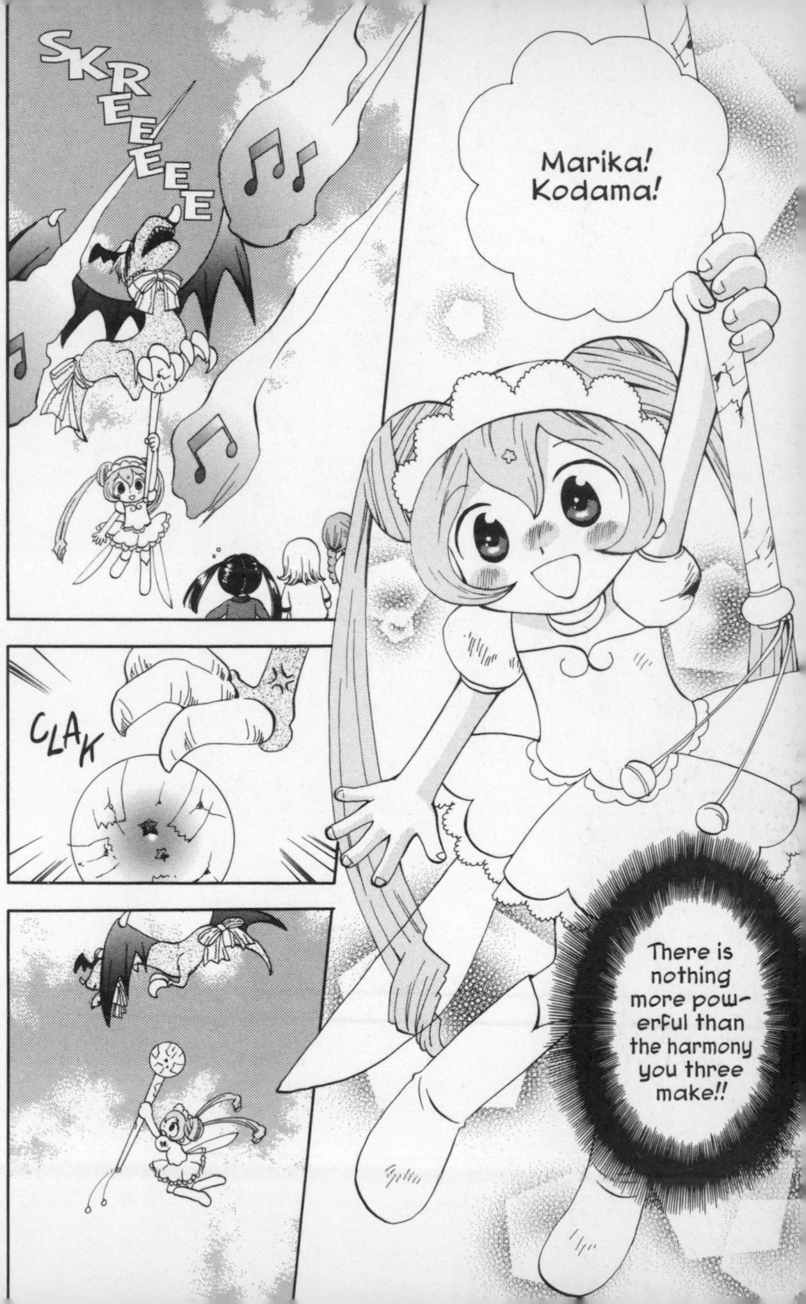
Marika! Kodama!
There is nothing more pow-erful than the harmony you three make!!
SKREEEEE
CLAK

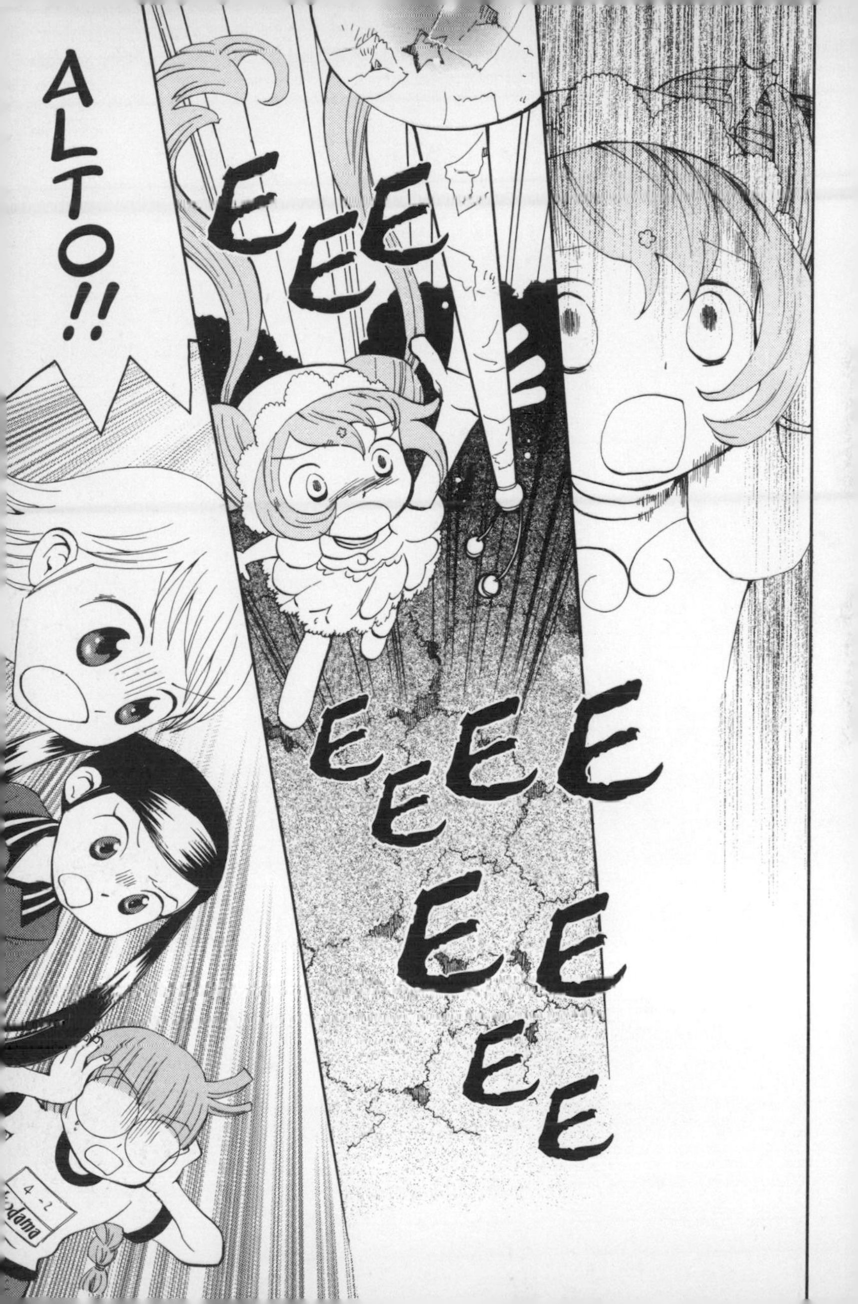
EEE
EEEEEEEEEE
ALTO!!
4-2

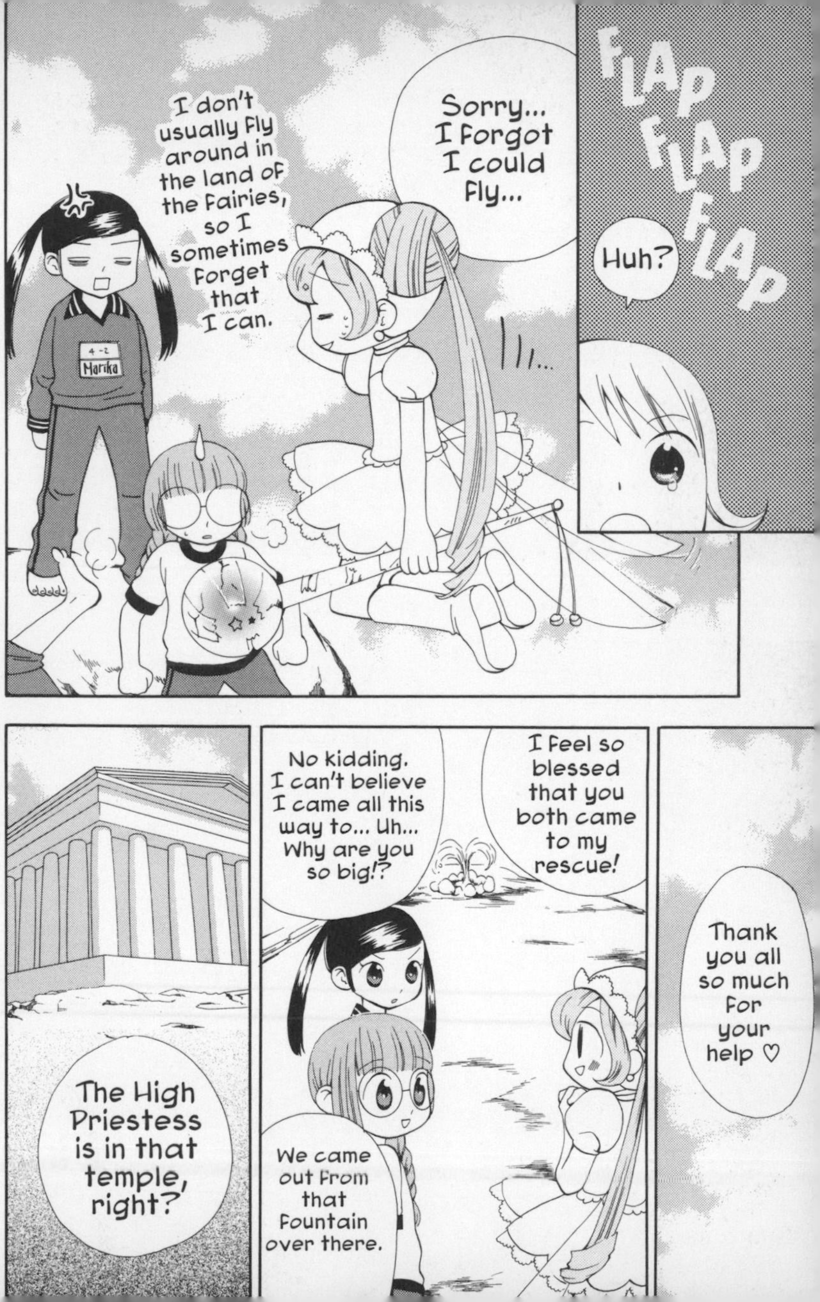
FLAP FLAP FLAP
Huh?
Sorry... I forgot I could fly...
I don't usually fly around in the land of the fairies, so I sometimes forget that I can.
4-2
Marika
Thank you all so much for your help ♡
I feel so blessed that you both came to my rescue!
No kidding. I can't believe I came all this way to... Uh... Why are you so big!?
We came out from that fountain over there.
The High Priestess is in that temple, right?

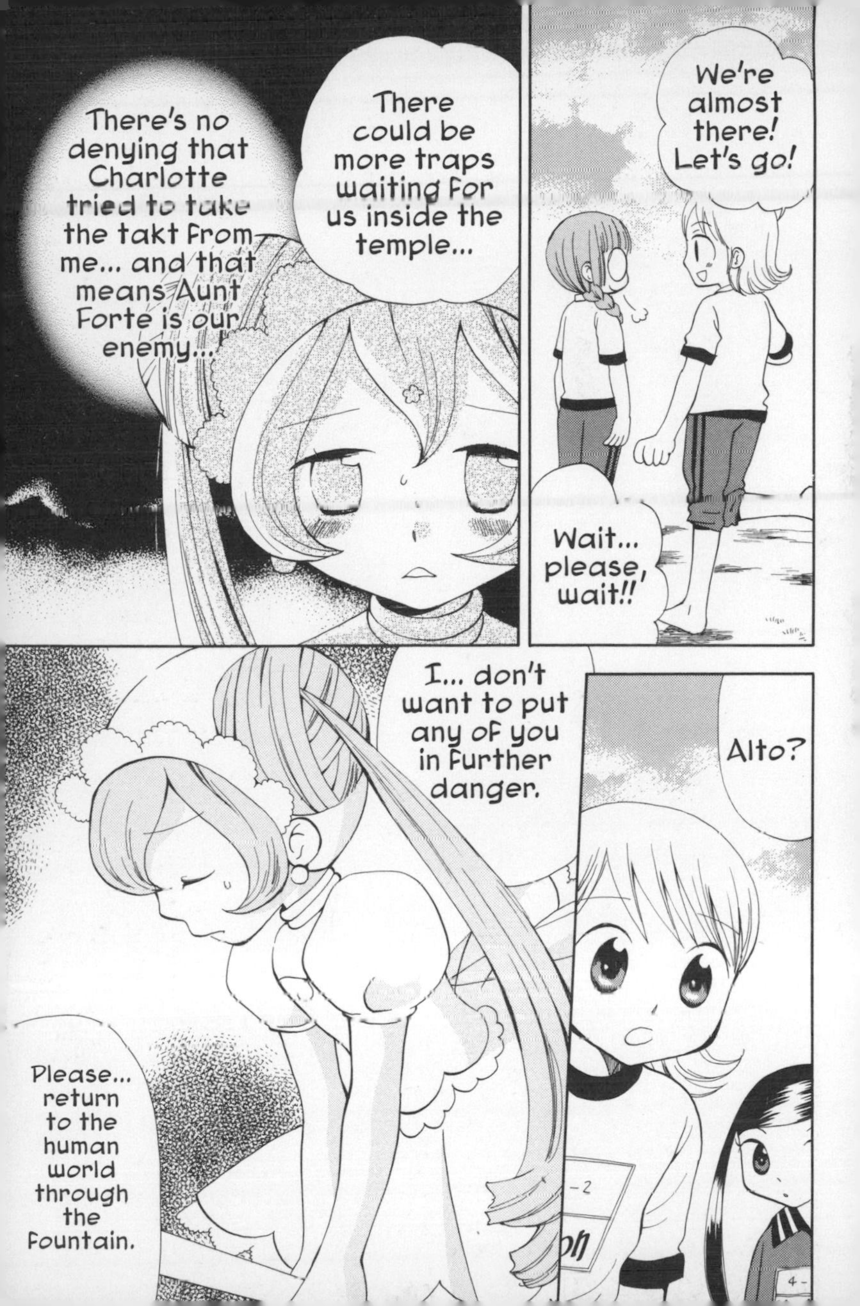
We're almost there! Let's go!
Wait... please, wait!!
There could be more traps waiting for us inside the temple...
There's no denying that Charlotte tried to take the takt from me... and that means Aunt Forte is our enemy...
Alto?
I... don't want to put any of you in further danger.
Please... return to the human world through the fountain.

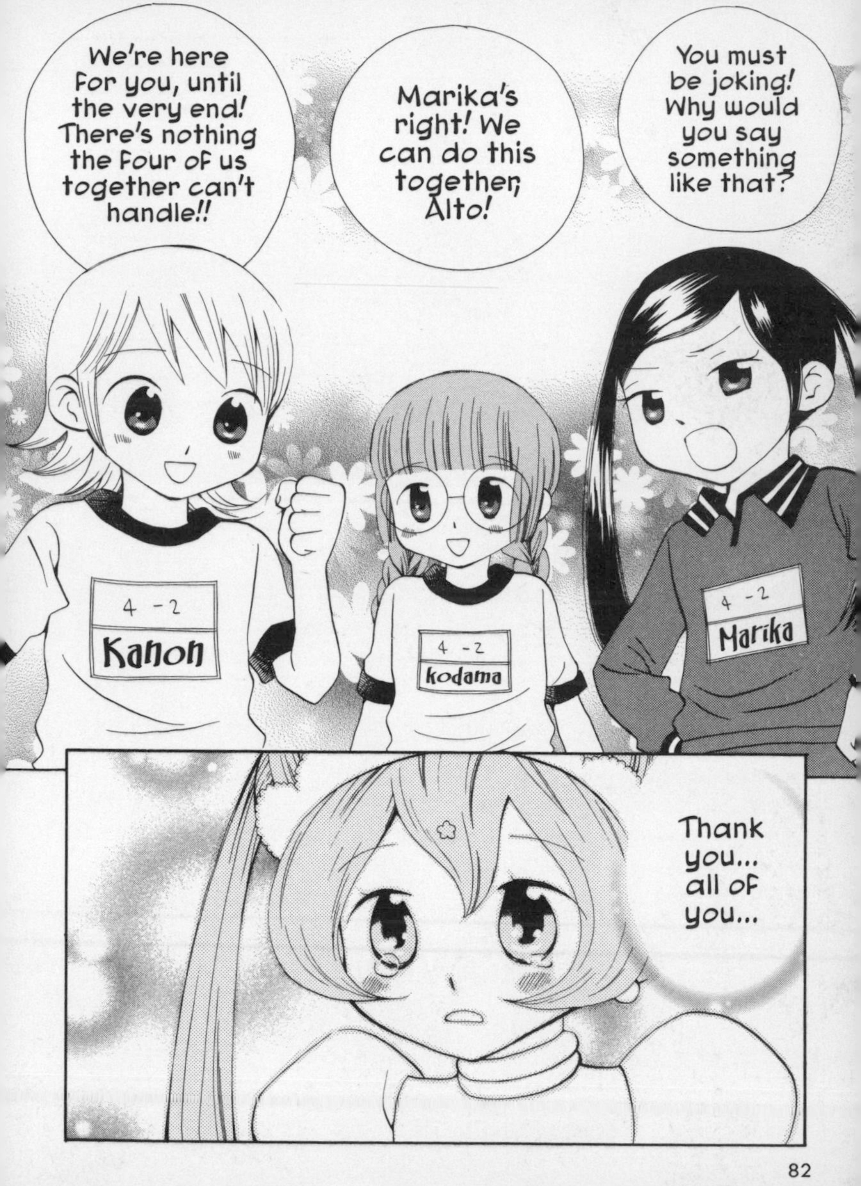
You must be joking! Why would you say something like that?
Marika's right! We can do this together, Alto!
We're here for you, until the very end! There's nothing the four of us together can't handle!!
4 -2
Marika
4 -2
kodama
4 -2
Kanon
Thank you... all of you...

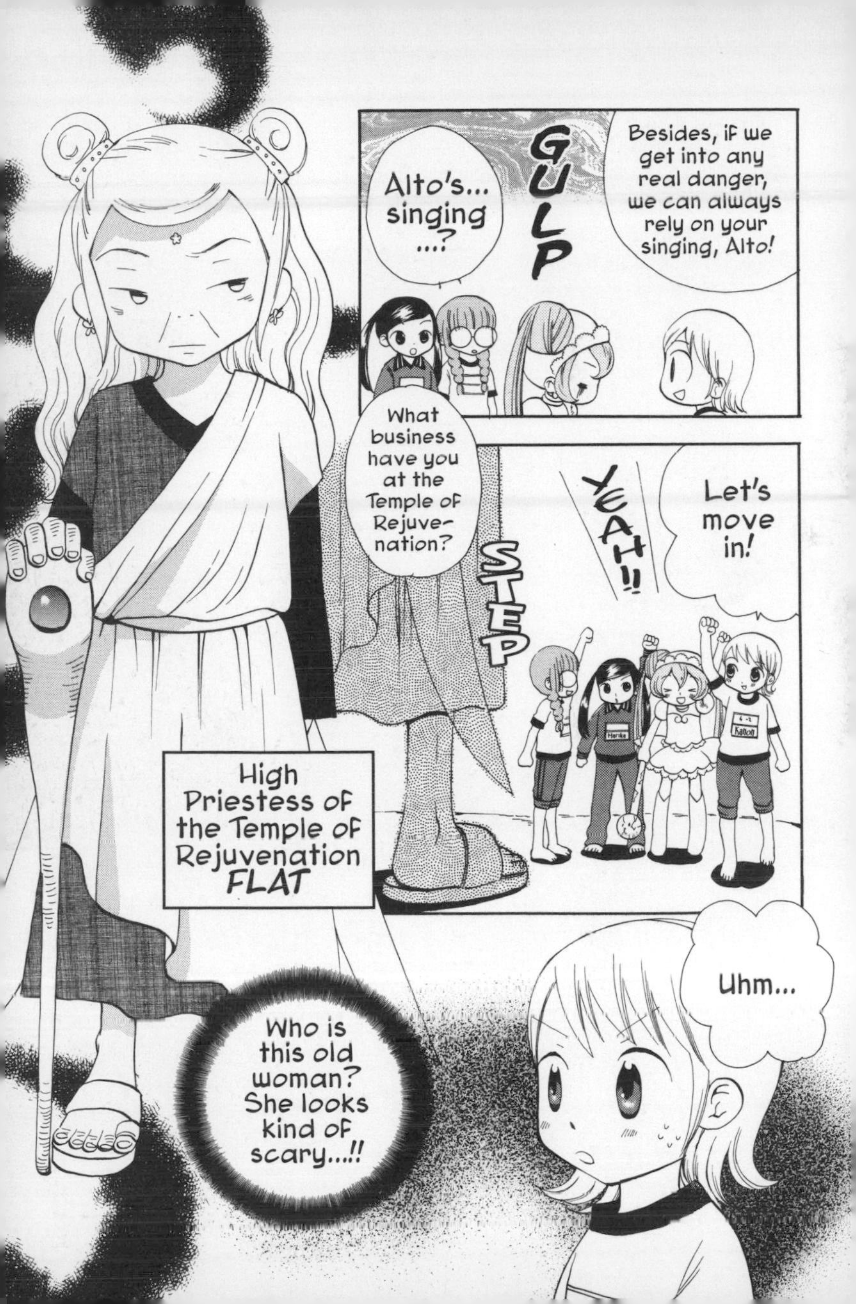
Besides, if we get into any real danger, we can always rely on your singing, Alto!
GULP
Alto's... singing ...?
Let's move in!
YEAH!!
What business have you at the Temple of Rejuvenation?
STEP
High Priestess of the Temple of Rejuvenation FLAT
Uhm...
Who is this old woman? She looks kind of scary...!!

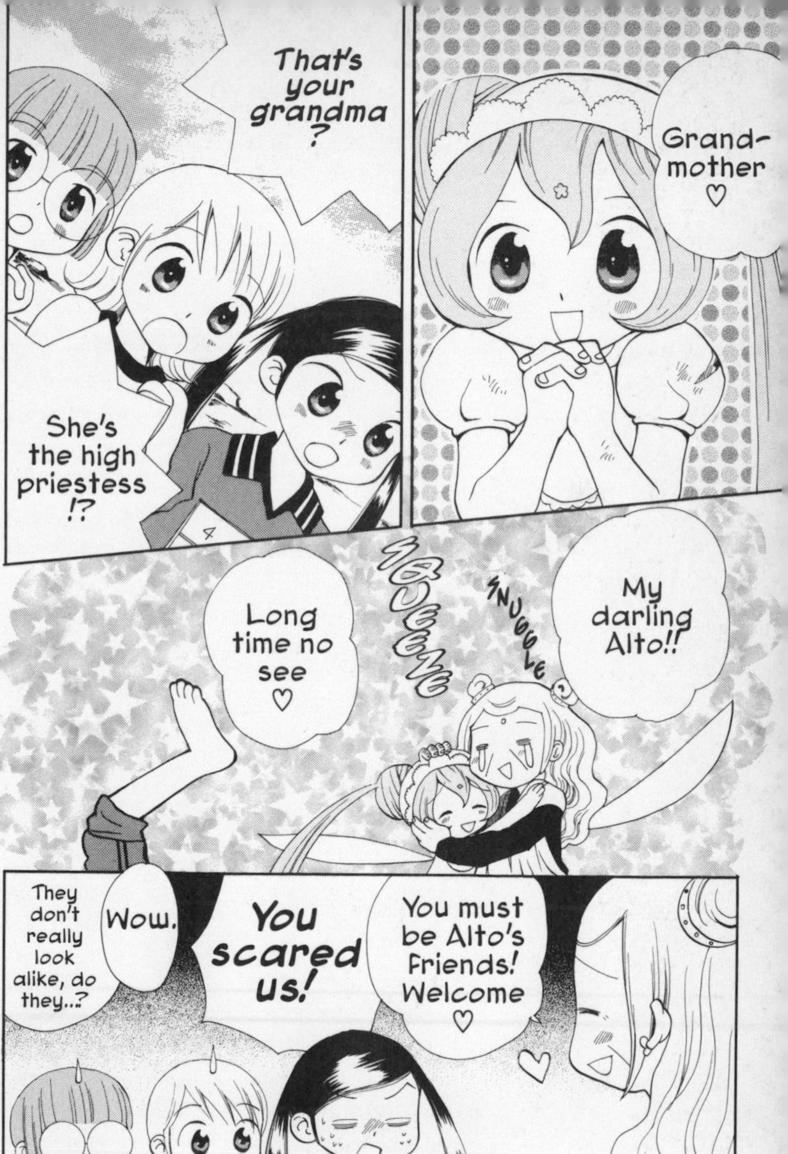
Grand-mother ♡
That's your grandma?
She's the high priestess!?
My darling Alto!!
SNUGGLE
SQUEEZE
Long time no see ♡
You must be Alto's friends! Welcome ♡
You scared us!
Wow.
They don't really look alike, do they..?

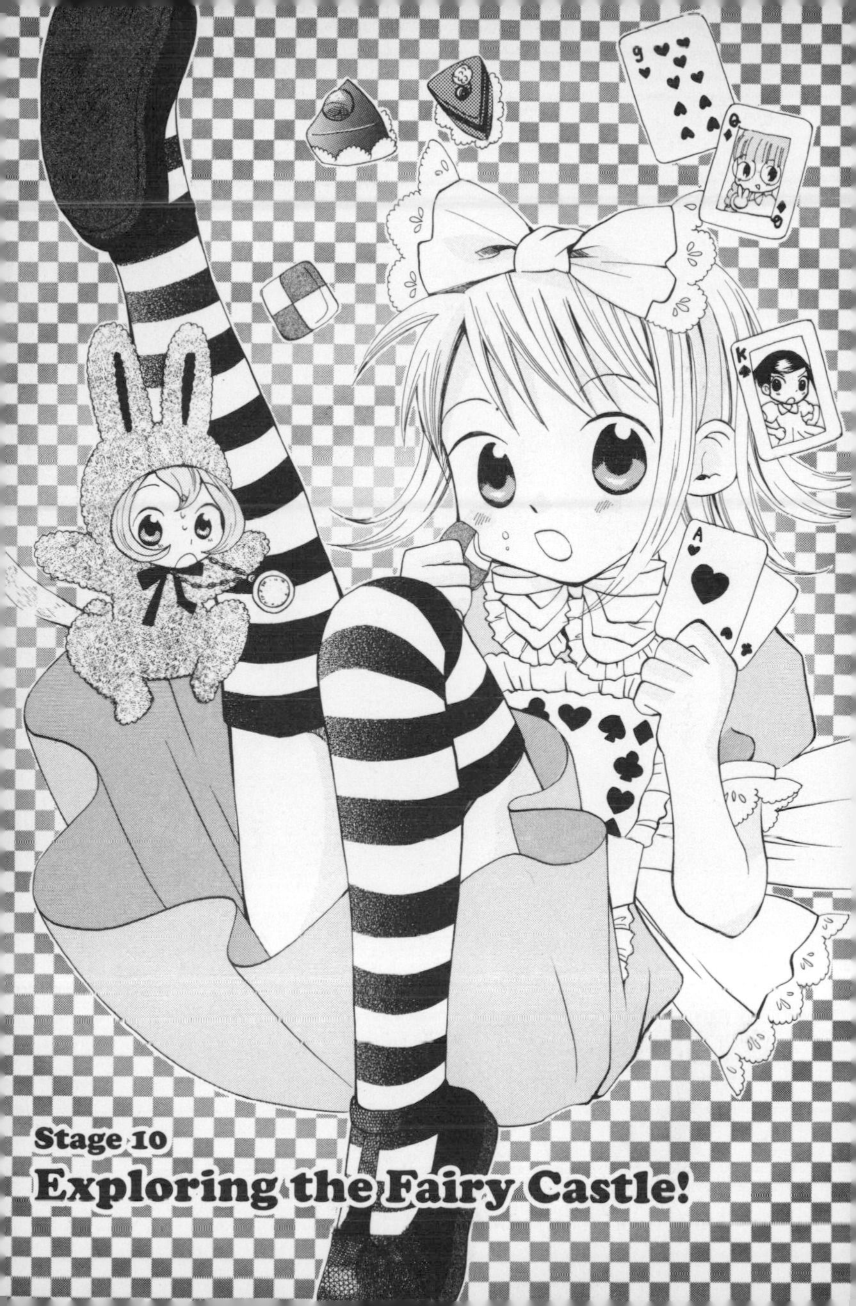

## Stage 10
# Exploring the Fairy Castle!

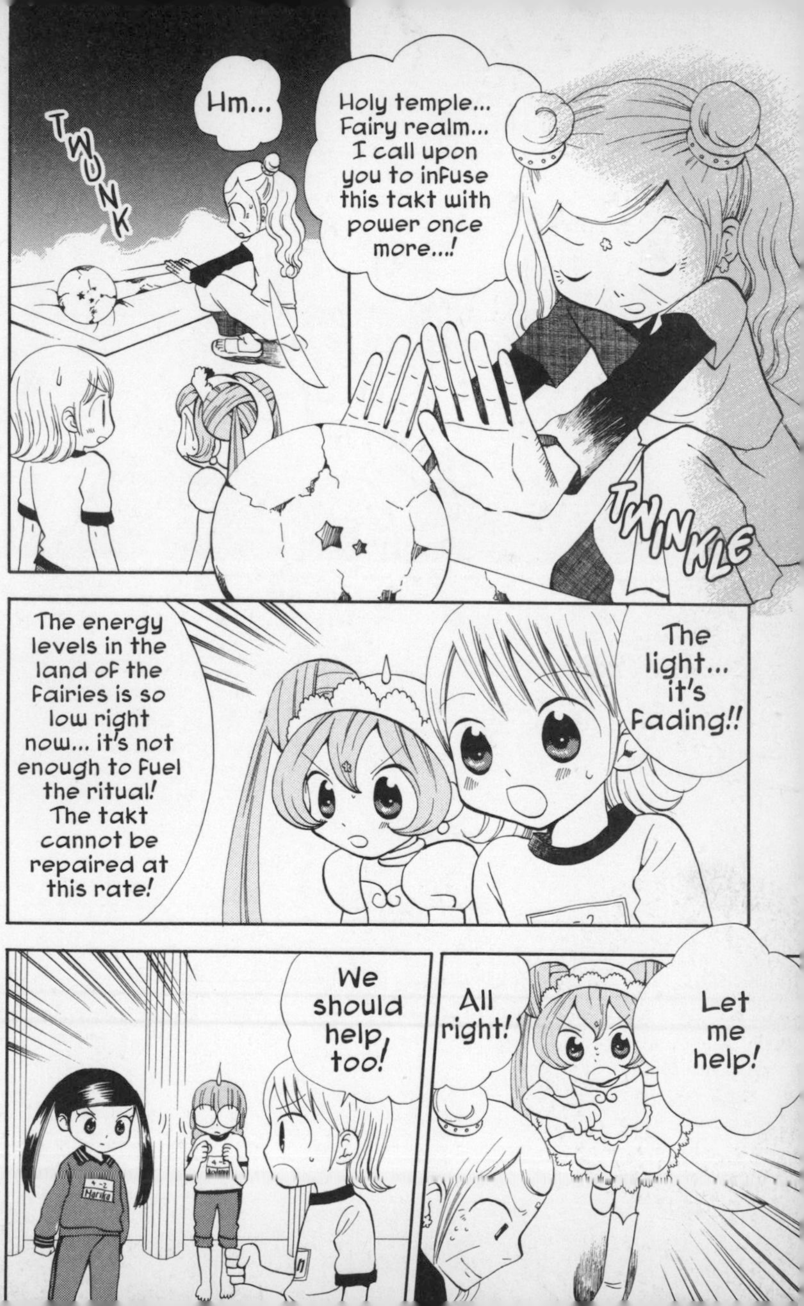
Holy temple... Fairy realm... I call upon you to infuse this takt with power once more...!
TWINKLE
Hm...
TWUNK
The light... it's fading!!
The energy levels in the land of the fairies is so low right now... it's not enough to fuel the ritual! The takt cannot be repaired at this rate!
Let me help!
All right!
We should help, too!

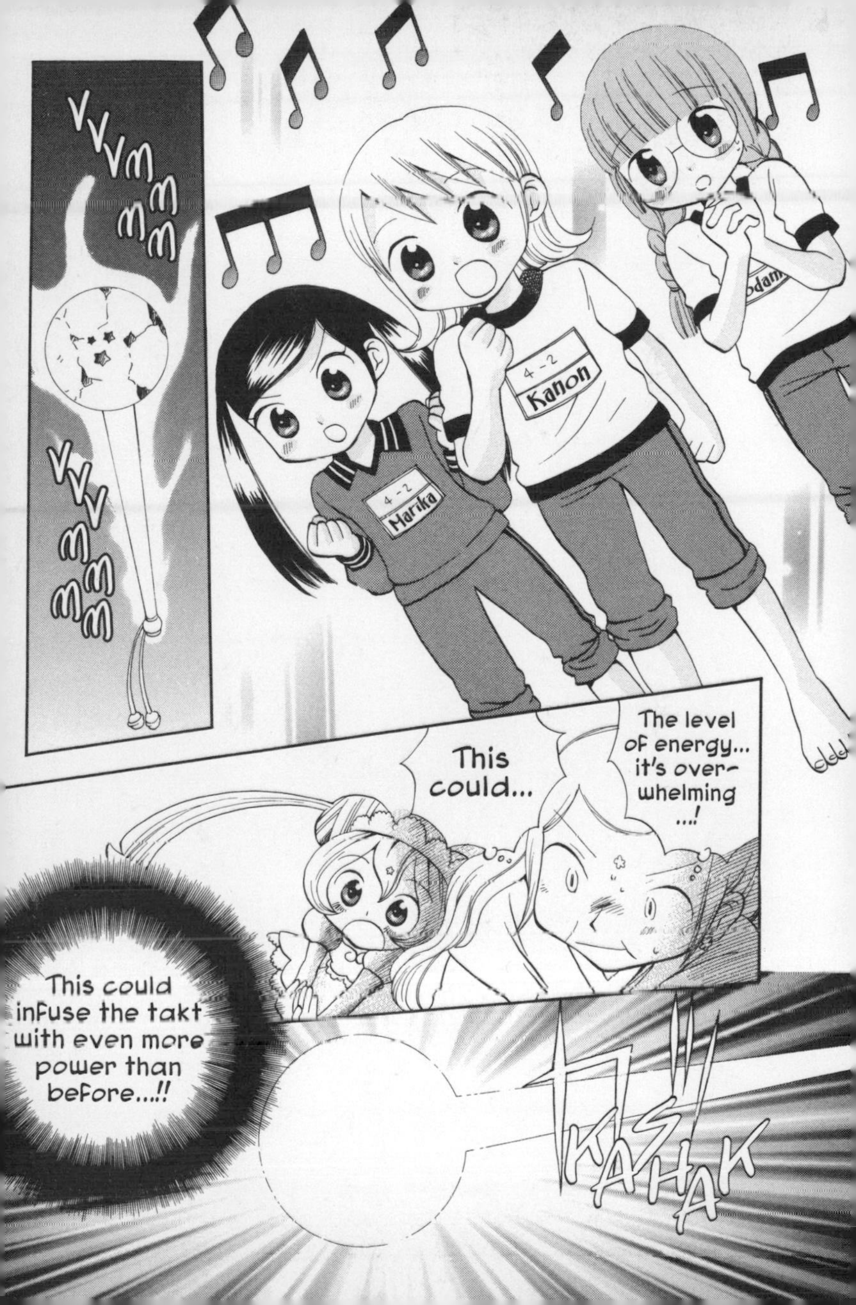
4-2 Kanon
4-2 Marika
VVVmmmmmm
VVVmmmmmm
The level of energy... it's over-whelming ...!
This could...
This could infuse the takt with even more power than before...!!
KASAHAK!!

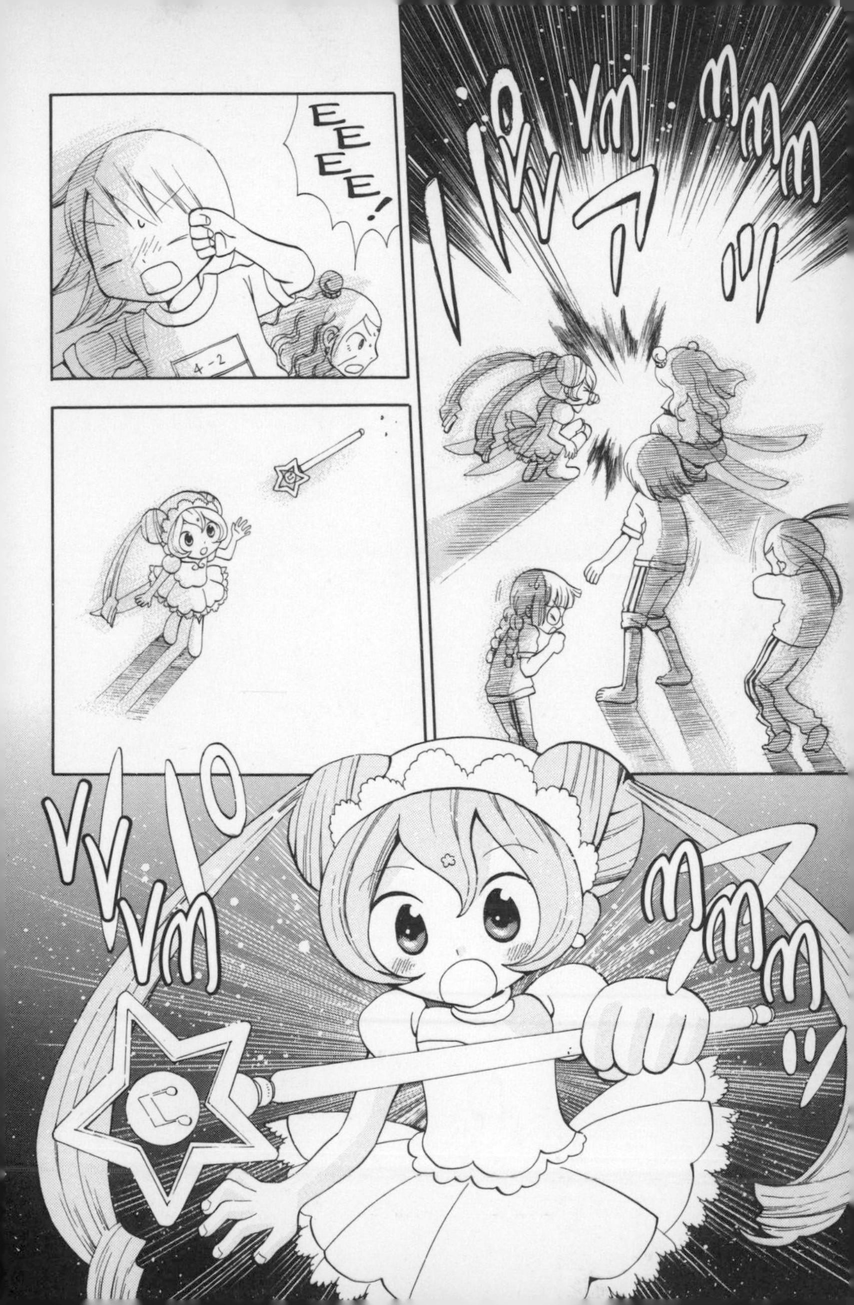

VVVVM MMMM
EEEEE!
VVVVM MMMM

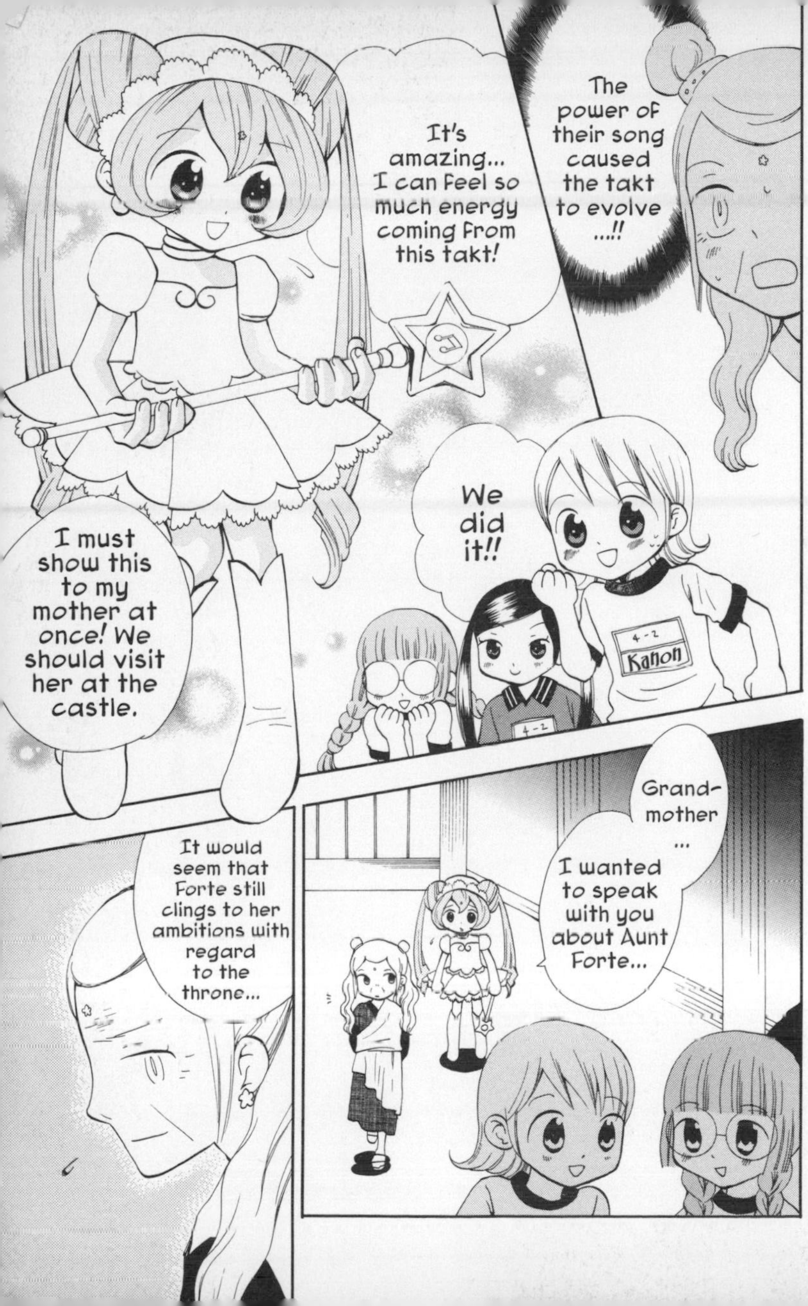
The power of their song caused the takt to evolve ...!!
We did it!!
It's amazing... I can feel so much energy coming from this takt!
I must show this to my mother at once! We should visit her at the castle.
4-2 Kanon
4-2
Grand-mother ...
I wanted to speak with you about Aunt Forte...
It would seem that Forte still clings to her ambitions with regard to the throne...

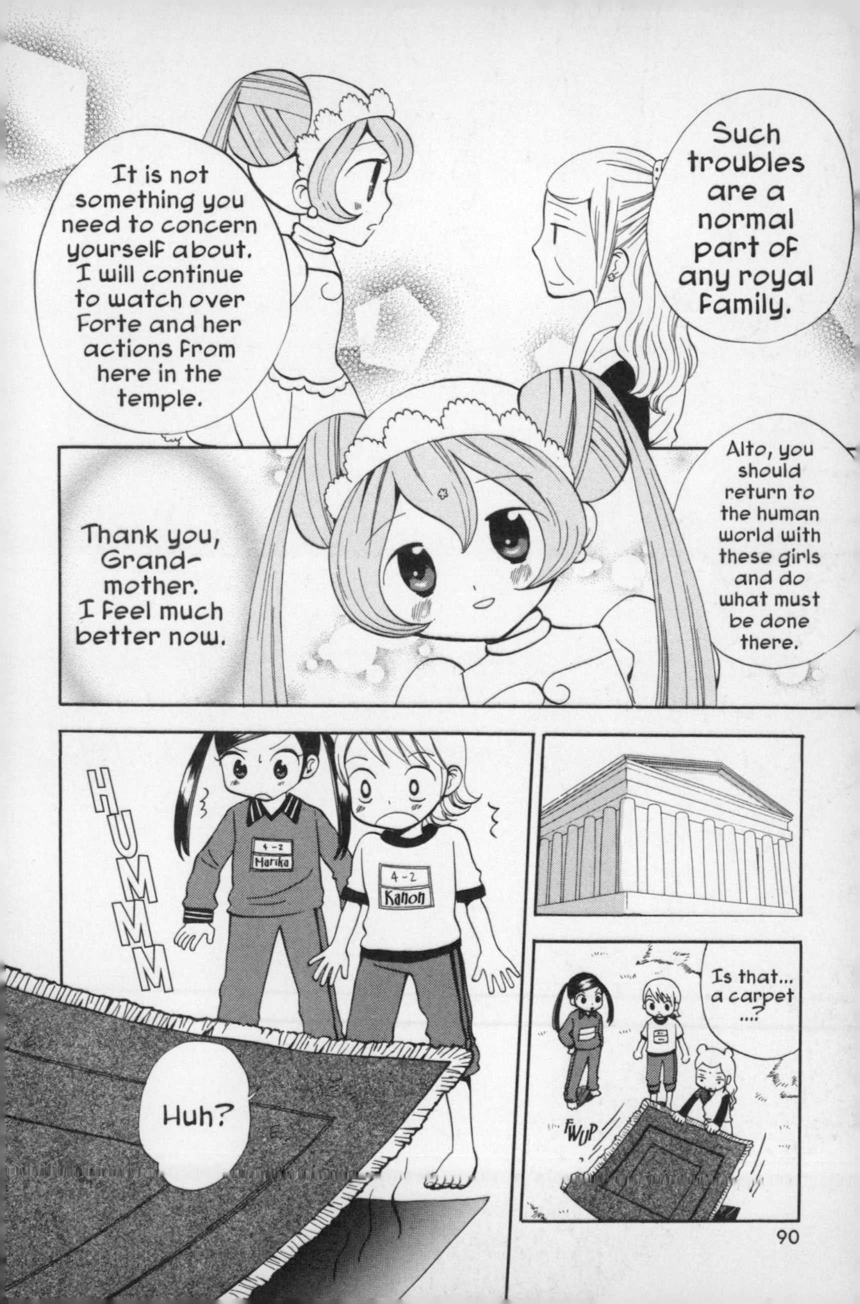
Such troubles are a normal part of any royal family.
It is not something you need to concern yourself about. I will continue to watch over Forte and her actions from here in the temple.
Alto, you should return to the human world with these girls and do what must be done there.
Thank you, Grand-mother. I feel much better now.
Is that... a carpet ...?
FWUP
4-2
Marika
4-2
Kanon
HUMMM
Huh?

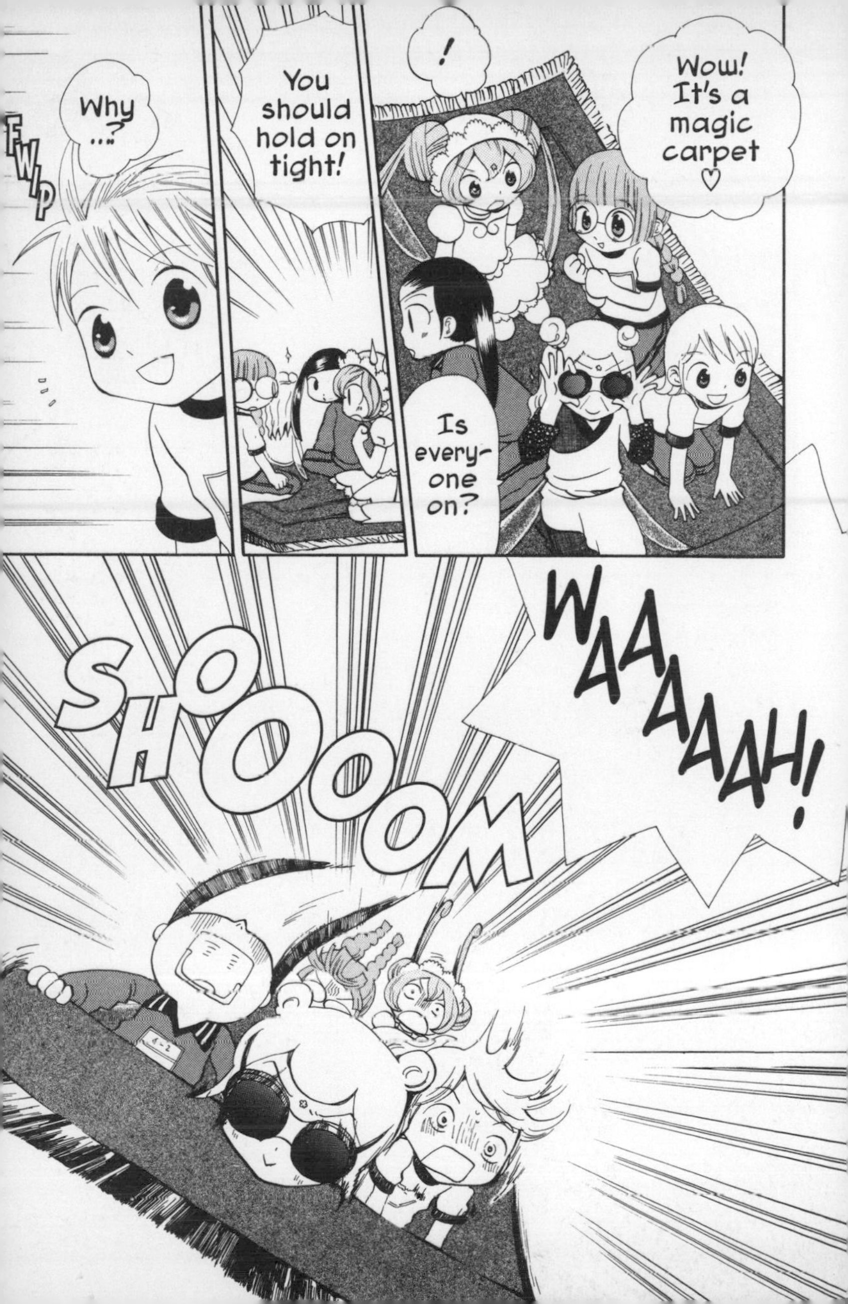
Wow! It's a magic carpet ♡
!
Is every-one on?
You should hold on tight!
Why ...?
FWIP
WAAAAAAH!
SHOOOOOM

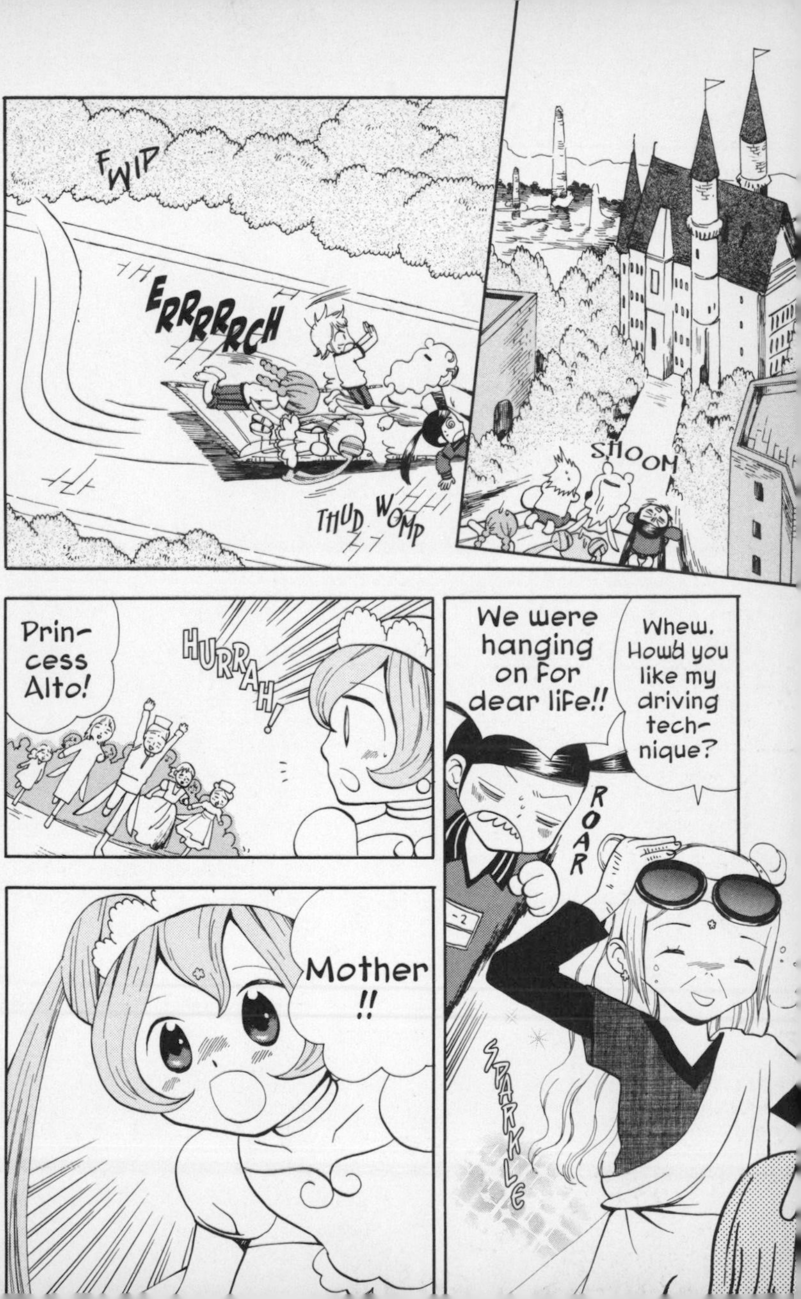

SHOOM
FWIP
ERRRRRCH
THUD
WOMP
Whew. How'd you like my driving tech-nique?
We were hanging on for dear life!!
ROAR
SPARKLE
HURRAH!
Prin-cess Alto!
Mother!!

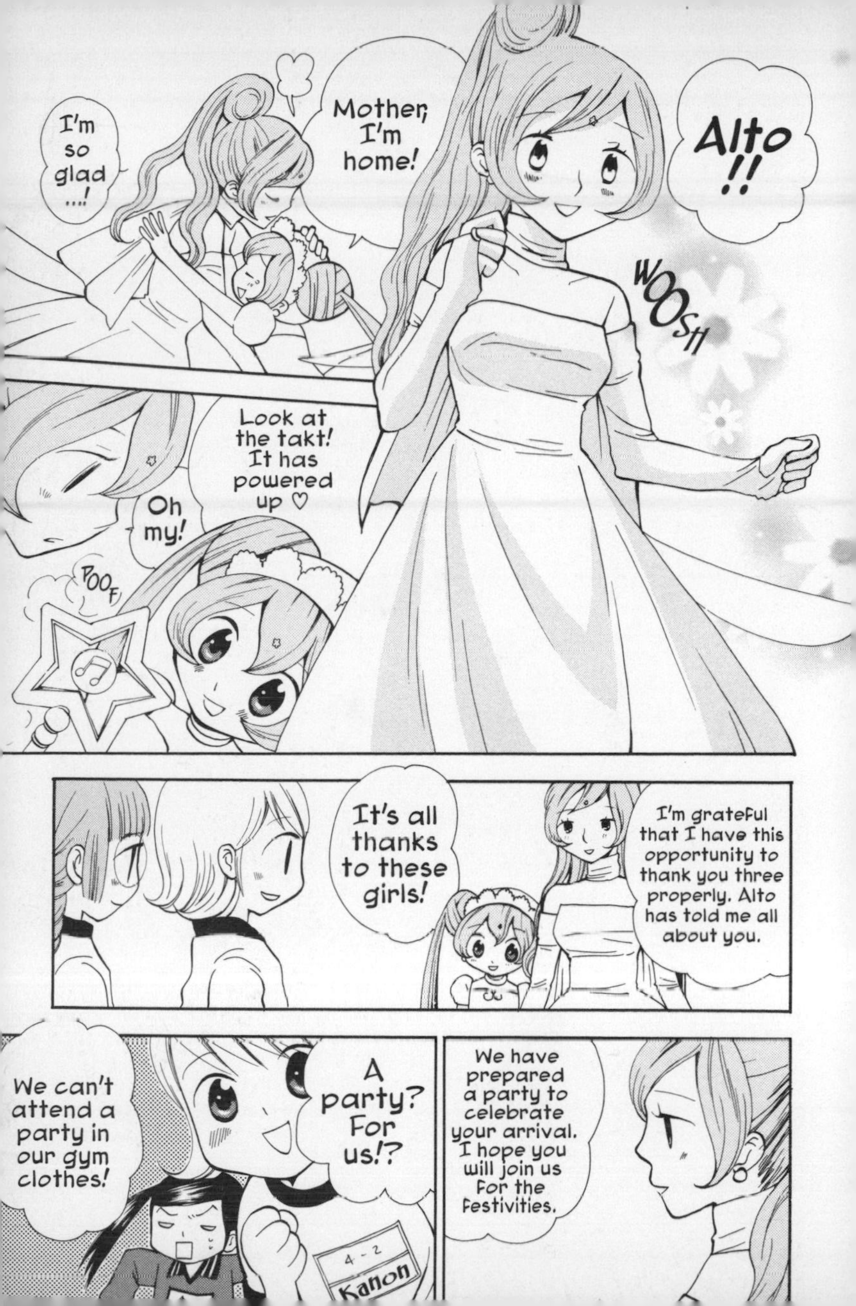
Alto!!
WOOSH
Mother, I'm home!
I'm so glad...!
Look at the takt! It has powered up ♡
Oh my!
POOF
I'm grateful that I have this opportunity to thank you three properly. Alto has told me all about you.
It's all thanks to these girls!
We have prepared a party to celebrate your arrival. I hope you will join us for the festivities.
A party? For us!?
We can't attend a party in our gym clothes!
4-2
Kanon

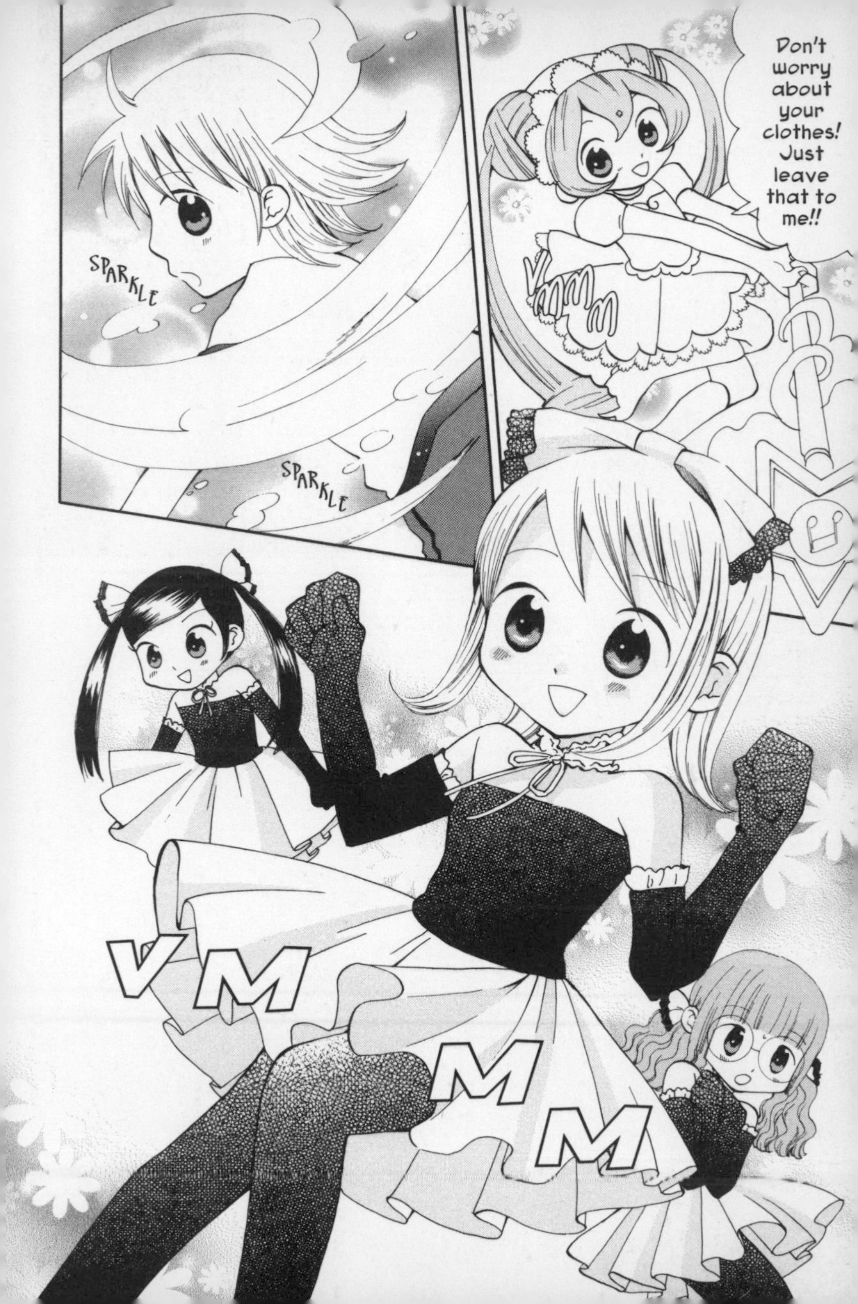
Don't worry about your clothes! Just leave that to me!!
Vmmm
SPARKLE
SPARKLE
VM
M
M

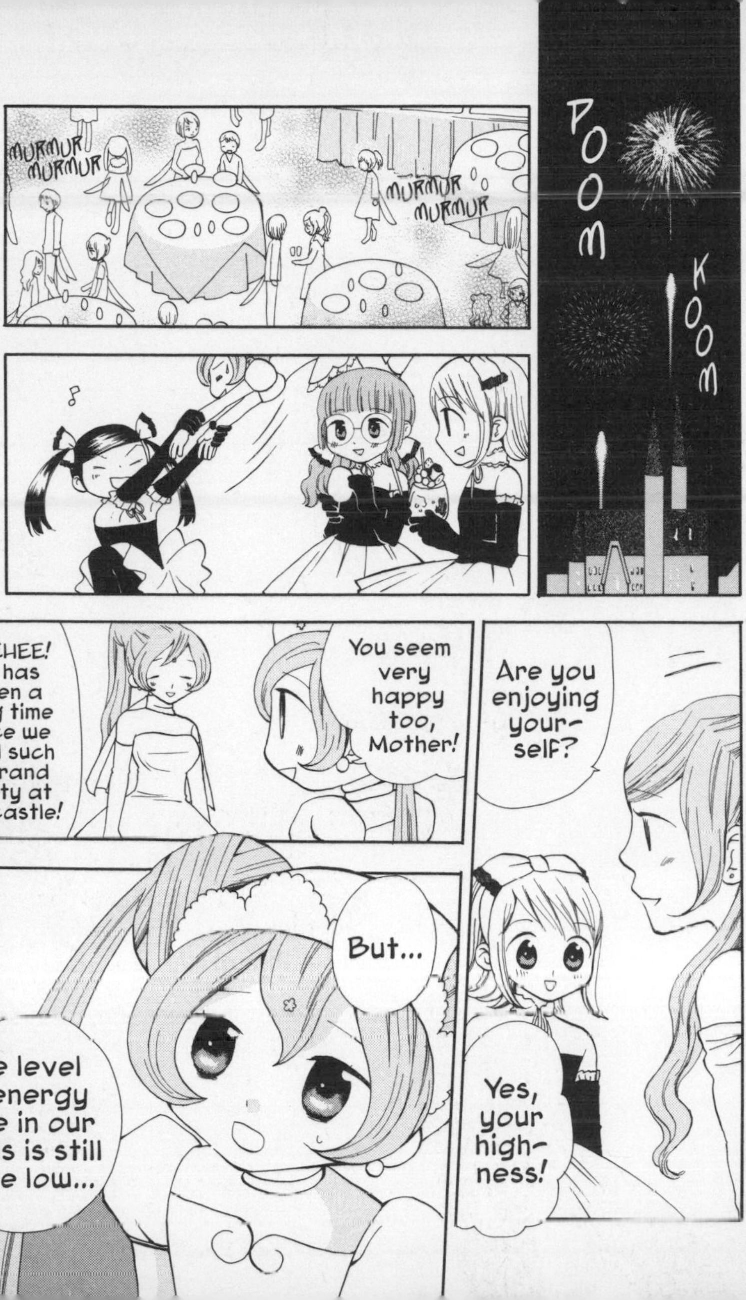
POOM
KOOM
MURMUR MURMUR
MURMUR MURMUR
Are you enjoying your-self?
Yes, your high-ness!
You seem very happy too, Mother!
TEEHEE! It has been a long time since we held such a grand party at the castle!
But...
The level of energy here in our lands is still quite low...

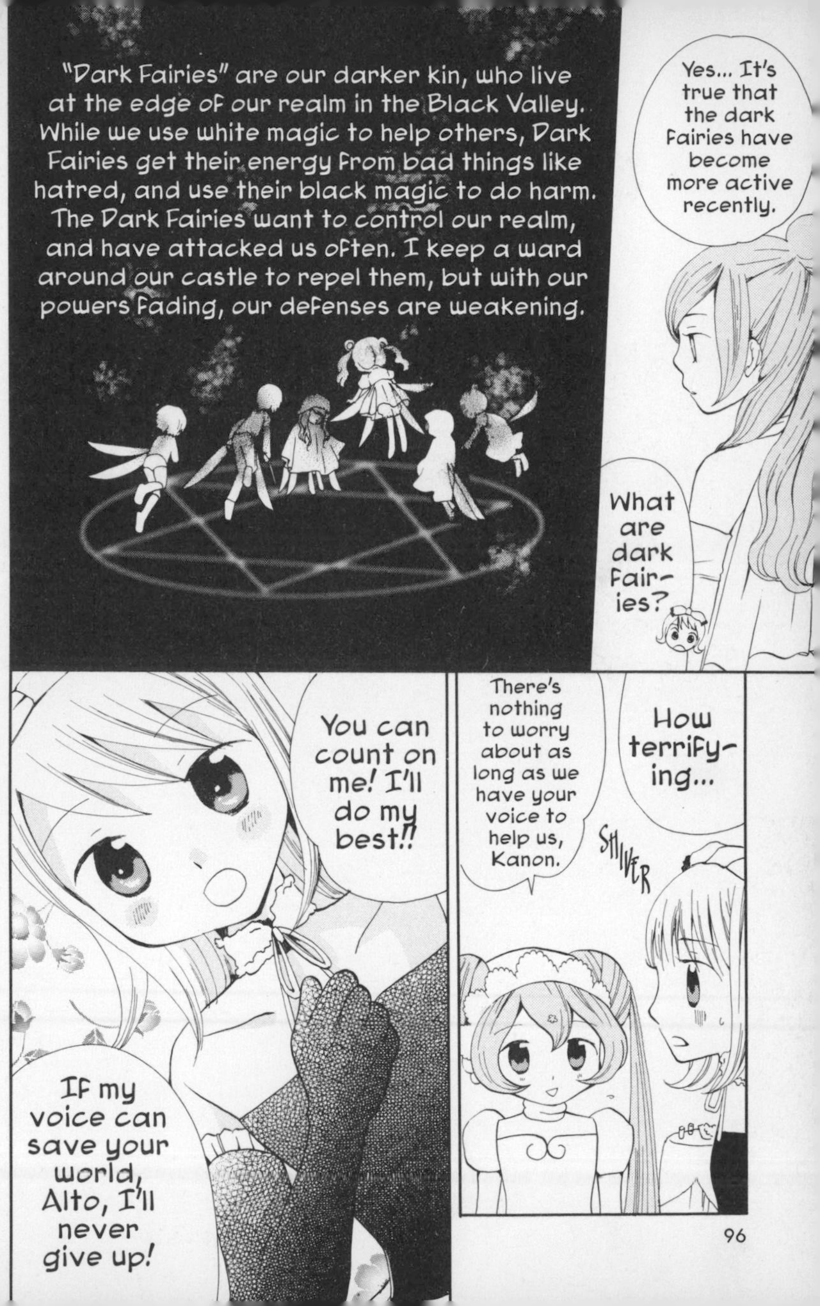
Yes... It's true that the dark fairies have become more active recently.
What are dark fairies?
"Dark Fairies" are our darker kin, who live at the edge of our realm in the Black Valley. While we use white magic to help others, Dark Fairies get their energy from bad things like hatred, and use their black magic to do harm. The Dark Fairies want to control our realm, and have attacked us often. I keep a ward around our castle to repel them, but with our powers fading, our defenses are weakening.
How terrify-ing...
SHIVER
There's nothing to worry about as long as we have your voice to help us, Kanon.
You can count on me! I'll do my best!!
If my voice can save your world, Alto, I'll never give up!

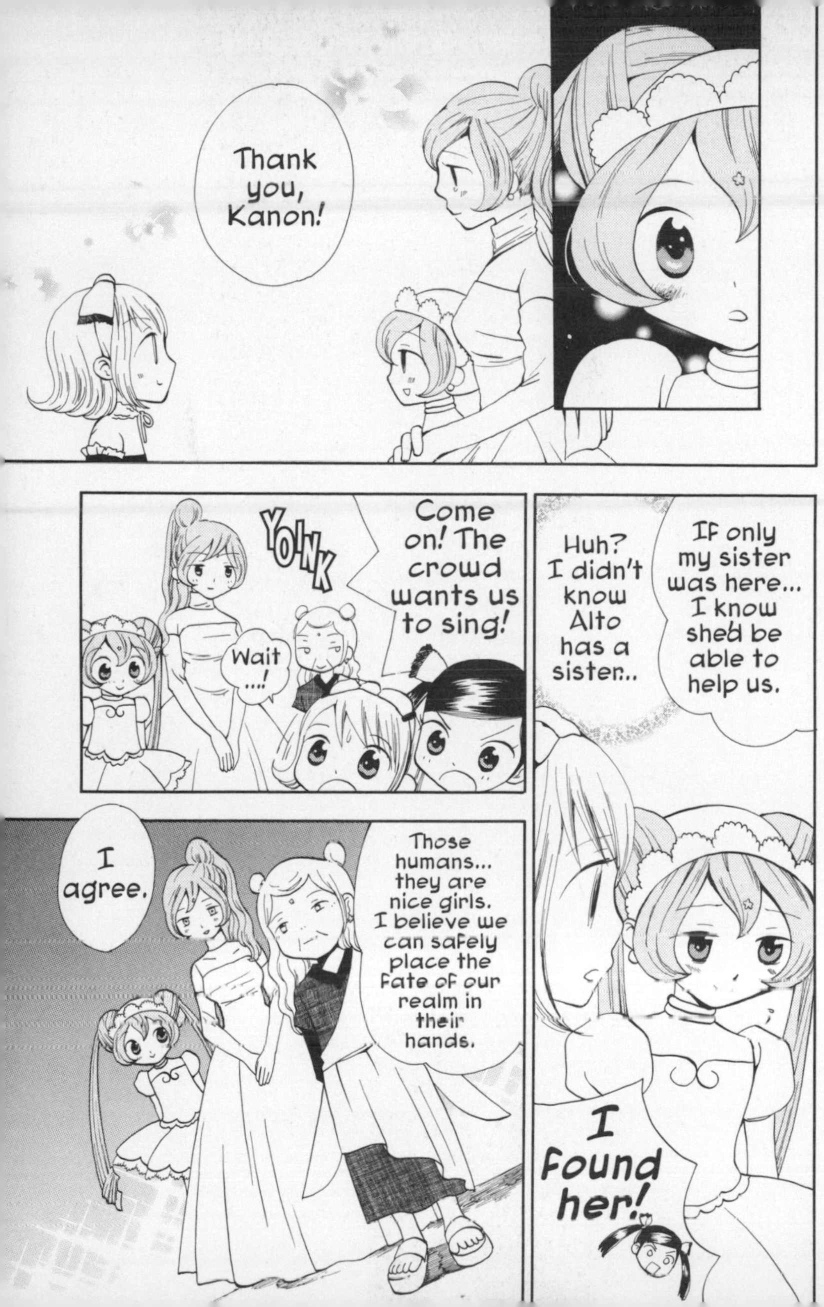
Thank you, Kanon!
If only my sister was here... I know she'd be able to help us.
Huh? I didn't know Alto has a sister...
I found her!
Come on! The crowd wants us to sing!
YOINK
Wait ...!
Those humans... they are nice girls. I believe we can safely place the fate of our realm in their hands.
I agree.

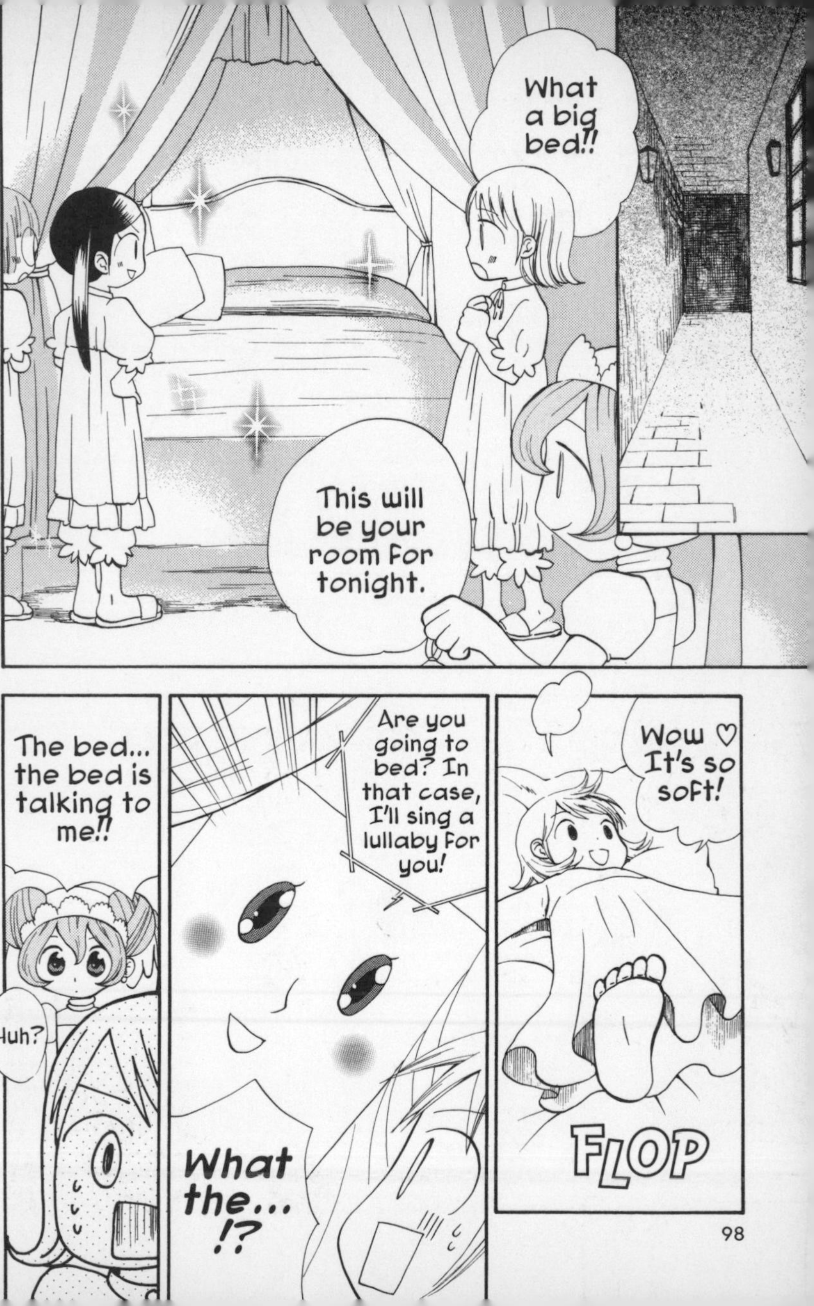
What a big bed!!
This will be your room for tonight.
Wow ♡ It's so soft!
FLOP
Are you going to bed? In that case, I'll sing a lullaby for you!
What the... !?
The bed... the bed is talking to me!!
Huh?

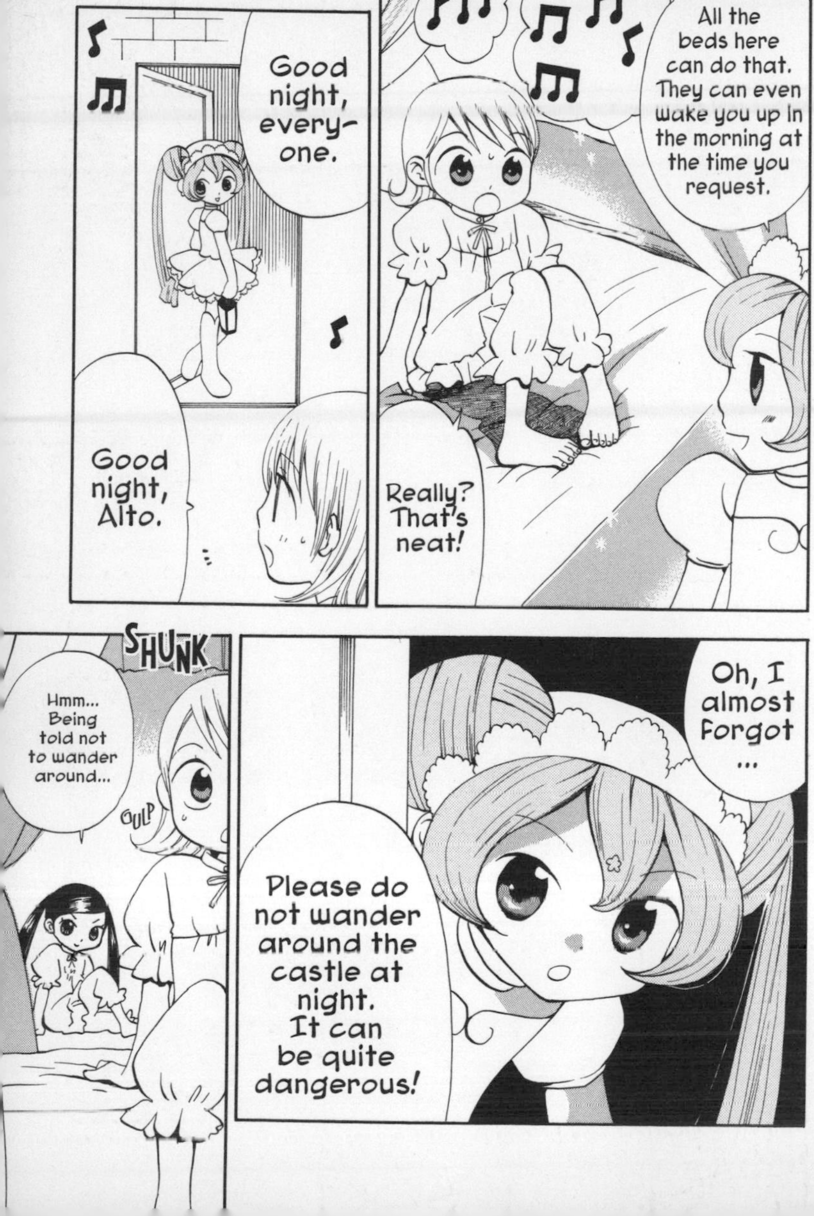
All the beds here can do that. They can even wake you up in the morning at the time you request.
Really? That's neat!
Good night, every-one.
Good night, Alto.
...
Oh, I almost forgot ...
Please do not wander around the castle at night. It can be quite dangerous!
SHUNK
Hmm... Being told not to wander around...
GULP

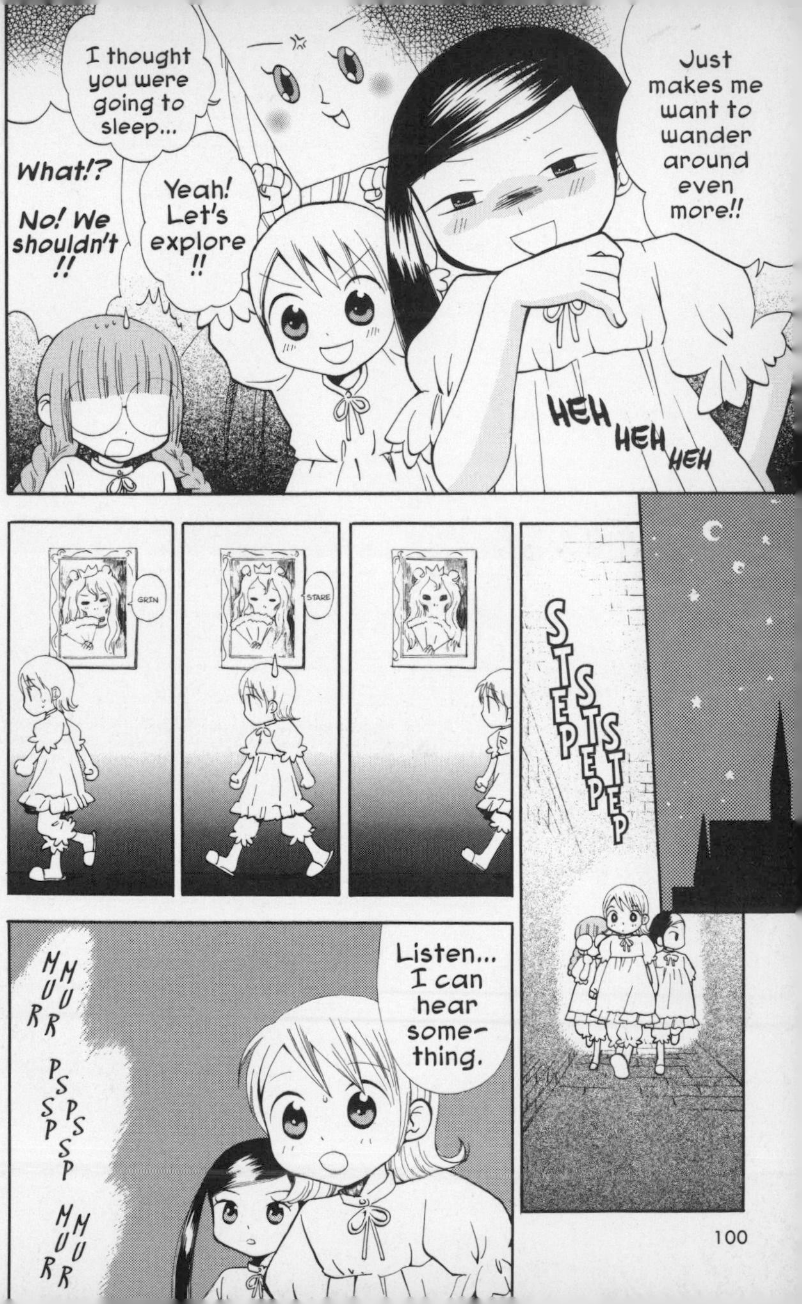
Just makes me want to wander around even more!!
I thought you were going to sleep...
Yeah! Let's explore!!
What!?
No! We shouldn't!!
HEH HEH HEH
STEP STEP STEP
STARE
GRIN
Listen... I can hear something.
MURR MURR
PSSP PSSP
MURR MURR

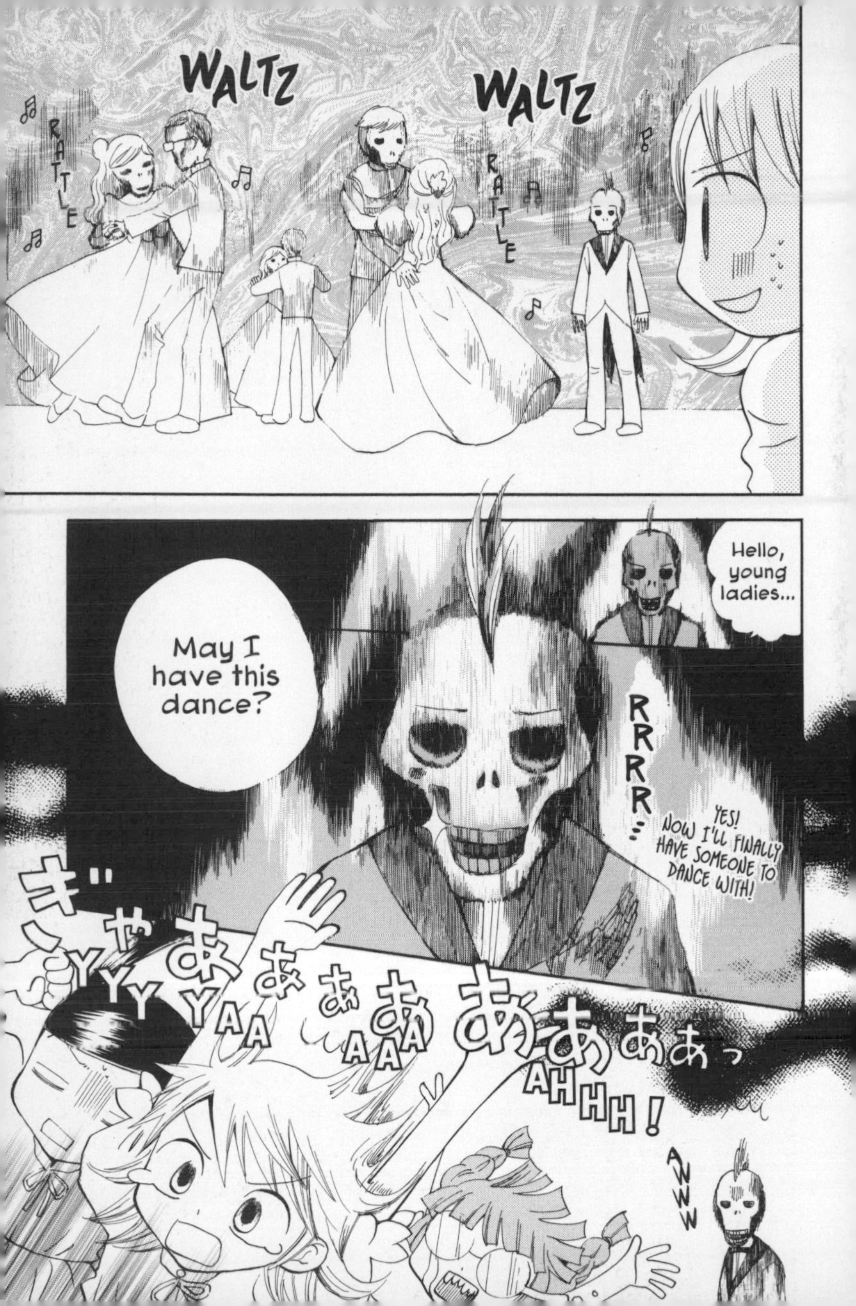
WALTZ
RATTLE
WALTZ
RATTLE
Hello, young ladies...
RRRR
YES! NOW I'LL FINALLY HAVE SOMEONE TO DANCE WITH!
May I have this dance?
ぎゃあぁぁあああああっ
YYYYAAAAAAHHHH!
AWWW

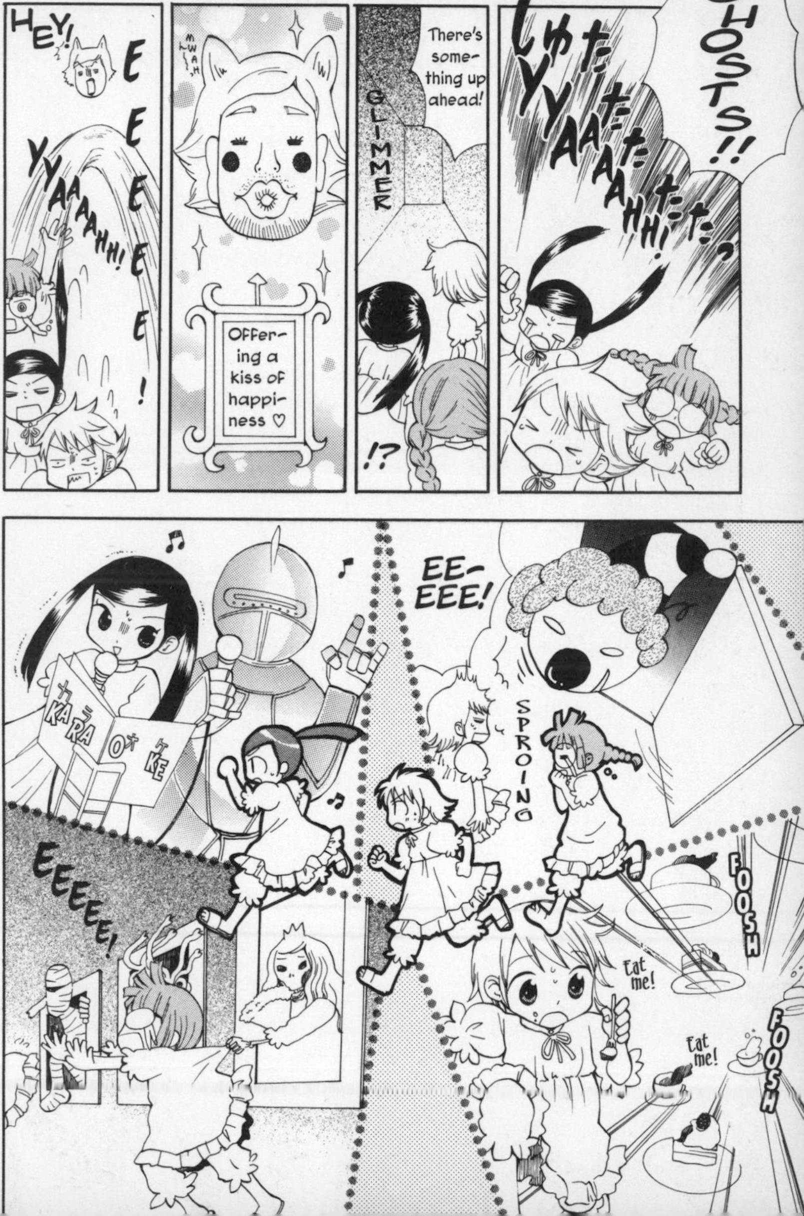
GHOSTS!!
しゅた
YYAAAAHH!
たたたたたっ
There's some-thing up ahead!
GLIMMER
!?
MWAH
Offer-ing a kiss of happi-ness ♡
HEY!
YYAAAAHH!
EEEEEE!
EE-EEE!
SPROING
FOOSH
Eat me!
Eat me!
FOOSH
カラオケ
KARAOKE
EEEEEE!

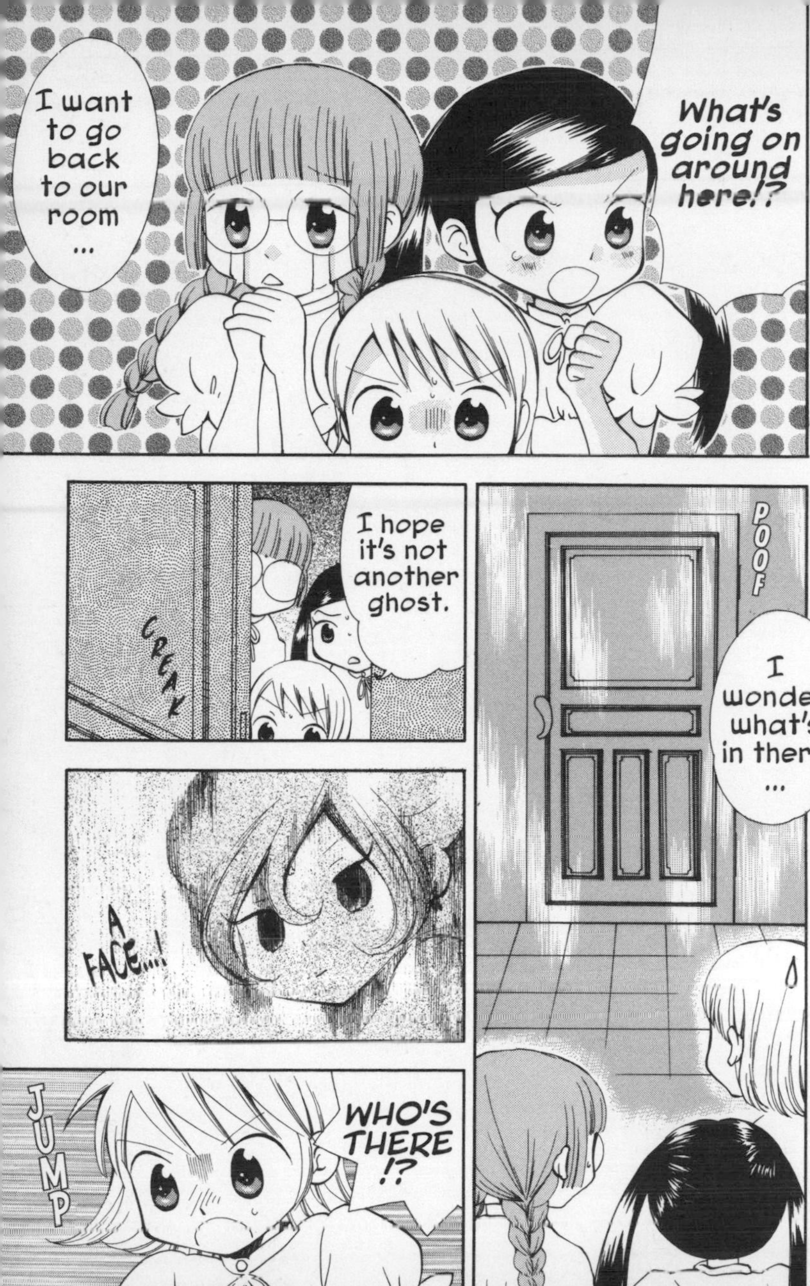
What's going on around here!?
I want to go back to our room ...
POOF
I wonder what's in there ...
CREAK
I hope it's not another ghost.
A FACE...!
JUMP
WHO'S THERE !?

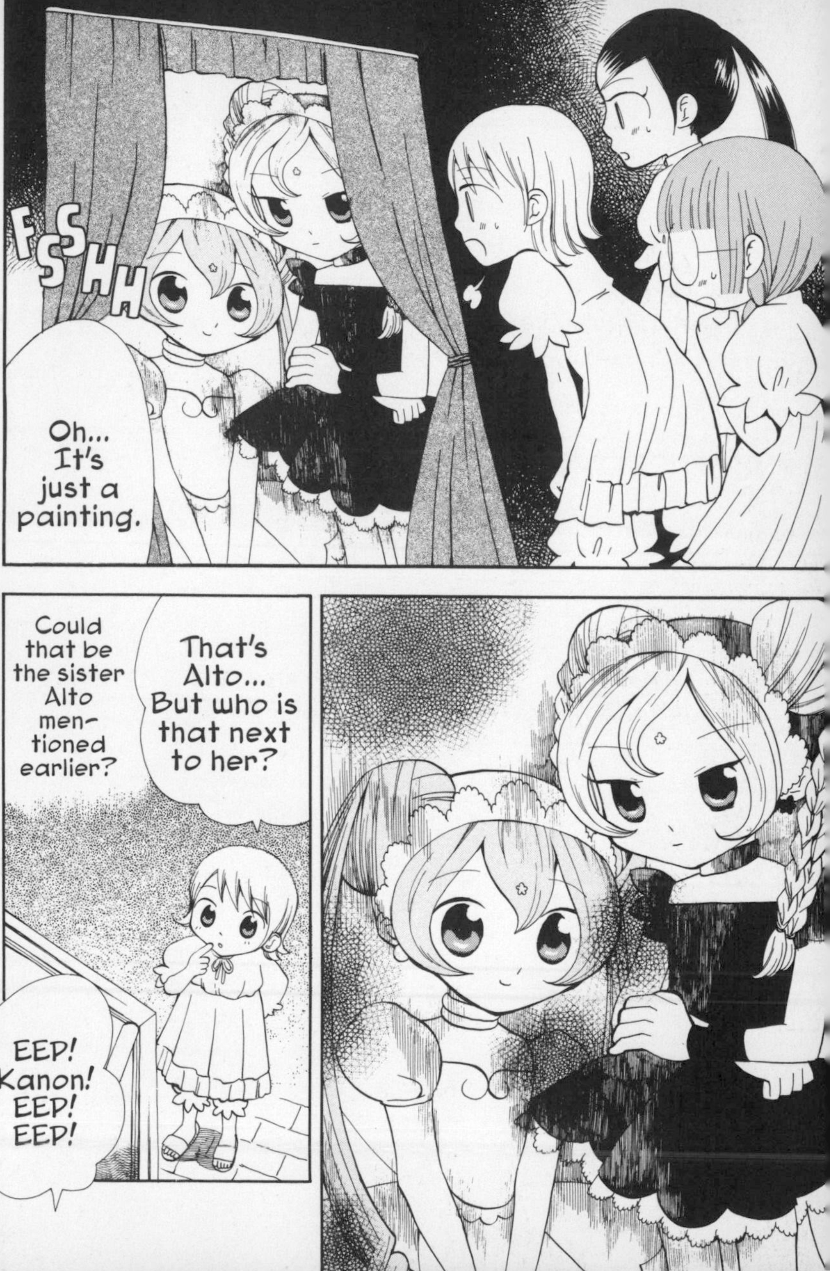
FSSHH
Oh... It's just a painting.
That's Alto... But who is that next to her?
Could that be the sister Alto mentioned earlier?
EEP! Kanon! EEP! EEP!

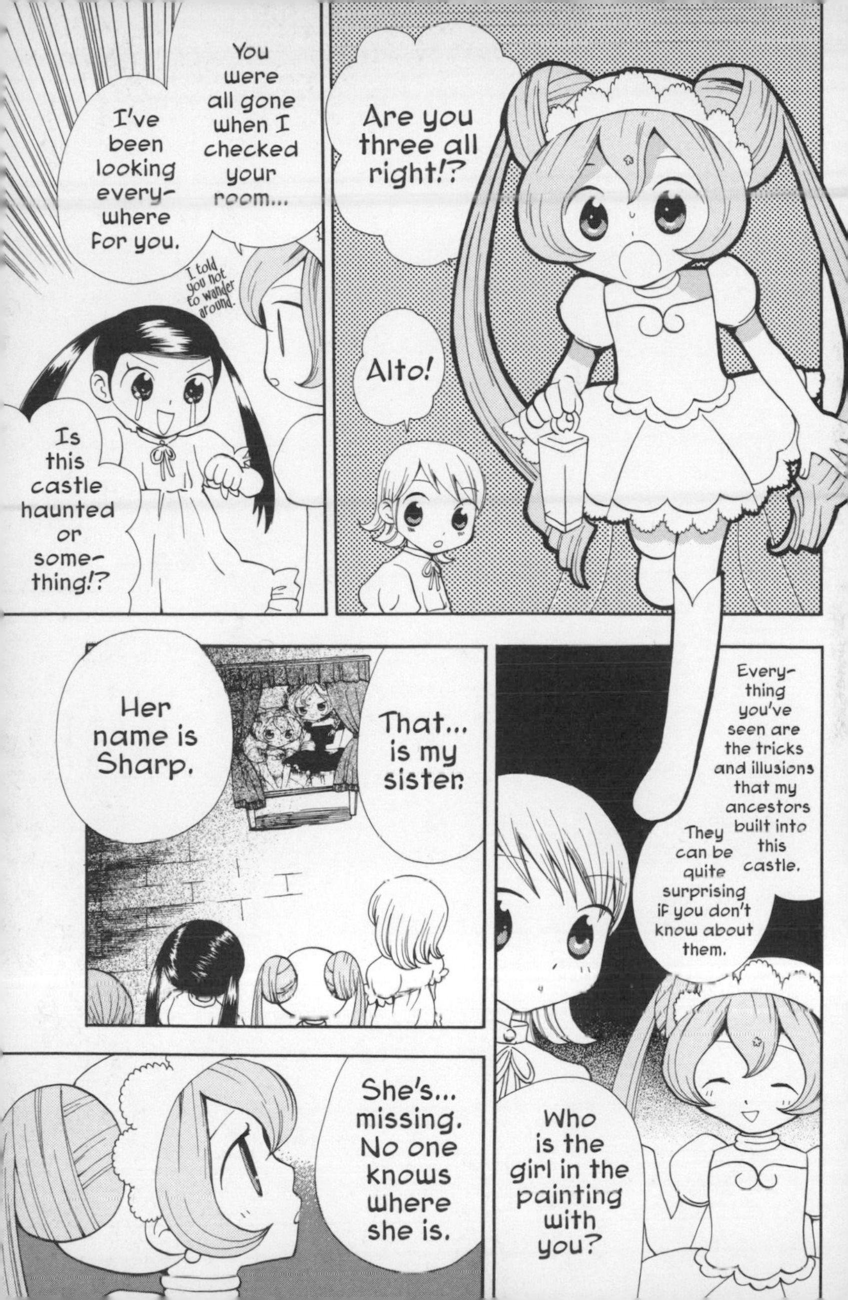
Are you three all right!?
Alto!
You were all gone when I checked your room...
I've been looking every-where for you.
I told you not to wander around.
Is this castle haunted or some-thing!?
Every-thing you've seen are the tricks and illusions that my ancestors built into this castle.
They can be quite surprising if you don't know about them.
Who is the girl in the painting with you?
That... is my sister.
Her name is Sharp.
She's... missing. No one knows where she is.

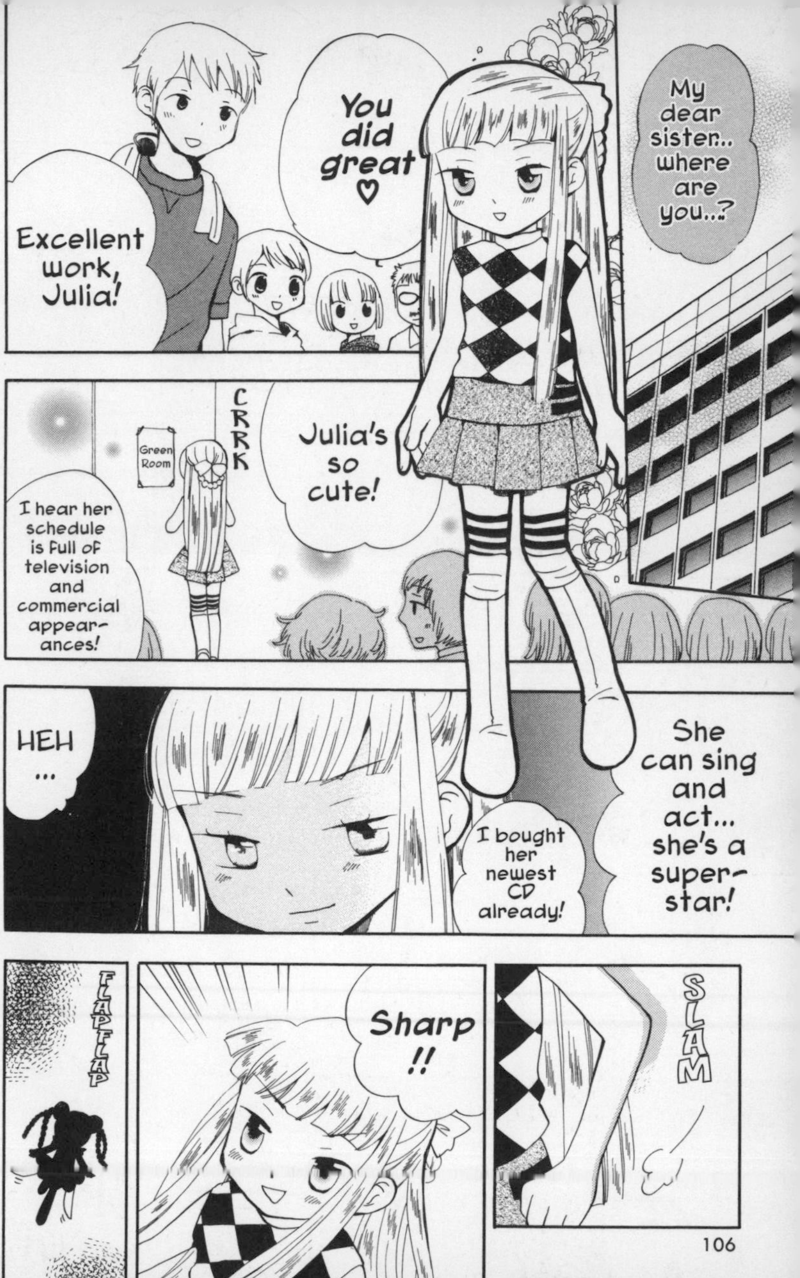

My dear sister... where are you...?
You did great ♥
Excellent work, Julia!
Julia's so cute!
CRRK
Green Room
I hear her schedule is full of television and commercial appearances!
She can sing and act... she's a superstar!
I bought her newest CD already!
HEH ...
SLAM
Sharp !!
FLAPFLAP

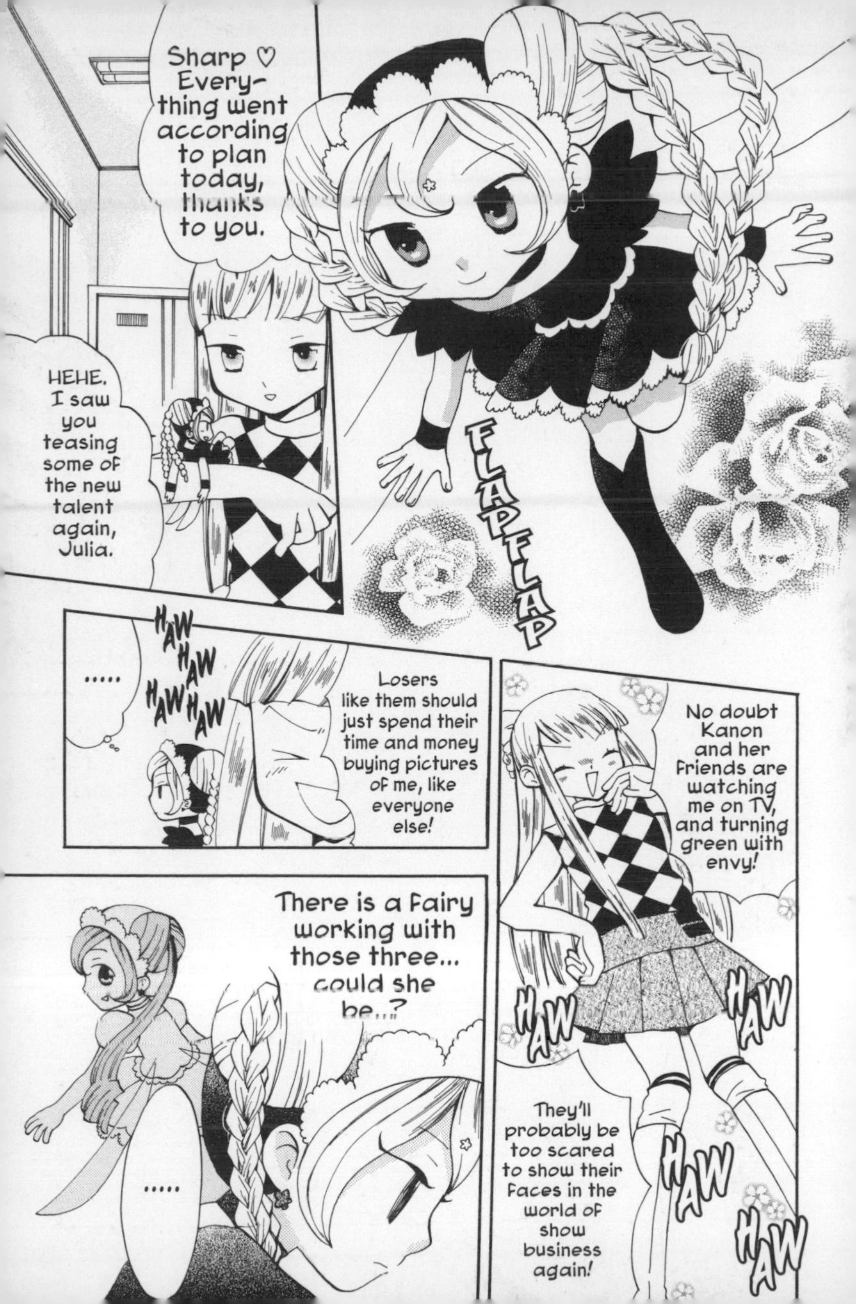
Sharp ♡ Every-thing went according to plan today, thanks to you.
HEHE. I saw you teasing some of the new talent again, Julia.
FLAPFLAP
No doubt Kanon and her friends are watching me on TV, and turning green with envy!
HAW HAW HAW HAW
They'll probably be too scared to show their faces in the world of show business again!
HAW HAW
HAW HAW HAW HAW
.....
Losers like them should just spend their time and money buying pictures of me, like everyone else!
There is a fairy working with those three... could she be...?
.....

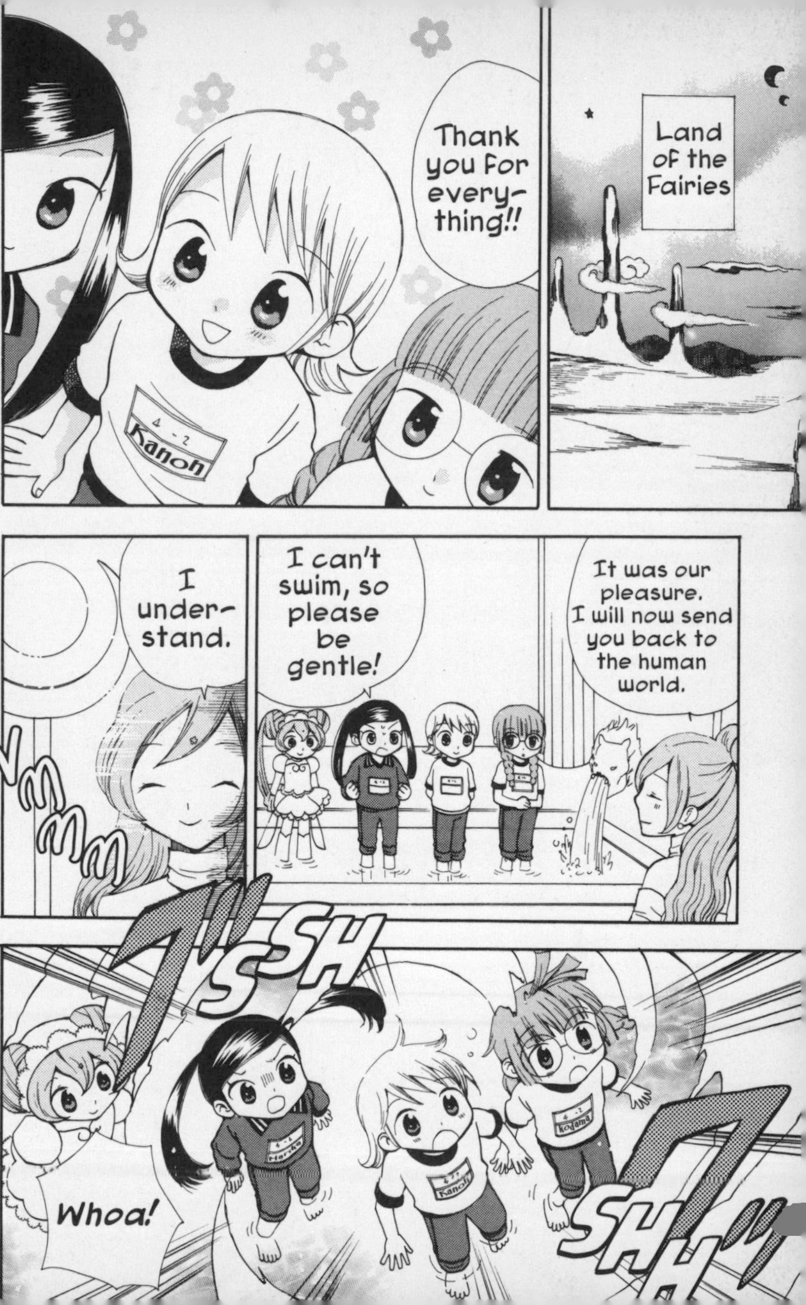
Land of the Fairies
Thank you for every-thing!!
4-2
Kanoh
It was our pleasure. I will now send you back to the human world.
I can't swim, so please be gentle!
I under-stand.
VMMM
Whoa!
SHH!!

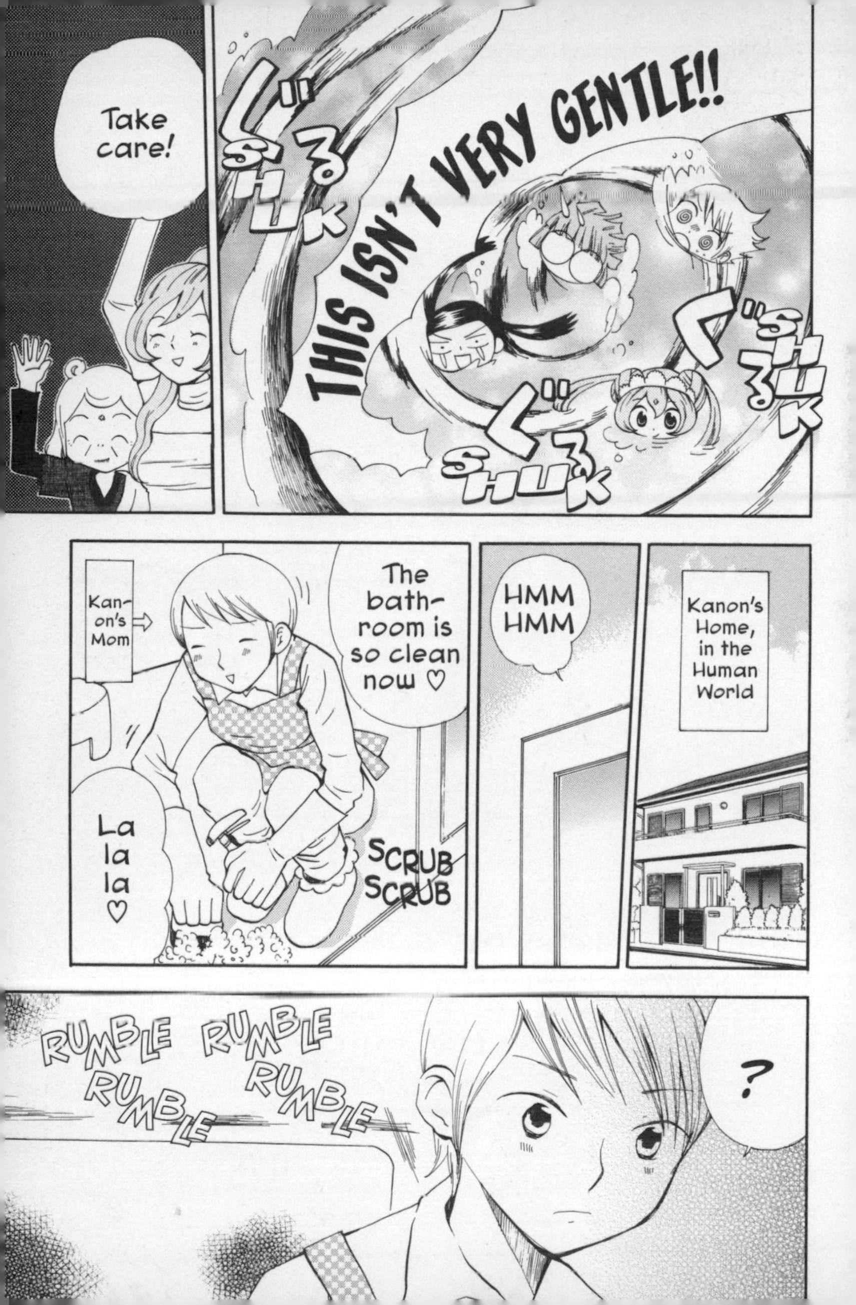
THIS ISN'T VERY GENTLE!!
SHUK
SHUK
SHUK
Take care!
Kanon's Home, in the Human World
HMM HMM
The bathroom is so clean now ♡
Kanon's Mom
SCRUB SCRUB
La la la ♡
?
RUMBLE RUMBLE
RUMBLE RUMBLE

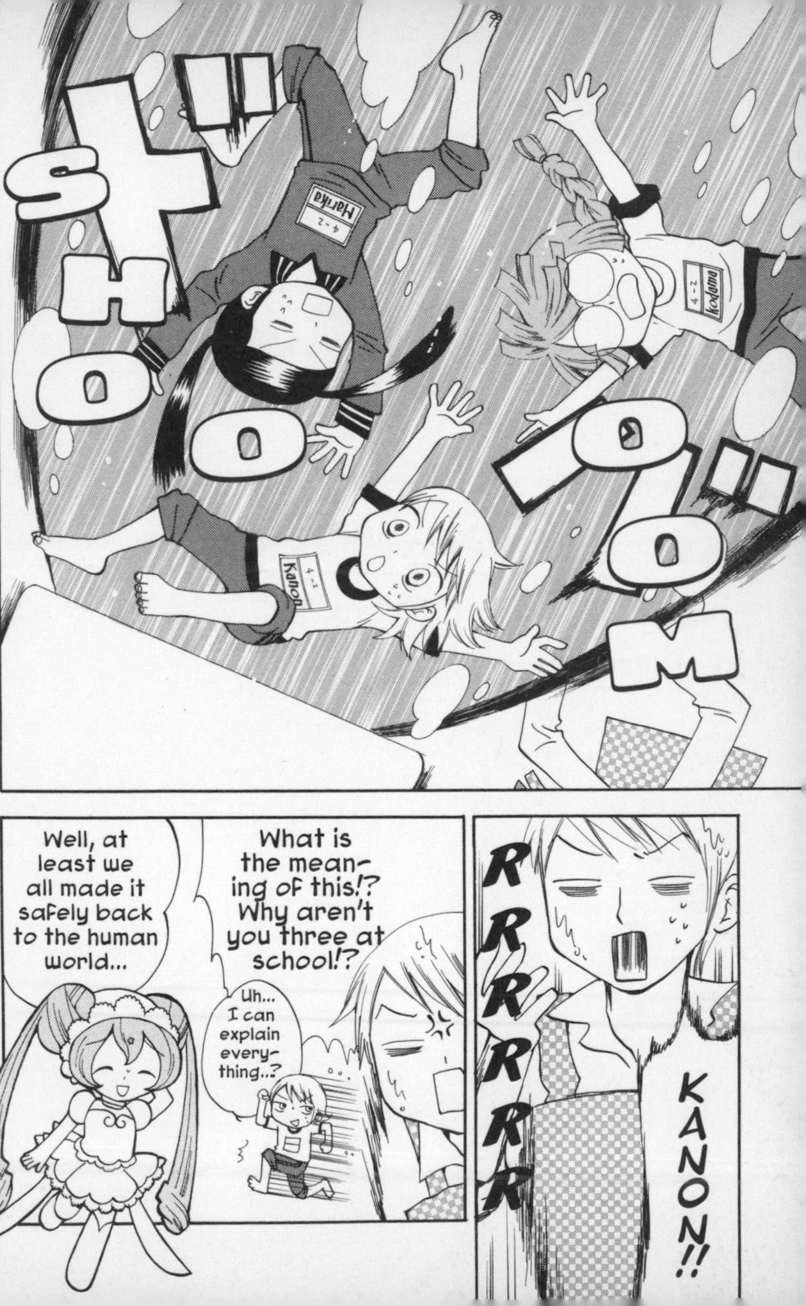
SHOOOOM!!
4-2 Marika
4-2 Kodama
4-2 Kanon
RRRRRRR
KANON!!
What is the meaning of this!? Why aren't you three at school!?
Uh... I can explain everything...?
Well, at least we all made it safely back to the human world...

## Stage 11
# Reunion

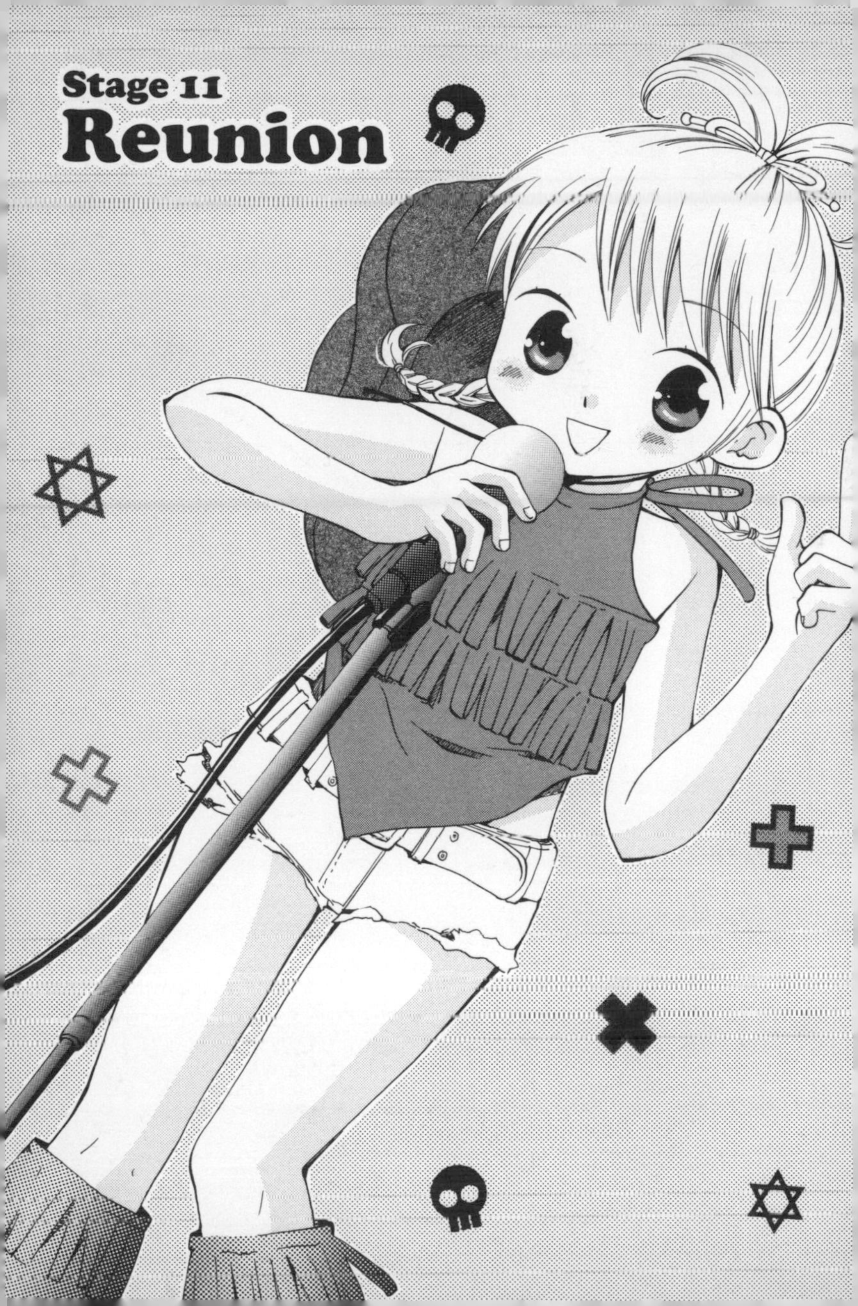

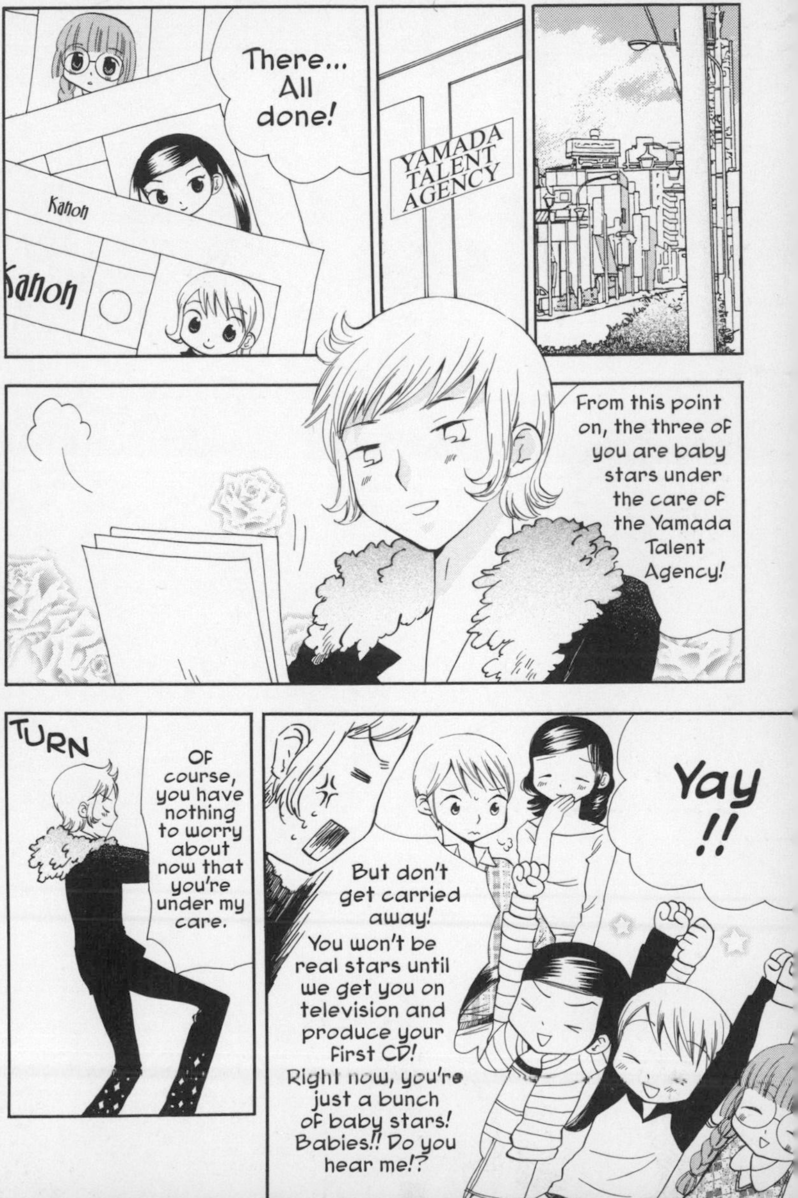
YAMADA TALENT AGENCY
There... All done!
Kanon
Kanon
From this point on, the three of you are baby stars under the care of the Yamada Talent Agency!
Yay!!
But don't get carried away! You won't be real stars until we get you on television and produce your first CD! Right now, you're just a bunch of baby stars! Babies!! Do you hear me!?
TURN
Of course, you have nothing to worry about now that you're under my care.

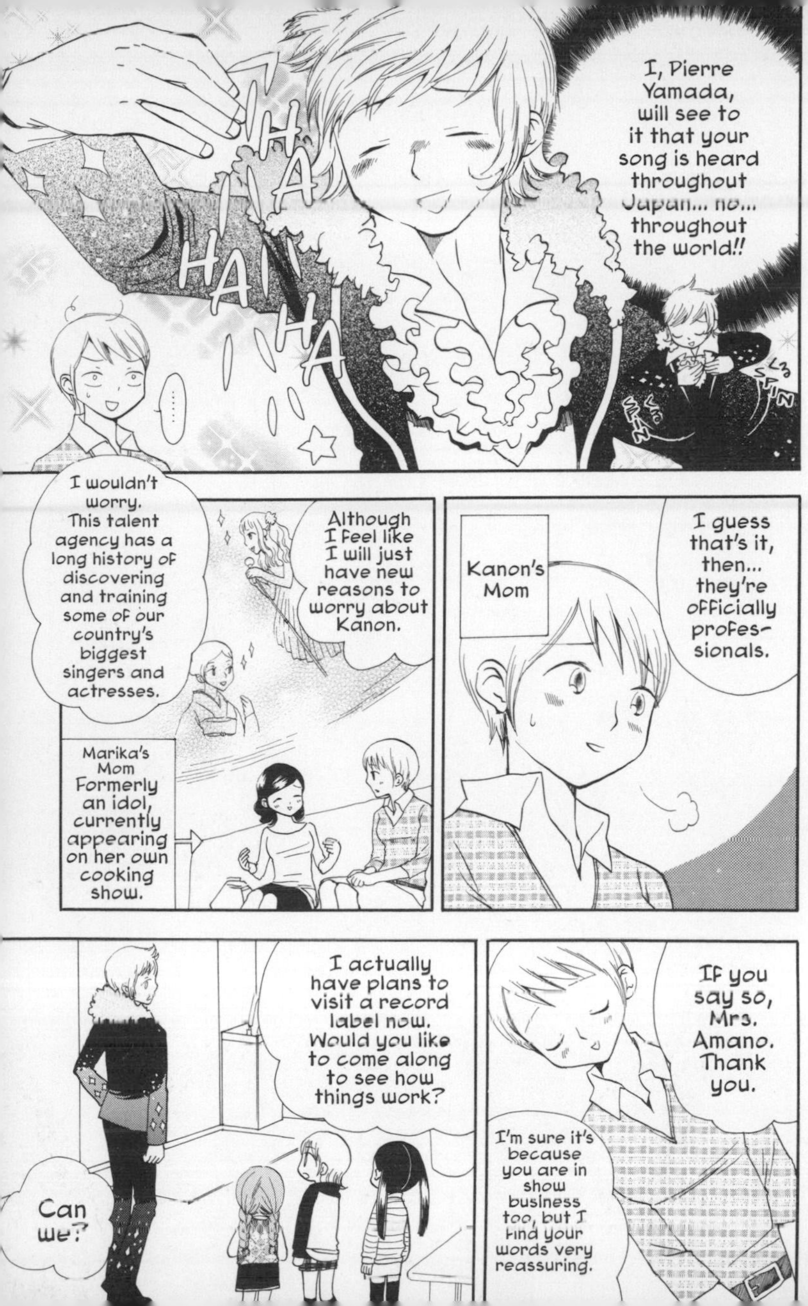
I, Pierre Yamada, will see to it that your song is heard throughout Japan... no... throughout the world!!
HA HA HA HA
SPIN SPIN
......
Kanon's Mom
I guess that's it, then... they're officially profes-sionals.
Although I feel like I will just have new reasons to worry about Kanon.
I wouldn't worry. This talent agency has a long history of discovering and training some of our country's biggest singers and actresses.
Marika's Mom Formerly an idol, currently appearing on her own cooking show.
If you say so, Mrs. Amano. Thank you.
I'm sure it's because you are in show business too, but I find your words very reassuring.
I actually have plans to visit a record label now. Would you like to come along to see how things work?
Can we?

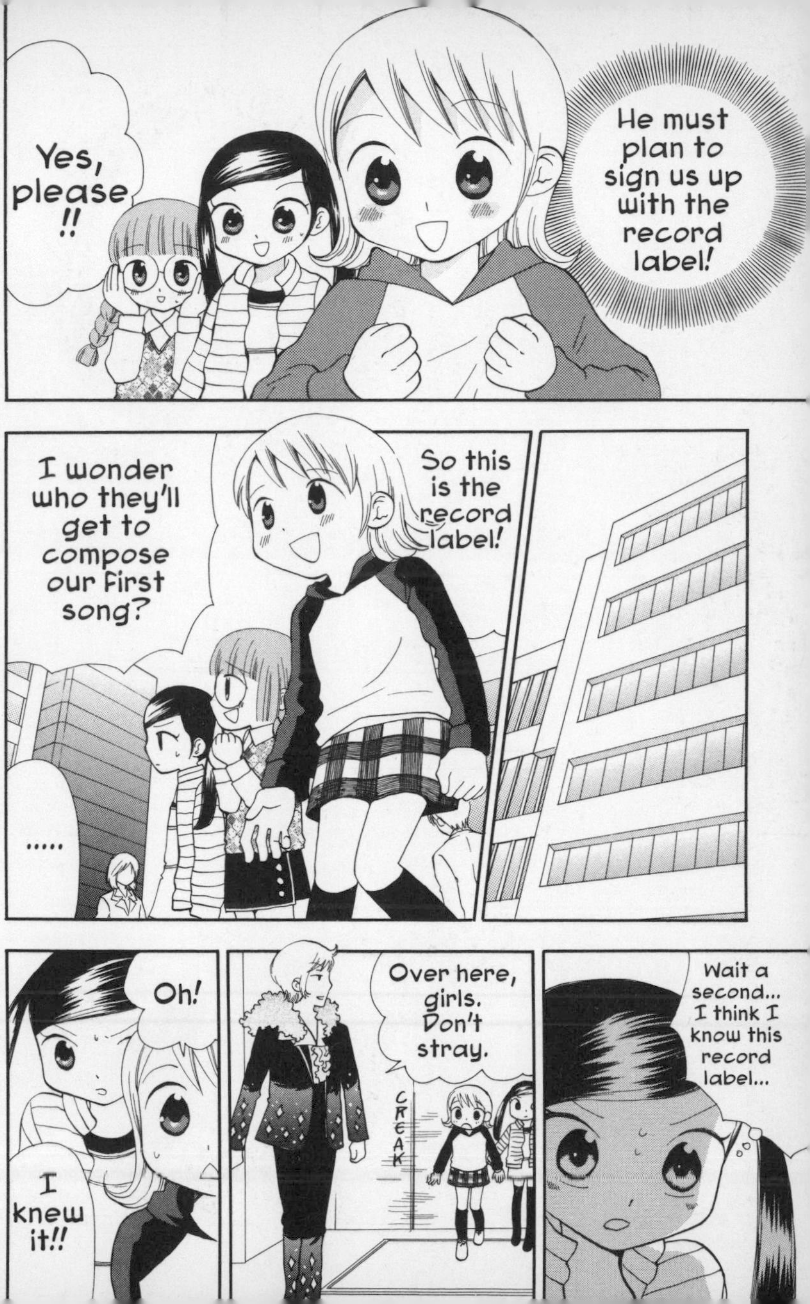
He must plan to sign us up with the record label!
Yes, please!!
So this is the record label!
I wonder who they'll get to compose our first song?
.....
Wait a second... I think I know this record label...
Over here, girls. Don't stray.
CREAK
Oh!
I knew it!!

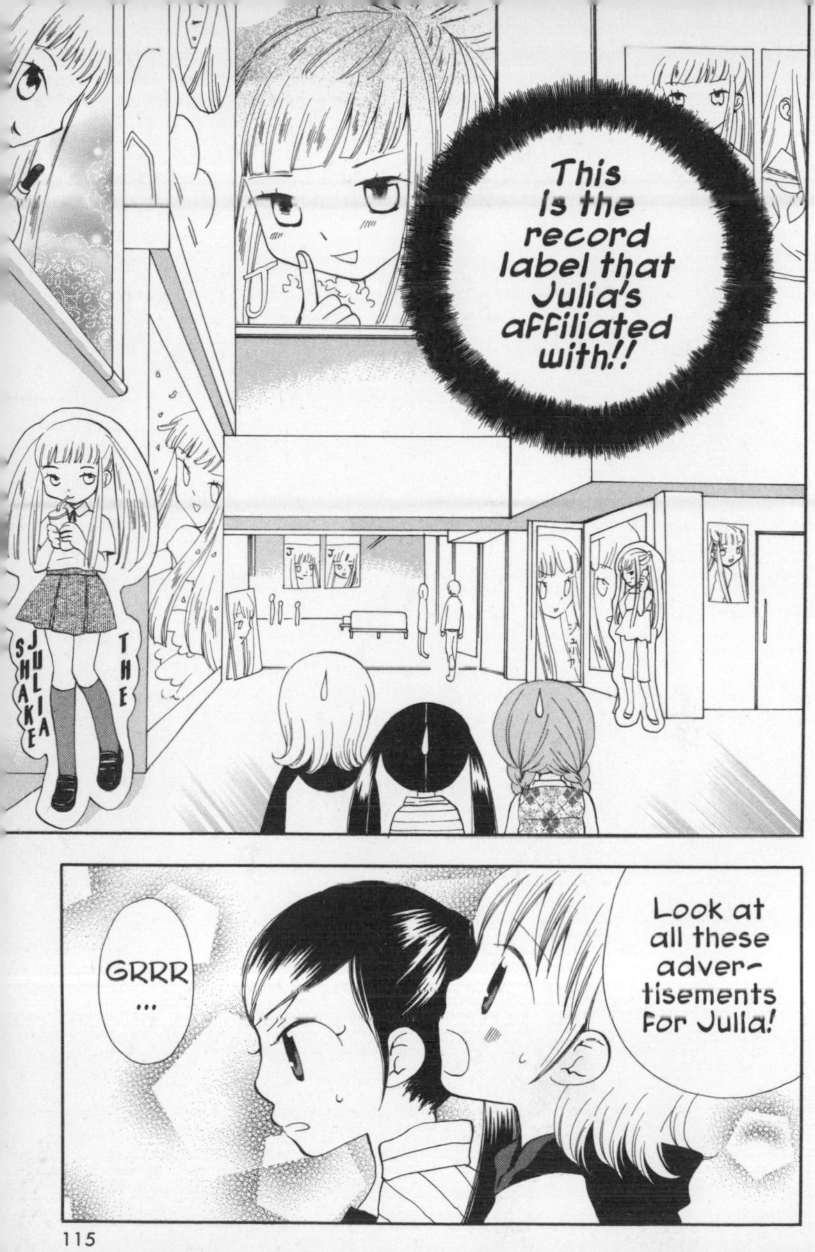
This is the record label that Julia's affiliated with!!
THE JULIA SHAKE
Look at all these adver-tisements for Julla!
GRRR ...

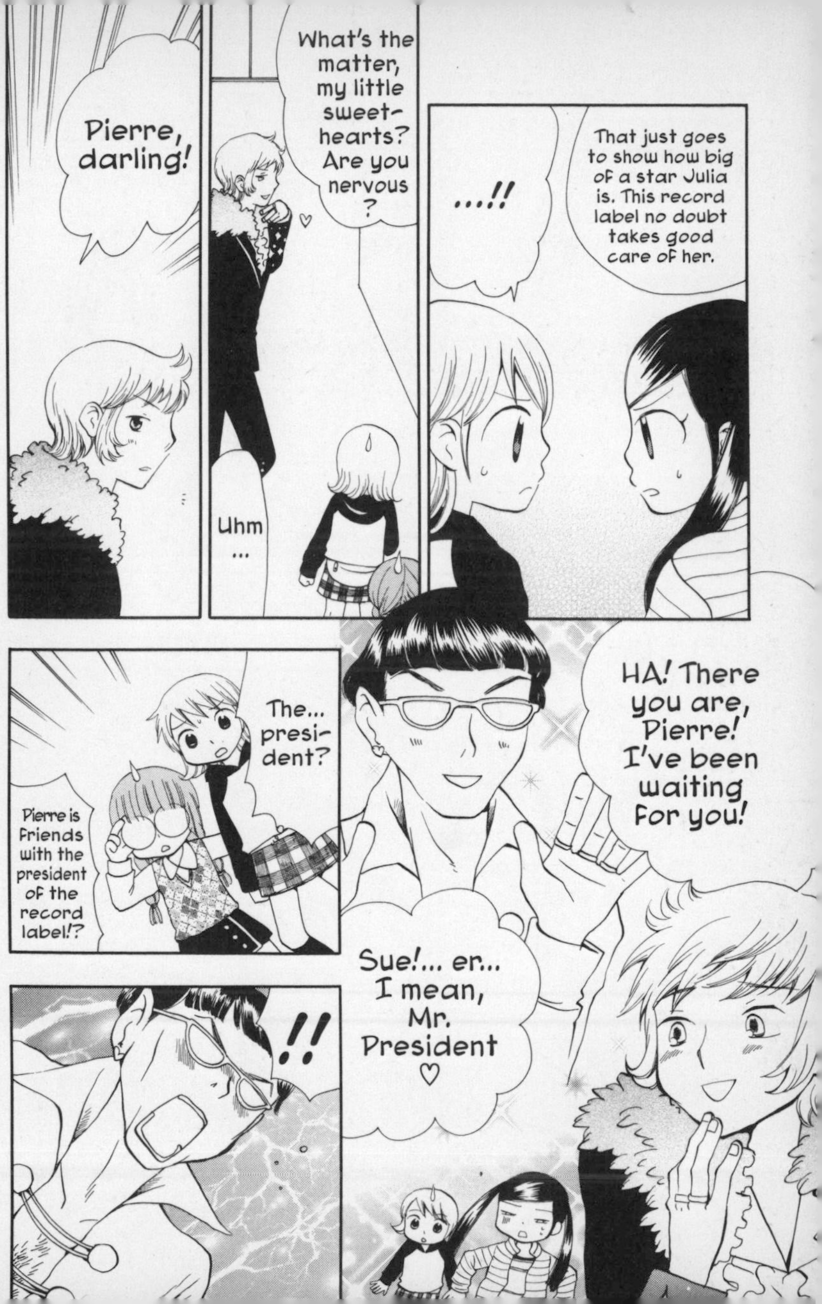

That just goes to show how big of a star Julia is. This record label no doubt takes good care of her.
...!!
What's the matter, my little sweet-hearts? Are you nervous?
Uhm...
Pierre, darling!
HA! There you are, Pierre! I've been waiting for you!
Sue!... er... I mean, Mr. President ♡
The... president?
Pierre is friends with the president of the record label!?
!!

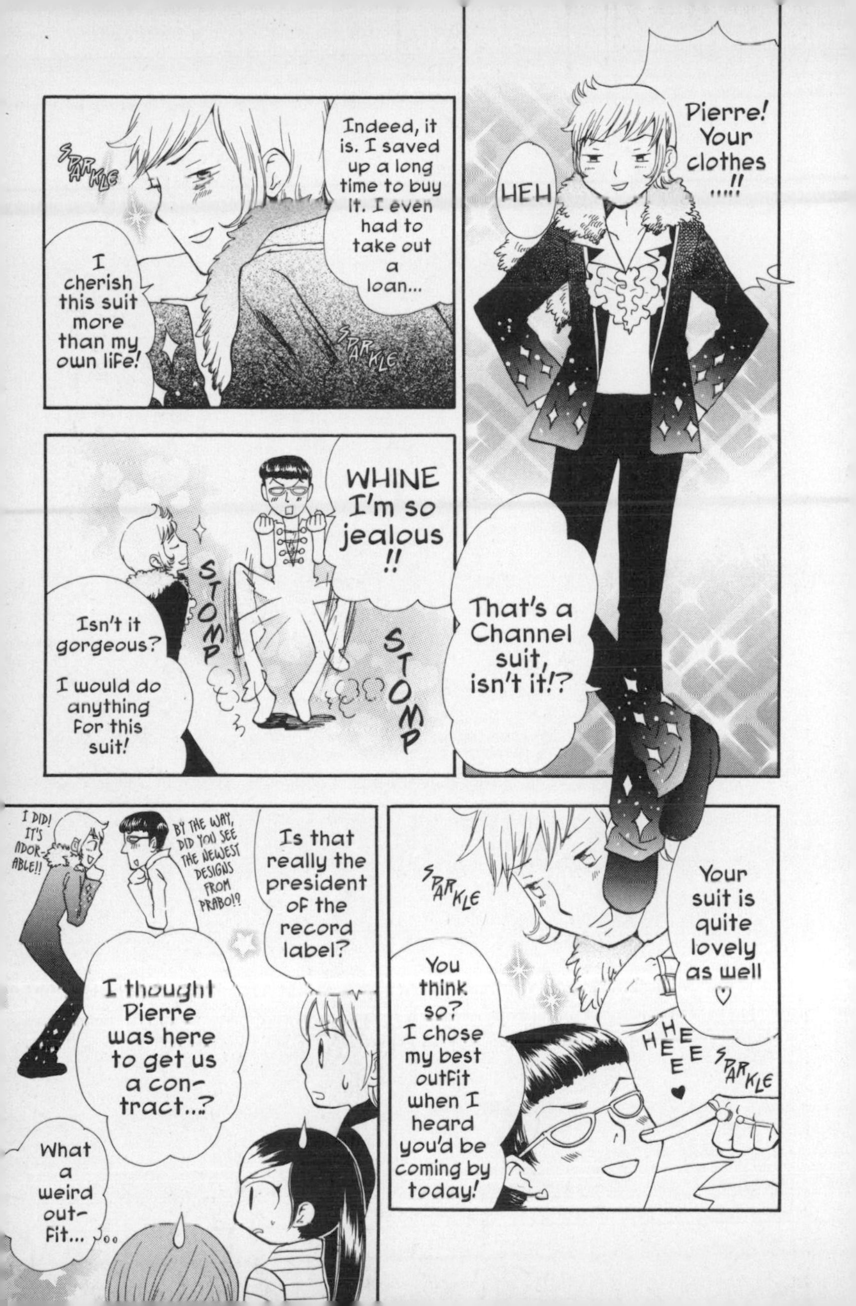

Pierre! Your clothes ....!!
HEH
That's a Channel suit, isn't it!?
Indeed, it is. I saved up a long time to buy it. I even had to take out a loan...
SPARKLE
I cherish this suit more than my own life!
SPARKLE
WHINE I'm so jealous!!
STOMP
STOMP
Isn't it gorgeous?
I would do anything for this suit!
Your suit is quite lovely as well ♡
SPARKLE
You think so? I chose my best outfit when I heard you'd be coming by today!
HEHEE
SPARKLE
BY THE WAY, DID YOU SEE THE NEWEST DESIGNS FROM PRABO!?
I DID! IT'S ADORABLE!!
Is that really the president of the record label?
I thought Pierre was here to get us a contract...?
What a weird outfit...

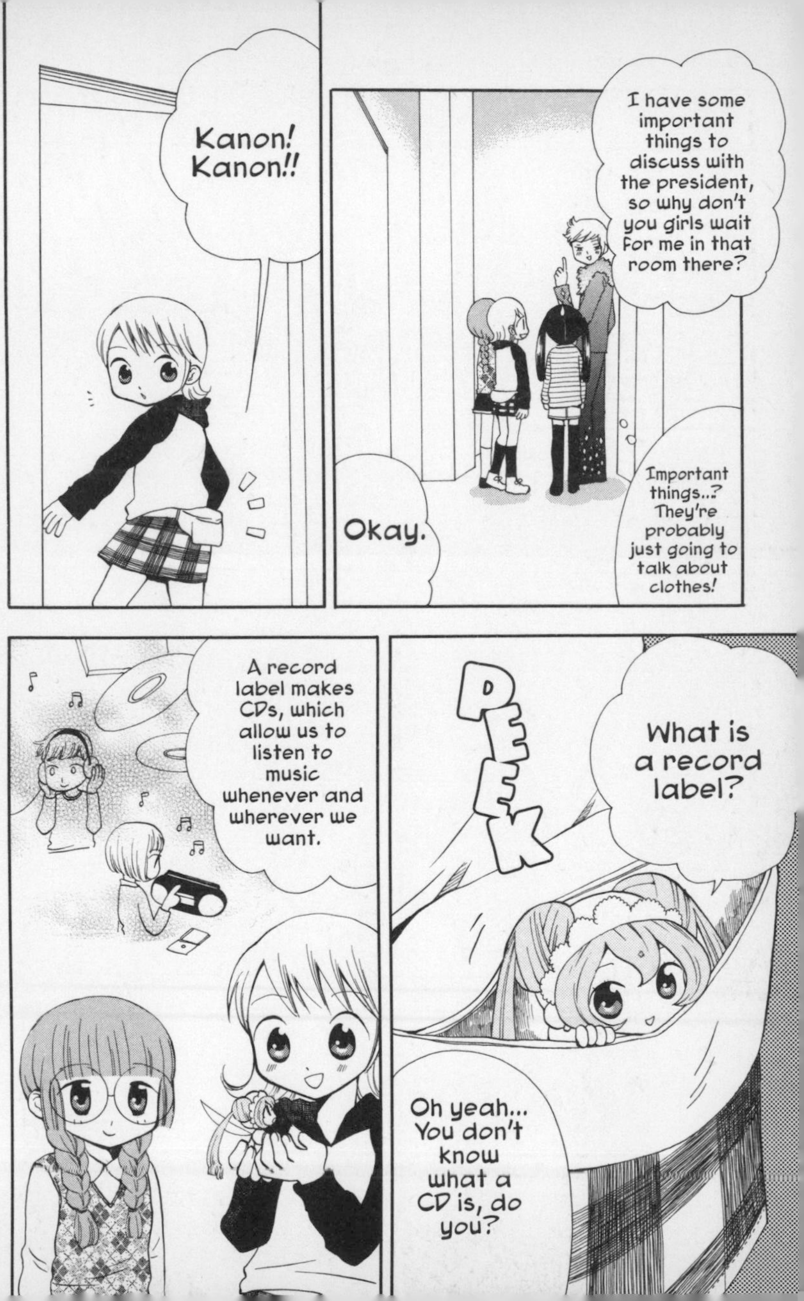
I have some important things to discuss with the president, so why don't you girls wait for me in that room there?
Important things...? They're probably just going to talk about clothes!
Okay.
Kanon! Kanon!!
PEEK
What is a record label?
Oh yeah... You don't know what a CD is, do you?
A record label makes CDs, which allow us to listen to music whenever and wherever we want.

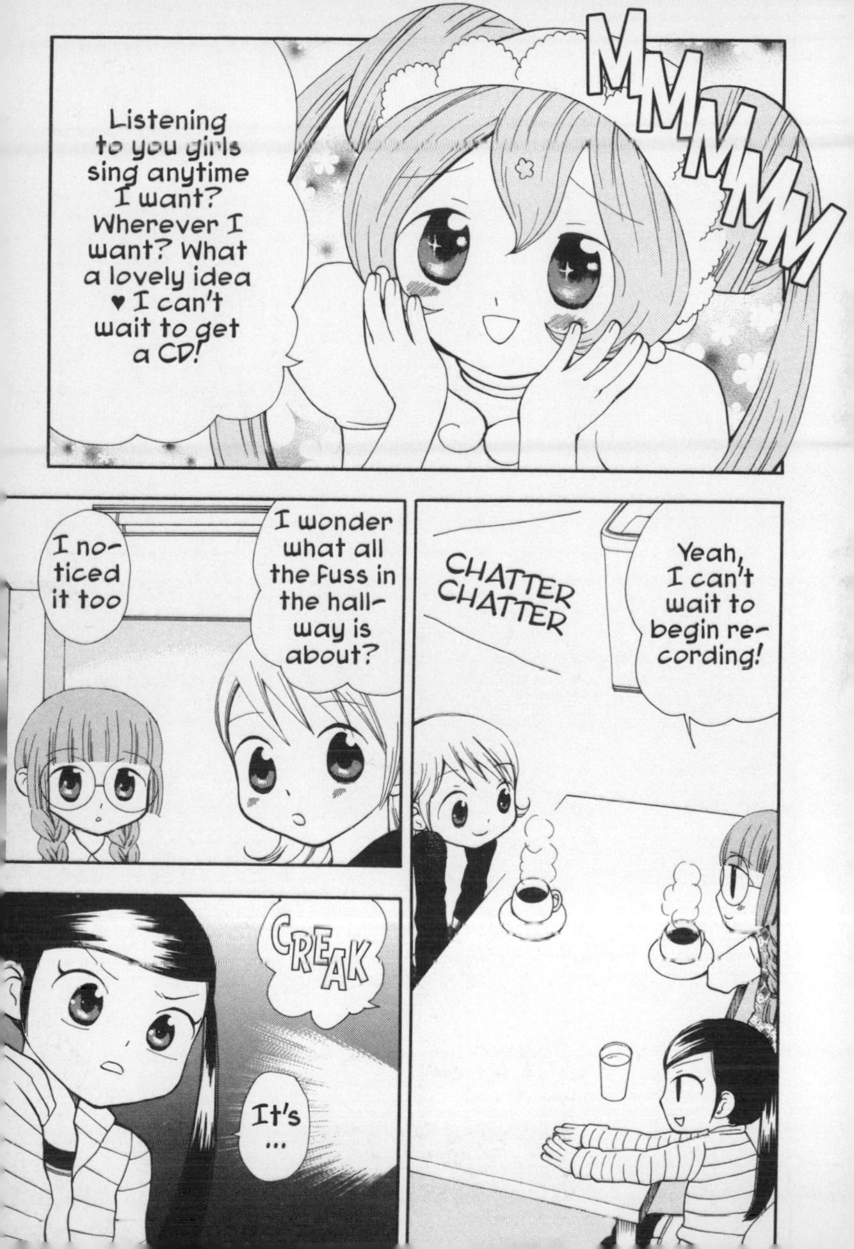
MMMMMMM
Listening to you girls sing anytime I want? Wherever I want? What a lovely idea ♥ I can't wait to get a CD!
Yeah, I can't wait to begin recording!
CHATTER CHATTER
I wonder what all the fuss in the hallway is about?
I noticed it too
CREAK
It's ...

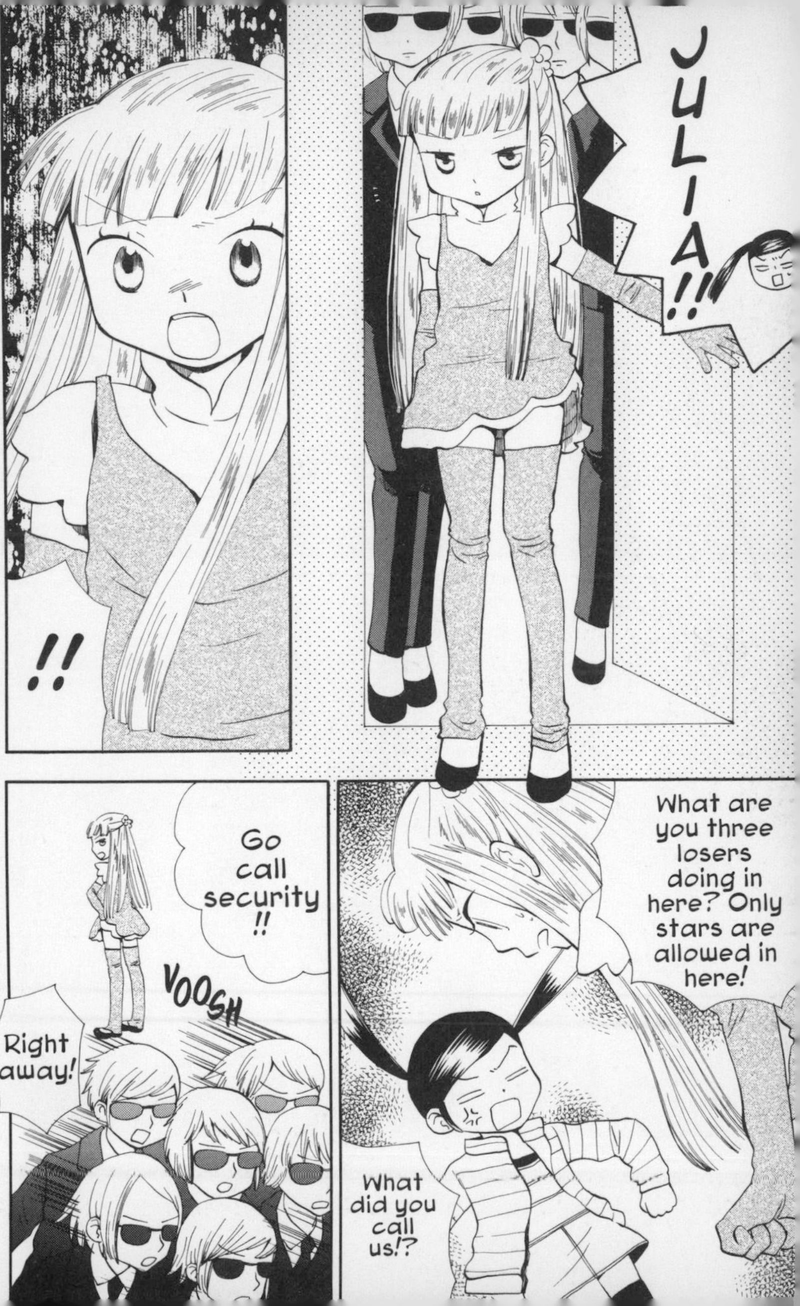
JULIA!!!
!!
What are you three losers doing in here? Only stars are allowed in here!
What did you call us!?
Go call security!!
VOOSH
Right away!

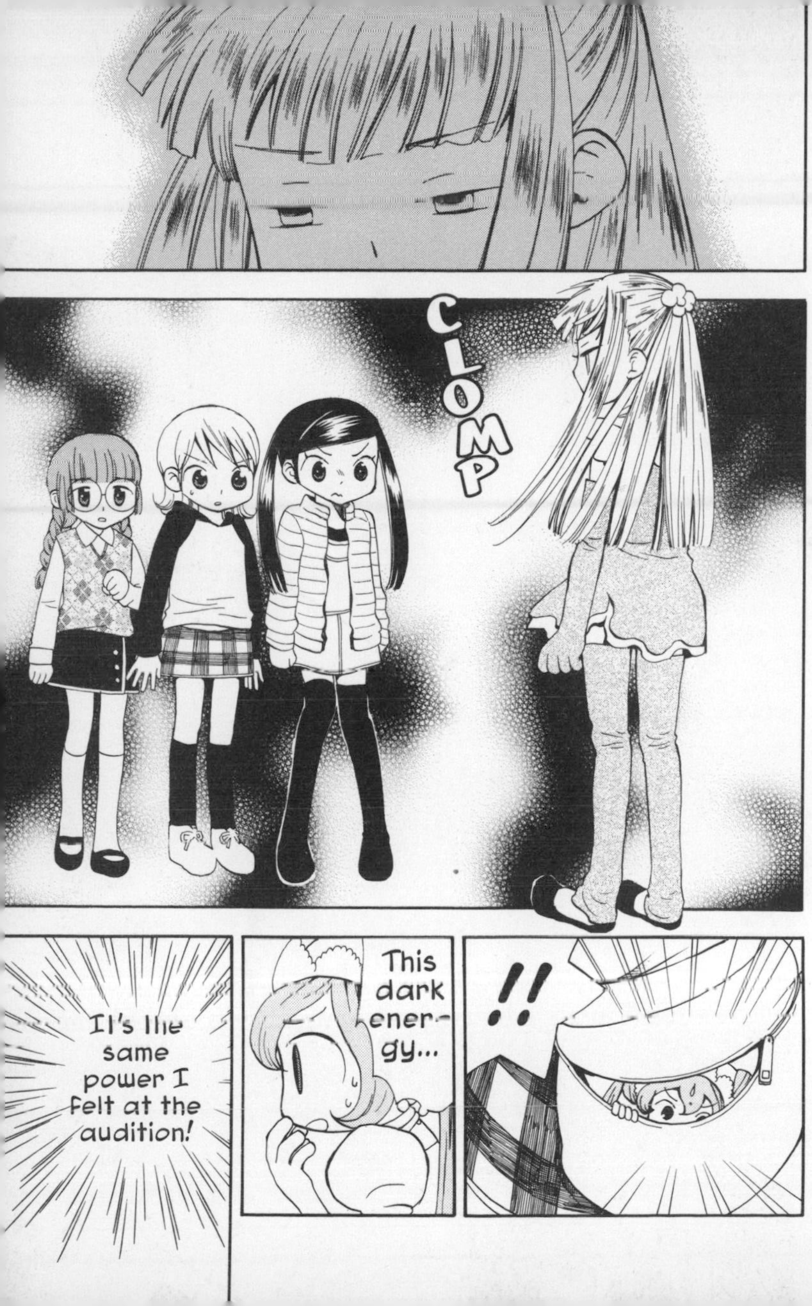
CLOMP
!!
This dark ener-gy...
It's the same power I felt at the audition!

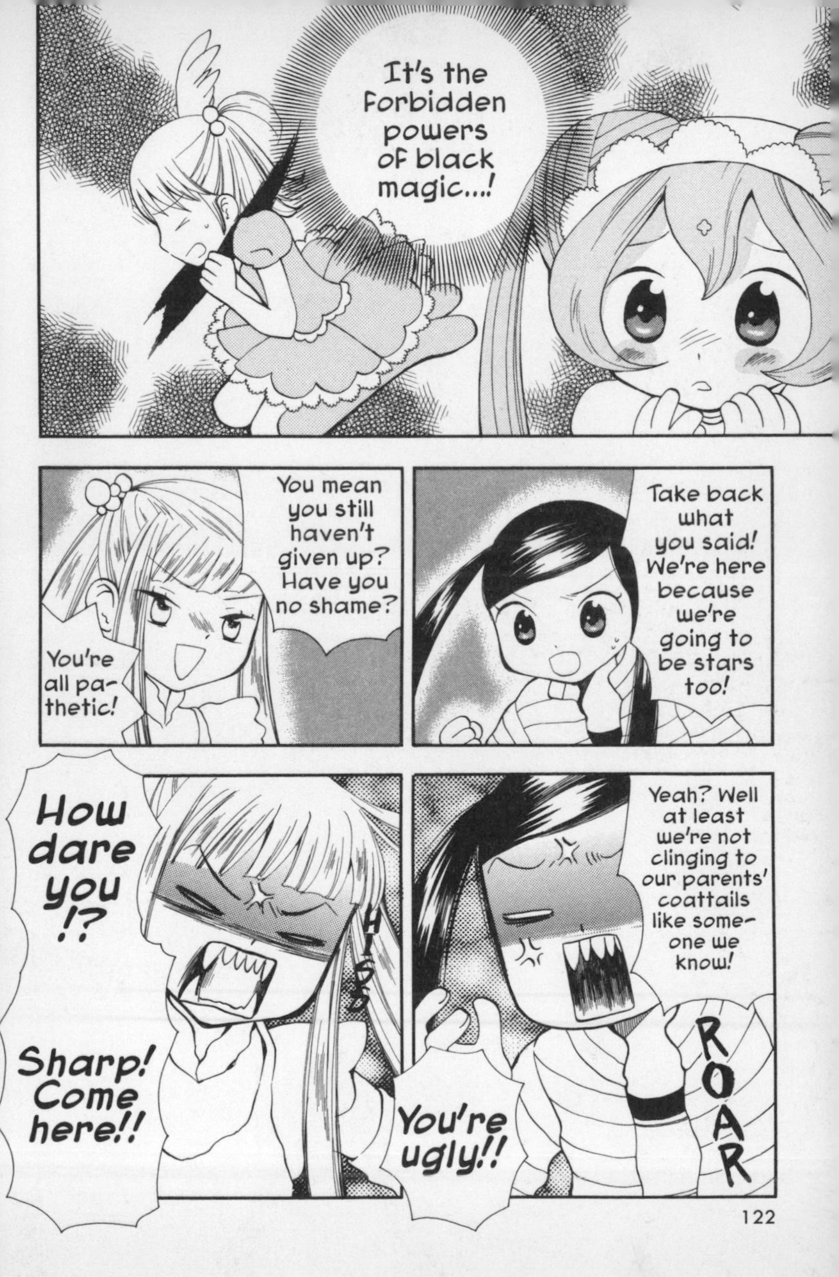
It's the forbidden powers of black magic...!
Take back what you said! We're here because we're going to be stars too!
You mean you still haven't given up? Have you no shame?
You're all pa-thetic!
Yeah? Well at least we're not clinging to our parents' coattails like some-one we know!
ROAR
You're ugly!!
How dare you!?
HISS
Sharp! Come here!!

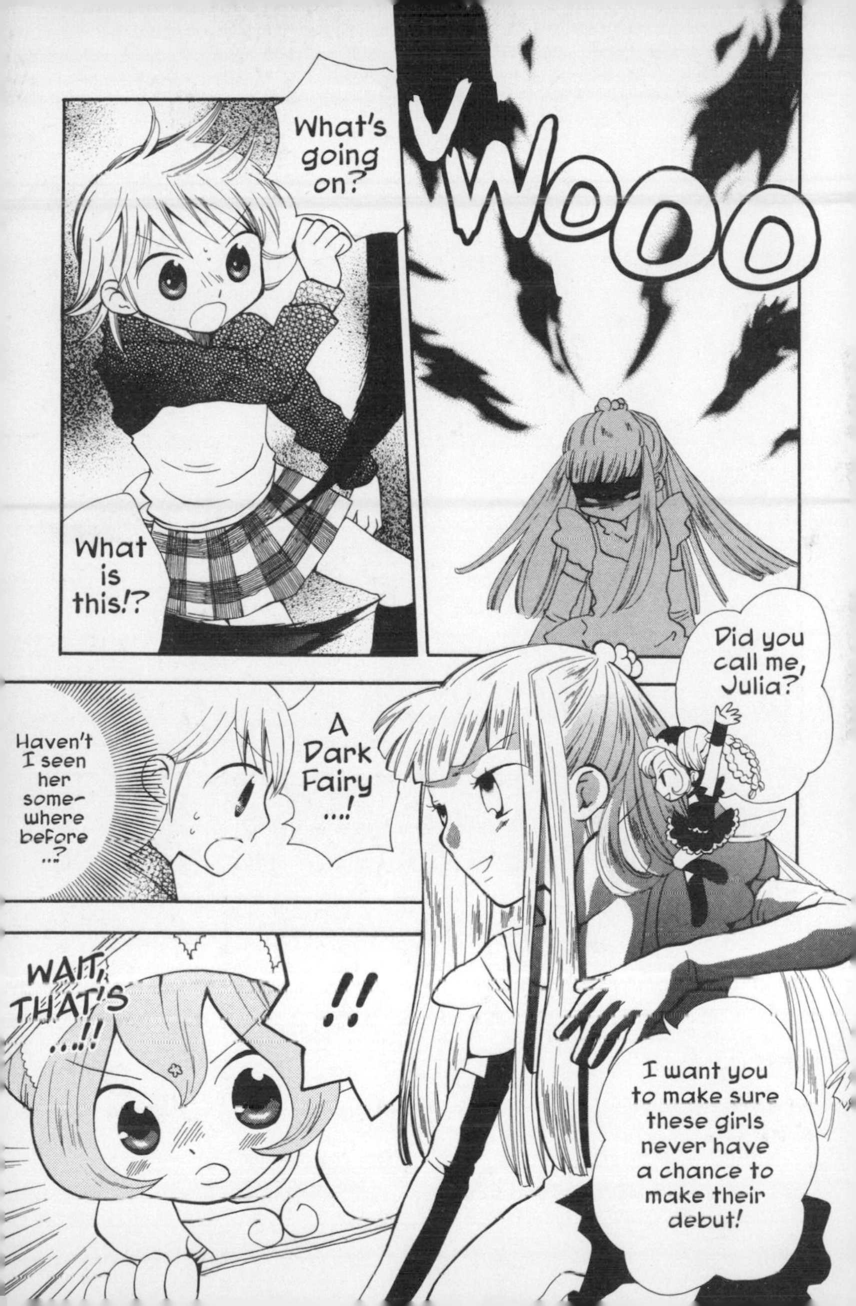
VWOOO
What's going on?
What is this!?
Did you call me, Julia?
I want you to make sure these girls never have a chance to make their debut!
A Dark Fairy ...!
Haven't I seen her some-where before ...?
WAIT, THAT'S ...!!
!!

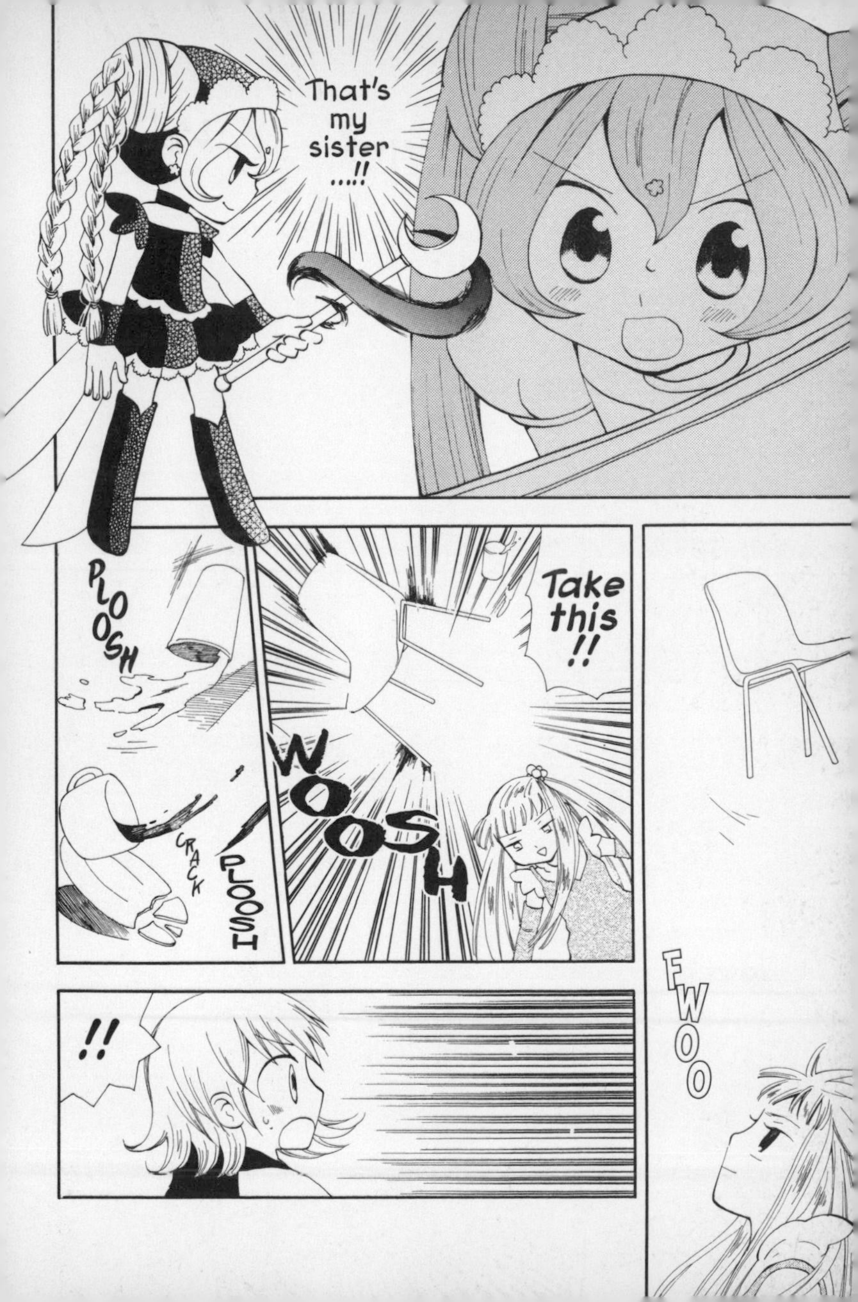
That's my sister ....!!
FWOOO
Take this!!
WOOSH
PLOOSH
CRACK
PLOOSH
!!

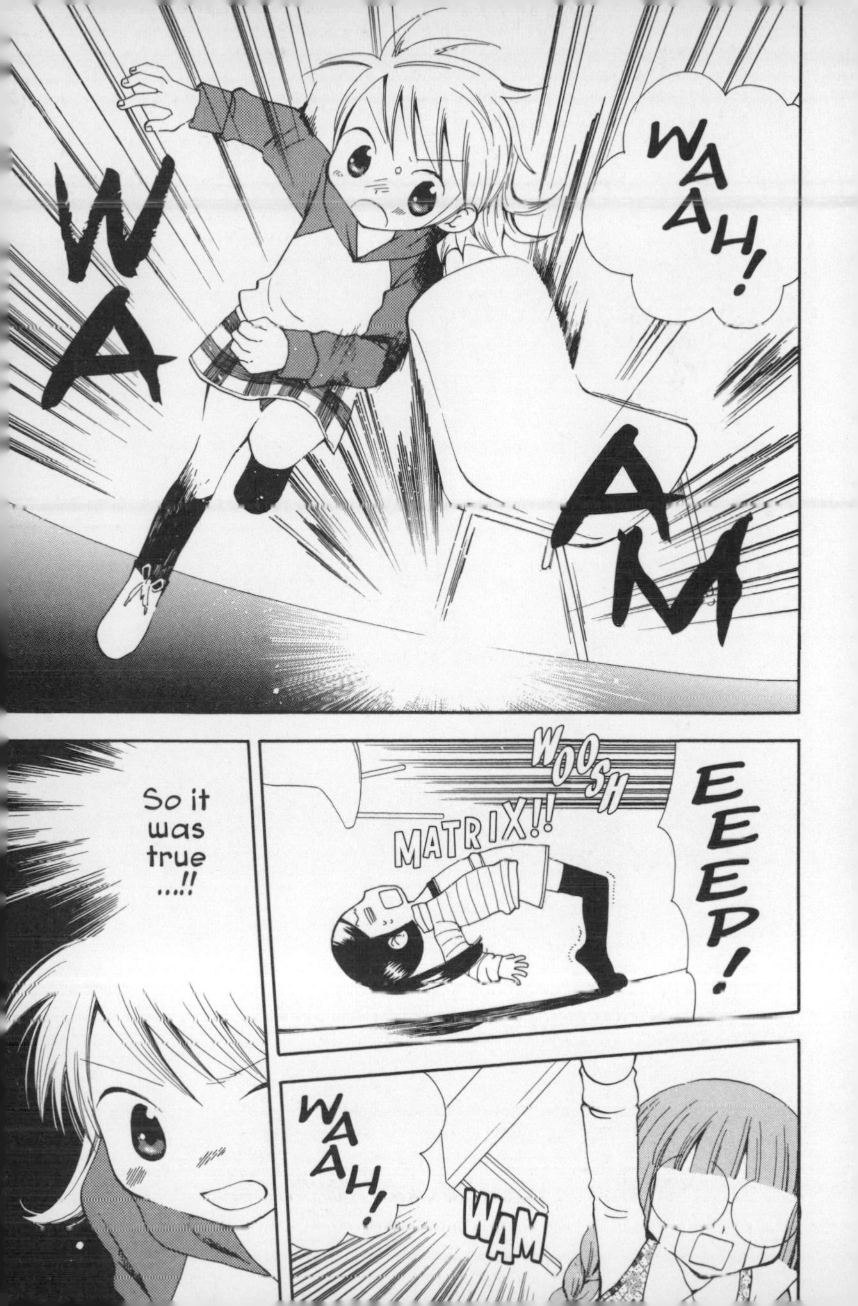
WAAH!
WAAAM
EEEEP!
WOOSH
MATRIX!!
WAAH!
WAM
So it was true ...!!

The rumors that Kodama told us about...

It was no coincidence that Julia's rivals were all injured and had to quit.

They weren't accidents at all! They were caused by this Dark Fairy!

Fwoo

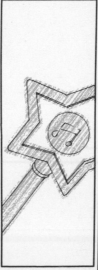

WOOOSH

!!

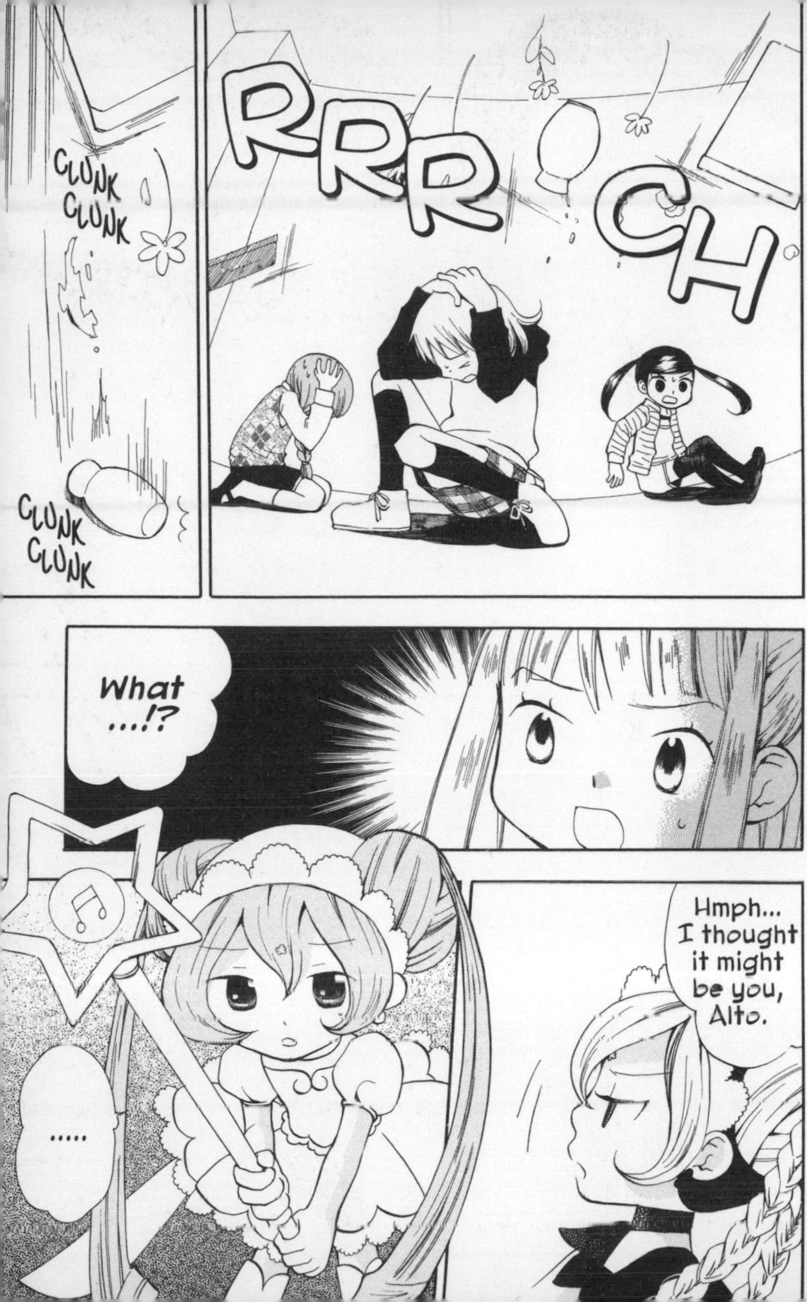
RRRRCH
CLUNK CLUNK
CLUNK CLUNK
What ...!?
Hmph... I thought it might be you, Alto.
.....

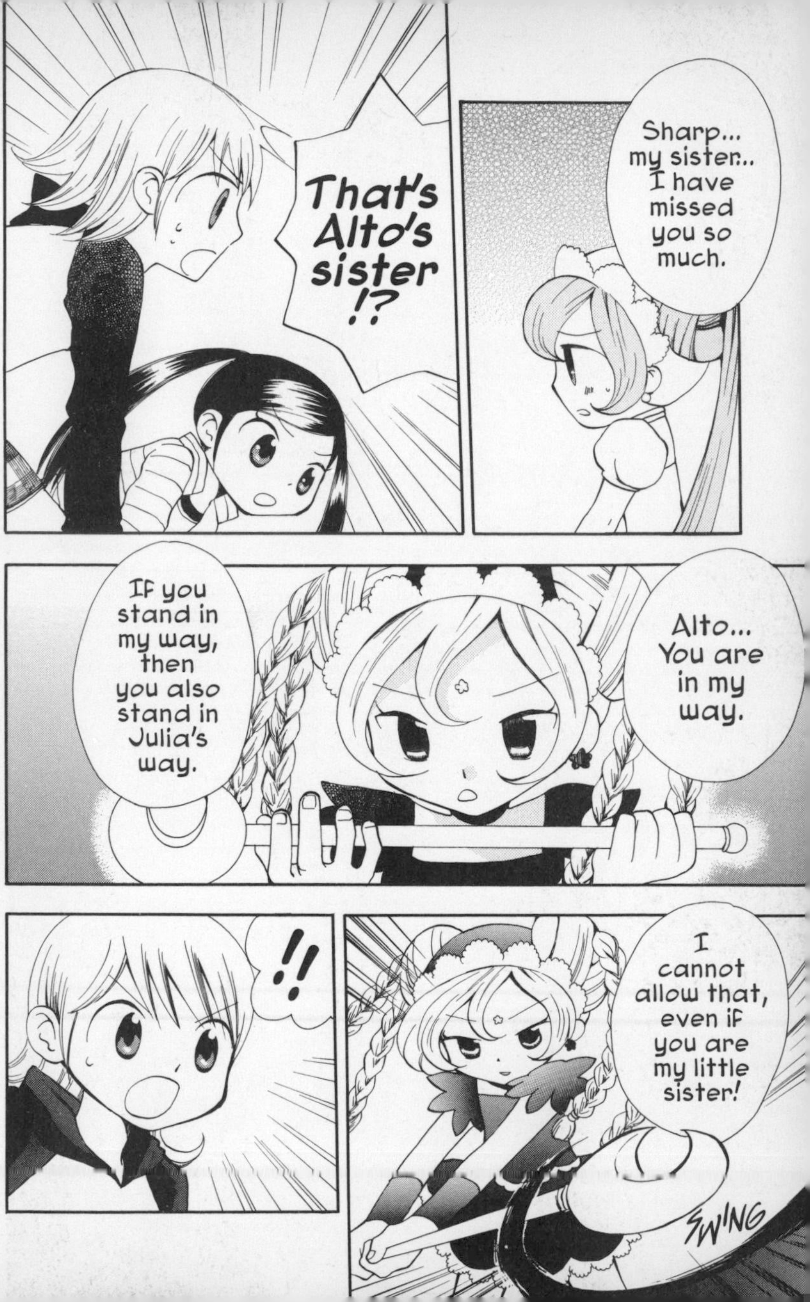
Sharp... my sister... I have missed you so much.
That's Alto's sister !?
Alto... You are in my way.
If you stand in my way, then you also stand in Julia's way.
I cannot allow that, even if you are my little sister!
SWING
!!

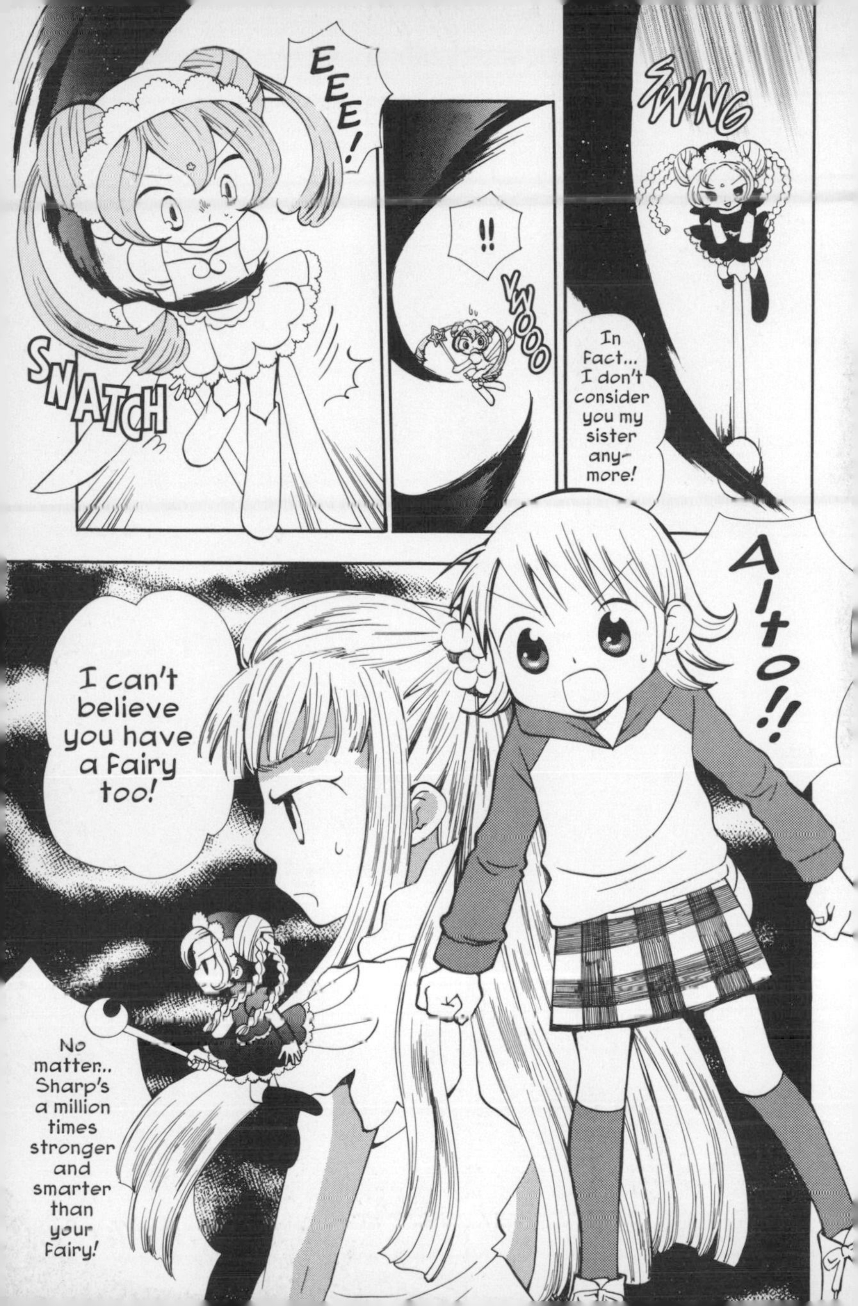
SWING
In fact... I don't consider you my sister anymore!
!!
VWOOO
EEE!
SNATCH
Aito!!
I can't believe you have a fairy too!
No matter... Sharp's a million times stronger and smarter than your fairy!

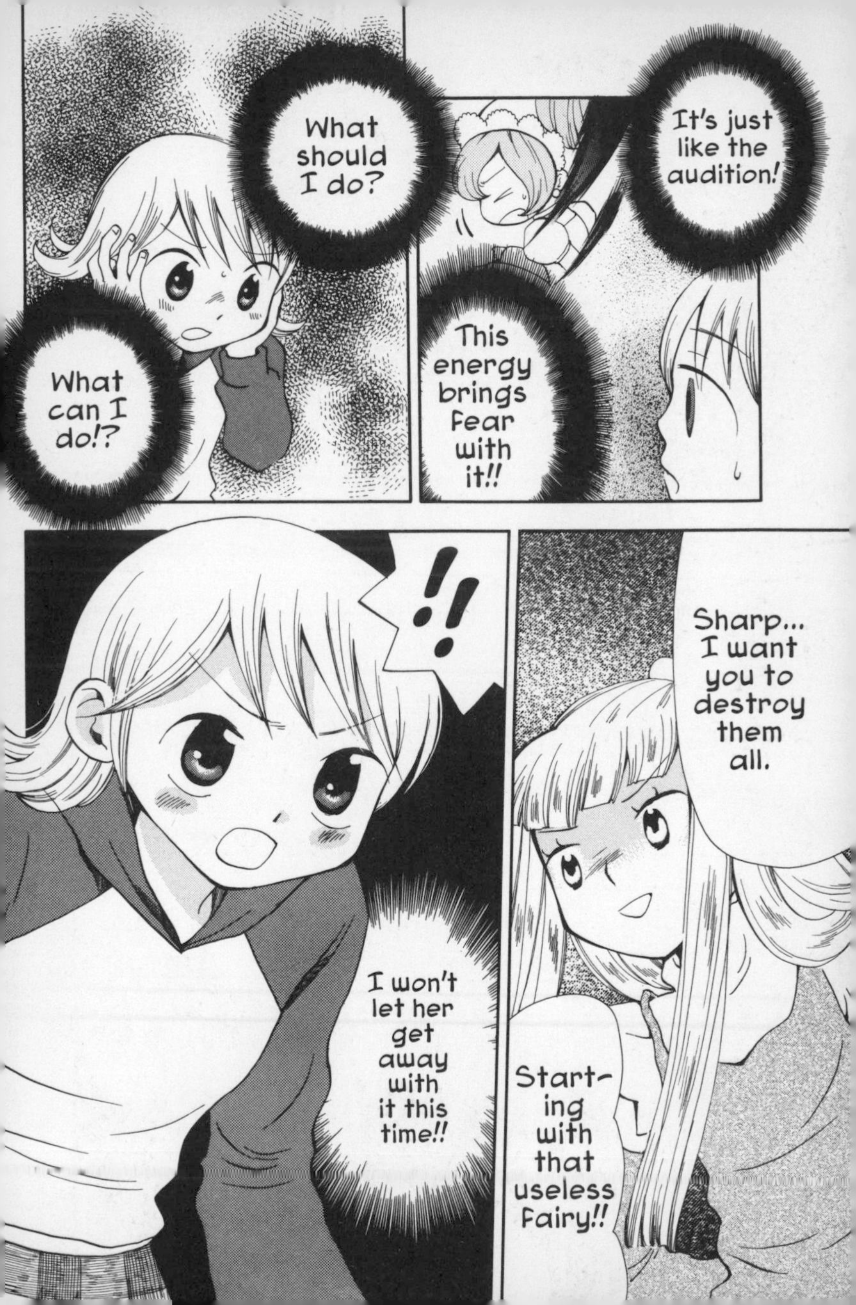
It's just like the audition!
This energy brings fear with it!!
What should I do?
What can I do!?
Sharp... I want you to destroy them all.
Starting with that useless Fairy!!
!!
I won't let her get away with it this time!!

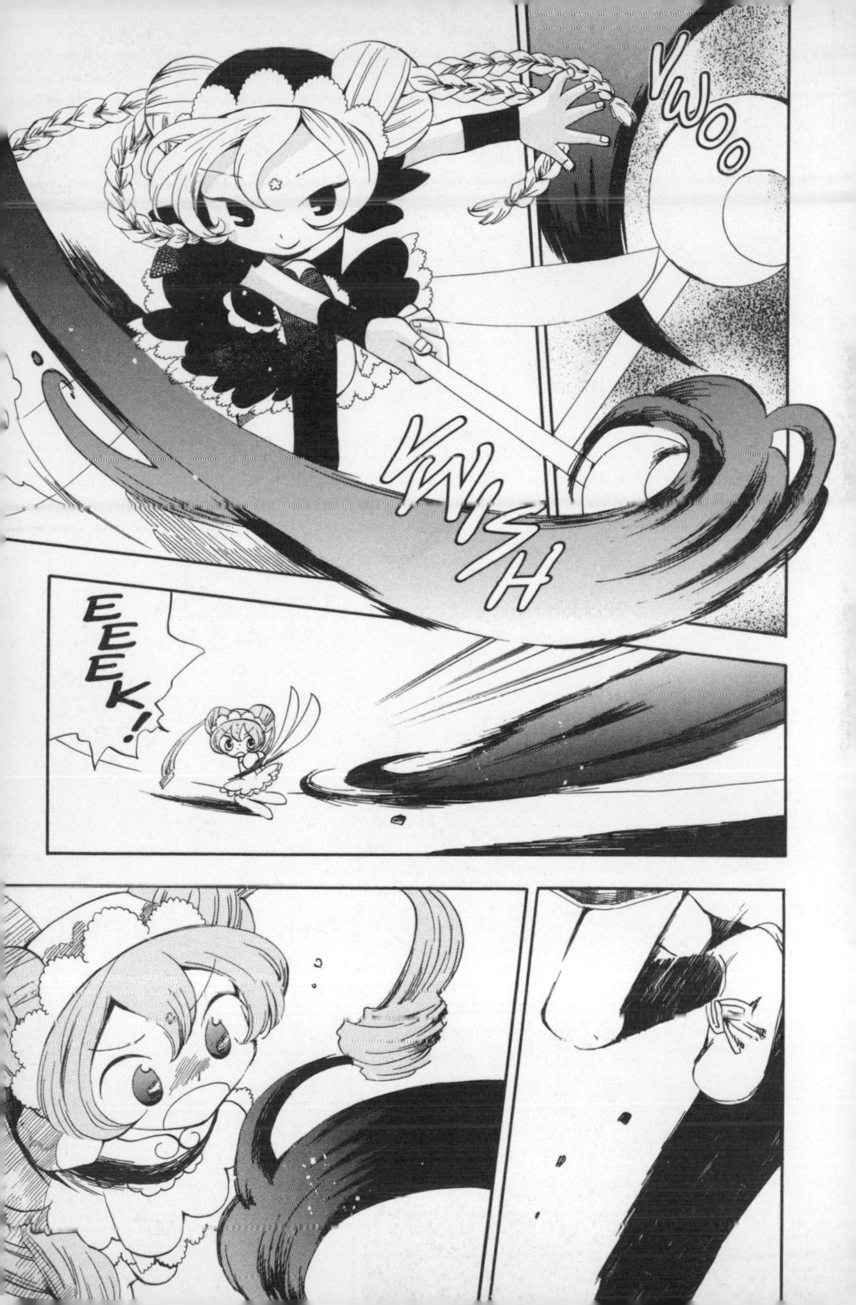
VWOO
VWISH
EEEEK!

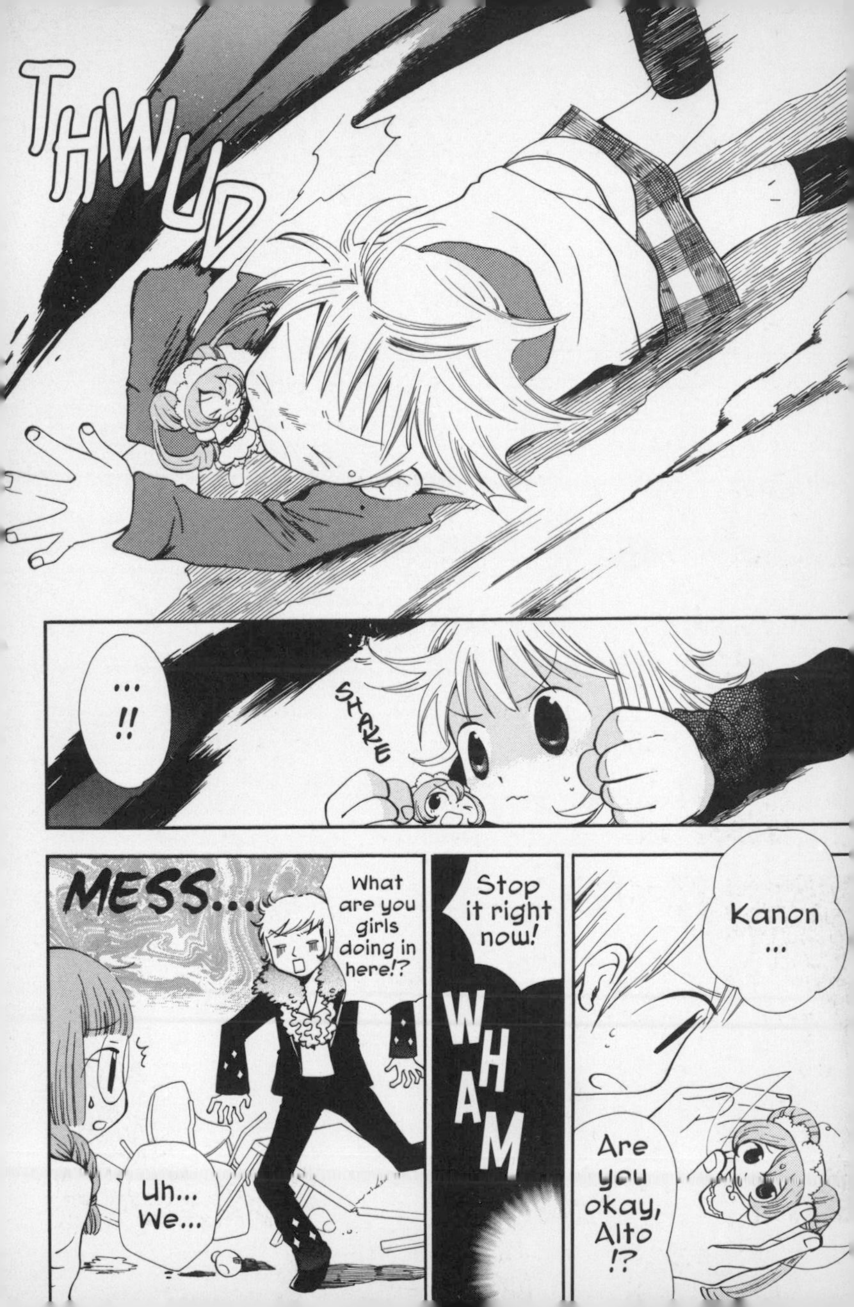
THWUD
SHAKE
...!!
Kanon ...
Are you okay, Alto!?
Stop it right now!
WHAM
MESS...
What are you girls doing in here!?
Uh... We...

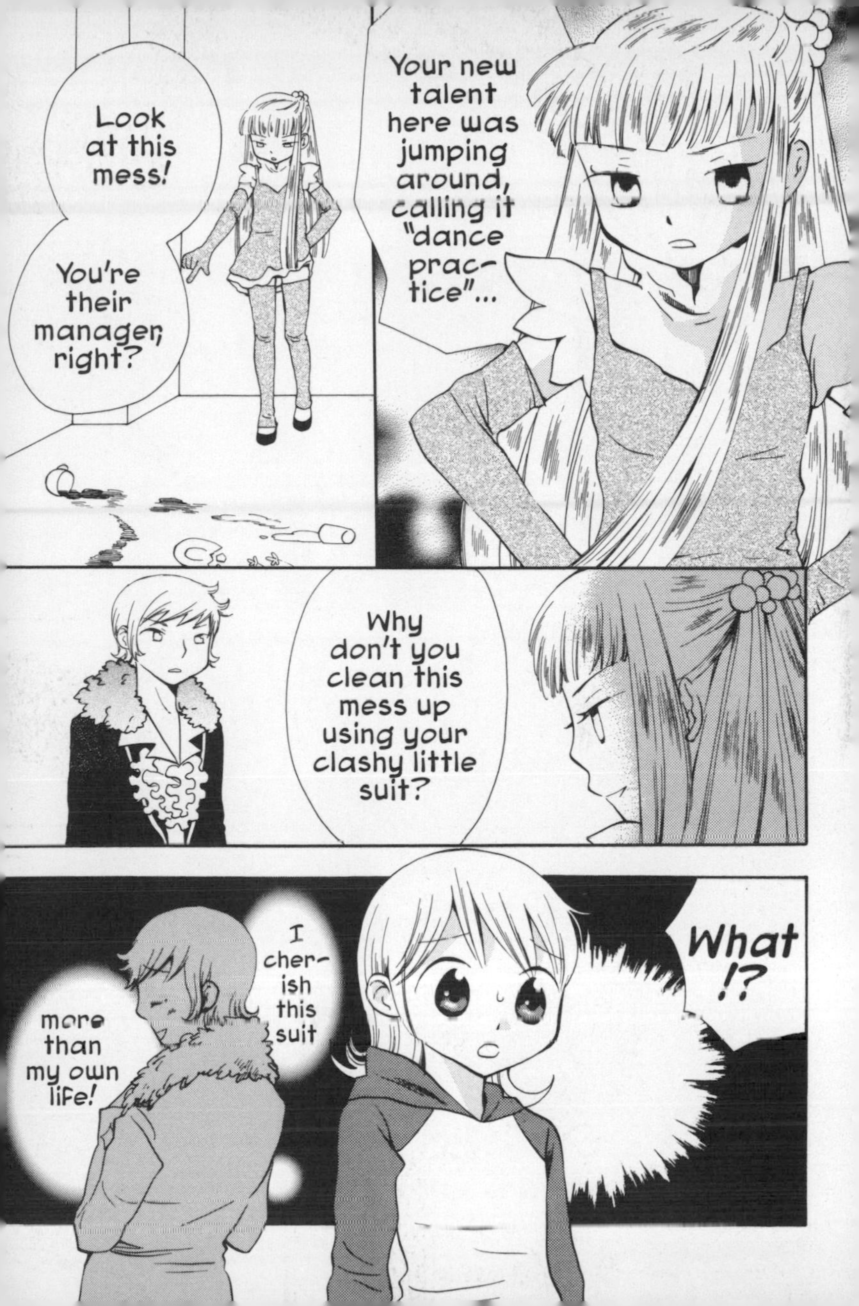
Your new talent here was jumping around, calling it "dance prac-tice"...
Look at this mess!
You're their manager, right?
Why don't you clean this mess up using your clashy little suit?
What!?
I cher-ish this suit
more than my own life!

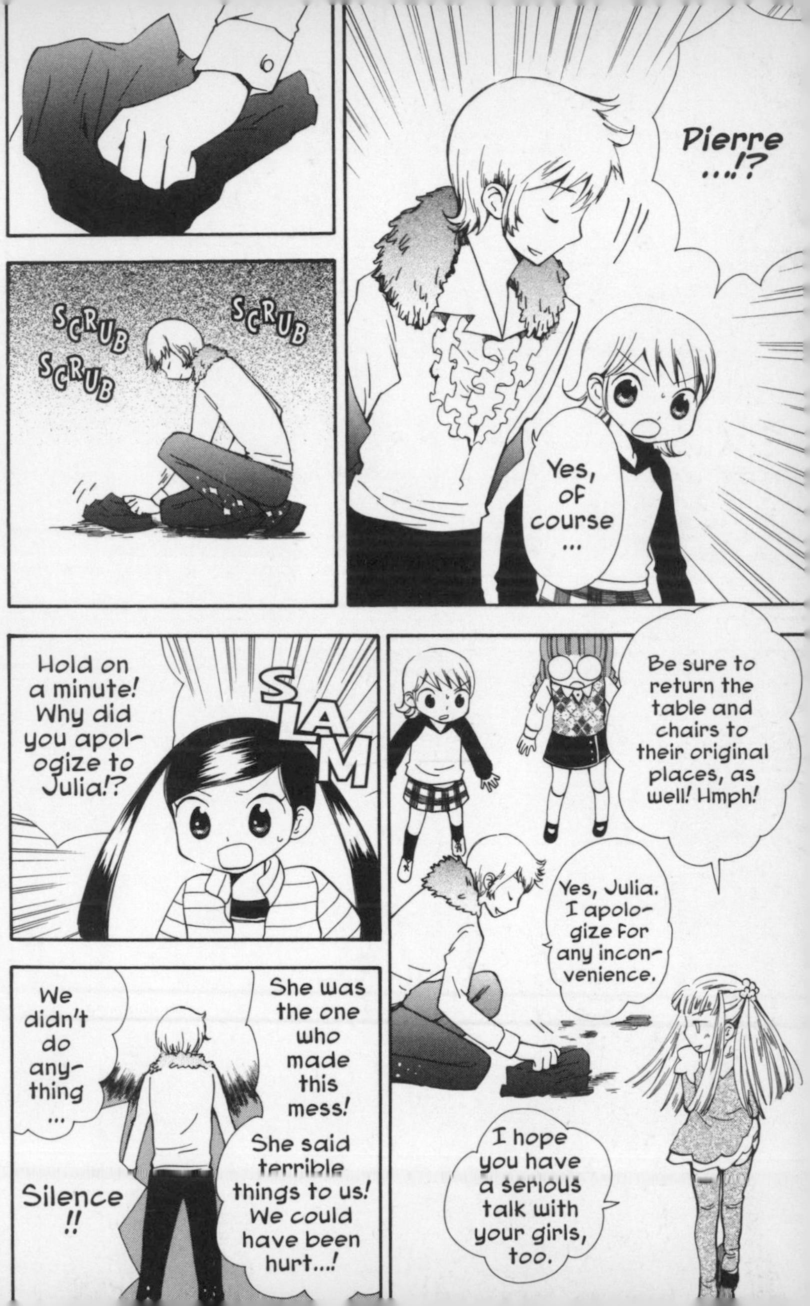

Pierre ...!?
Yes, of course ...
SCRUB
SCRUB
SCRUB
Be sure to return the table and chairs to their original places, as well! Hmph!
Yes, Julia. I apologize for any inconvenience.
I hope you have a serious talk with your girls, too.
Hold on a minute! Why did you apologize to Julia!?
SLAM
She was the one who made this mess!
We didn't do anything ...
She said terrible things to us! We could have been hurt...!
Silence !!

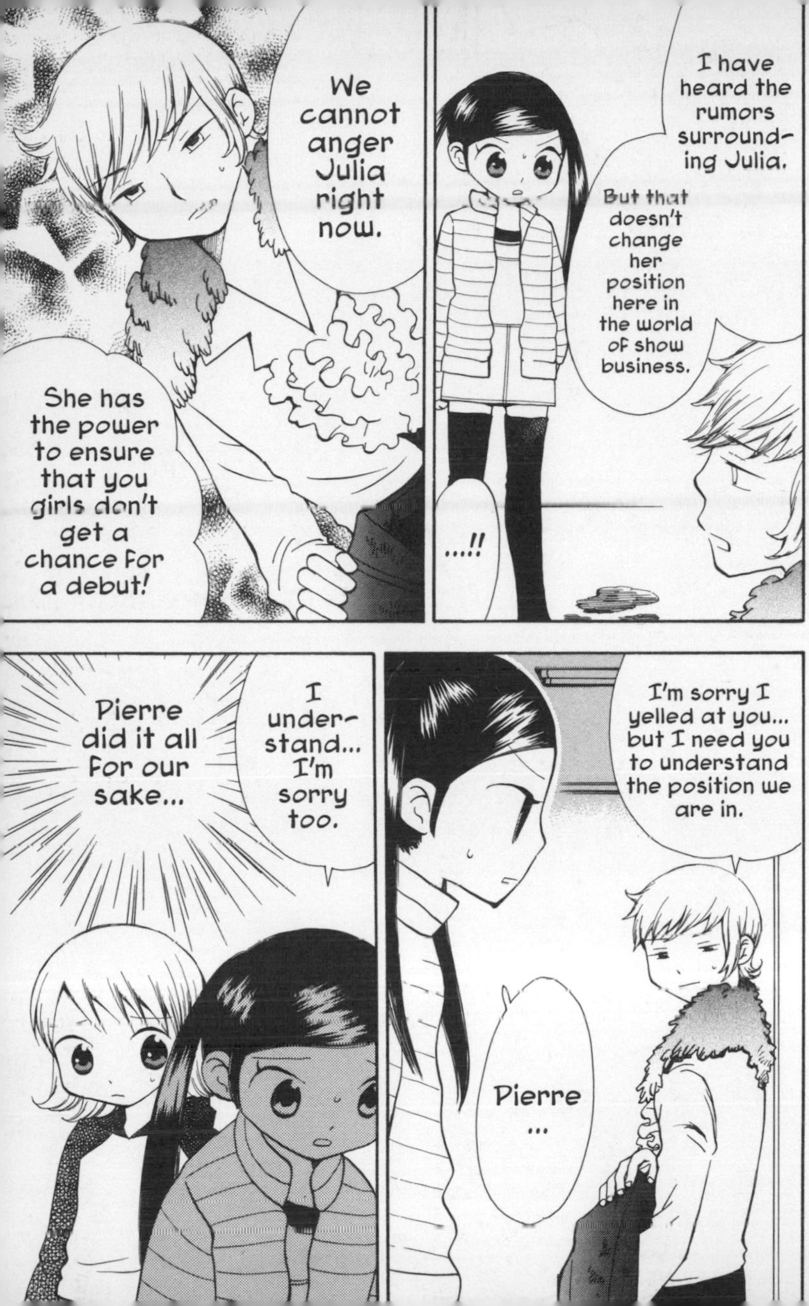
I have heard the rumors surrounding Julia.
But that doesn't change her position here in the world of show business.
...!!
We cannot anger Julia right now.
She has the power to ensure that you girls don't get a chance for a debut!
I'm sorry I yelled at you... but I need you to understand the position we are in.
Pierre ...
I understand... I'm sorry too.
Pierre did it all for our sake...

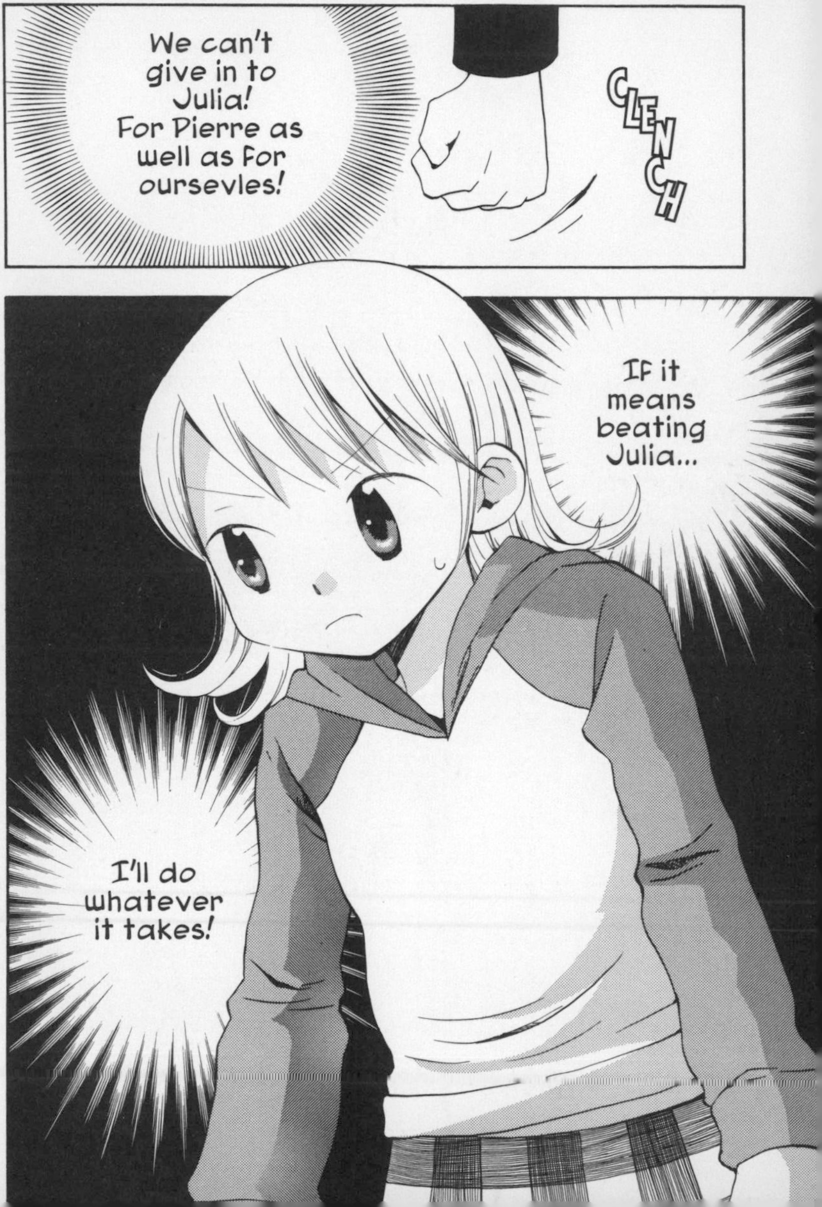
CLENCH
We can't give in to Julia! For Pierre as well as for oursevles!
If it means beating Julia...
I'll do whatever it takes!

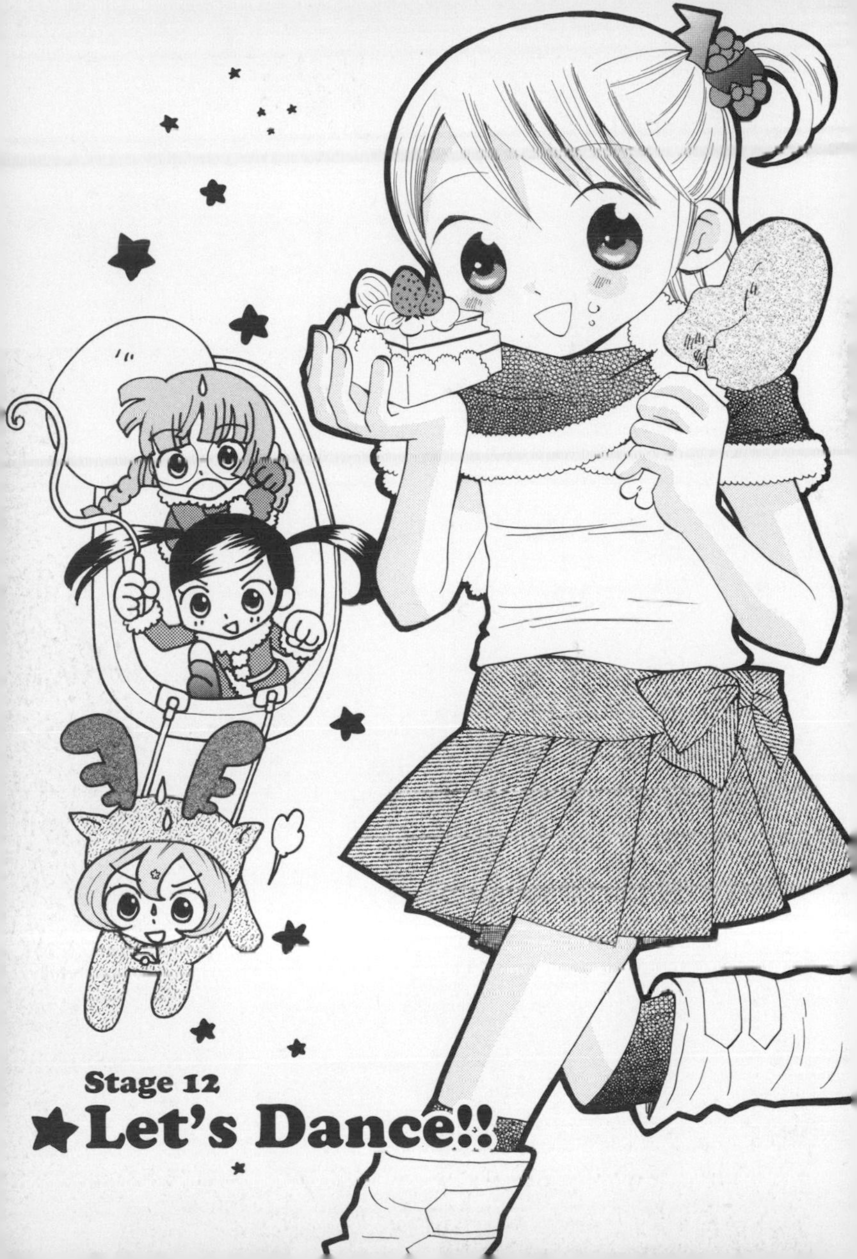

## Stage 12
# ★Let's Dance!!

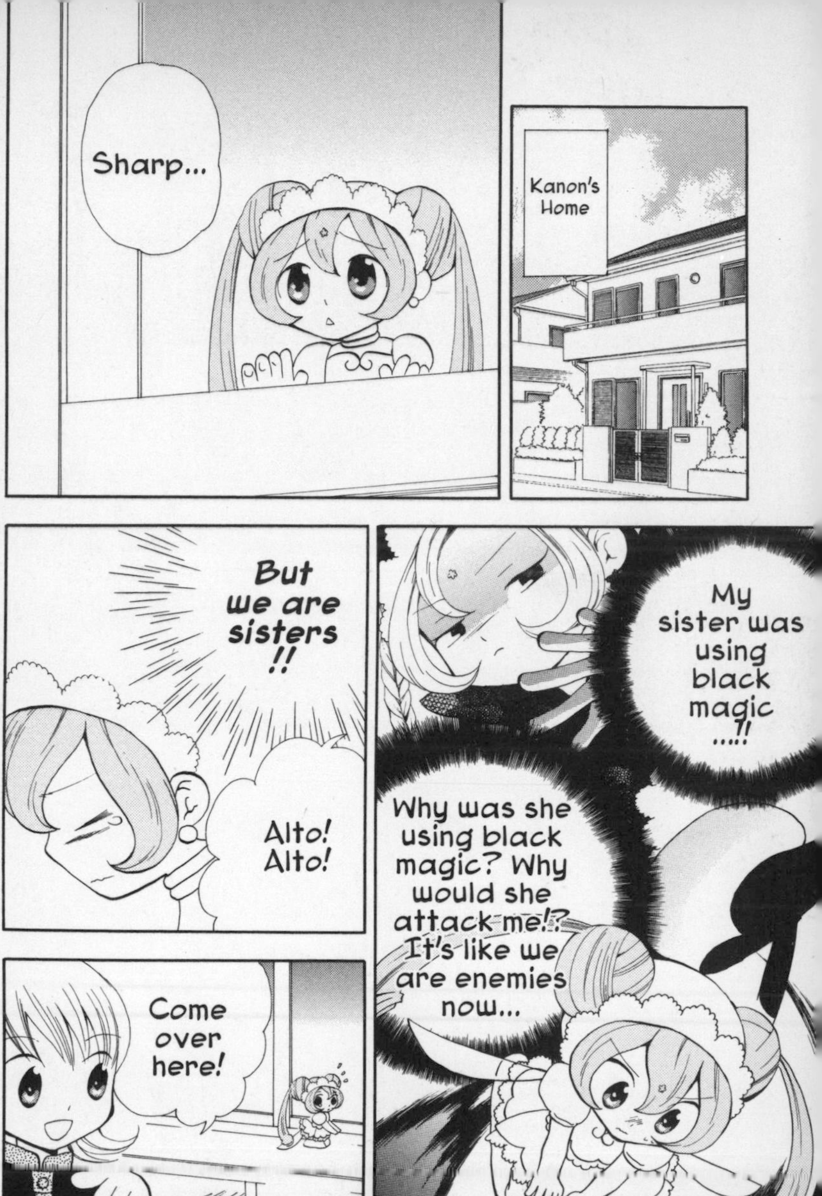
Kanon's Home
Sharp...
My sister was using black magic ...!!
Why was she using black magic? Why would she attack me!? It's like we are enemies now...
But we are sisters !!
Alto! Alto!
Come over here!

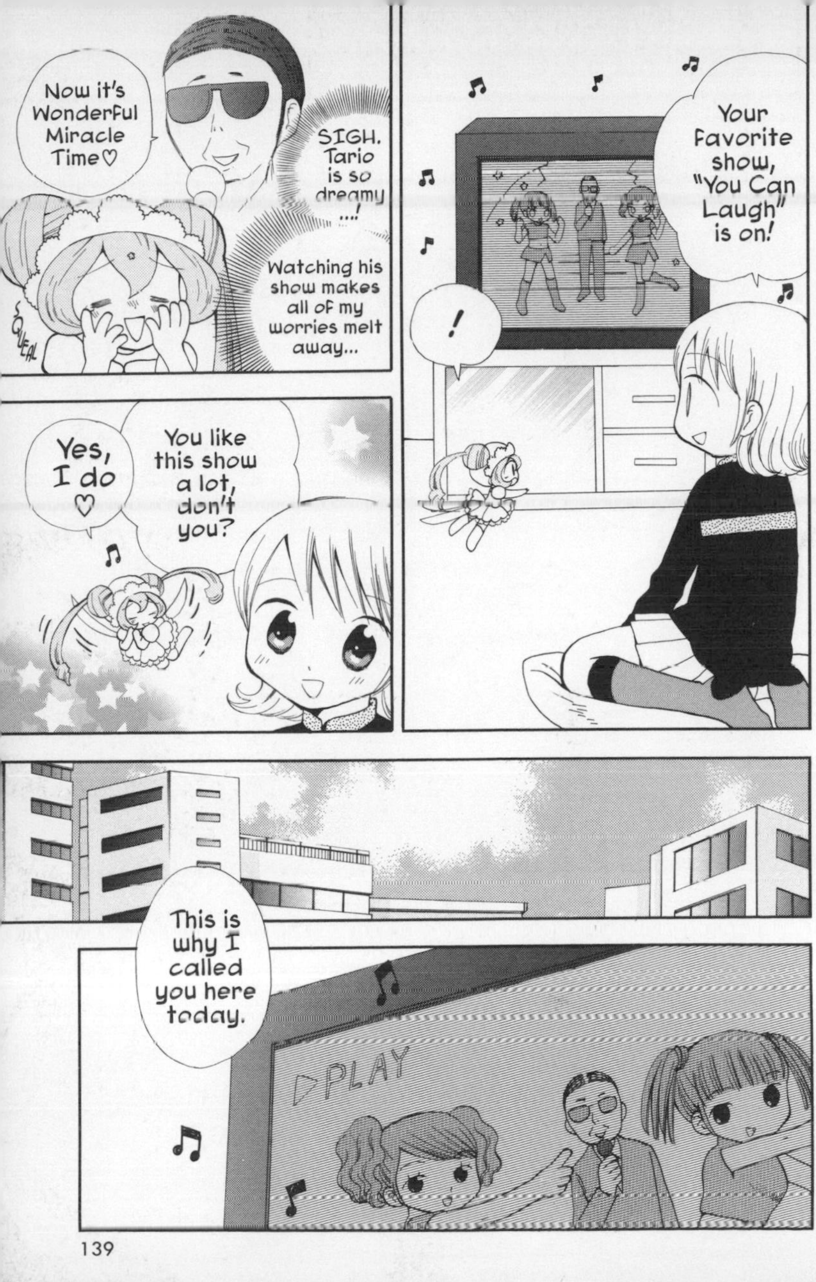
Your favorite show, "You Can Laugh" is on!
!
Now it's Wonderful Miracle Time♡
SIGH. Tario is so dreamy ...!
Watching his show makes all of my worries melt away...
SQUEAL
You like this show a lot, don't you?
Yes, I do ♡
This is why I called you here today.
▷PLAY

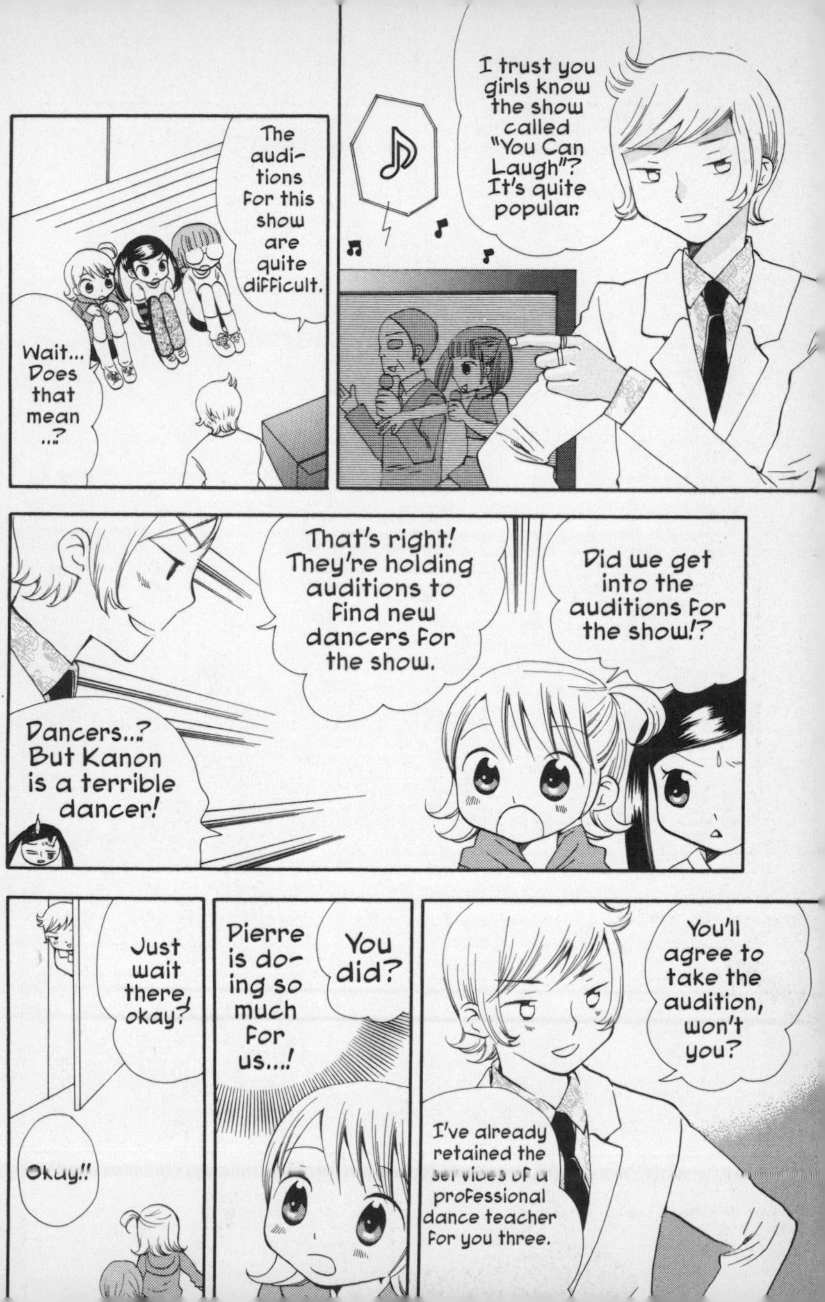
I trust you girls know the show called "You Can Laugh"? It's quite popular.
The audi-tions for this show are quite difficult.
Wait... Does that mean ...?
Did we get into the auditions for the show!?
That's right! They're holding auditions to find new dancers for the show.
Dancers...? But Kanon is a terrible dancer!
You'll agree to take the audition, won't you?
I've already retained the services of a professional dance teacher for you three.
You did?
Pierre is do-ing so much for us...!
Just wait there, okay?
Okay!!

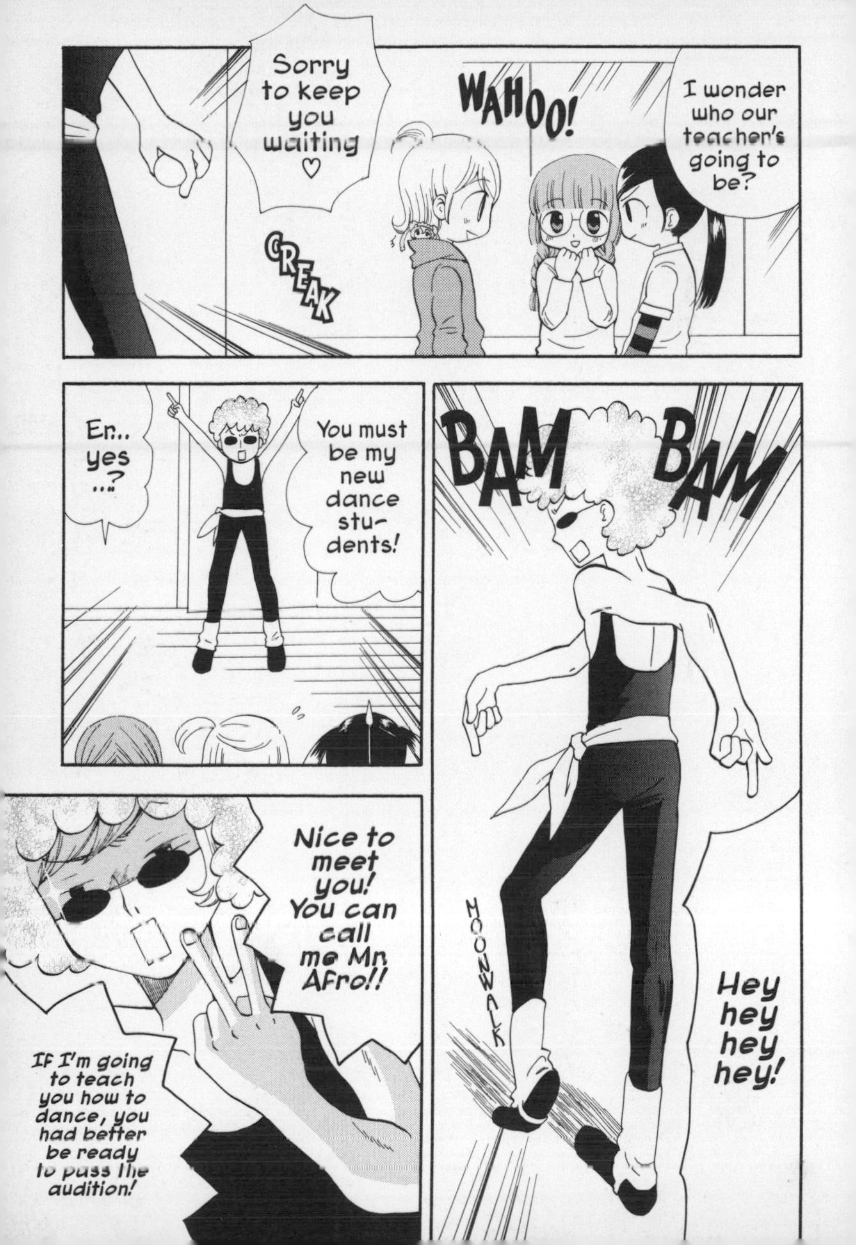
I wonder who our teacher's going to be?
WAHOO!
Sorry to keep you waiting ♡
CREAK
BAM BAM
Hey hey hey hey!
MOONWALK
You must be my new dance stu-dents!
Er.. yes ...?
Nice to meet you! You can call me Mr. Afro!!
If I'm going to teach you how to dance, you had better be ready to pass the audition!

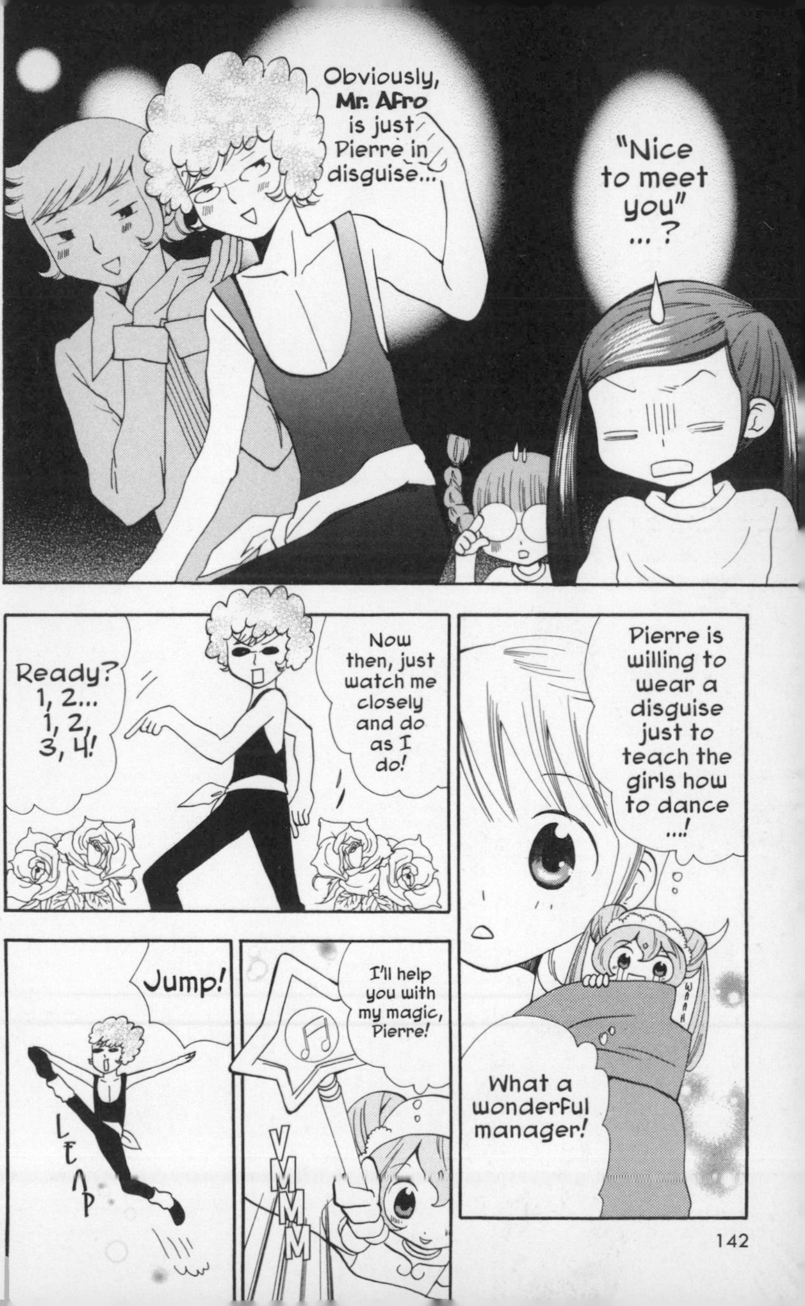
"Nice to meet you" ... ?
Obviously, **Mr. Afro** is just Pierre in disguise...
Pierre is willing to wear a disguise just to teach the girls how to dance ...!
What a wonderful manager!
Now then, just watch me closely and do as I do!
Ready? 1, 2... 1, 2, 3, 4!
I'll help you with my magic, Pierre!
VMMMM
Jump!
LEAP

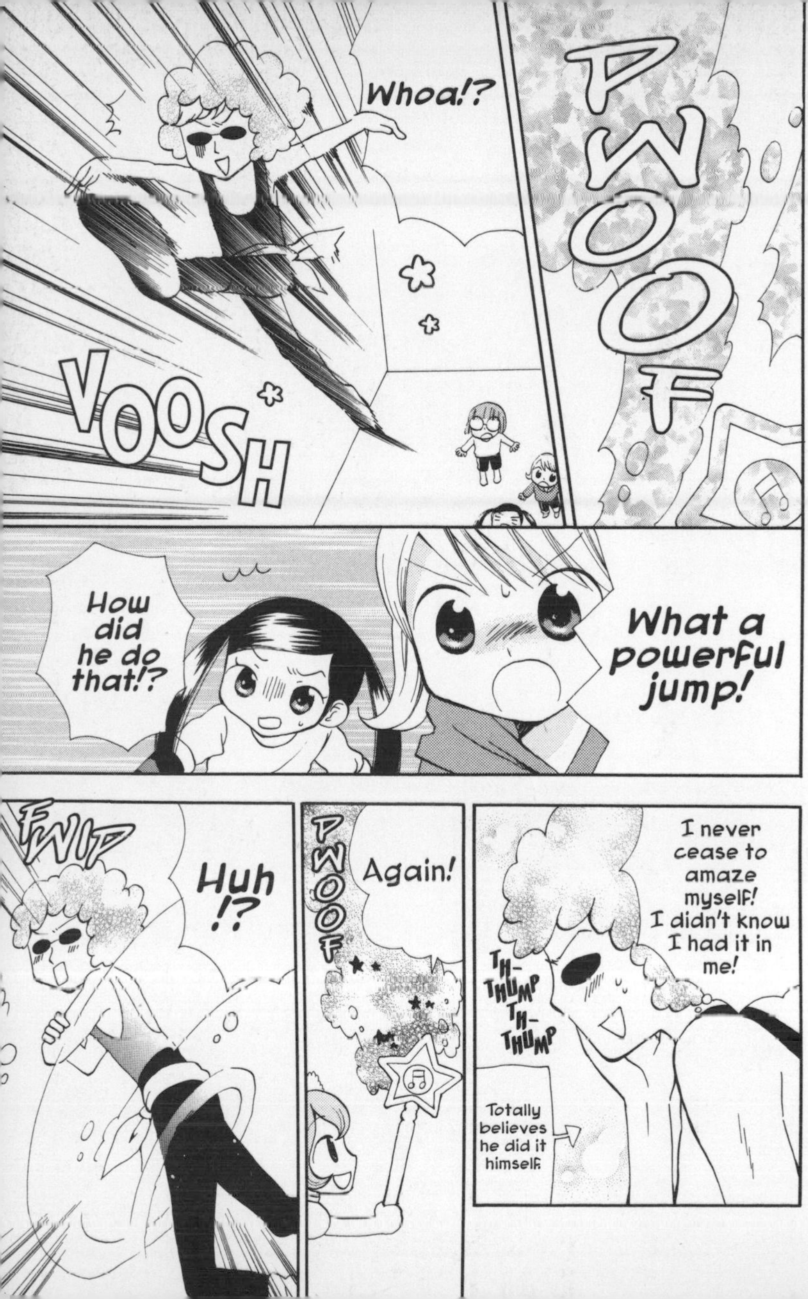
PWOOF
Whoa!?
VOOSH
What a powerful jump!
How did he do that!?
I never cease to amaze myself! I didn't know I had it in me!
TH-THUMP TH-THUMP
Totally believes he did it himself.
Again!
PWOOF
FWIP
Huh!?

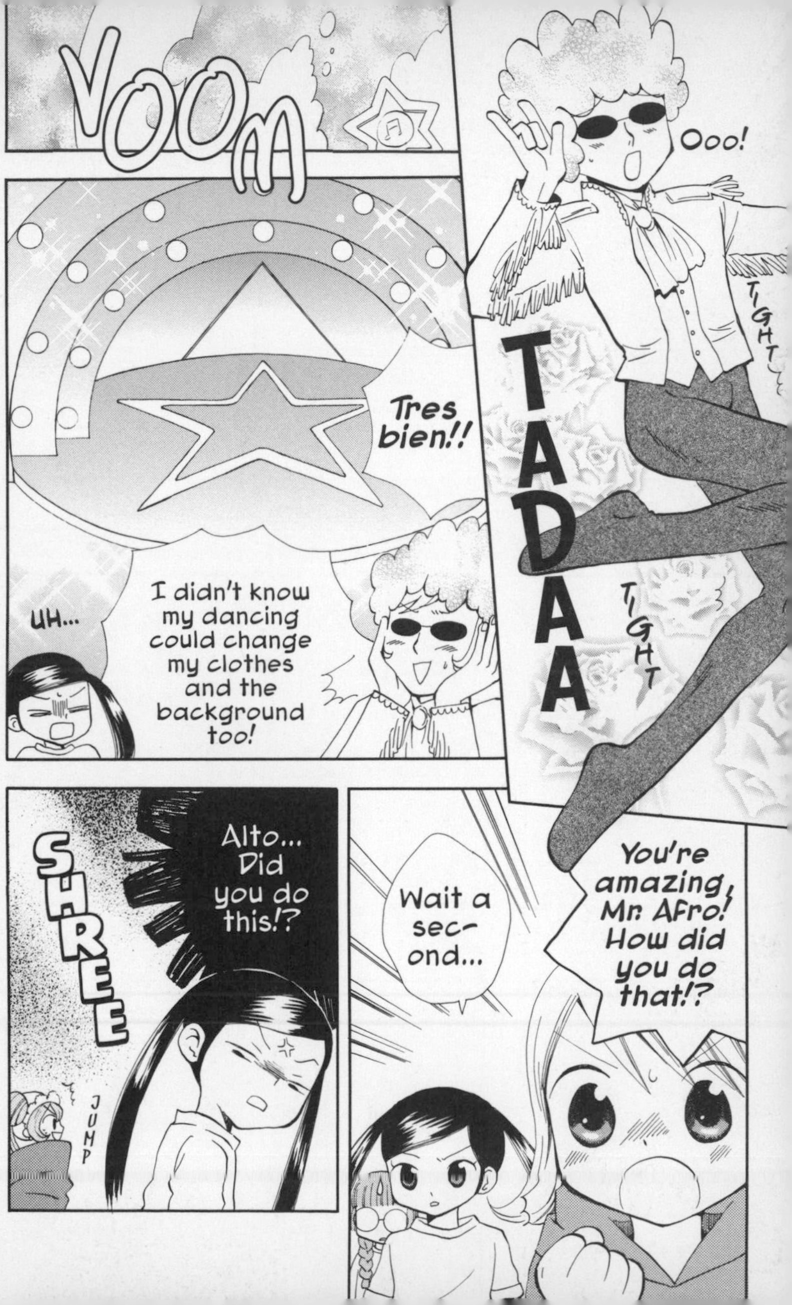
Ooo!
TADAA
TIGHT
TIGHT
VOOM
Tres bien!!
I didn't know my dancing could change my clothes and the background too!
UH...
You're amazing, Mr. Afro! How did you do that!?
Wait a sec-ond...
Alto... Did you do this!?
SHREE
JUMP

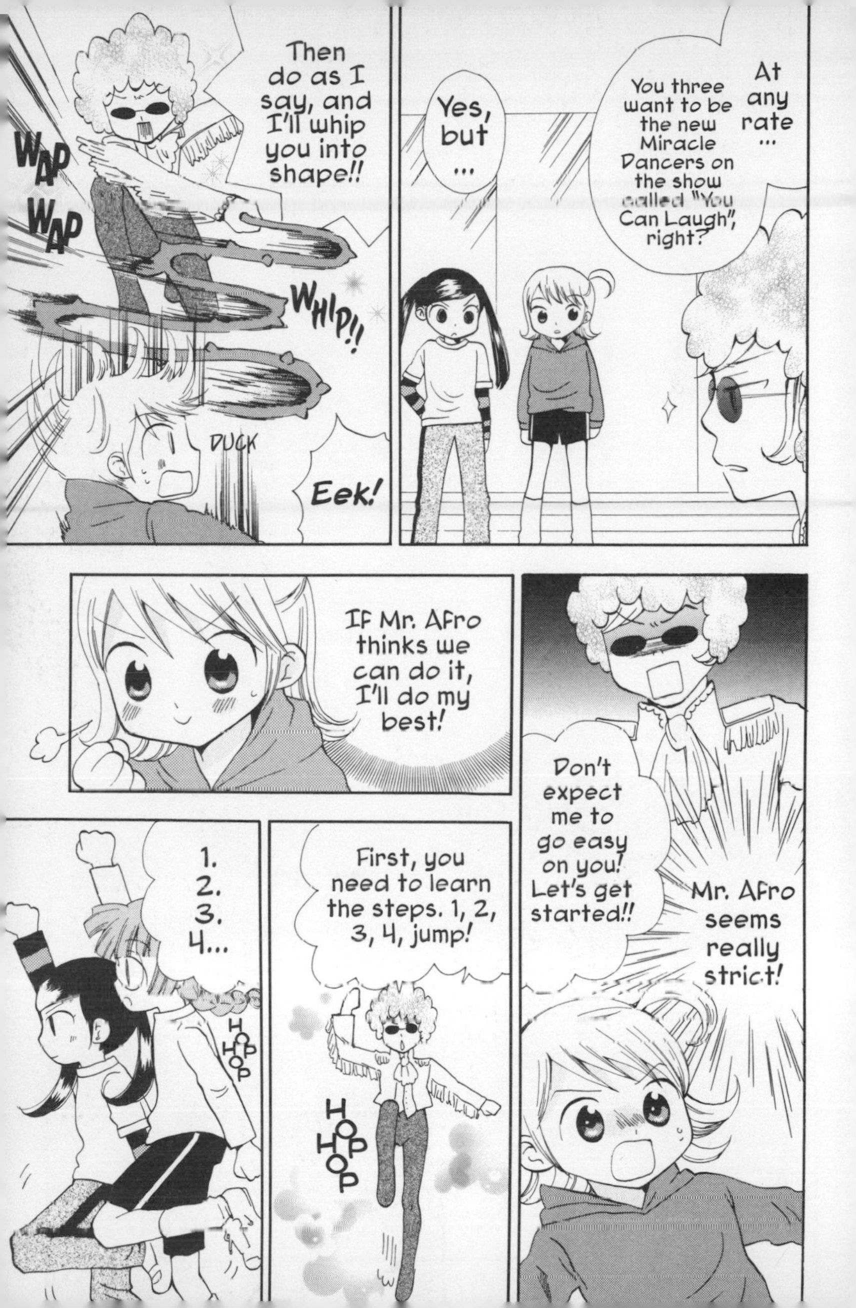
At any rate ...
You three want to be the new Miracle Dancers on the show called "You Can Laugh", right?
Yes, but ...
Then do as I say, and I'll whip you into shape!!
WAP
WAP
WHIP!!
DUCK
Eek!
Don't expect me to go easy on you! Let's get started!!
Mr. Afro seems really strict!
If Mr. Afro thinks we can do it, I'll do my best!
First, you need to learn the steps. 1, 2, 3, 4, jump!
HOP HOP
1. 2. 3. 4...
HOP HOP

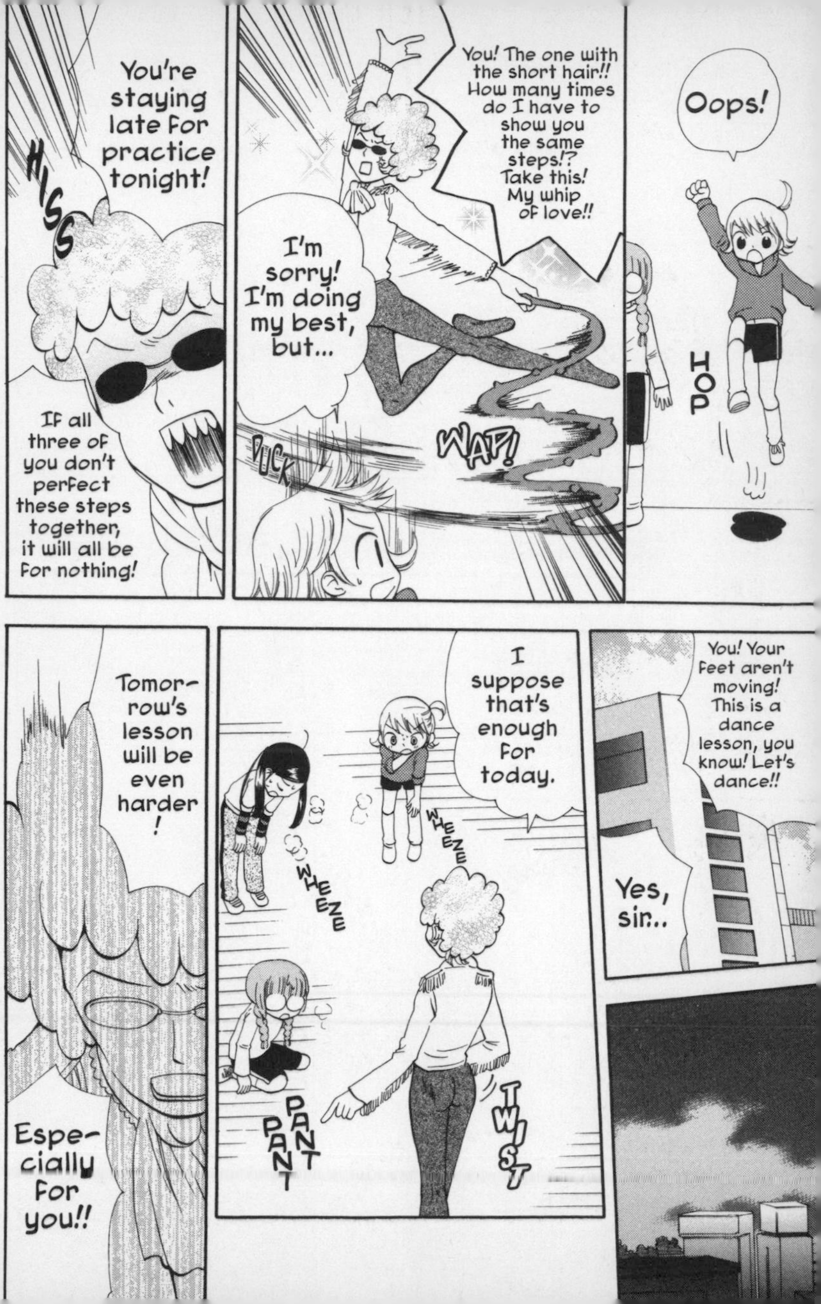
Oops!
HOP
You! The one with the short hair!! How many times do I have to show you the same steps!? Take this! My whip of love!!
I'm sorry! I'm doing my best, but...
WAP!
DUCK
You're staying late for practice tonight!
HISS
If all three of you don't perfect these steps together, it will all be for nothing!
You! Your feet aren't moving! This is a dance lesson, you know! Let's dance!!
Yes, sir..
I suppose that's enough for today.
WHEEZE
WHEEZE
PANT PANT
TWIST
Tomorrow's lesson will be even harder!
Especially for you!!

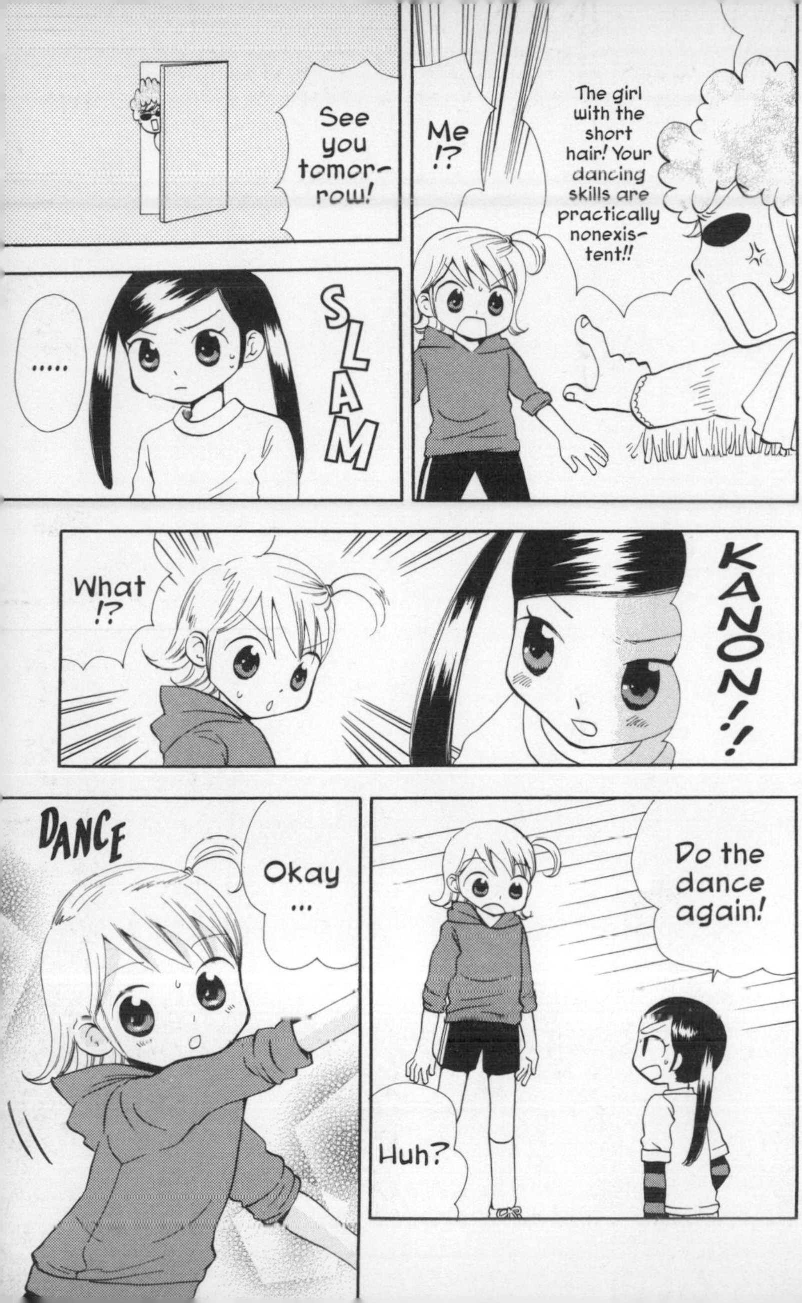

The girl with the short hair! Your dancing skills are practically nonexistent!!
Me !?
See you tomorrow!
SLAM
.....
KANON!!
What !?
Do the dance again!
Huh?
Okay ...
DANCE

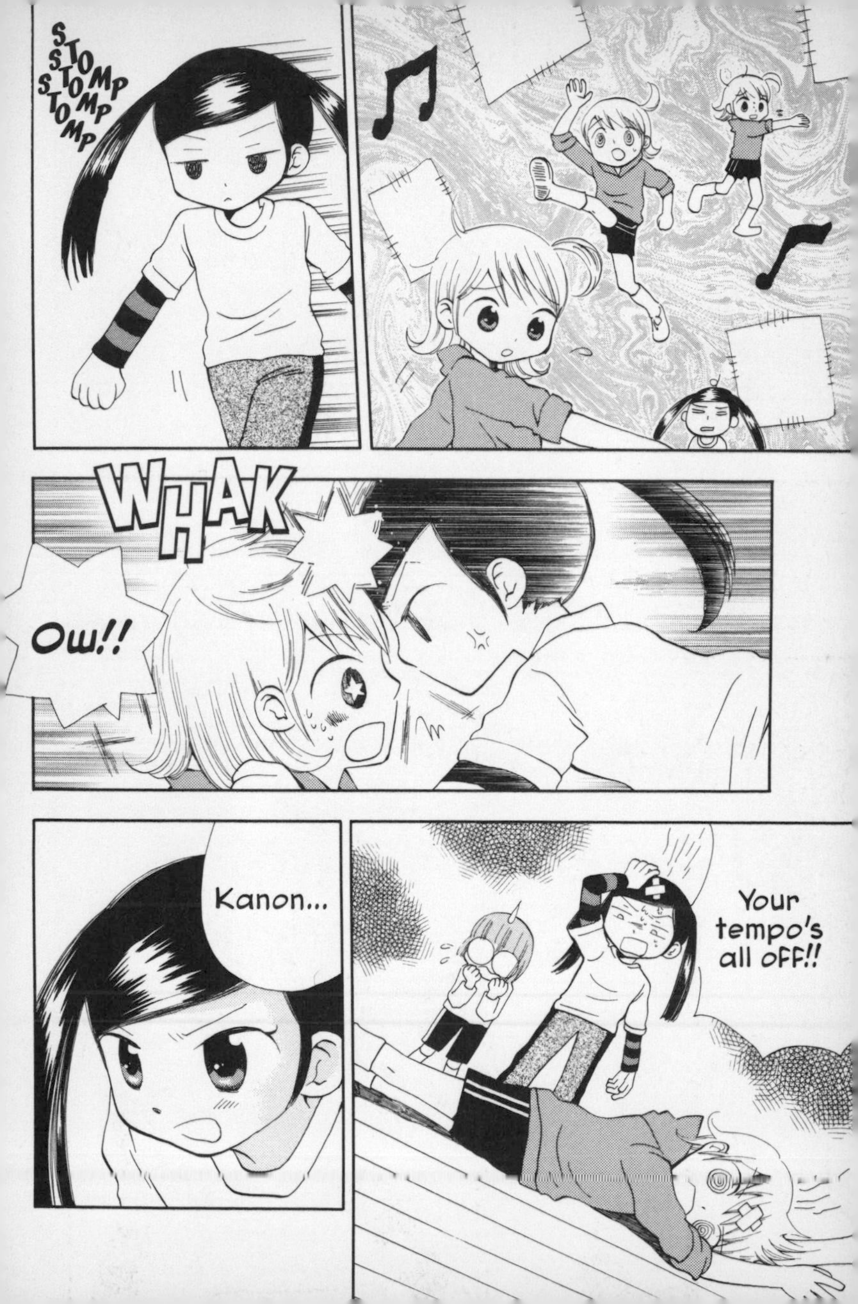
STOMP STOMP STOMP
WHAK
Ow!!
Your tempo's all off!!
Kanon...

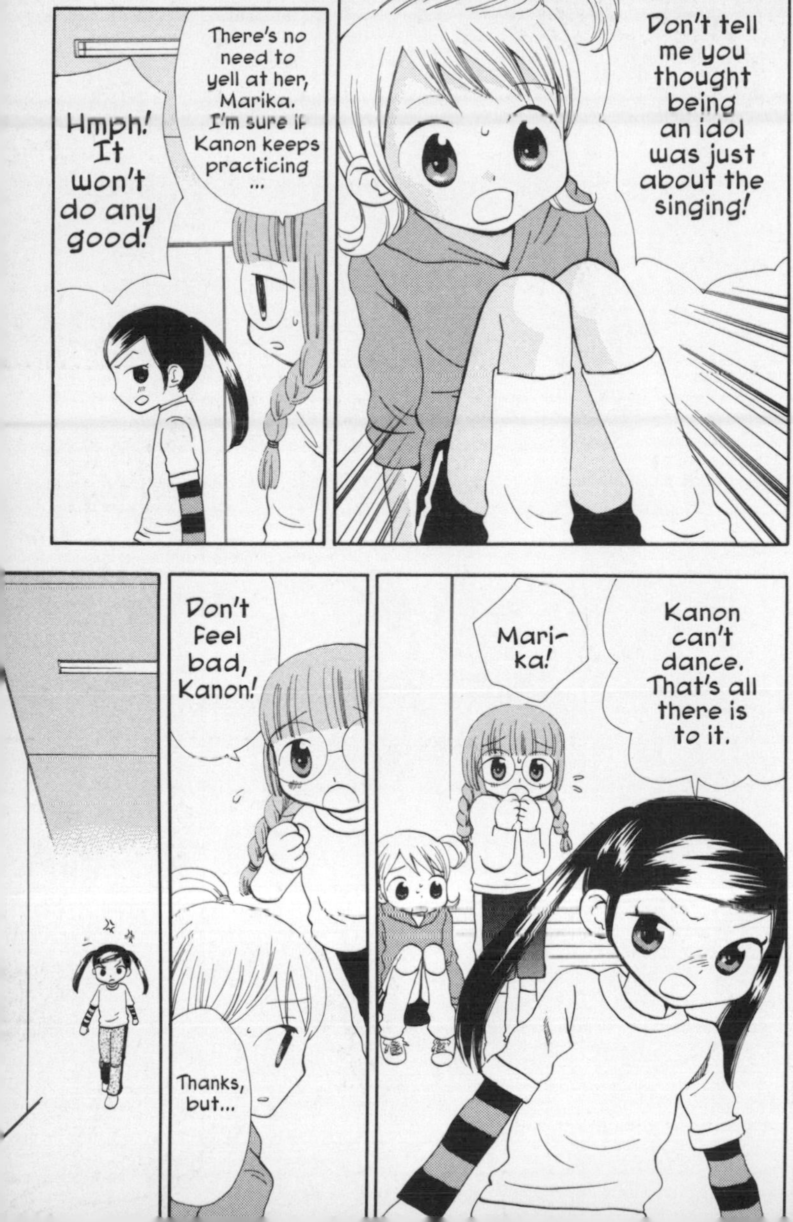
Don't tell me you thought being an idol was just about the singing!
There's no need to yell at her, Marika. I'm sure if Kanon keeps practicing ...
Hmph! It won't do any good!
Kanon can't dance. That's all there is to it.
Mari-ka!
Don't feel bad, Kanon!
Thanks, but...

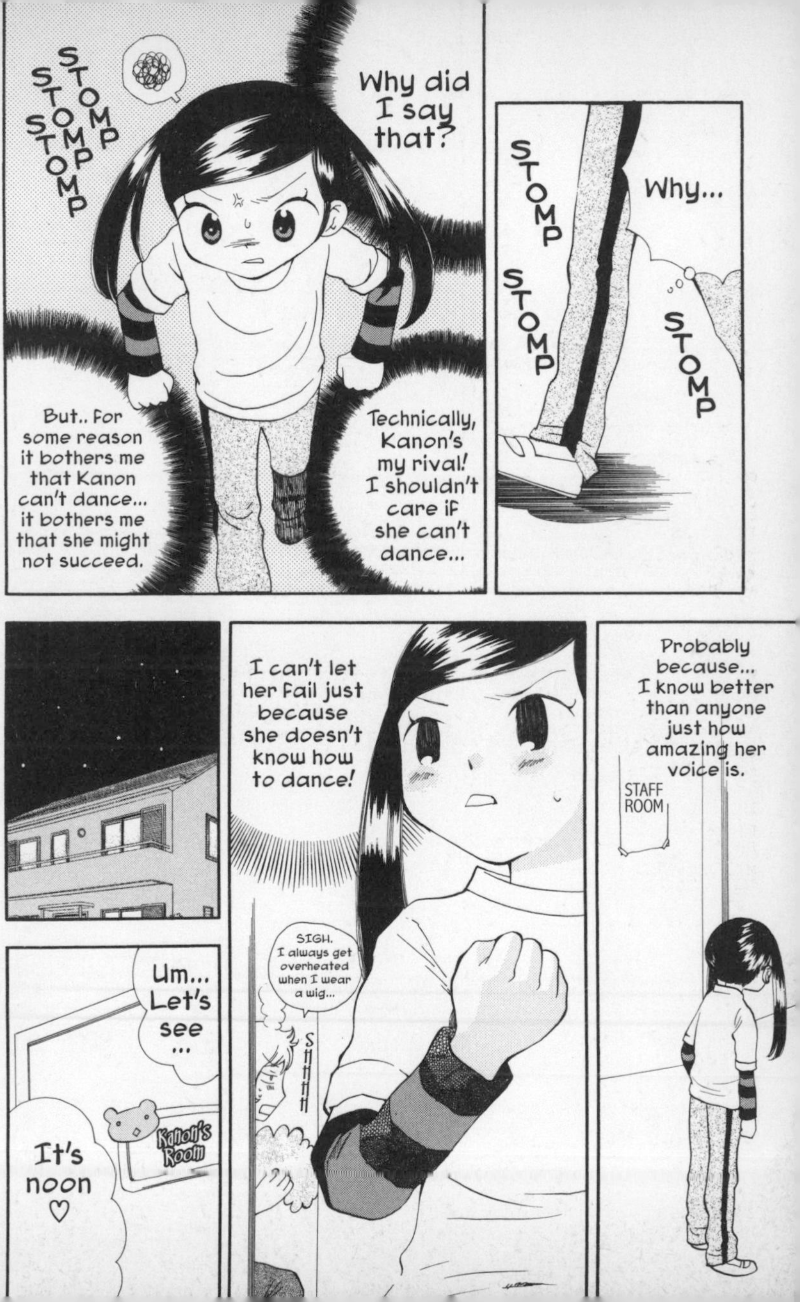
Why...
STOMP
STOMP
STOMP
Why did I say that?
STOMP
STOMP
STOMP
STOMP
Technically, Kanon's my rival! I shouldn't care if she can't dance...
But.. for some reason it bothers me that Kanon can't dance... it bothers me that she might not succeed.
Probably because... I know better than anyone just how amazing her voice is.
STAFF ROOM
I can't let her fail just because she doesn't know how to dance!
SIGH. I always get overheated when I wear a wig...
SHHHH
Um... Let's see ...
Kanon's Room
It's noon ♡

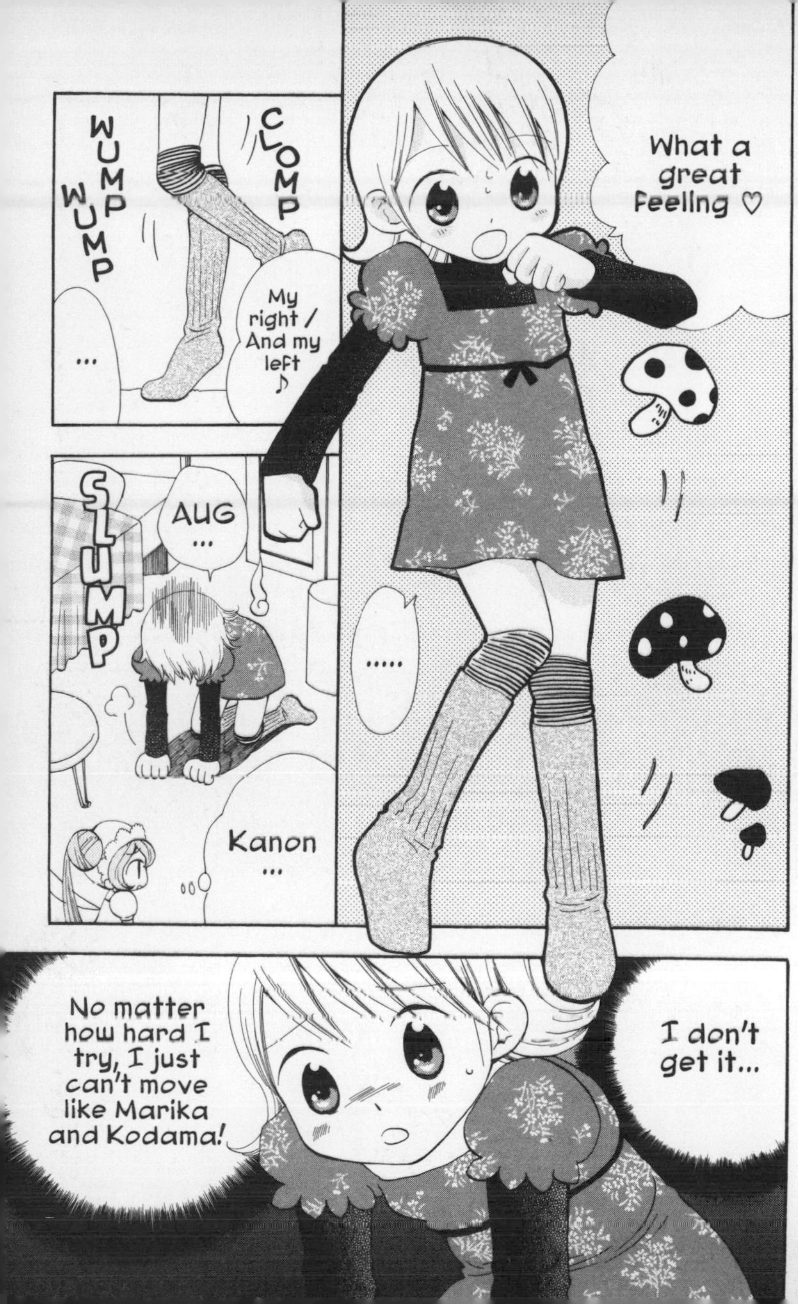
What a great feeling ♡
......
CLOMP
My right / And my left ♪
WUMP WUMP
...
AUG ...
SLUMP
Kanon ...
I don't get it...
No matter how hard I try, I just can't move like Marika and Kodama!

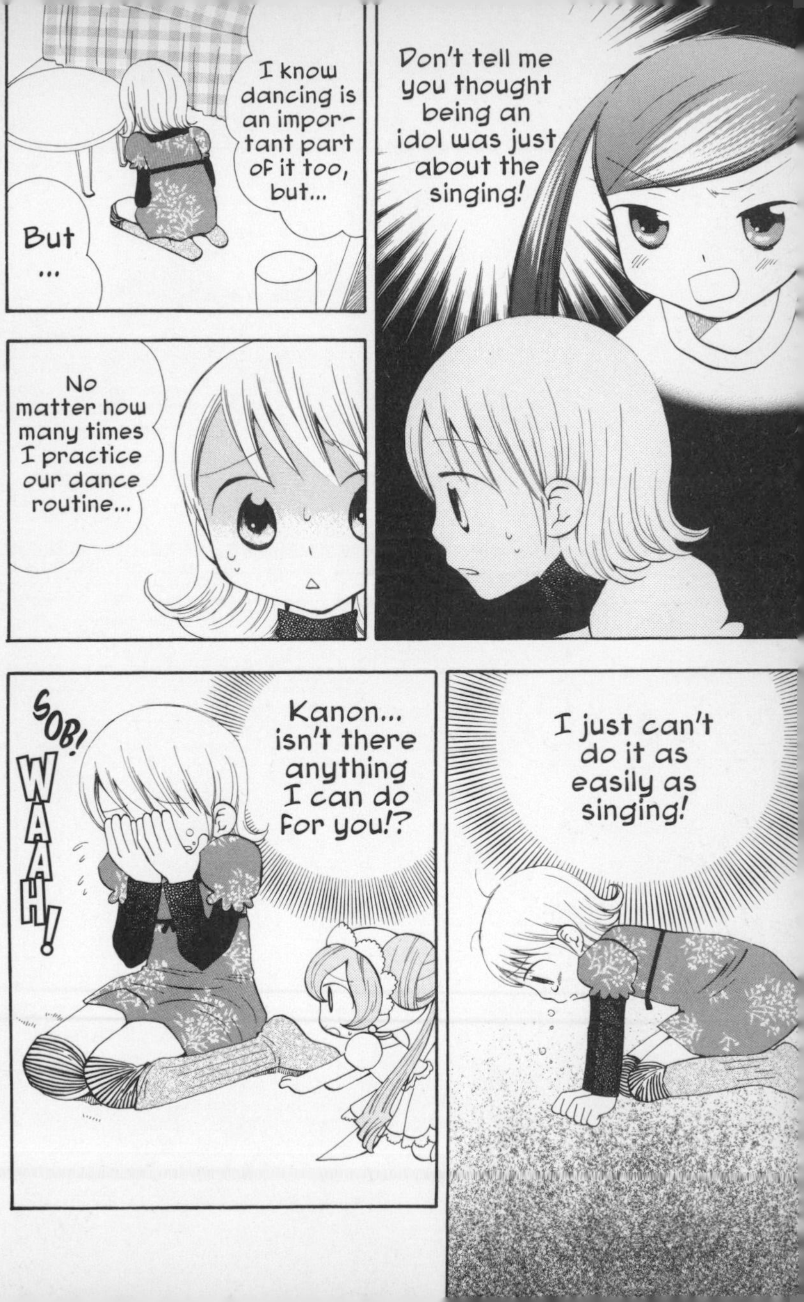
Don't tell me you thought being an idol was just about the singing!
I know dancing is an important part of it too, but...
But ...
No matter how many times I practice our dance routine...
I just can't do it as easily as singing!
Kanon... isn't there anything I can do for you!?
SOB!
WAAAH!

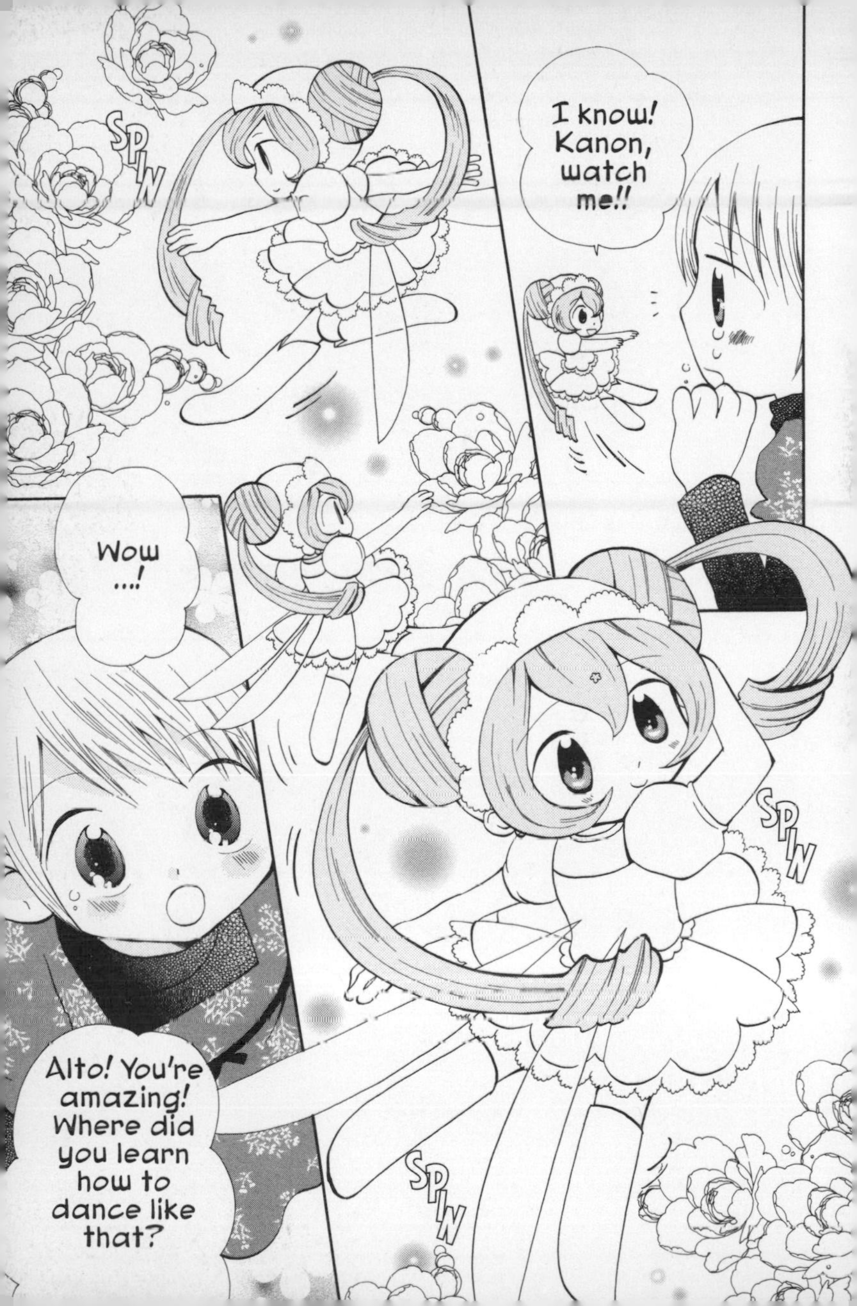
I know! Kanon, watch me!!
SPIN
SPIN
SPIN
Wow ...!
Alto! You're amazing! Where did you learn how to dance like that?

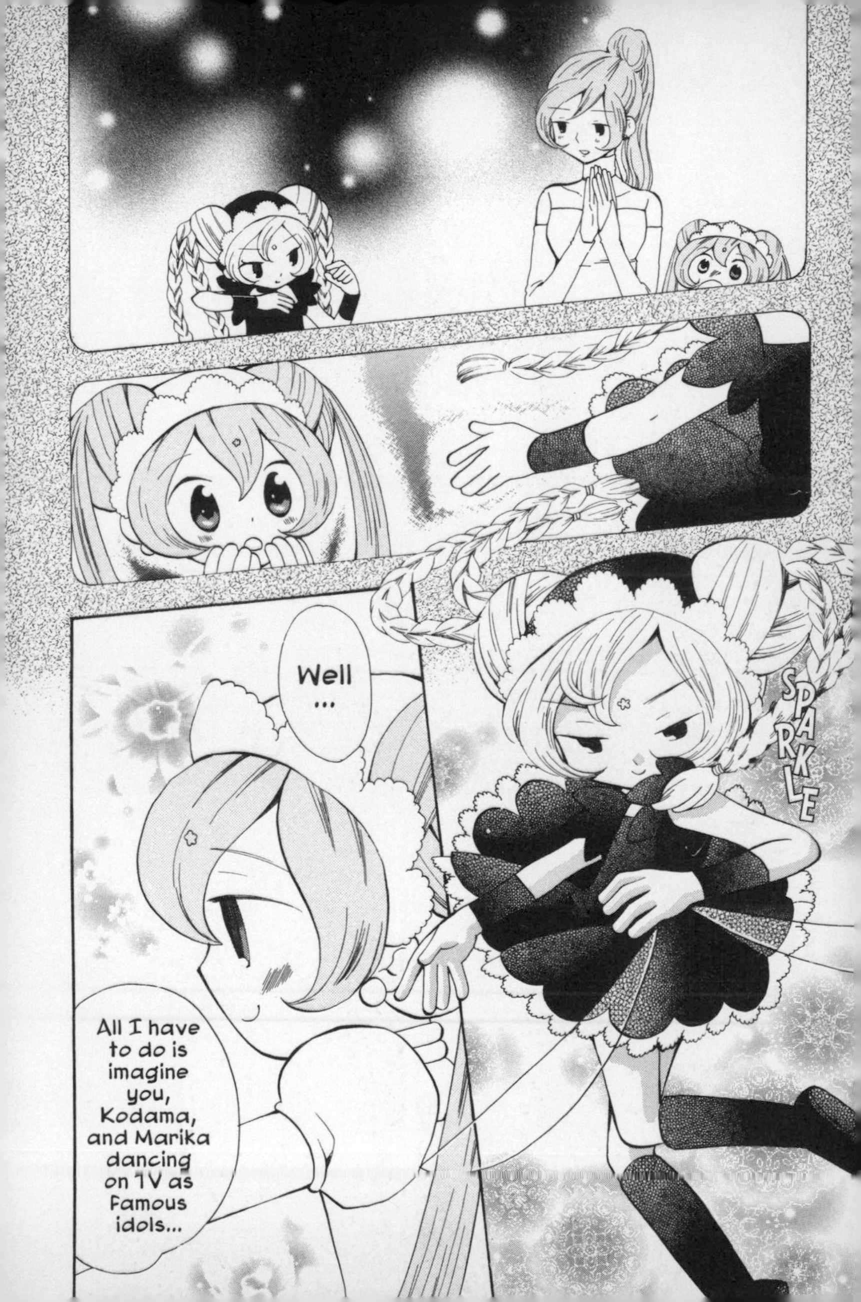
SPARKLE
Well ...
All I have to do is imagine you, Kodama, and Marika dancing on TV as famous idols...

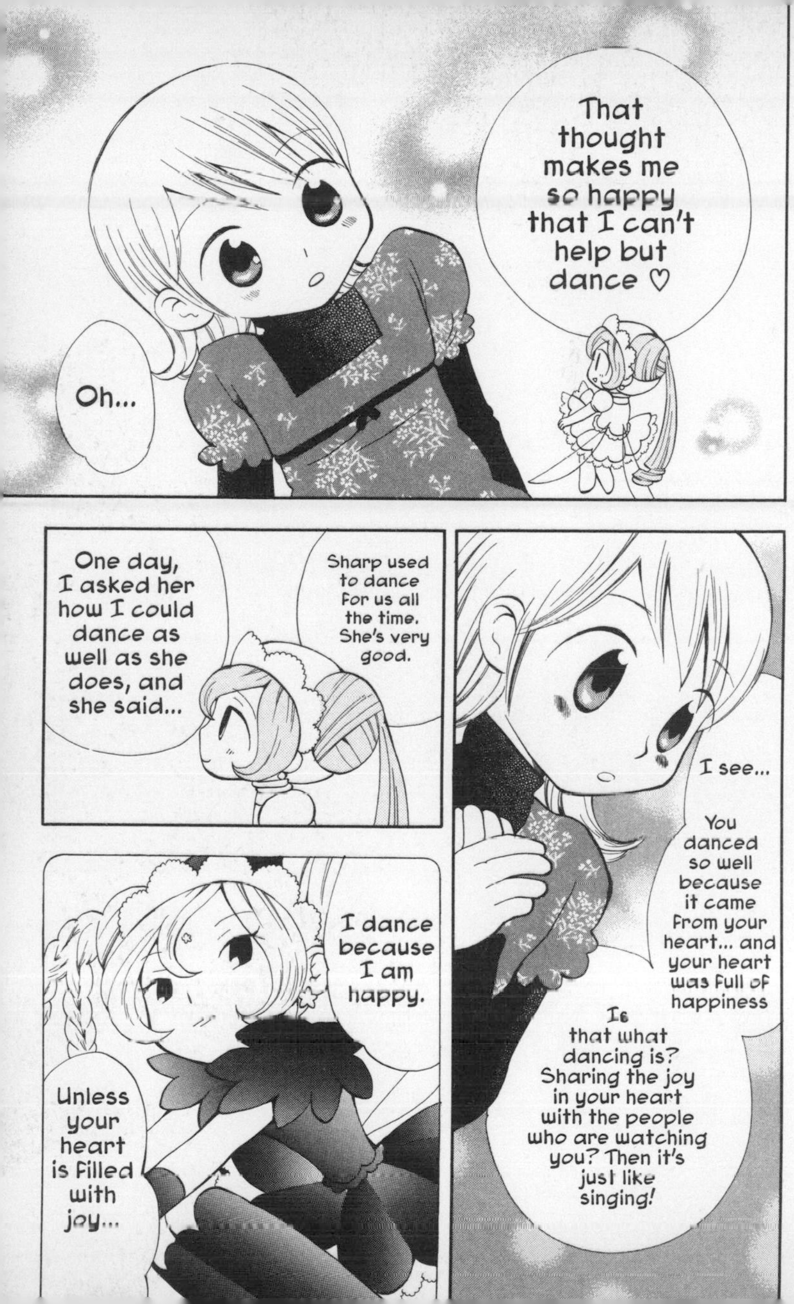
That thought makes me so happy that I can't help but dance ♡
Oh...
I see...
You danced so well because it came from your heart... and your heart was full of happiness
Is that what dancing is? Sharing the joy in your heart with the people who are watching you? Then it's just like singing!
Sharp used to dance for us all the time. She's very good.
One day, I asked her how I could dance as well as she does, and she said...
I dance because I am happy.
Unless your heart is filled with joy...

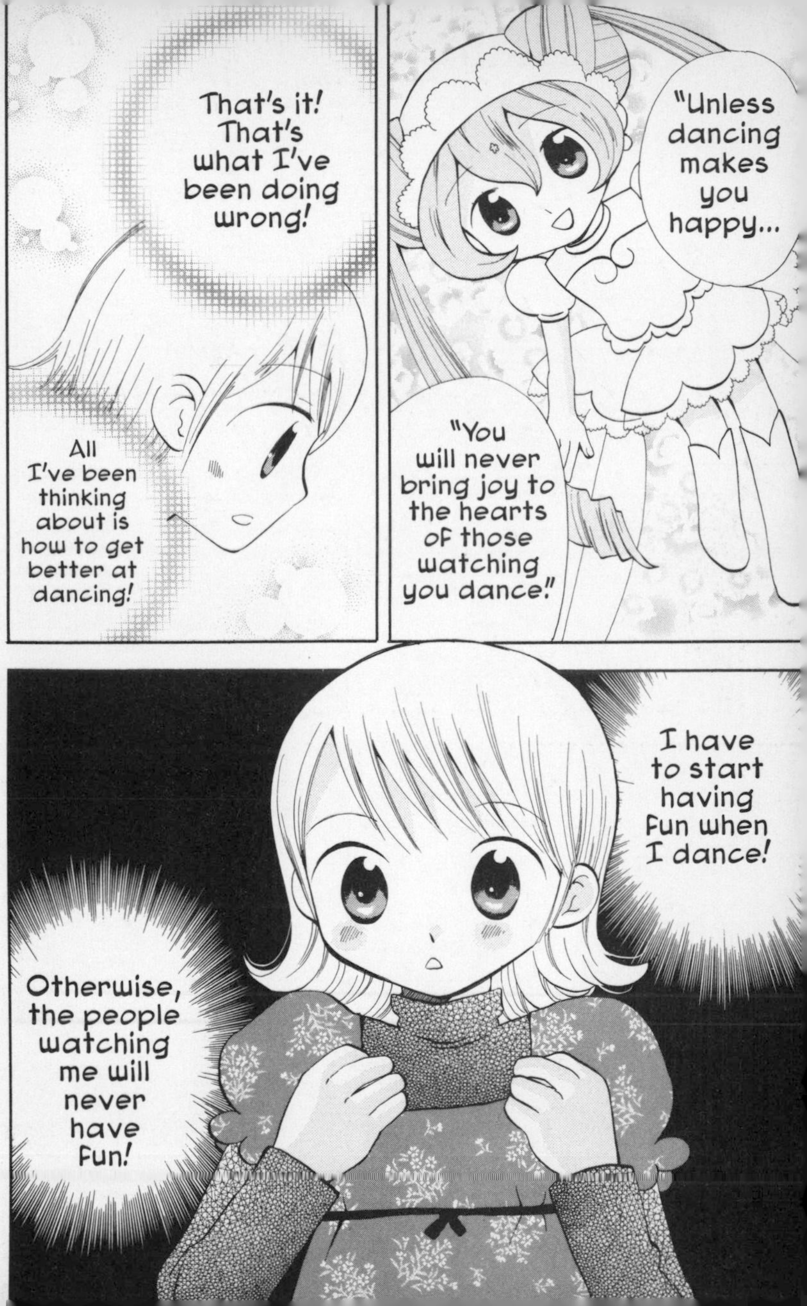
"Unless dancing makes you happy...
"You will never bring joy to the hearts of those watching you dance!"
That's it! That's what I've been doing wrong!
All I've been thinking about is how to get better at dancing!
I have to start having fun when I dance!
Otherwise, the people watching me will never have fun!

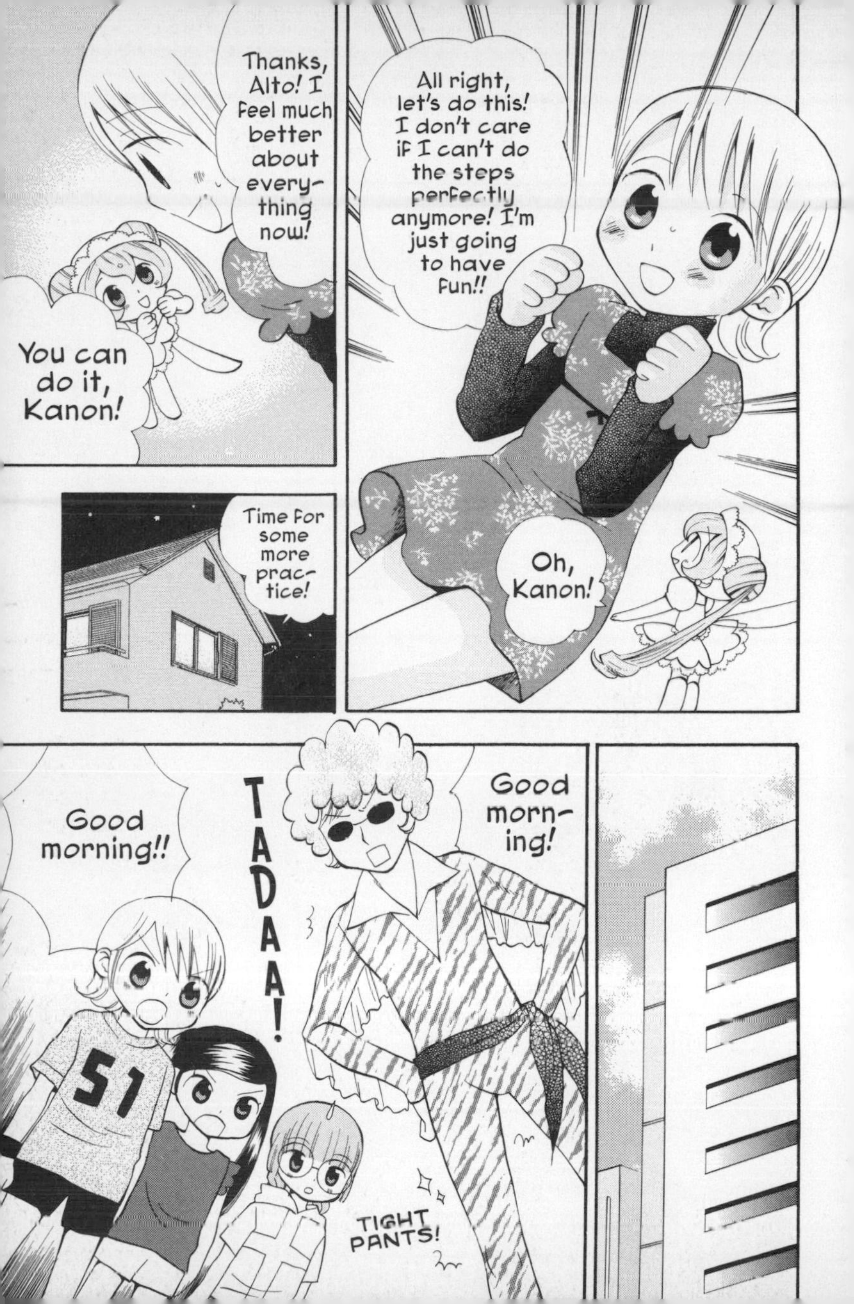
All right, let's do this! I don't care if I can't do the steps perfectly anymore! I'm just going to have fun!!
Oh, Kanon!
Thanks, Alto! I feel much better about every-thing now!
You can do it, Kanon!
Time for some more prac-tice!
Good morn-ing!
TADAA!
Good morning!!
TIGHT PANTS!

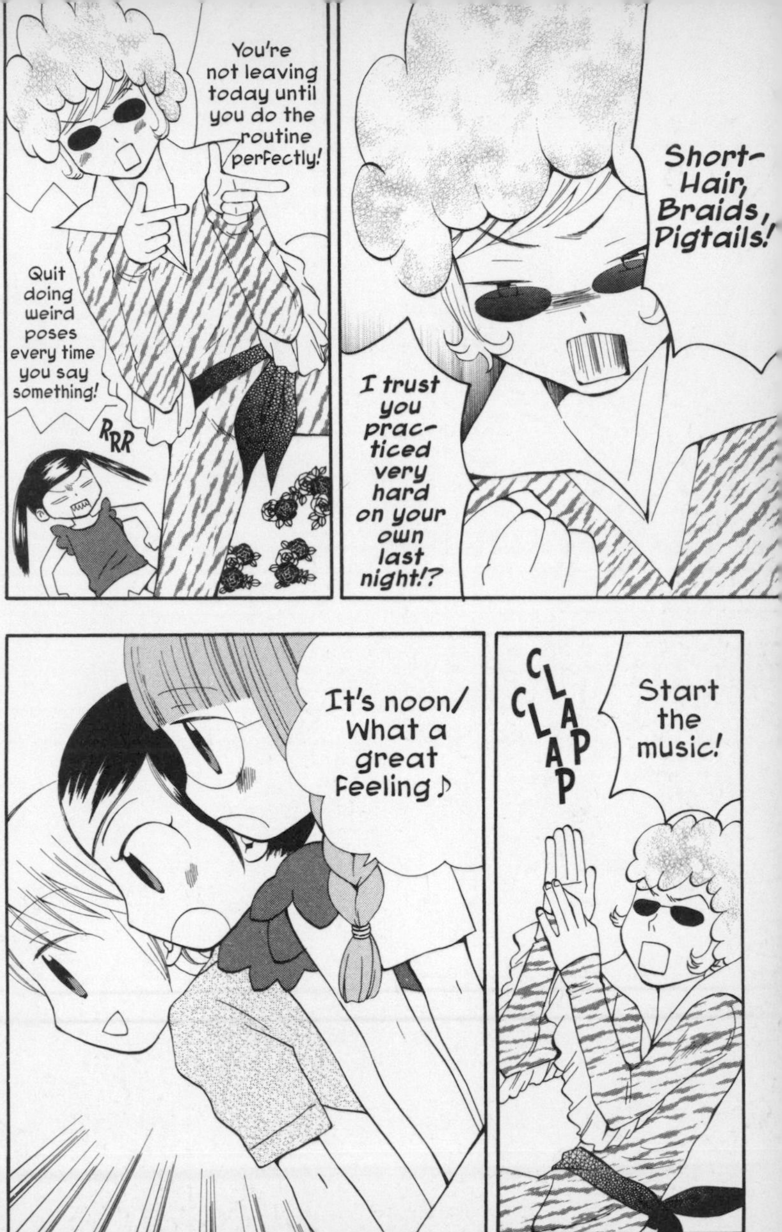
Short-Hair, Braids, Pigtails!
I trust you practiced very hard on your own last night!?
You're not leaving today until you do the routine perfectly!
Quit doing weird poses every time you say something!
RRR
CLAP CLAP
Start the music!
It's noon/ What a great feeling♪

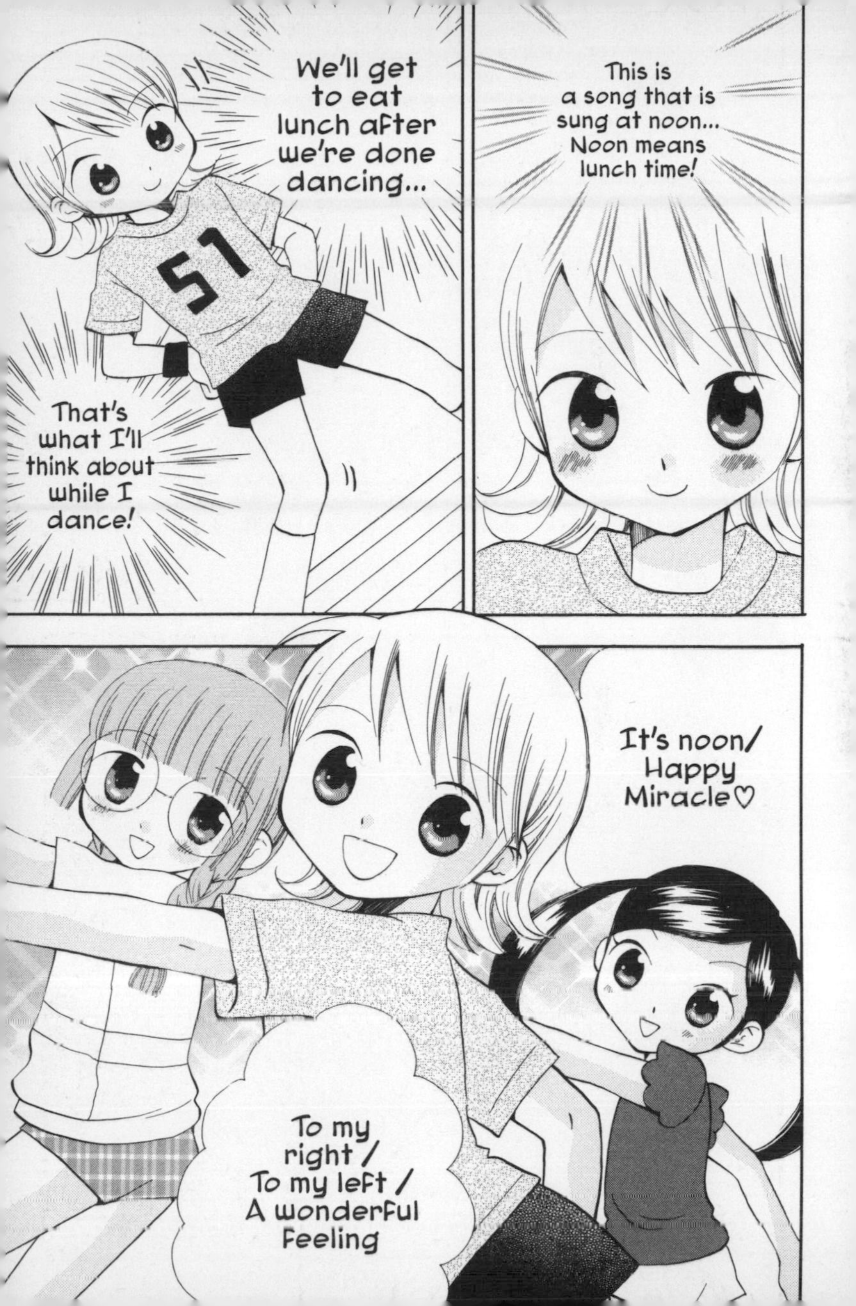
This is a song that is sung at noon... Noon means lunch time!
We'll get to eat lunch after we're done dancing...
That's what I'll think about while I dance!
It's noon/ Happy Miracle♡
To my right / To my left / A wonderful Feeling

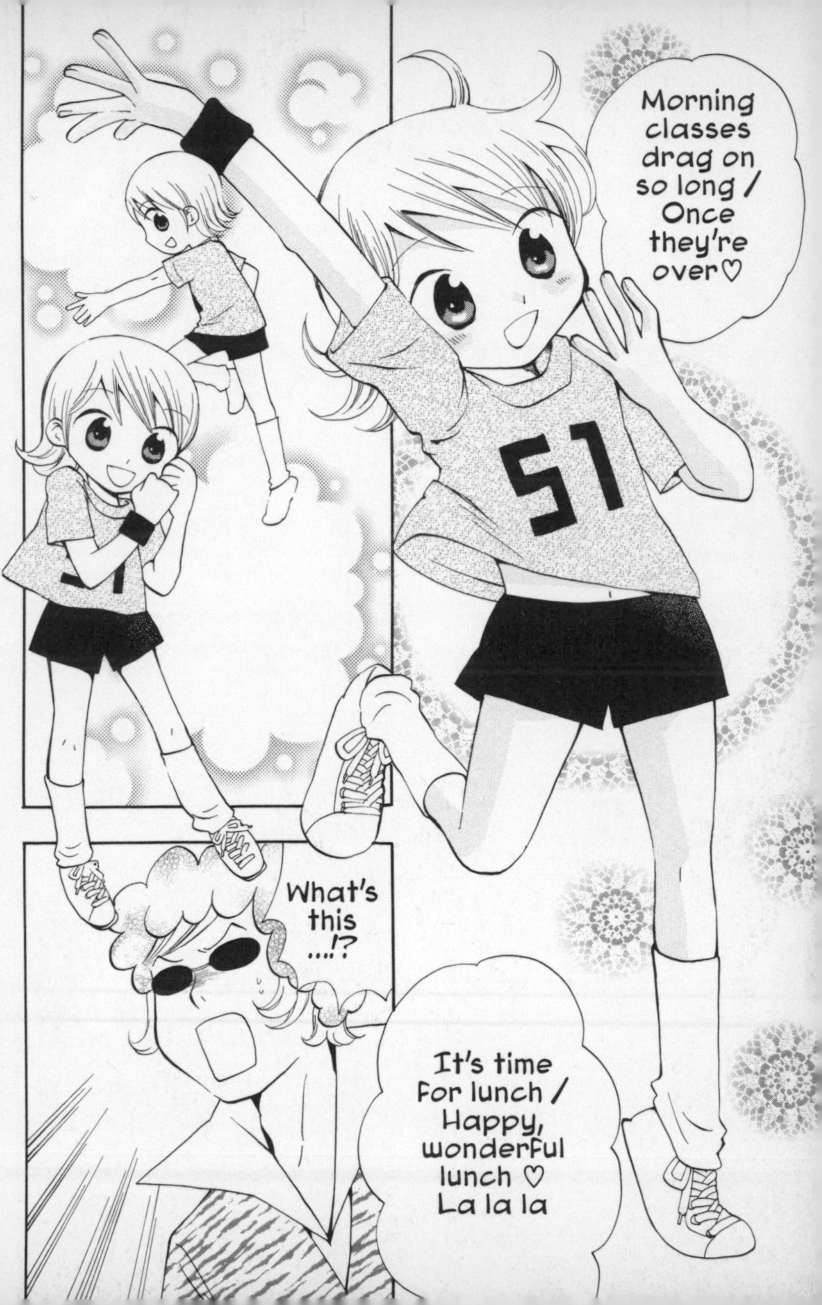
Morning classes drag on so long / Once they're over♡
It's time for lunch / Happy, wonderful lunch ♡ La la la
What's this ...!?

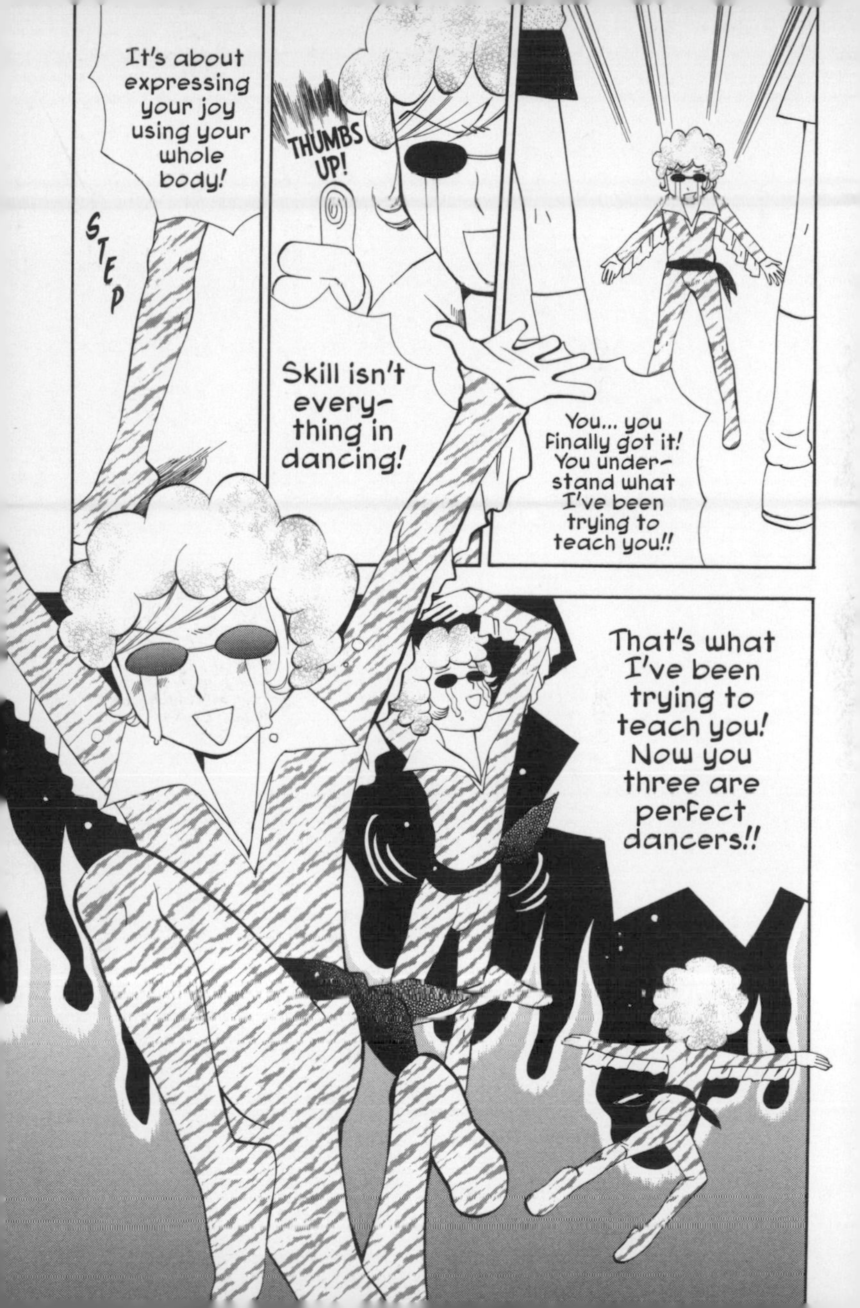
You... you finally got it! You under-stand what I've been trying to teach you!!
THUMBS UP!
Skill isn't every-thing in dancing!
It's about expressing your joy using your whole body!
STEP
That's what I've been trying to teach you! Now you three are perfect dancers!!

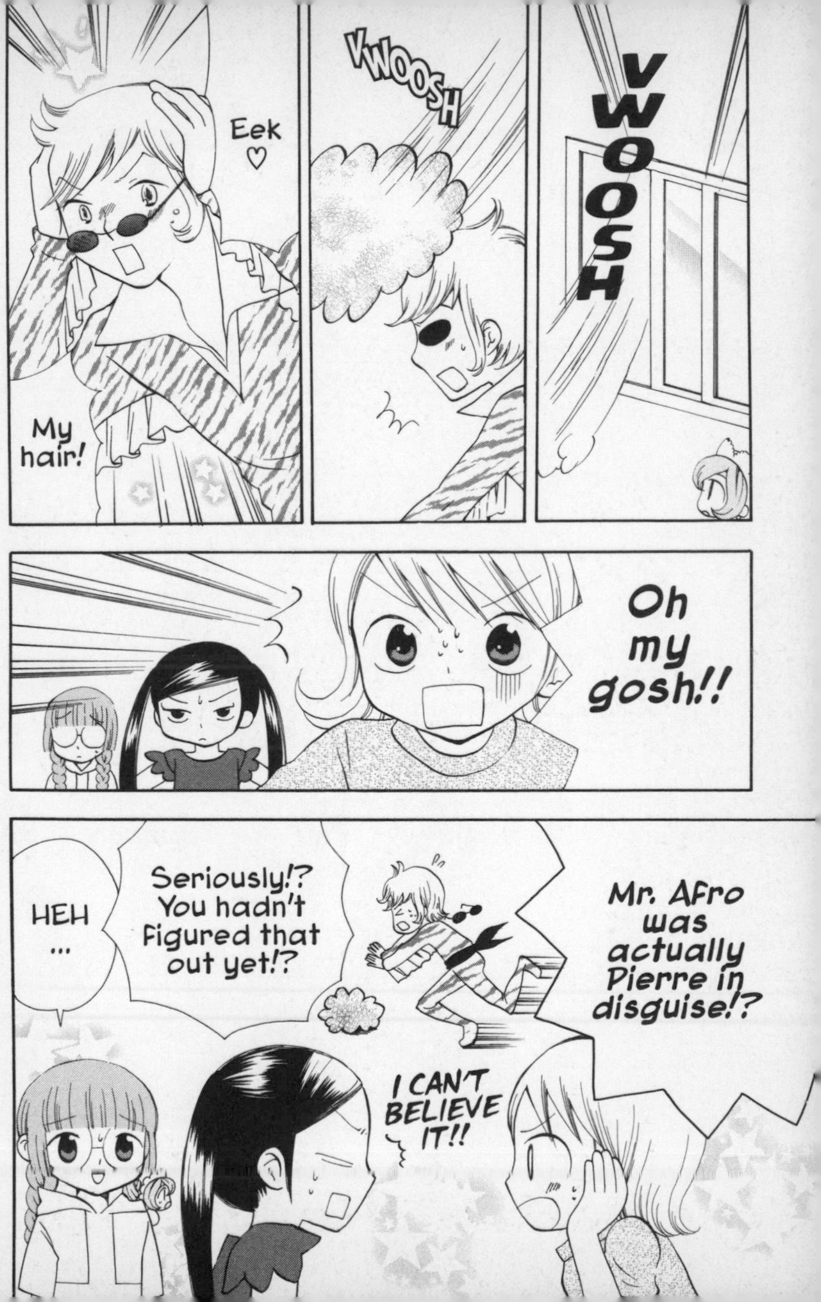
VWOOSH
VWOOSH
Eek ♡
My hair!
Oh my gosh!!
Mr. Afro was actually Pierre in disguise!?
I CAN'T BELIEVE IT!!
Seriously!? You hadn't figured that out yet!?
HEH ...

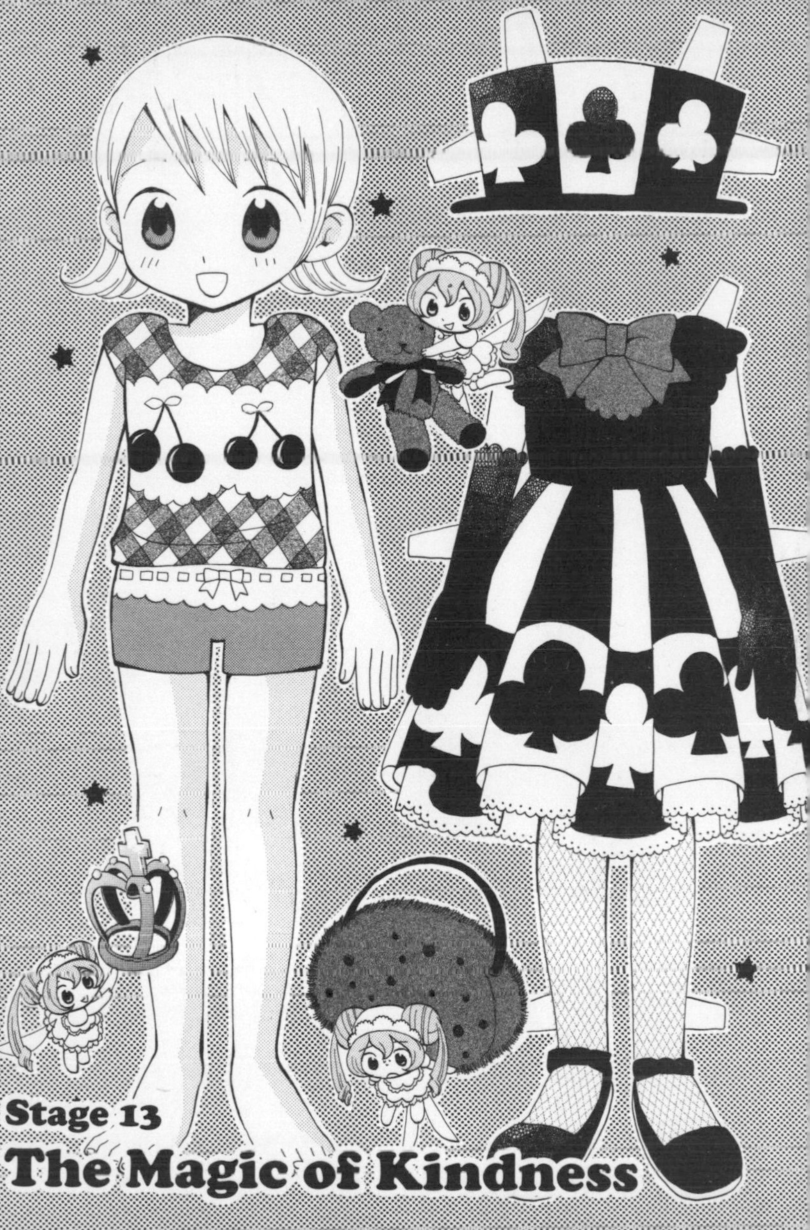

## Stage 13
# The Magic of Kindness

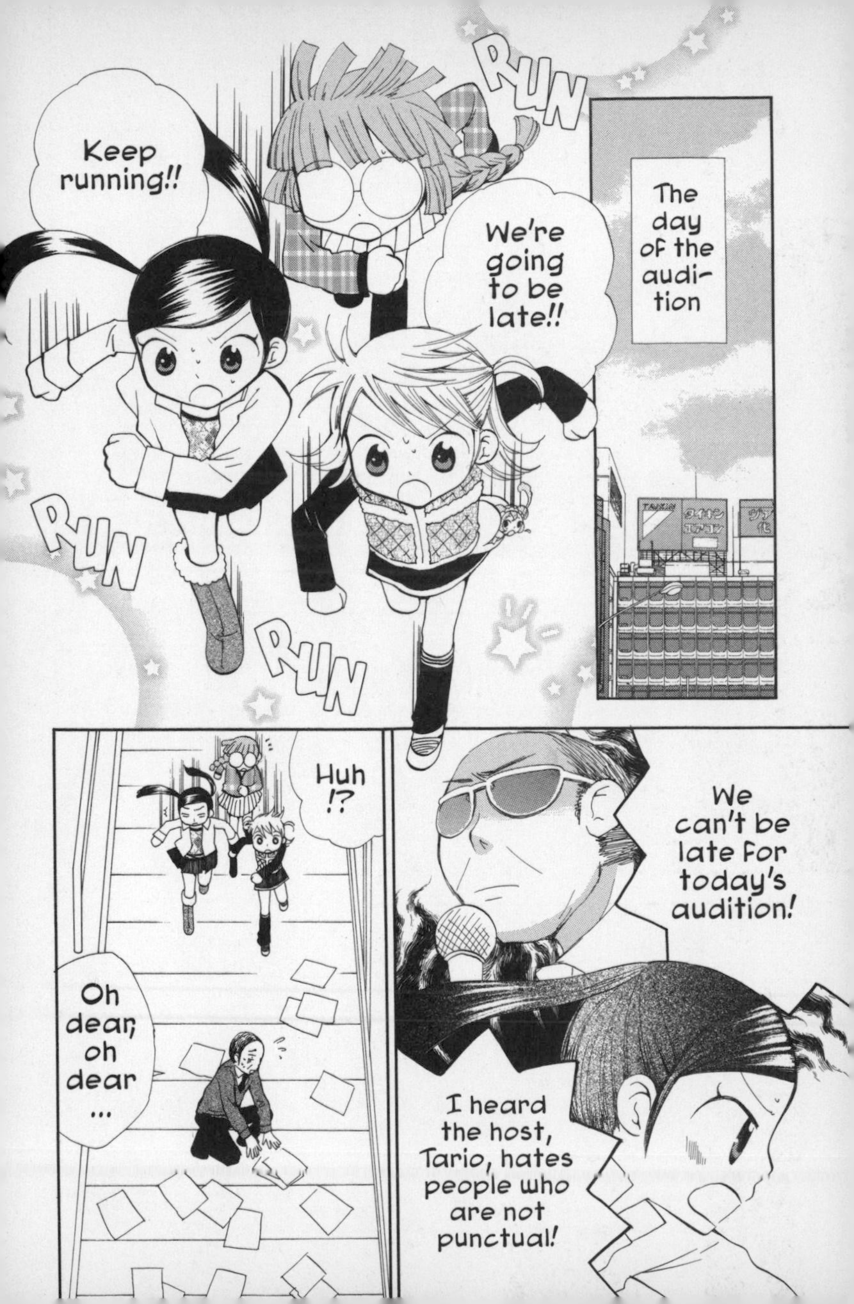
The day of the audition
RUN
We're going to be late!!
Keep running!!
RUN
RUN
We can't be late for today's audition!
I heard the host, Tario, hates people who are not punctual!
Huh!?
Oh dear, oh dear ...

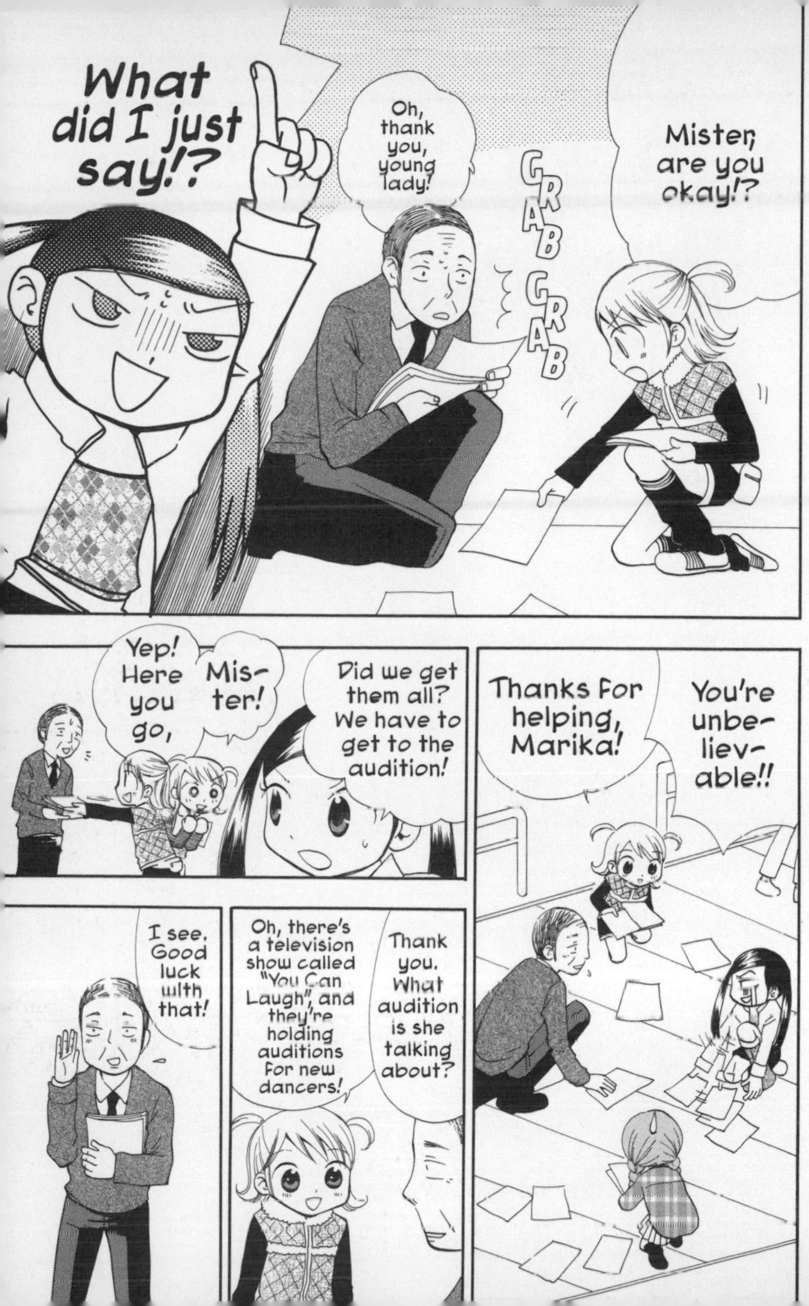
Mister, are you okay!?
GRAB GRAB
Oh, thank you, young lady!
What did I just say!?
You're unbe-liev-able!!
Thanks for helping, Marika!
Did we get them all? We have to get to the audition!
Yep! Here you go,
Mis-ter!
Thank you. What audition is she talking about?
Oh, there's a television show called "You Can Laugh", and they're holding auditions for new dancers!
I see. Good luck with that!

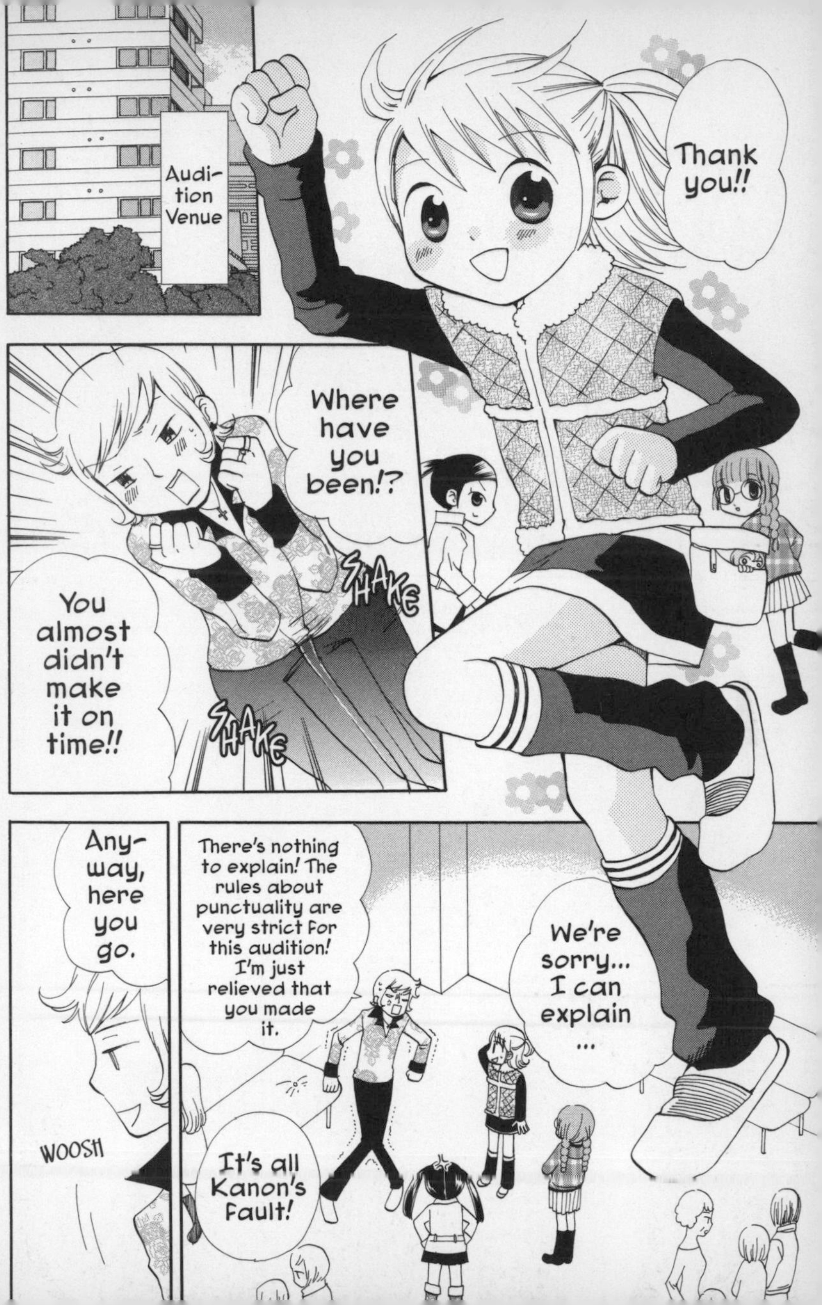
Thank you!!
Audition Venue
Where have you been!?
SHAKE
You almost didn't make it on time!!
SHAKE
We're sorry... I can explain ...
There's nothing to explain! The rules about punctuality are very strict for this audition! I'm just relieved that you made it.
It's all Kanon's fault!
Anyway, here you go.
WOOSH

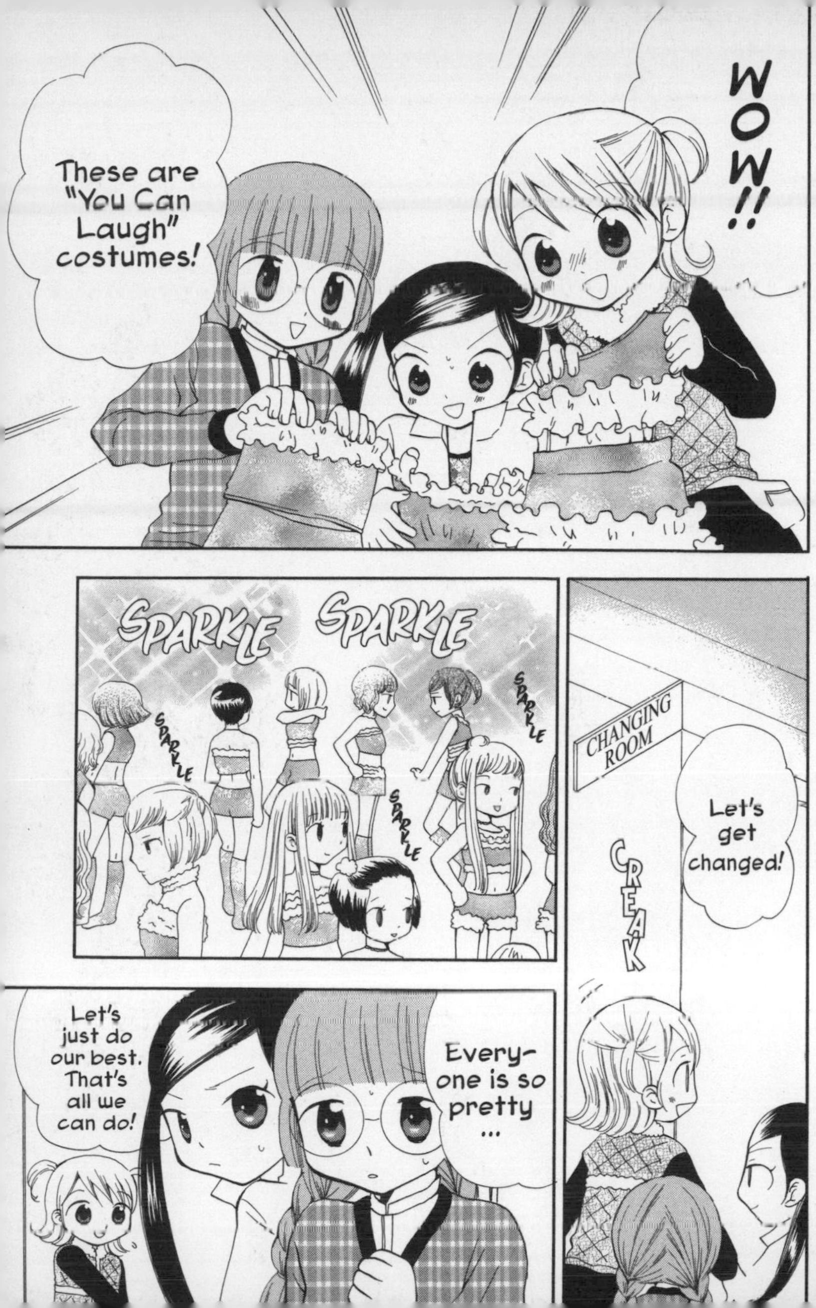
WOW!!
These are "You Can Laugh" costumes!
CHANGING ROOM
Let's get changed!
CREAK
SPARKLE SPARKLE
SPARKLE
SPARKLE
SPARKLE
Every-one is so pretty ...
Let's just do our best. That's all we can do!

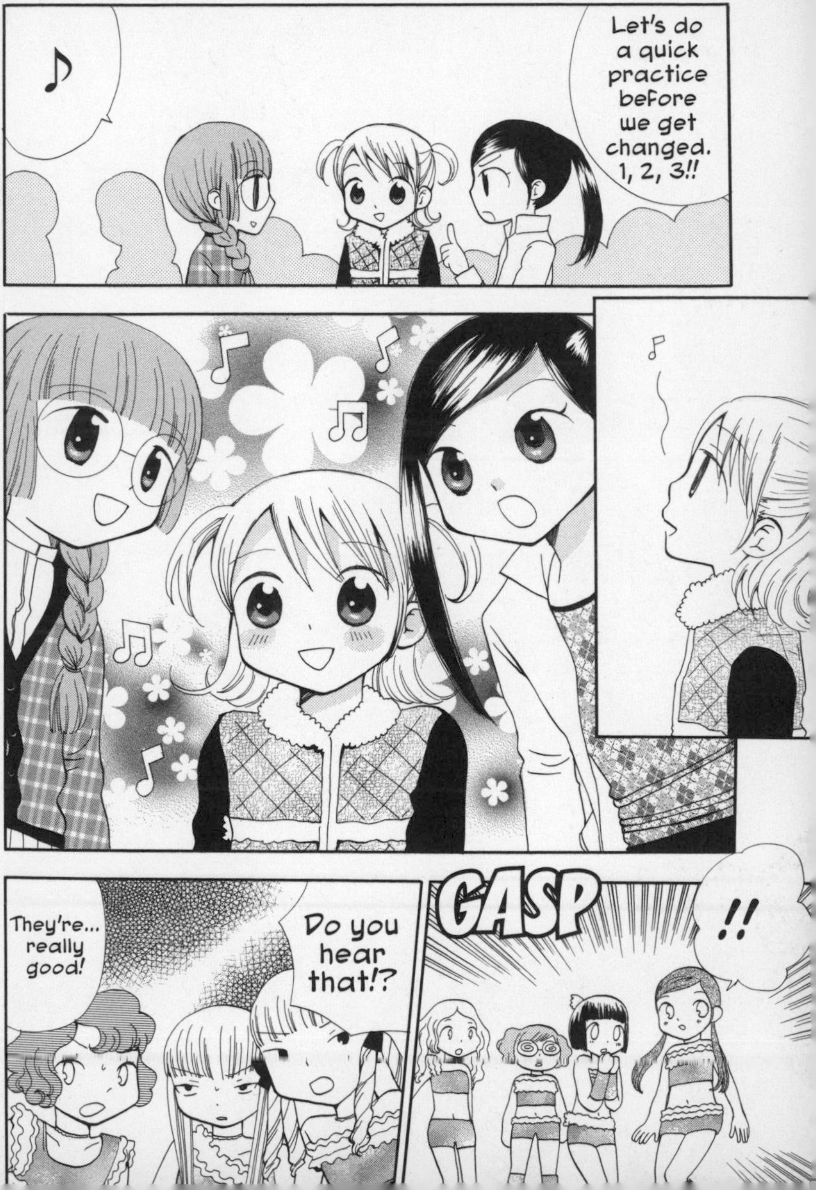
Let's do a quick practice before we get changed. 1, 2, 3!!
♪
!!
GASP
Do you hear that!?
They're... really good!

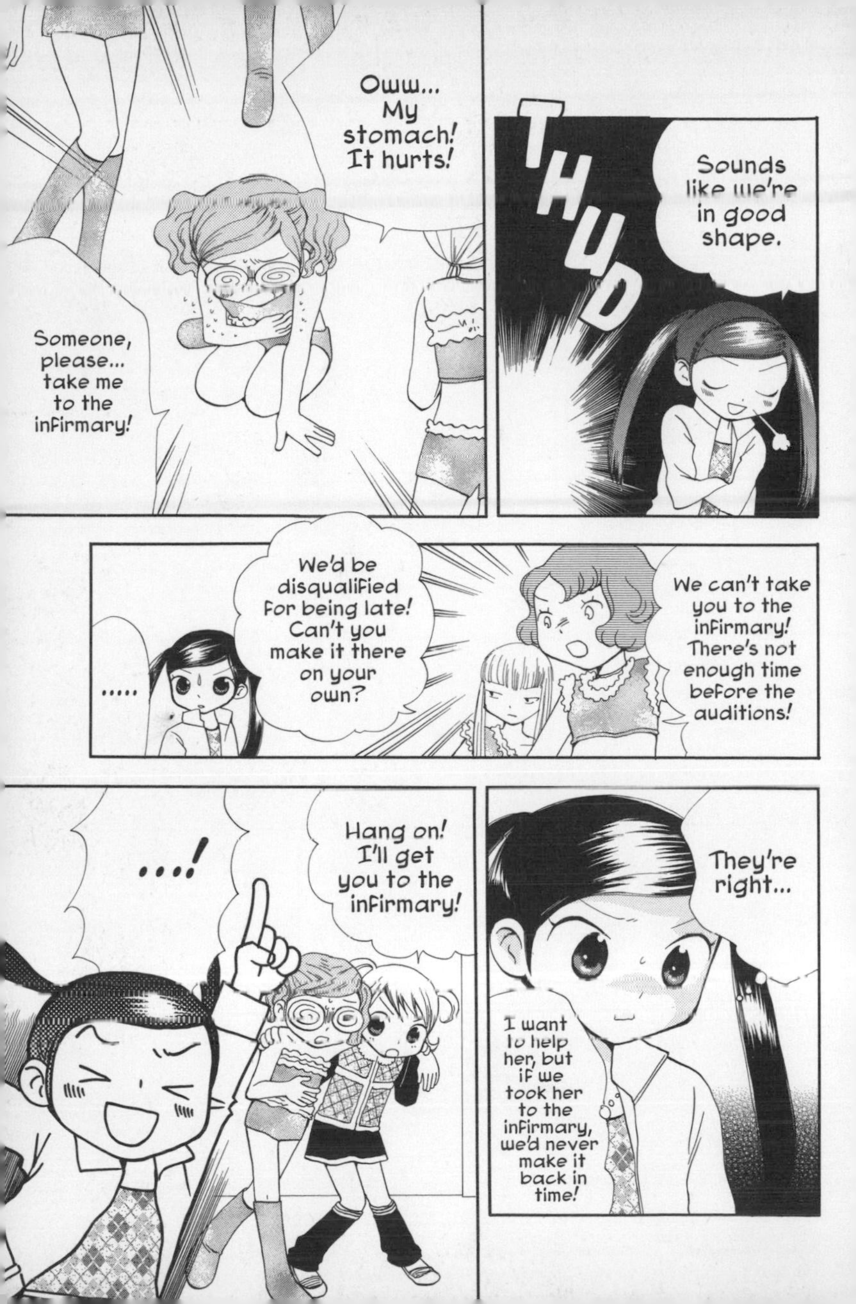
THUD
Sounds like we're in good shape.
Oww... My stomach! It hurts!
Someone, please... take me to the infirmary!
We can't take you to the infirmary! There's not enough time before the auditions!
We'd be disqualified for being late! Can't you make it there on your own?
.....
They're right...
I want to help her, but if we took her to the infirmary, we'd never make it back in time!
Hang on! I'll get you to the infirmary!
...!

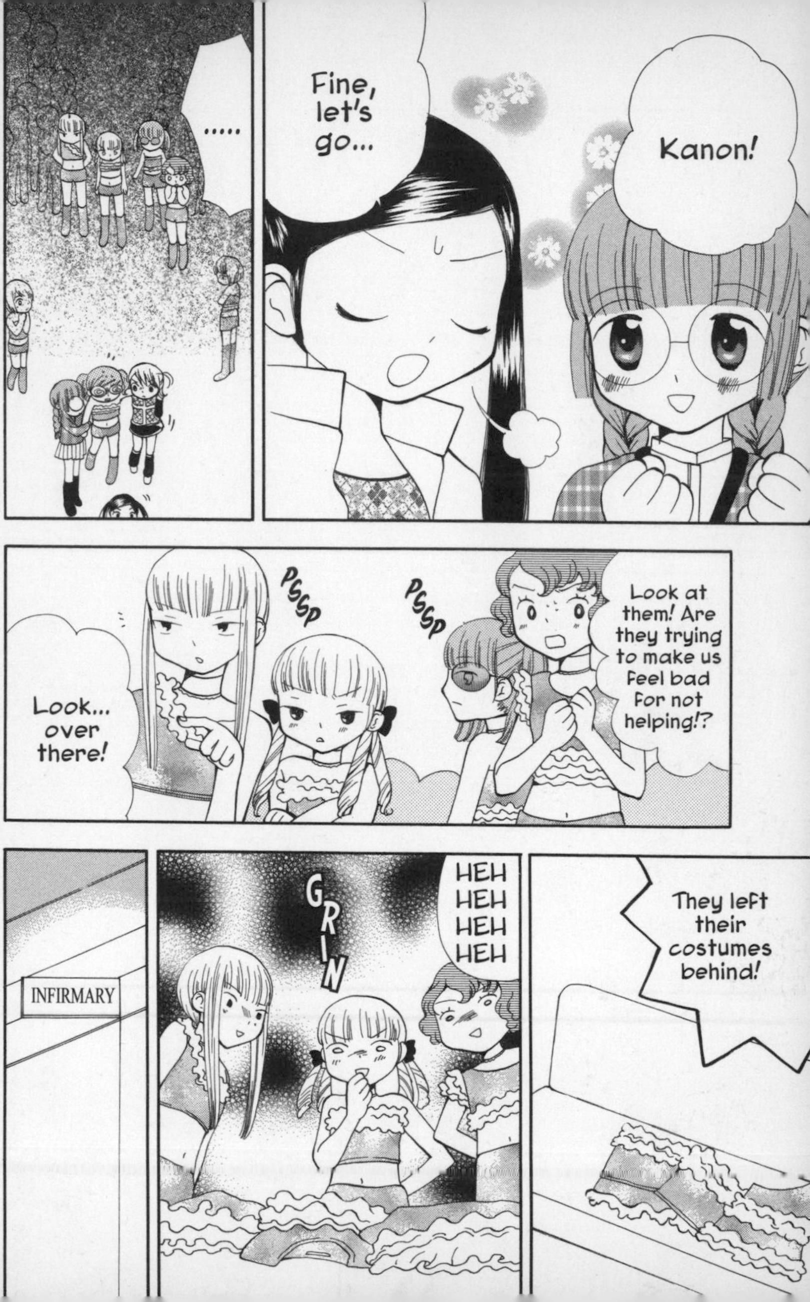
Kanon!
Fine, let's go...
.....
Look at them! Are they trying to make us feel bad for not helping!?
PSSP
PSSP
Look... over there!
They left their costumes behind!
HEH HEH HEH HEH
GRIN
INFIRMARY

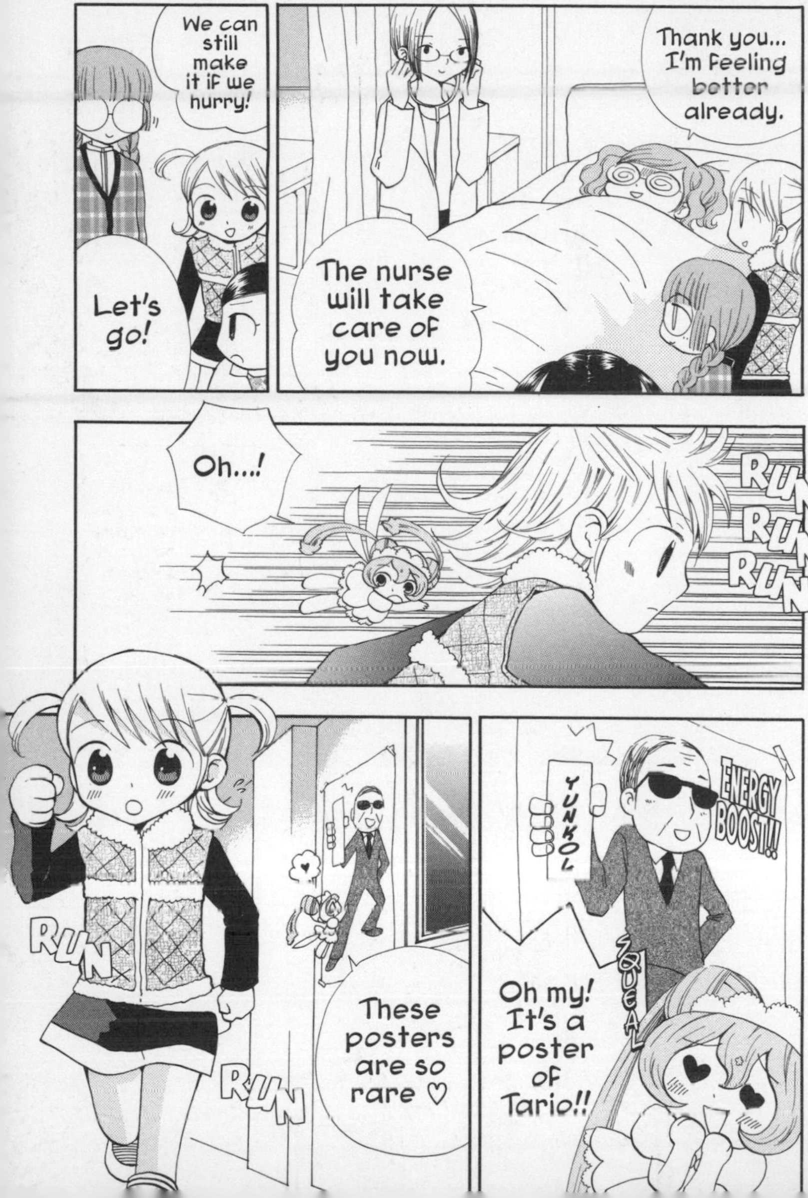
Thank you... I'm feeling better already.
The nurse will take care of you now.
We can still make it if we hurry!
Let's go!
Oh...!
RUN
RUN
RUN
YUNKOL
ENERGY BOOST!!
Oh my! It's a poster of Tario!!
SQUEAL
These posters are so rare ♡
RUN
RUN

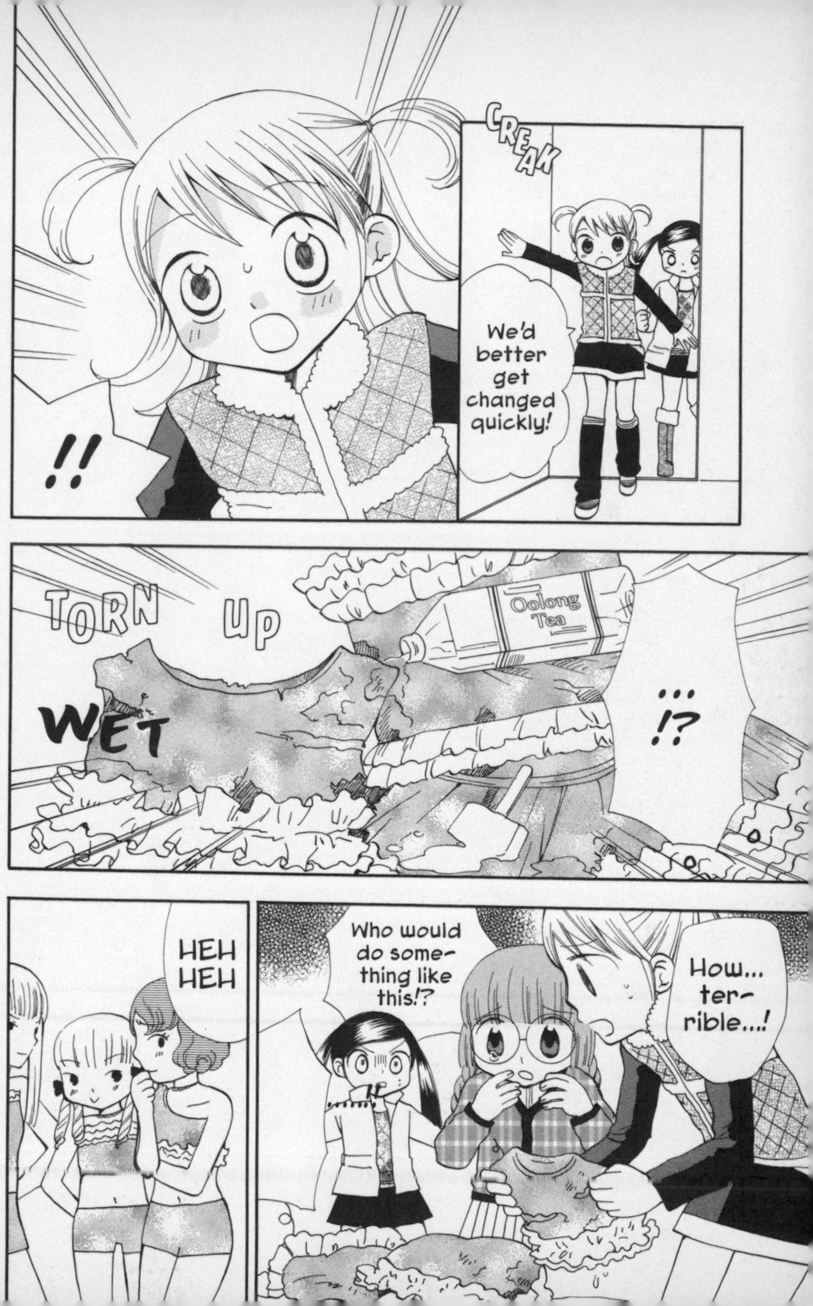
CREAK
We'd better get changed quickly!
!!
Oolong Tea
...!?
TORN UP
WET
How... terrible...!
Who would do something like this!?
HEH HEH

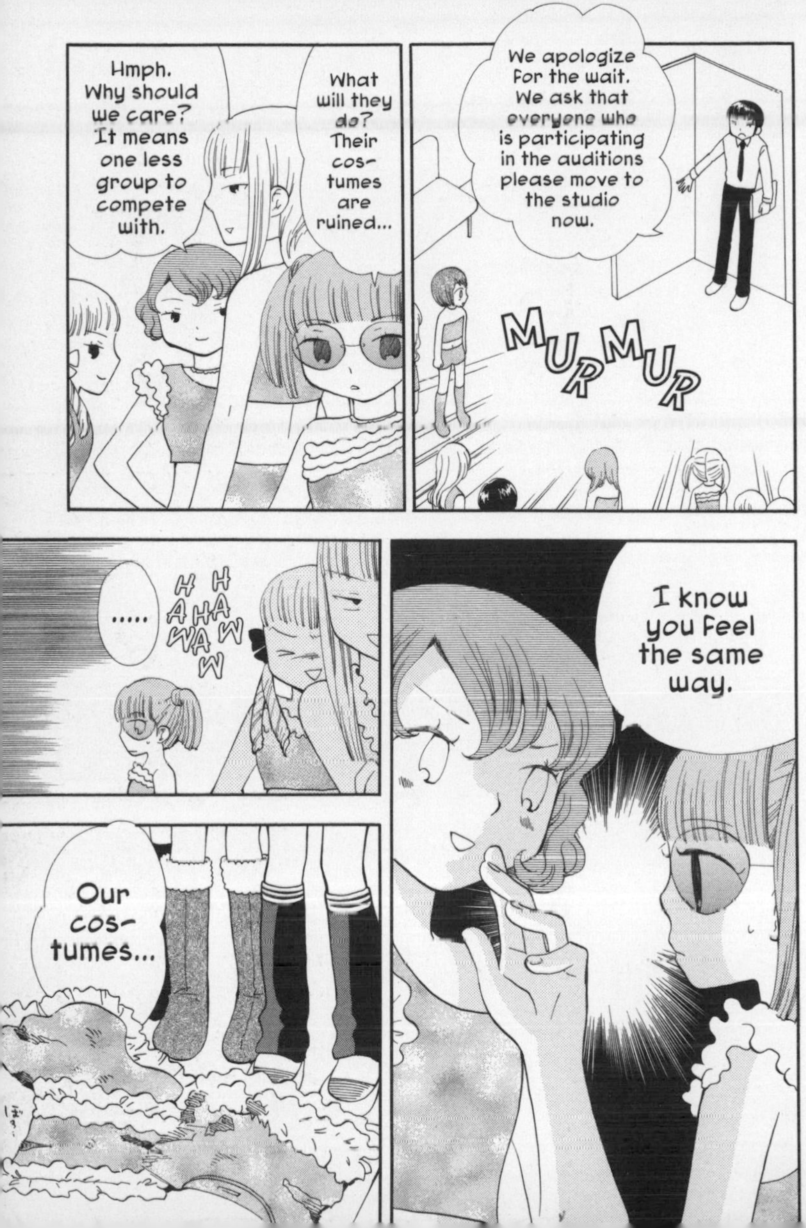
We apologize for the wait. We ask that everyone who is participating in the auditions please move to the studio now.
MURMUR MURMUR
What will they do? Their cos-tumes are ruined...
Hmph. Why should we care? It means one less group to compete with.
I know you feel the same way.
.....
Our cos-tumes...

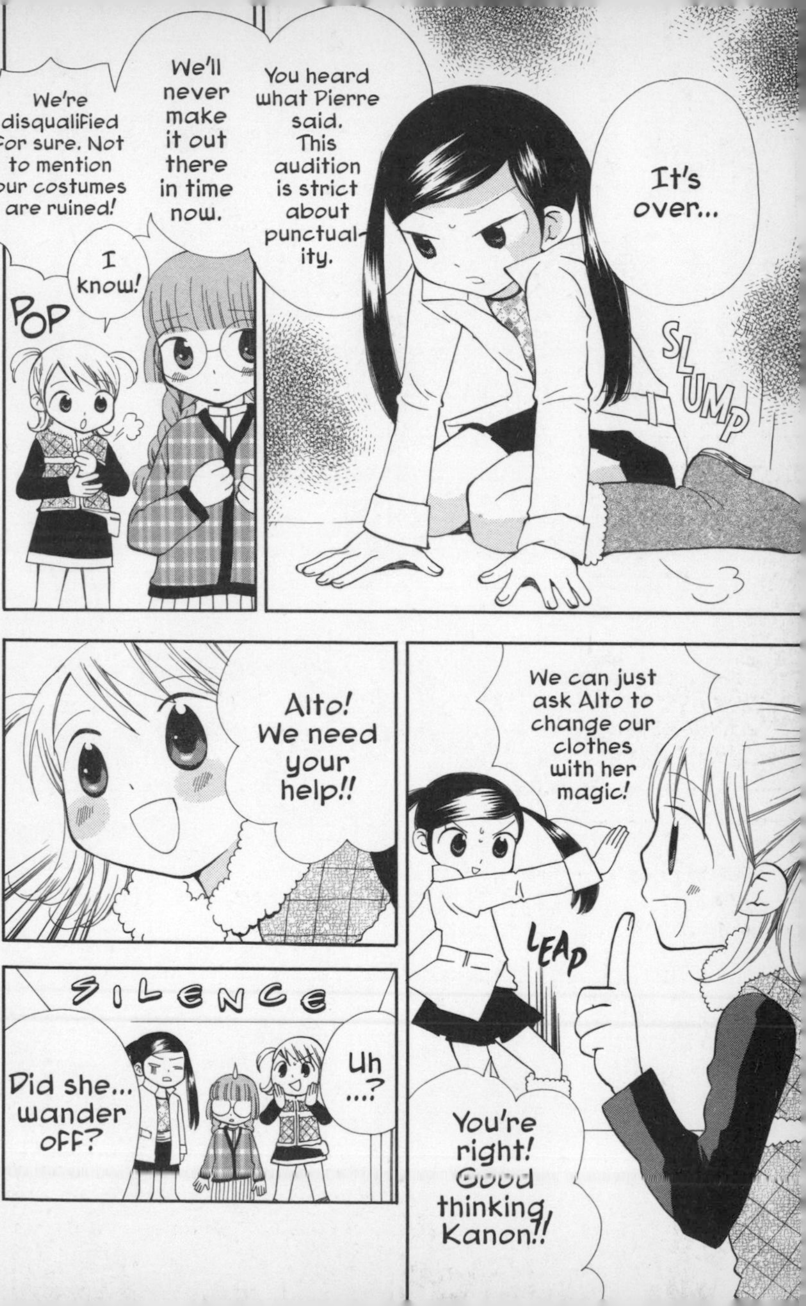

It's over...
SLUMP
You heard what Pierre said. This audition is strict about punctuality.
We'll never make it out there in time now.
We're disqualified for sure. Not to mention our costumes are ruined!
I know!
POP
We can just ask Alto to change our clothes with her magic!
LEAP
You're right! Good thinking, Kanon!!
Alto! We need your help!!
SILENCE
Uh ...?
Did she... wander off?

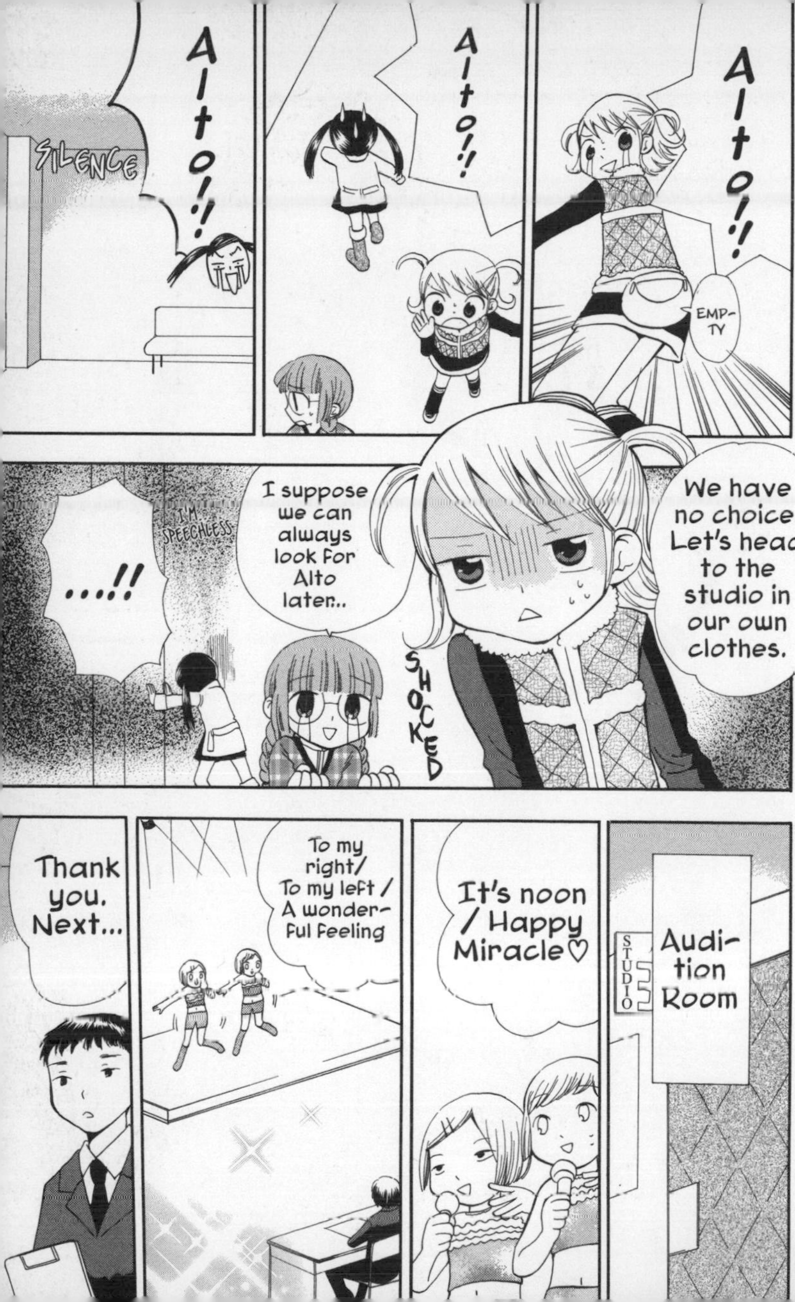
Alto!!
EMP-TY
Alto!!
Alto!!
SILENCE
We have no choice. Let's head to the studio in our own clothes.
SHOCKED
I suppose we can always look for Alto later...
I'M SPEECHLESS
...!!
Audi-tion Room
STUDIO 3
It's noon / Happy Miracle♡
To my right/ To my left / A wonder-ful feeling
Thank you. Next...

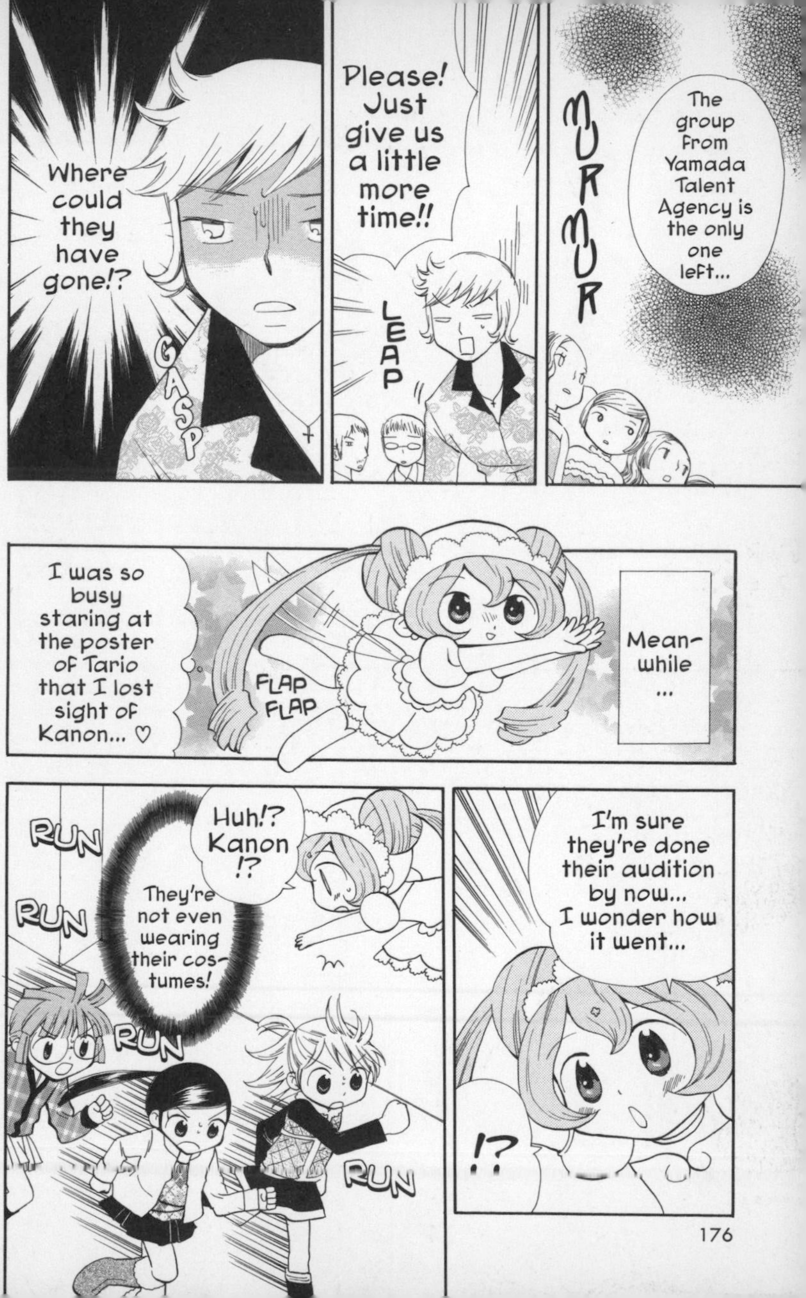
MURMUR
The group from Yamada Talent Agency is the only one left...
Please! Just give us a little more time!!
LEAP
Where could they have gone!?
GASP
Mean-while ...
I was so busy staring at the poster of Tario that I lost sight of Kanon... ♡
FLAP FLAP
I'm sure they're done their audition by now... I wonder how it went...
!?
Huh!? Kanon !?
They're not even wearing their cos-tumes!
RUN
RUN
RUN
RUN

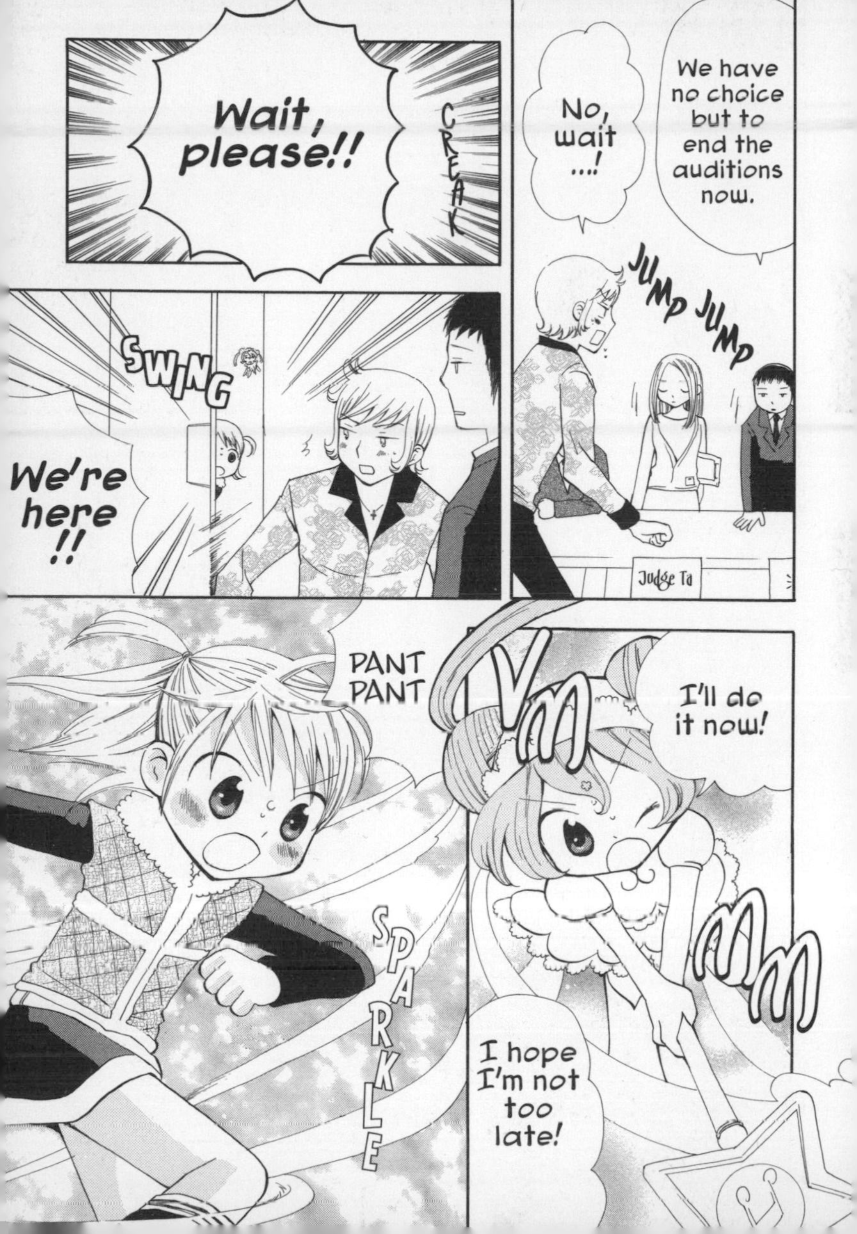

We have no choice but to end the auditions now.
No, wait ...!
JUMP JUMP
Judge Ta
Wait, please!!
CREAK
SWING
We're here!!
VMMM
I'll do it now!
I hope I'm not too late!
PANT PANT
SPARKLE

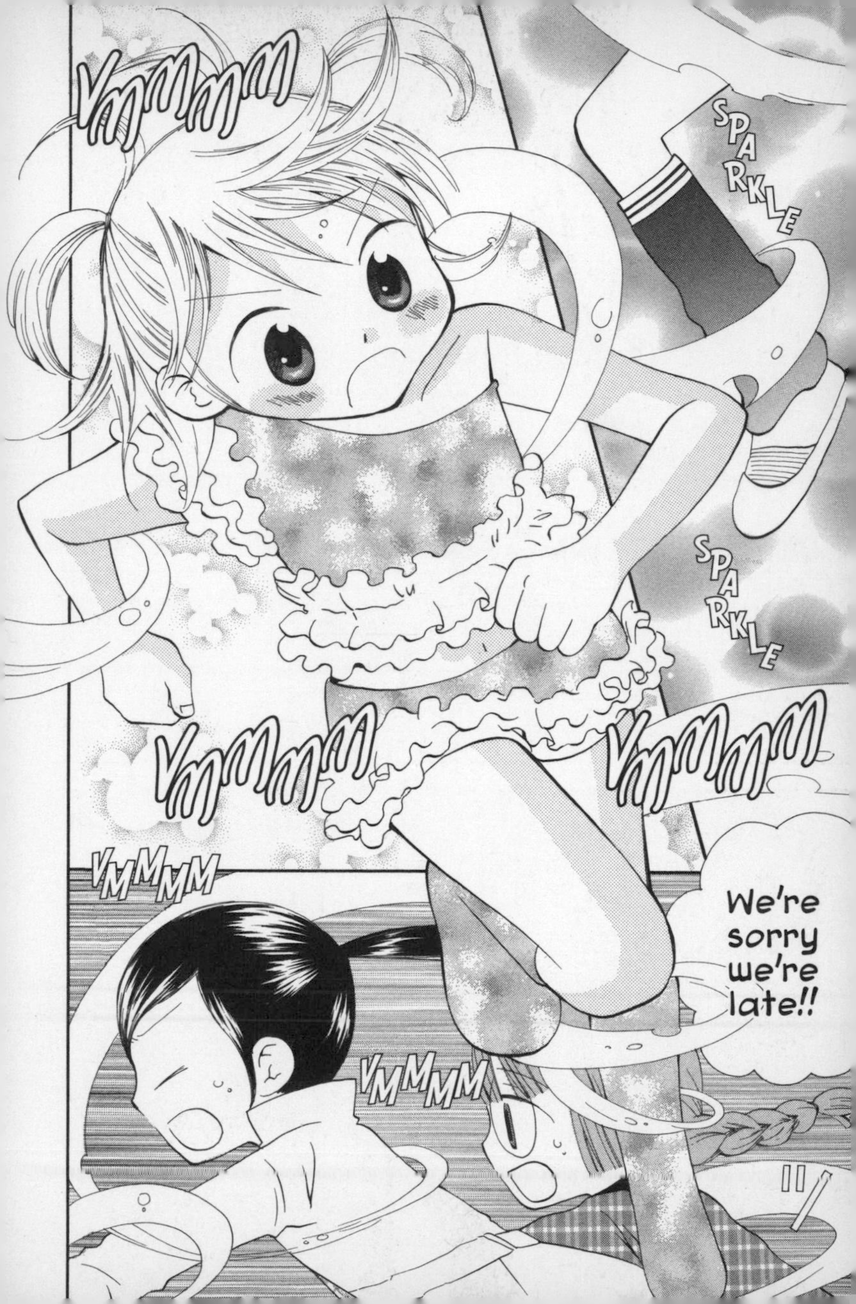
SPARKLE
VMMMM
SPARKLE
VMMMM
VMMMM
We're sorry we're late!!
VMMMM
VMMMM

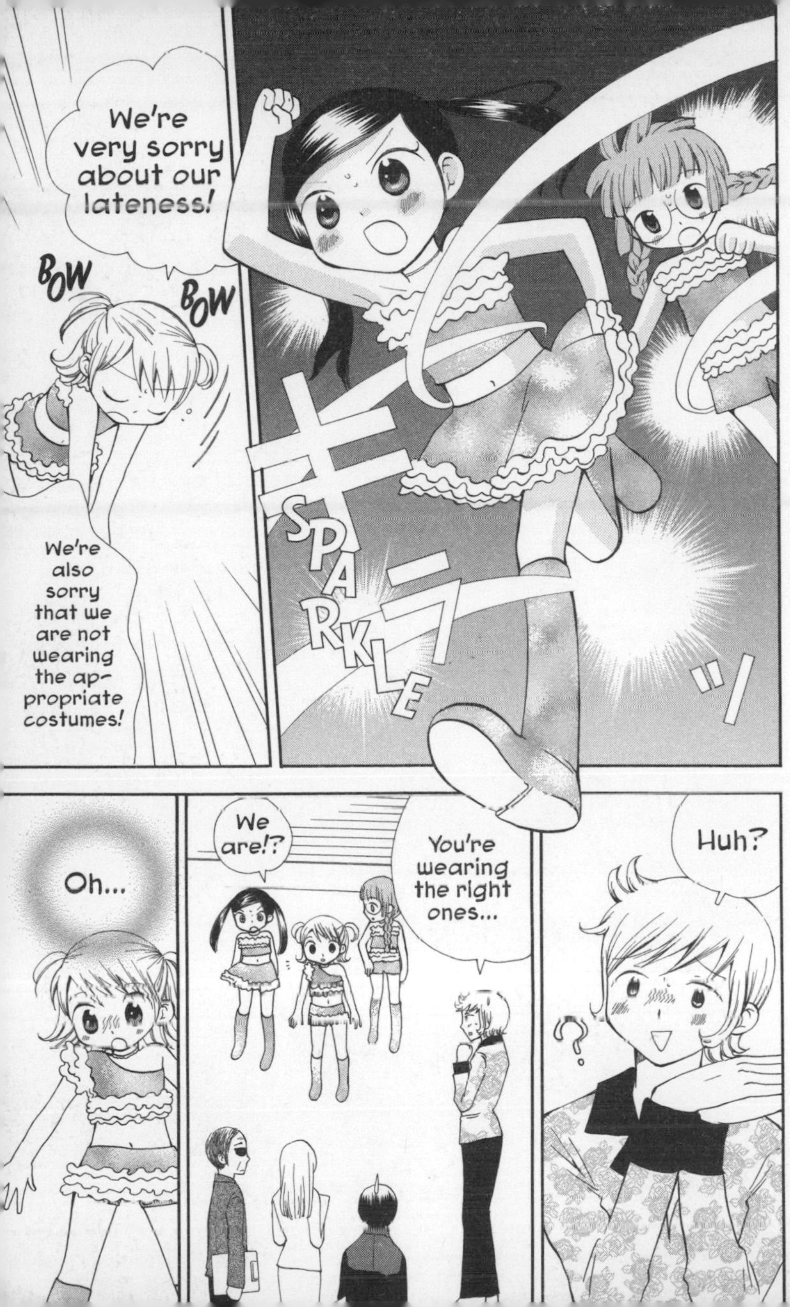
SPARKLE
We're very sorry about our lateness!
BOW BOW
We're also sorry that we are not wearing the ap-propriate costumes!
Huh?
You're wearing the right ones...
We are!?
Oh...

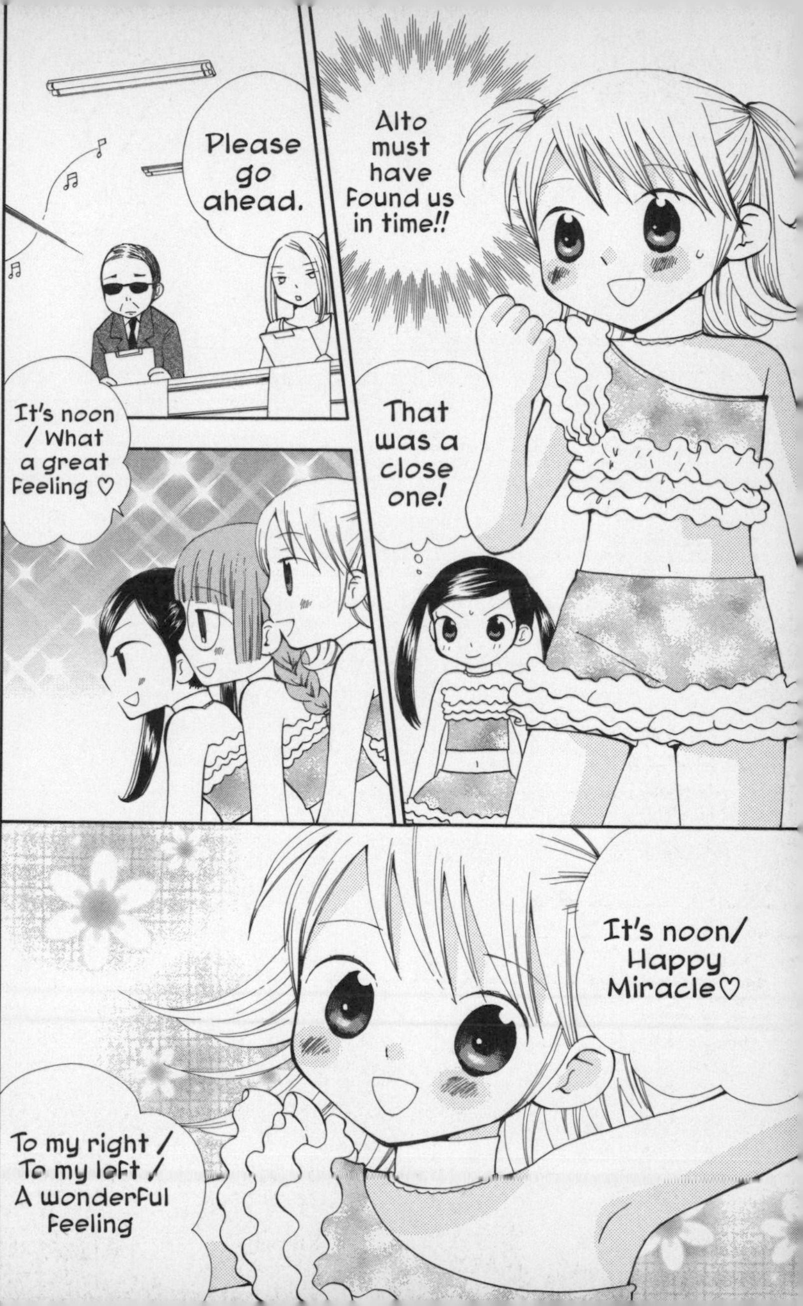
Alto must have found us in time!!
That was a close one!
Please go ahead.
It's noon / What a great feeling ♡
It's noon/ Happy Miracle♡
To my right / To my left / A wonderful feeling

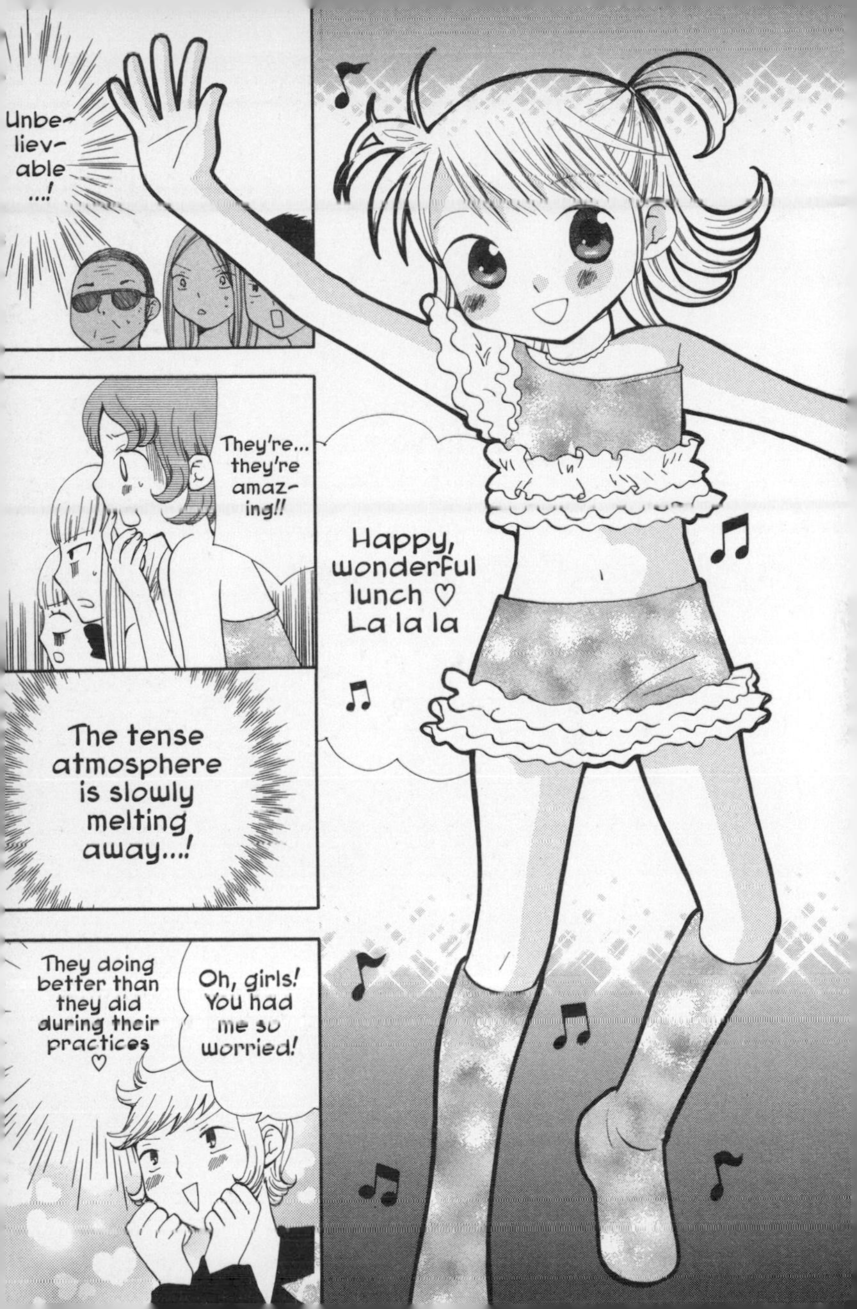
Happy, wonderful lunch ♡ La la la
Unbe-liev-able ...!
They're... they're amaz-ing!!
The tense atmosphere is slowly melting away...!
Oh, girls! You had me so worried!
They doing better than they did during their practices ♡

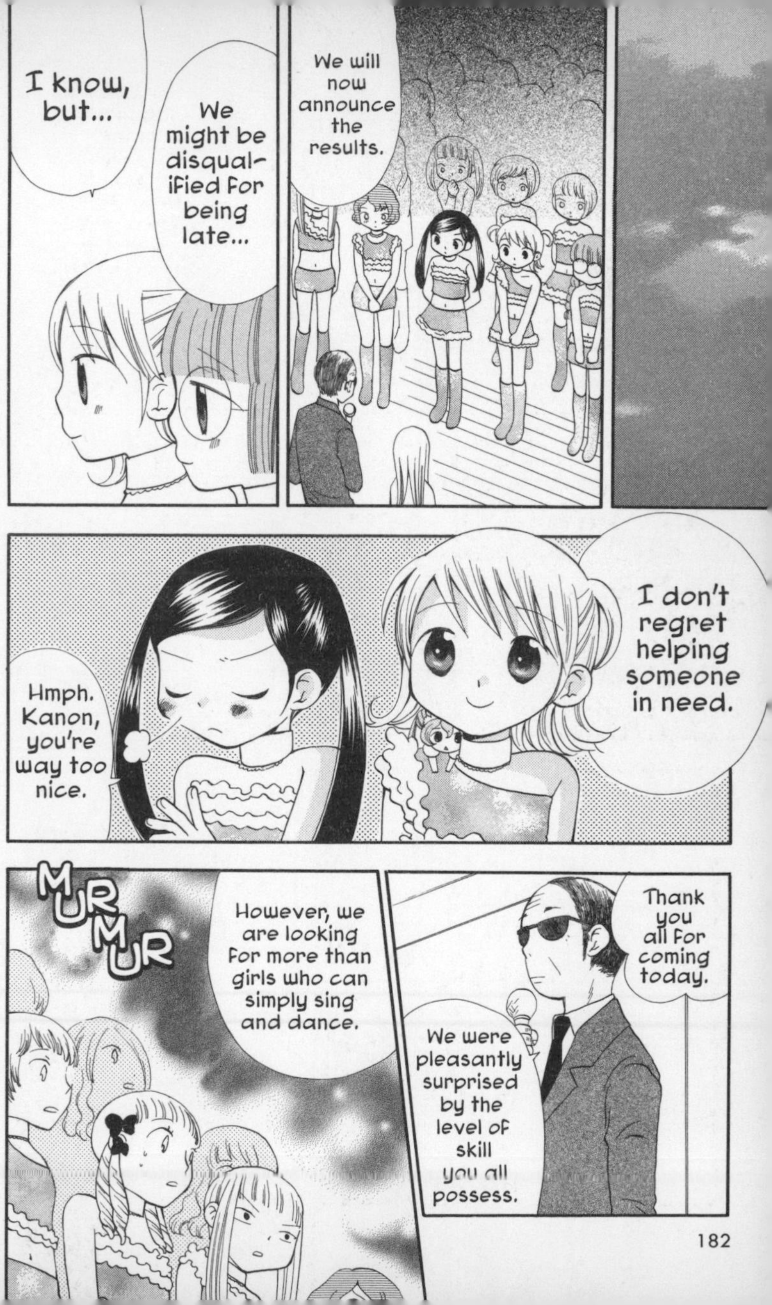
We will now announce the results.
We might be disqualified for being late...
I know, but...
I don't regret helping someone in need.
Hmph. Kanon, you're way too nice.
Thank you all for coming today.
We were pleasantly surprised by the level of skill you all possess.
However, we are looking for more than girls who can simply sing and dance.
MURMUR

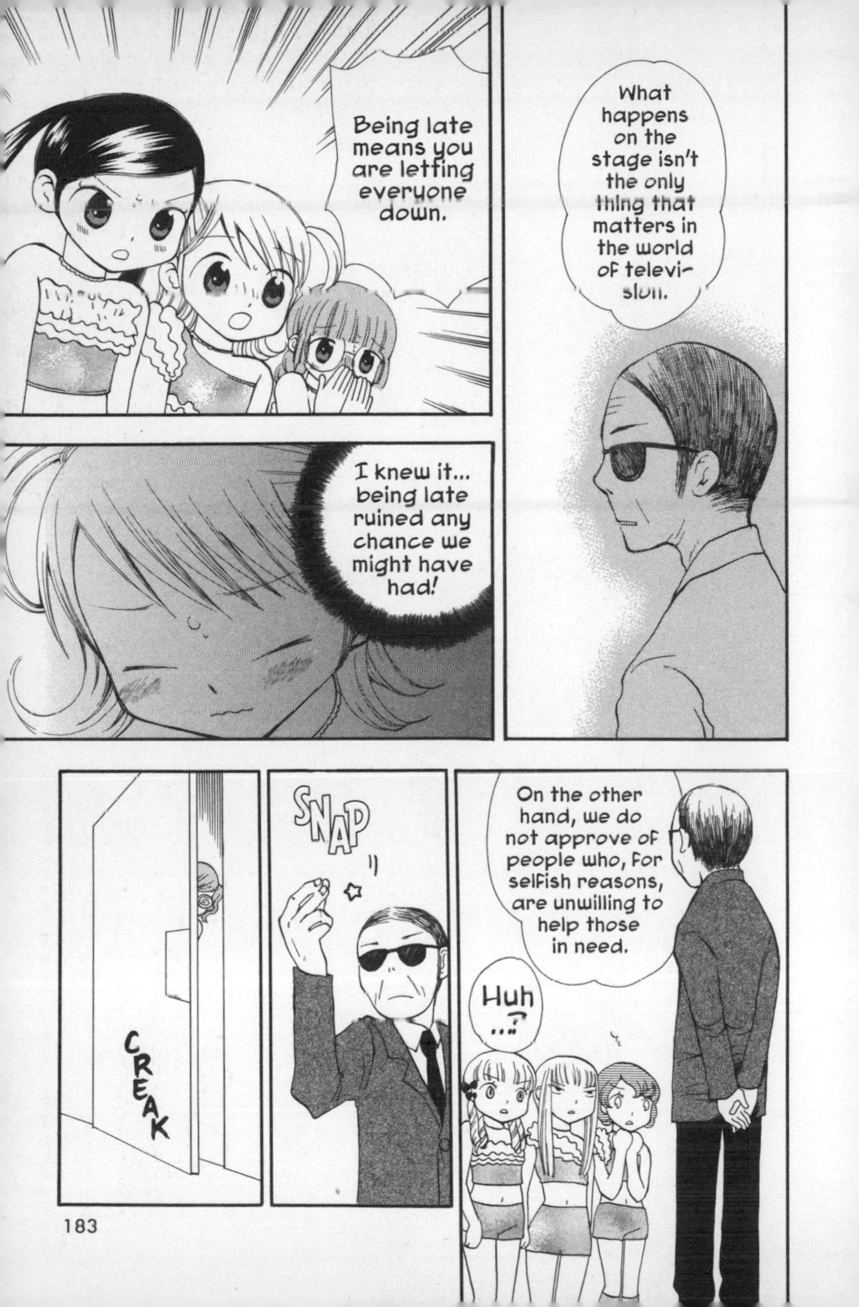
What happens on the stage isn't the only thing that matters in the world of televi-sion.
Being late means you are letting everyone down.
I knew it... being late ruined any chance we might have had!
On the other hand, we do not approve of people who, for selfish reasons, are unwilling to help those in need.
Huh ...?
SNAP
CREAK

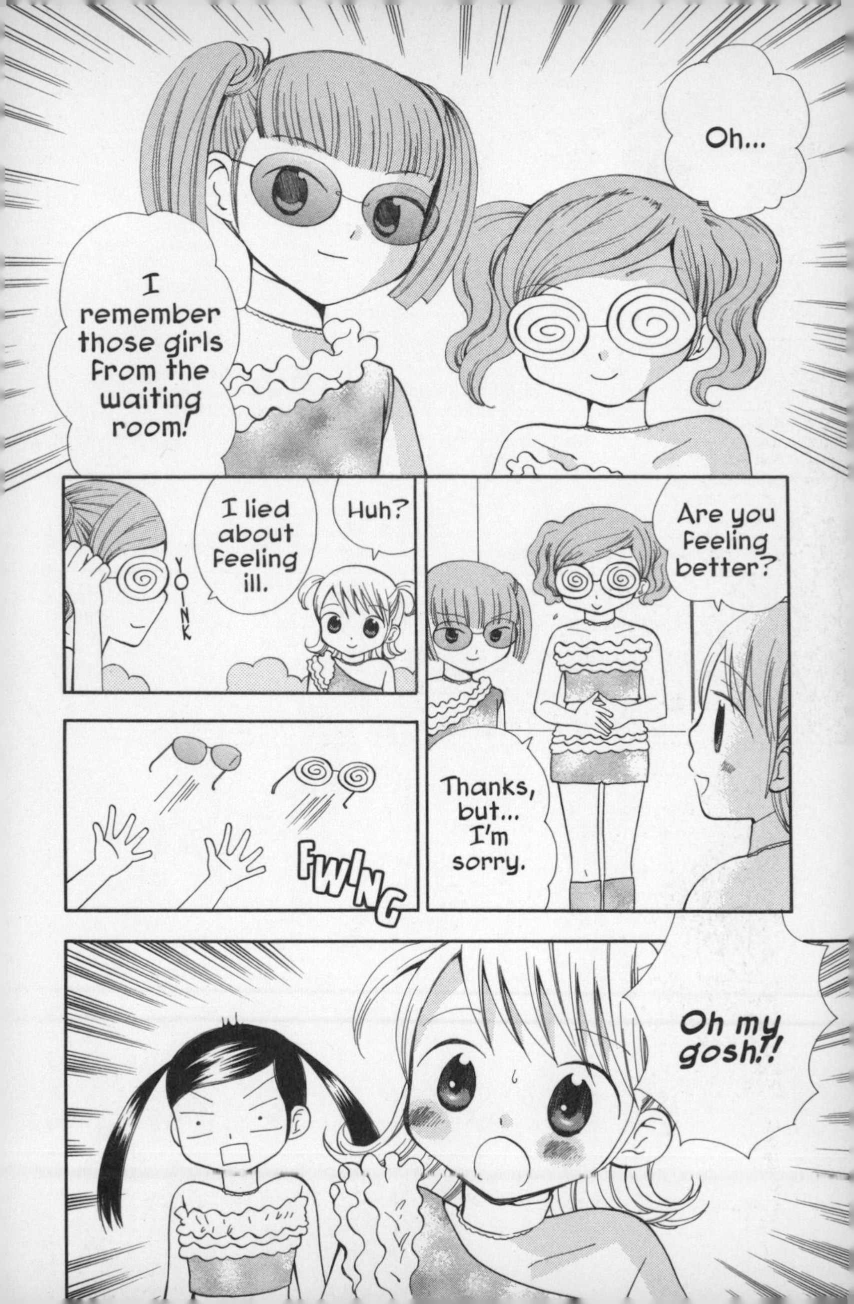
Oh...
I remember those girls from the waiting room!
Are you feeling better?
Thanks, but... I'm sorry.
Huh?
I lied about feeling ill.
YOINK
FWING
Oh my gosh!!

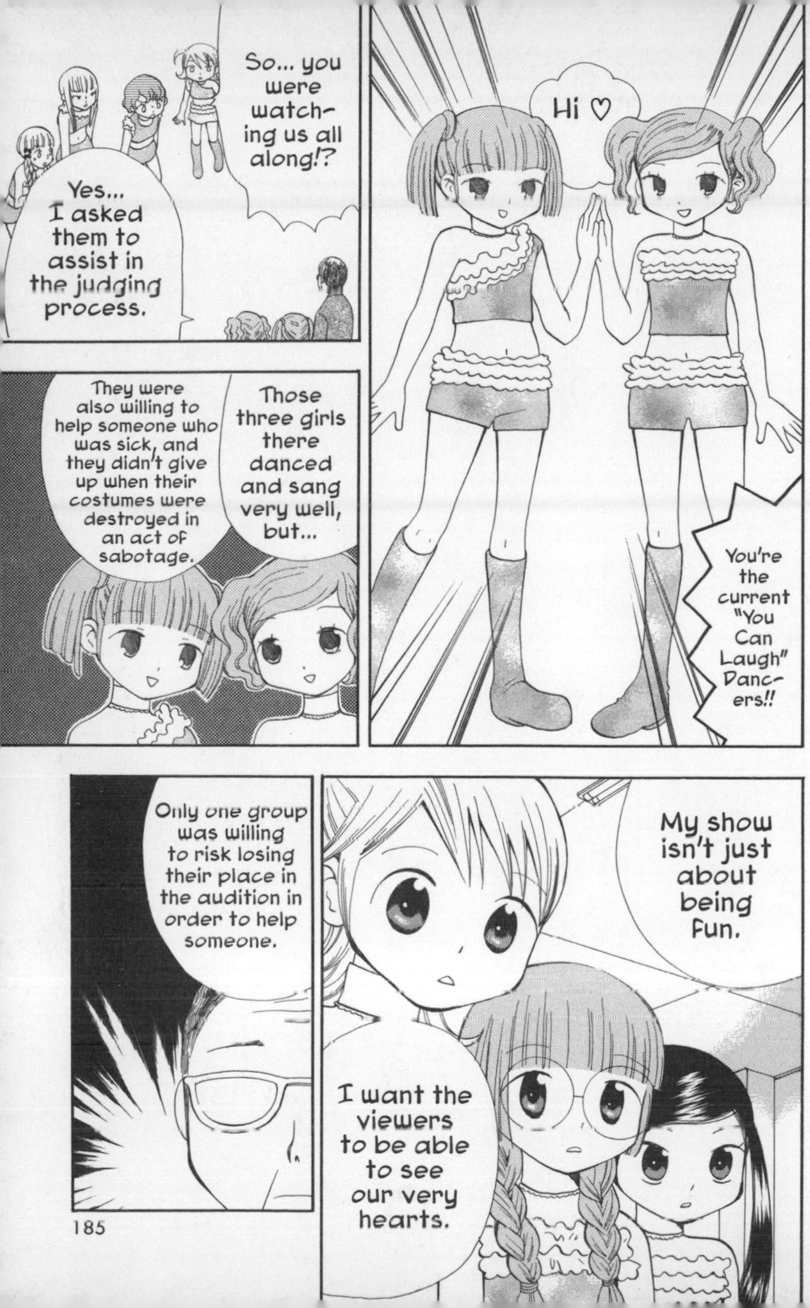
Hi ♡
You're the current "You Can Laugh" Dancers!!
So... you were watching us all along!?
Yes... I asked them to assist in the judging process.
Those three girls there danced and sang very well, but...
They were also willing to help someone who was sick, and they didn't give up when their costumes were destroyed in an act of sabotage.
My show isn't just about being fun.
I want the viewers to be able to see our very hearts.
Only one group was willing to risk losing their place in the audition in order to help someone.

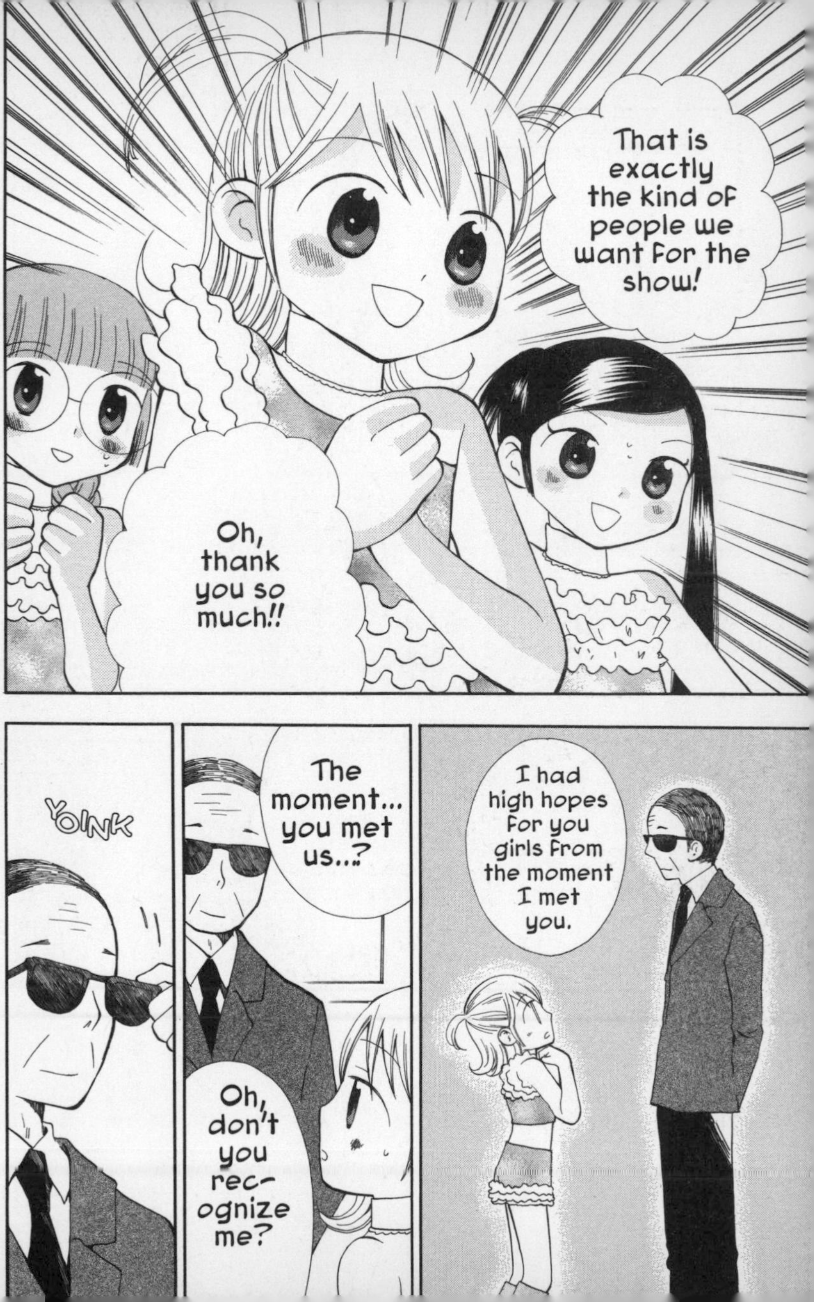
That is exactly the kind of people we want for the show!
Oh, thank you so much!!
I had high hopes for you girls from the moment I met you.
The moment... you met us...?
Oh, don't you recognize me?
YOINK

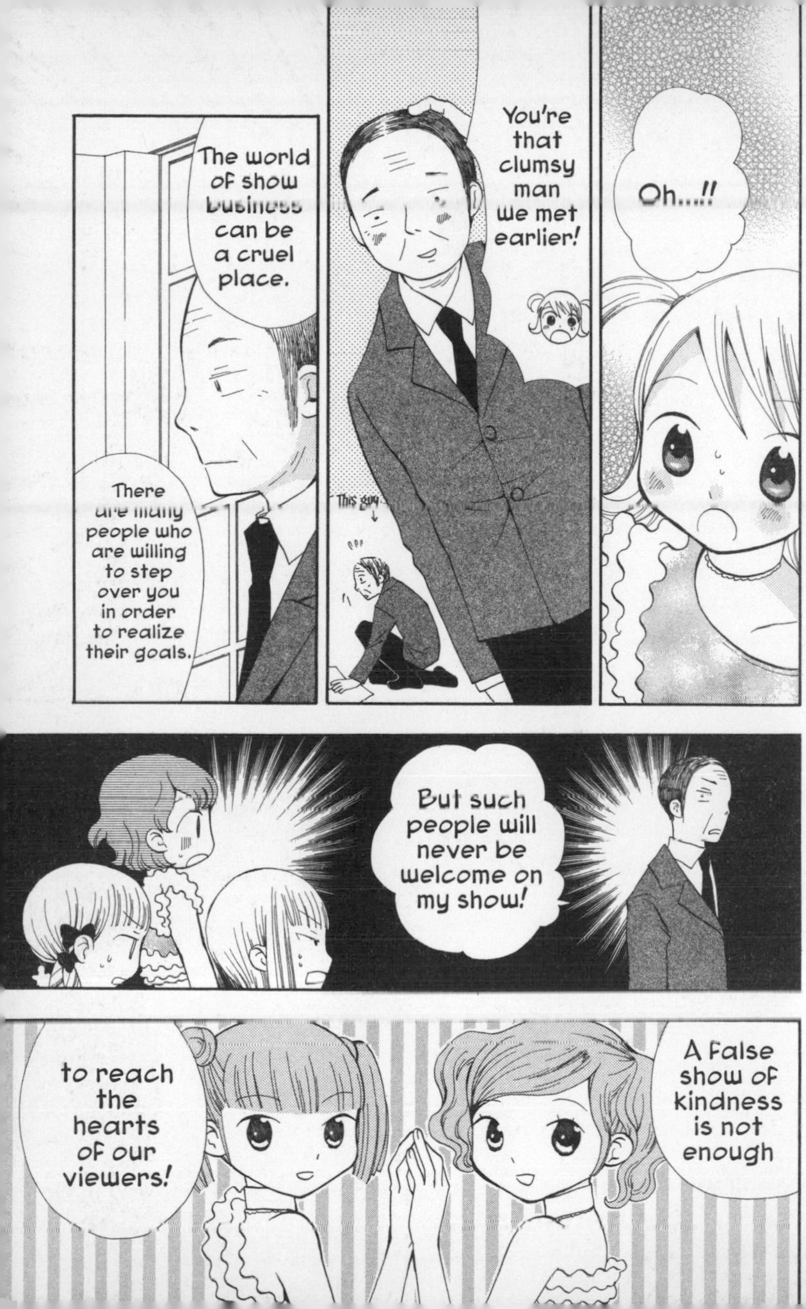
Oh...!!
You're that clumsy man we met earlier!
This guy
The world of show business can be a cruel place.
There are many people who are willing to step over you in order to realize their goals.
But such people will never be welcome on my show!
A false show of kindness is not enough
to reach the hearts of our viewers!

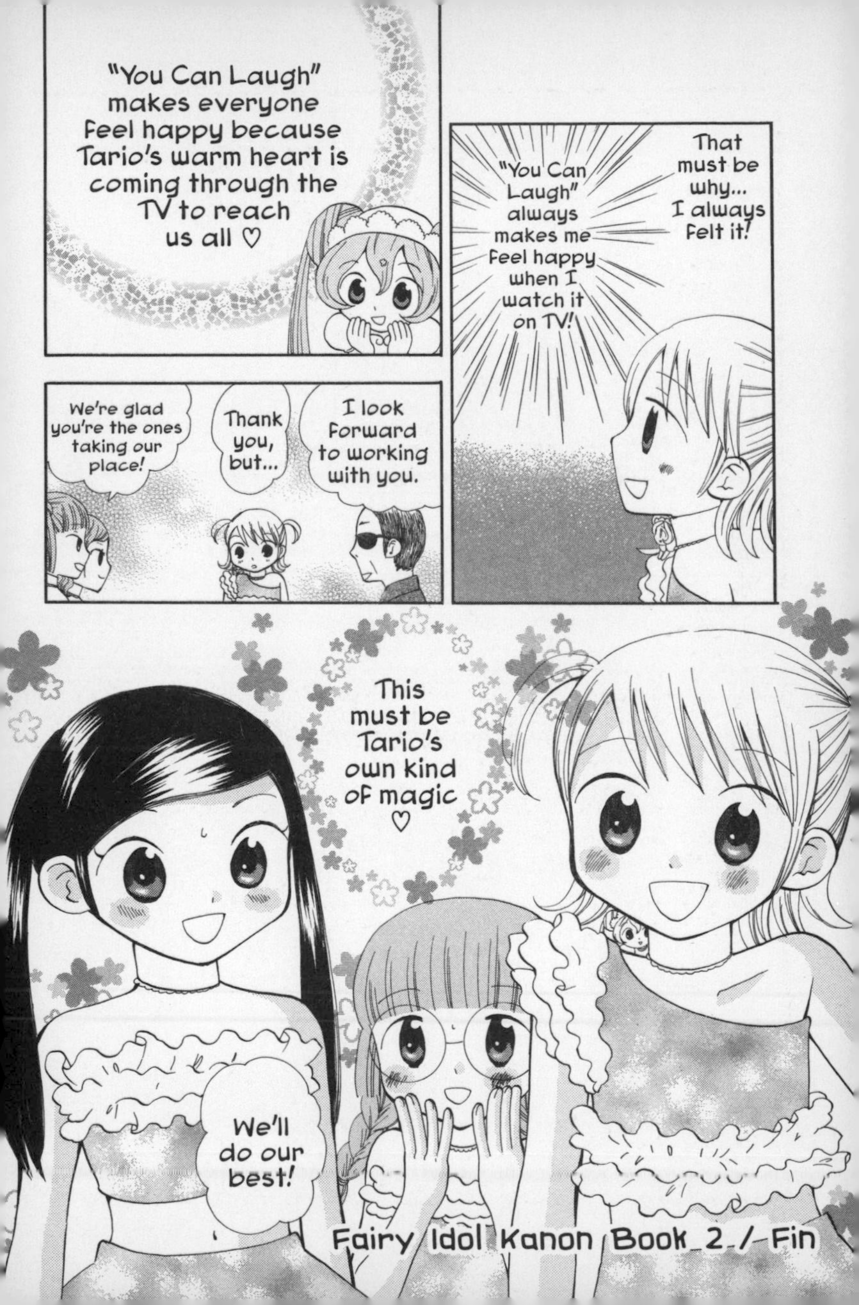
That must be why... I always felt it!
"You Can Laugh" always makes me feel happy when I watch it on TV!
"You Can Laugh" makes everyone feel happy because Tario's warm heart is coming through the TV to reach us all ♡
I look forward to working with you.
Thank you, but...
We're glad you're the ones taking our place!
This must be Tario's own kind of magic ♡
We'll do our best!
Fairy Idol Kanon Book 2 / Fin

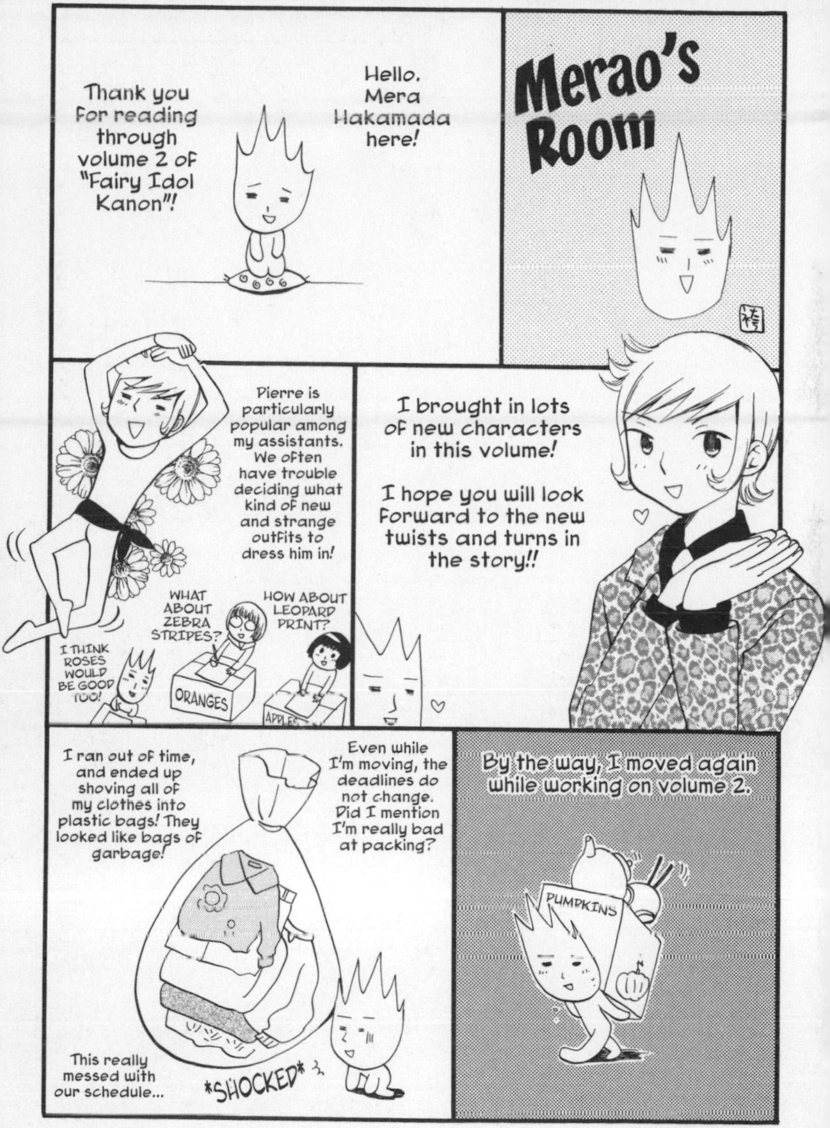
Merao's Room
Hello. Mera Hakamada here!
Thank you for reading through volume 2 of "Fairy Idol Kanon"!
I brought in lots of new characters in this volume!
I hope you will look forward to the new twists and turns in the story!!
Pierre is particularly popular among my assistants. We often have trouble deciding what kind of new and strange outfits to dress him in!
HOW ABOUT LEOPARD PRINT?
WHAT ABOUT ZEBRA STRIPES?
I THINK ROSES WOULD BE GOOD TOO!
ORANGES
By the way, I moved again while working on volume 2.
PUMPKINS
Even while I'm moving, the deadlines do not change. Did I mention I'm really bad at packing?
I ran out of time, and ended up shoving all of my clothes into plastic bags! They looked like bags of garbage!
*SHOCKED*
This really messed with our schedule...

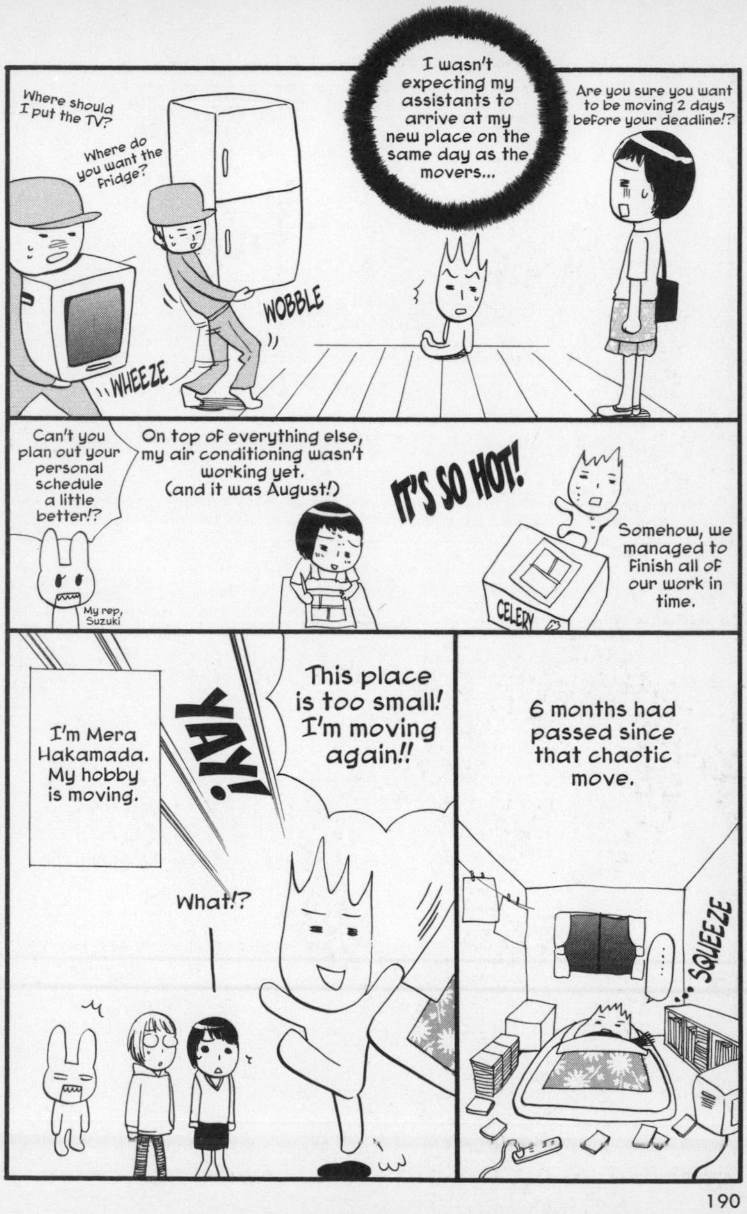
Are you sure you want to be moving 2 days before your deadline!?
I wasn't expecting my assistants to arrive at my new place on the same day as the movers...
Where should I put the TV?
Where do you want the fridge?
WOBBLE
WHEEZE
Somehow, we managed to finish all of our work in time.
IT'S SO HOT!
CELERY
On top of everything else, my air conditioning wasn't working yet. (and it was August!)
Can't you plan out your personal schedule a little better!?
My rep, Suzuki
6 months had passed since that chaotic move.
....
SQUEEZE
This place is too small! I'm moving again!!
YAY!
I'm Mera Hakamada. My hobby is moving.
What!?

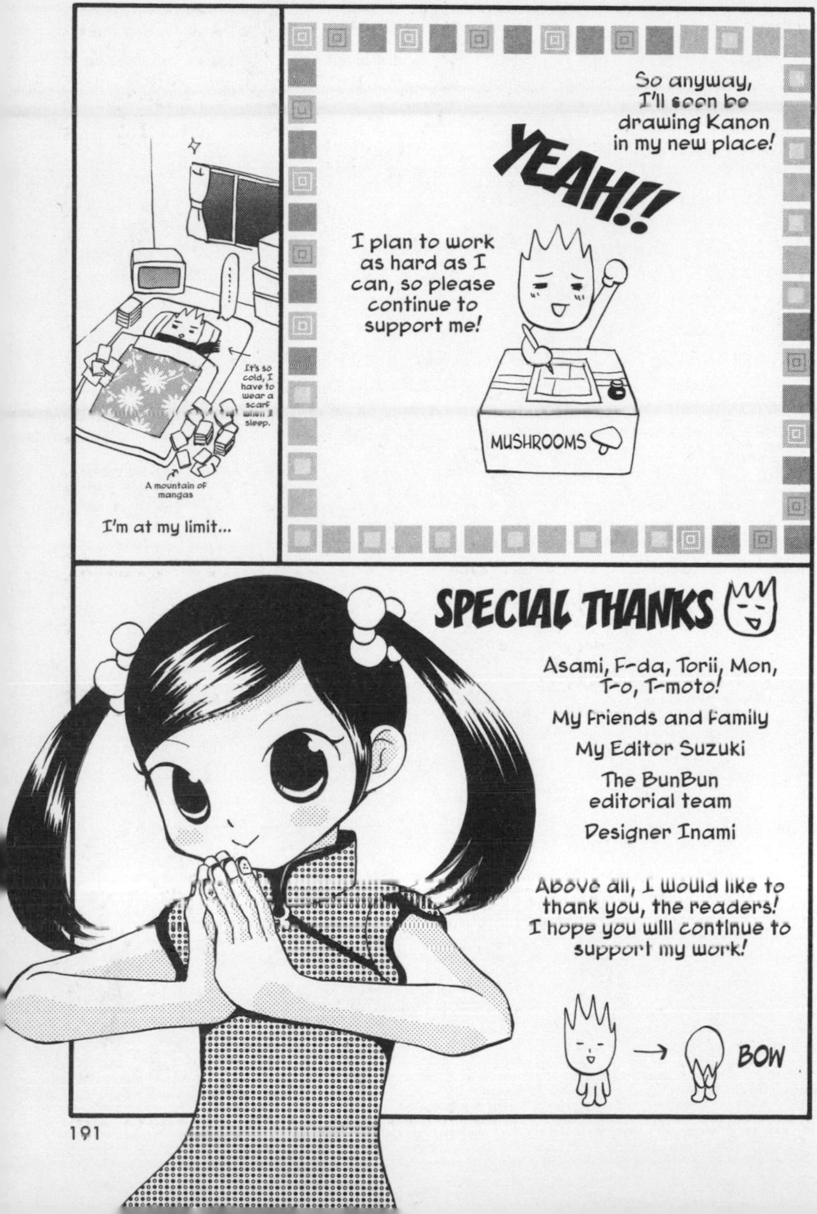
So anyway, I'll soon be drawing Kanon in my new place!
YEAH!!
I plan to work as hard as I can, so please continue to support me!
MUSHROOMS
It's so cold, I have to wear a scarf when I sleep.
A mountain of mangas
I'm at my limit...
SPECIAL THANKS
Asami, F-da, Torii, Mon, T-o, T-moto!
My friends and family
My Editor Suzuki
The BunBun editorial team
Designer Inami
Above all, I would like to thank you, the readers! I hope you will continue to support my work!
BOW

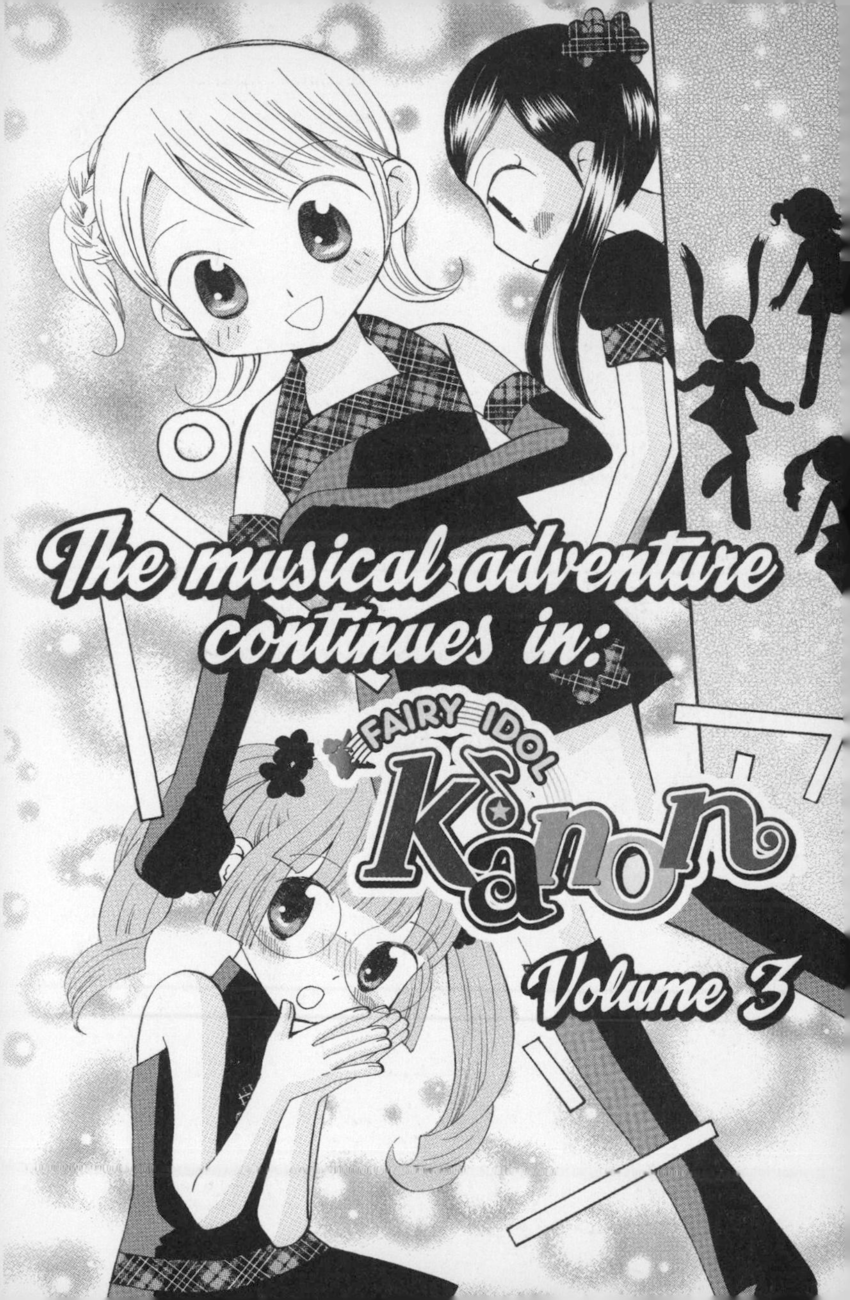
The musical adventure continues in:
FAIRY IDOL
Kanon
Volume 3

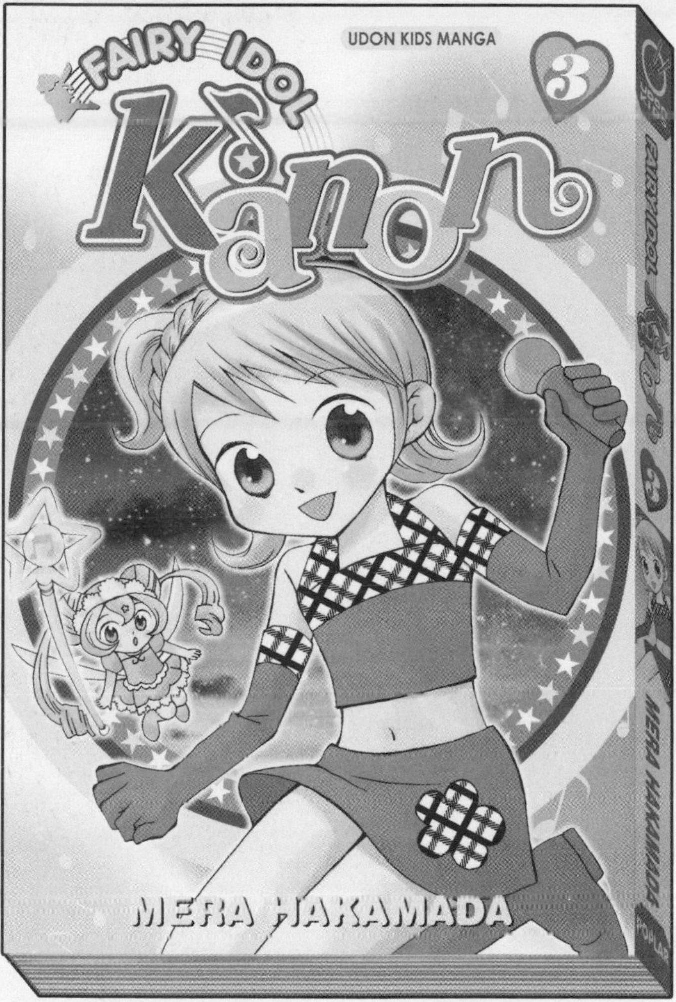
UDON KIDS MANGA
FAIRY IDOL
Kanon
3
MERA HAKAMADA
FAIRY IDOL KANON 3 MERA HAKAMADA
POPLAR

# THE GALAXY HAS SOME NEW BEST FRIENDS!

# SWANS in SPACE

## SCI-FI ADVENTURES FOR GIRLS!

SWANS IN SPACE Vol.1
ISBN: 978-1-897376-93-5

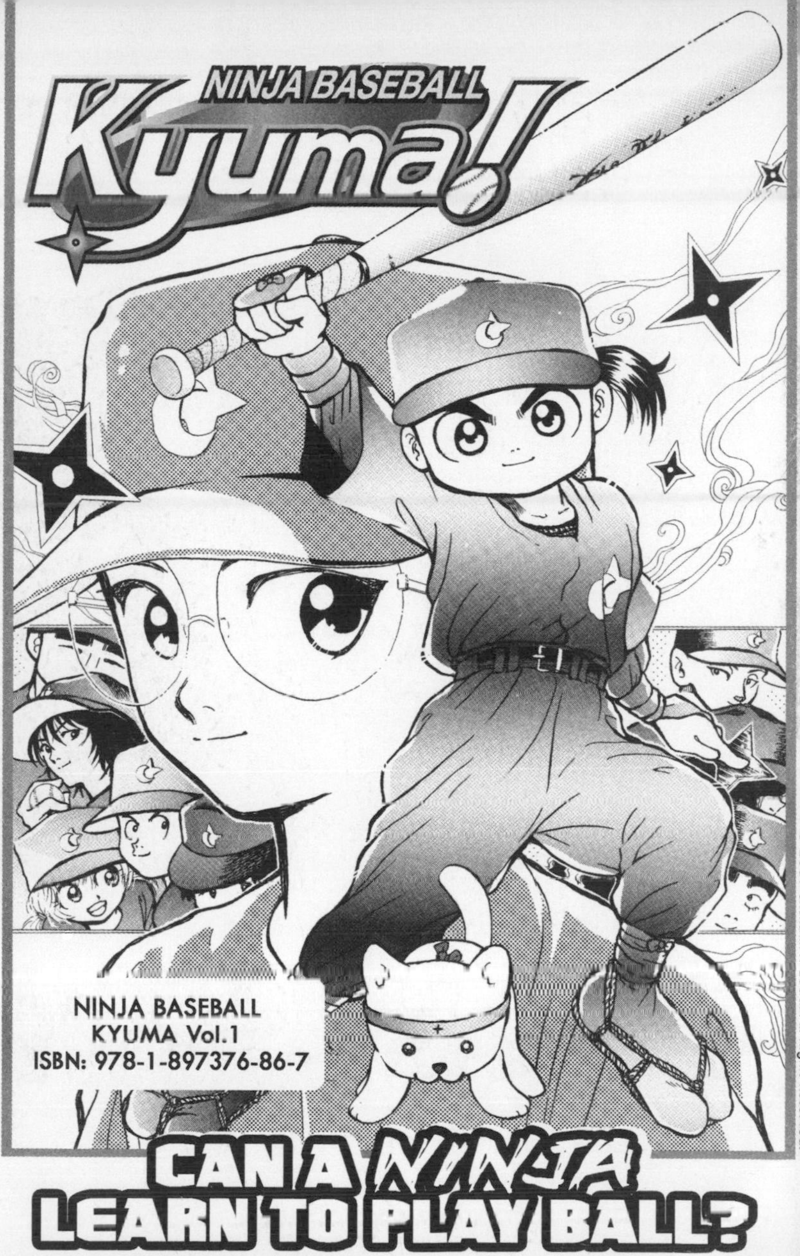
NINJA BASEBALL
Kyuma!

NINJA BASEBALL
KYUMA Vol.1
ISBN: 978-1-897376-86-7

**CAN A NINJA LEARN TO PLAY BALL?**

GET READY FOR
FRIENDSHIP AND ADVENTURE
IN THE LAND OF MAGIC!

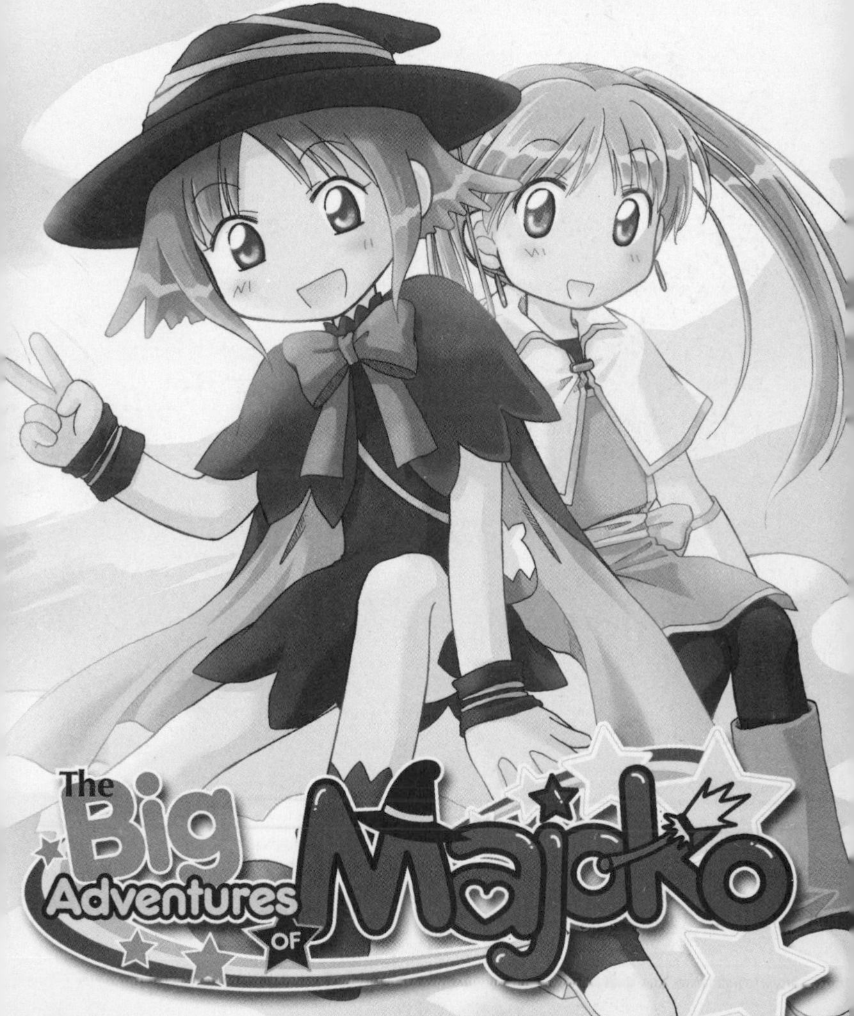
The Big Adventures of Majoko

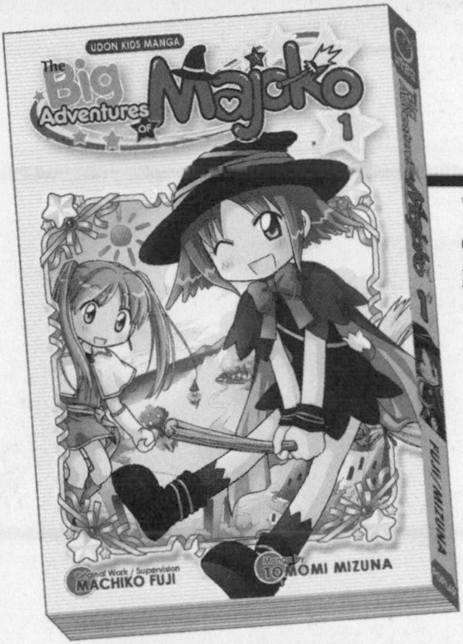
UDON KIDS MANGA
The Big Adventures of Majoko
1
Original Work / Supervision
MACHIKO FUJI
Manga by
TOMOMI MIZUNA
FUJI / MIZUNA

THE BIG ADVENTURES OF MAJOKO Vol.1

ISBN: 978-1-897376-81-2

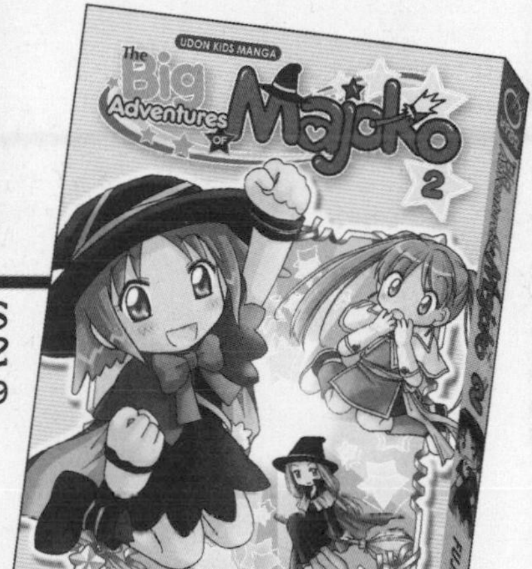
UDON KIDS MANGA
The Big Adventures of Majoko
2
Original Work / Supervision
MACHIKO FUJI
Manga by
TOMOMI MIZUNA
FUJI / MIZUNA

THE BIG ADVENTURES OF MAJOKO Vol.2

ISBN:978-1-897376-82-9

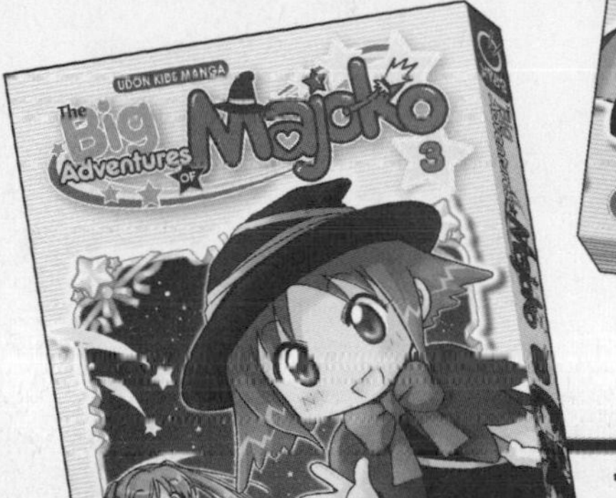
UDON KIDS MANGA
The Big Adventures of Majoko
3
Manga by
TOMOMI MIZUNA
MACHIKO FUJI
FUJI / MIZUNA

THE BIG ADVENTURES OF MAJOKO Vol.3

ISBN: 978-1-897376-83-6